TRUST AND DECEPTION

By the Same Author:

THE ATOM BOMB
THE U-BOAT FILLED WITH GOLD
SHELL-SHOCK
FIVE WARS, FIVE NAMES
THE PROPHET OF PATMOS
THE PROPHECIES OF REVELATION
THE THEORY AND PRACTICE OF PASTORAL CARE
EFFECTIVE COMMUNICATION IN THE CHURCH
HOW TO MANAGE A FLOURISHING CHURCH

ADELBERT SCHOLTZ

TRUST AND DECEPTION

A WAR STRORY WITH A TWIST

RESOURCE *Publications* · Eugene, Oregon

TRUST AND DECEPTION
A War Story with a Twist

Resource Publications
An Imprint of Wipf and Stock Publishers
199 W. 8th Ave., Suite 3
Eugene, OR 97401

www.wipfandstock.com

PAPERBACK ISBN: 979-8-3852-4401-0
HARDCOVER ISBN: 979-8-3852-4402-7
EBOOK ISBN: 979-8-3852-4403-4

READ THIS FIRST

This story is a work of fiction, within a real historical setting. Some of the characters mentioned in this book really lived, but most of the actions and words ascribed to them are nothing but fantasy. The other characters are purely the inventions of the author. If a picture of a certain person appears in this book, it may be assumed that that person existed.

Most of the places where this story unfolds are real places, although the Hagdale Estate in Hampshire never existed. Photos of many of the real places appear in this book. Most military units, which play a role in this story, did take part in the various wars mentioned in this story, although there never was a No 323 Squadron of the Royal Air Force.

Liberties were taken with the description of certain historical events to make the story more interesting, although care was taken to make this story as credible as possible. Although this book mentions characters in the Bible and deals with religious topics, it should not be regarded as a serious theological work.

A few parts of this story run parallel with a previous war novel of the present author, namely Five Wars, Five Names. The reason is that the main character in the present story is the sister of the main character in the previous story and they shared some experiences. Characters from previous novels by the present author make brief appearances in this story.

A glossary of Afrikaans and German words and expressions with their English equivalents is to be found at the end of the book, together with an explanation of the rank structures of the British Armed Forces during both World Wars.

CONTENTS

EPILOGUE AS A PROLOGUE 1

THE BOER WAR 11

THE GREAT WAR 145

THE SILENT WAR 315

THE SECOND WORLD WAR 451

THE COLD WAR 569

POSTSCRIPTUM 603

GLOSSARY 607

RANK STRUCTURES 611

LIST OF ILLUSTRATIONS 613

EPILOGUE AS A PROLOGUE

Southampton, Tuesday, 31 May 1955

The idea of a deathbed confession never seemed practical or attractive or desirable to me. All the dying people I've seen in my life had either lily-white consciences with nothing to confess, or they were unconscious or sedated or hallucinating and, therefore, could confess sweet blow-all.

However, according to the medical magicians, I am now lying on my deathbed and I have the urgent need to confess. For that reason, I summoned to my hospital bed my husband, Brigadier (retired) Viscount Hector de Hacqueville, and my brother, David Davidsohn, who ended his military career as an officer in the German Wehrmacht under the assumed name of Generalmajor a.D.[1] Thomas Freiherr[2] von Traubenstein. I am lying in the Nuffield Health Wessex Hospital, just outside Southampton, not far from our estate Hagdale, near the village of Hursley.

David flew in haste from South Africa after Hector had sent him an urgent telegram.

I have prepared a long speech in my mind and I start: "David, thank you for finding the time to visit me on this day, your sixty-third birthday. I was always seven years older than you, but that head-start will certainly disappear one of these days. That is to say, if we can believe the quacks and pill-pushers. This cancer is getting me and I can only carry on with strong pain killers. You were always my little brother, although you have managed to become a general in the German Army during the war, despite being of Jewish descent. I am proud of you."

---

[1] Generalmajor a.D. – Major General (retired). The abbreviation a.D. stands for "außer Dienst" – outside service.
[2] Freiherr: the German title for a baron.

David responds: "I immediately booked a flight when Hector sent me a telegram. He didn't inform you because he wanted my presence to be a surprise."

"No, it's not really a surprise. I just knew you were on your way here. Hector, thank you for summoning my little brother to my hospital bed. I'm grateful. Anyway, Hector, I fell in love with you when I had my first date with you on New Year's Eve 1900, during the Boer[3] War, although I was already convinced that you fell for me like a bag of rocks. You were supposed to be the enemy, a lieutenant in the blooming bloated British Army, while my father was fighting for our freedom as a member of a Boer commando. Nevertheless, you stole my heart and I was never sorry that we got married.

"But, my dear husband, I doubt whether I will be able to live another few days if things go on as at present. Or, that is what the learned witch doctors and miracle workers here tell me. However, my strength is getting less and less by the hour. If I wait another day or two, I will be too weak to tell you what I must tell you."

Hector: "My dear, darling, lovely, wonderful wife Dora, let me hold your hand. I am already weeping because I know I am losing you. Thank you for this occasion where the three of us can be together for a last time. I believe you have much on your mind, but I can assure you that I never doubted your love for me. The memory of our love and our mutual trust will carry me through the days to come, even after you have departed from this world."

I wave my hand to silence him: "Hector, thank you for your

---

[3] The name "Boer" literally means "farmer" in Dutch and Afrikaans. The descendants of the original Dutch and German settlers who came to the Dutch colony of the Cape of God Hope during the seventeenth century and later, were mostly farmers. The name "Boer" was later used for the white Afrikaans-speaking inhabitants of the Cape Colony and other parts of South Africa that were settled during the first half of the 19th century.

kind words. Please allow me to push a little more morphine into my sick, suffering, smarting anatomy. Aaah. This cursed cancer is a very cruel and cumbersome way to go. It's really killing me."

David: "Just tell us what we can do to make you more comfortable."

"All I want at this moment is your attention, although you may also hold my other hand, David. I have many things on my heart, things that I must confess. Hector, thank you that you always trusted me, as you said."

Hector: "I never doubted your devotion and loyalty to me and to our three sons."

"Thanks. But now I must confess that I broke your trust. Repeatedly. Over many years. Actually, from the very start when we became friends. No, it's not necessary to look so shocked. I didn't have any affairs or adventures or amorous antics with other men. You need not look at me with those big eyes. I would never have done that, although there were temptations. Many of them. You were the only man to whom I belonged, although my father and my brother and our three boys occupied special places in my heart – and that's why I'm glad that David is here today."

David squeezes my hand and places his other hand on my fore-arm: "I know you well enough. You would never have cheated on Hector, even if you were often separated for long periods during both World Wars."

"That's the point. I repeatedly broke Hector's trust during the three wars I've lived through. And this what I must confess."

Hector whispers: "My dear, darling Dora, don't work yourself so up. I don't think there can be anything to confess."

"Oh, there is! Yes, there is! Lots of it! Heaps of it! Hector, I have been able to keep this secret from you, but I was a spy."

Hector blinks his eyes: "Of course, you were a spy of sorts.

You helped me to gather intelligence on the German Military before the war and also during the war. You may certainly call yourself a spy. And I am proud of how you helped me. And grateful."

"My dear Hector! Of course, I aided you. But I was rather a spy for the enemies of bloody Britain. I was a spy for the Boers and David knows of that. And for Germany during both World Wars. Don't roll your eyes like that. I'm not hallucinating. I'm not high on anything, except for this morphine."

"My wonderful wife, I can't believe what I'm hearing now. There were never any opportunities for helping the enemies of Great Britain."

"You must have been blind, not to have noticed it. David knows of my role during the Boer War, but he was blissfully unaware of how I aided the Germans. I just couldn't forget my German roots. After all, German was one of our home languages where I grew up over there in Pretoria. Hector, you even learnt some German to be able to talk to my dad so much more easily, which you could use whenever we visited Germany before and again after the war."

David: "That's why I joined the German Schutztruppe[4] in South West in 1914. That's why I joined the German Army when I and my family settled in Germany after the First World War."

"Hector, I really hoodwinked you. I deceived you. I double-crossed you. By being a Boer spy and a German agent, while you were serving the British Army dutifully. My spying career started on our first date when you took me along to a formal dinner at the officers' club in Pretoria. I listened carefully at all the gossip and boasting of the other officers. I reported all of it to my father, who was also a spy for the Boers.

"Ha, I see that I'm shocking you now. You never suspected

---

[4] Schutztruppe: Protection troops in English

the real reason why my mother agreed to that first date. It was my job to keep my ears open while those blasted British officers drank too much and talked too much."

I can see how puzzled Hector is. David nods with his head to confirm my words, because he was also involved.

"I often lamented the fact that you were never promoted to the rank of major general. You deserved it. I abused my position as an English viscountess and the wife of a British brigadier to aid the enemies of ghastly Great Britain. You could have been a widower if I were ever caught and shot with a bullet through my heart or my head or somewhere as a traitor or a spy or an enemy agent or a saboteur or something. There were a few near brushes.

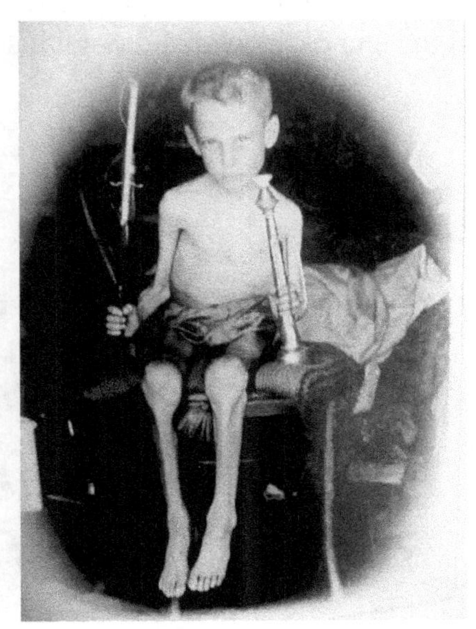

"I was the kingpin of a successful spy ring during the last war. I had three very valuable helpers. I won't betray them by naming them. If they choose to tell you who they are and what they did, then it's up to them.

"I could never forget what the British did with their concentration camps during the Boer War when thousands and thousands of Boer women and children died of starvation and ill health. That was a case of genocide, purely and simply. That was also the fate of thousands upon thousands of poor black people who were suspected of aiding the Boers. Every time when I hear the winter wind blowing through the trees and around the corners of our country home, I hear those poor Boer infants cry. Those crying and dying children pursued me in my dreams. You are aware that I rescued one of those babies from one of those contemptible concentration camps after an innocent Boer girl was raped by English soldiers. You saw that baby in our home in Pretoria towards the end of the war, although his full story was never revealed to you.

"I could never forget how that lousy and low-life Lord Kitchener destroyed all the farms belonging to Boers, whether they were fighting for their freedom, or whether they decided to become Joiners and help the blinking Brits. He did his best to annihilate and wreck our people's livelihood.

"All this suffering was caused by the British wish to gain control of our gold mines and diamond mines. The Boer republics had to be plundered, just as India and other conquered countries were looted and robbed by greedy Great Britain.

"Hector, I see tears in your eyes and I love you for that. I know you are ashamed about what your Army did in South Africa. What I am confessing now, must be a shock. Although I was married to an English nobleman, I could never forgive the Englishmen for all their war crimes in my country. I just had to aid their enemies, my dad's people, and my mom's people. And you unwittingly helped me by teaching me the Morse Code, by buying me an airplane, and helping me to get familiar with a radio set."

Hector bows his head and looks at the floor. I know that his mind is working at maximum revolutions to digest this news.

"And, my dear husband, I was more than just a spy. I was an active saboteur. I had a few plane crashes while ferrying new or repaired aircraft to various destinations. Those crashes were not ordinary accidents. I actively caused those planes to be wrecked to stop them from being used against German cities."

David: "Hell, Dora! What are you telling us? Did you really wreck RAF planes?"

"Yes, I did. And I also have another shock for you, Hector. David, please tell Hector something about our family history."

David: "Is it really necessary? What difference will that make?"

"It is my wish, my fervent wish as a dying woman. Please do it."

David: "Well, all right, Dora. Hector, listen carefully. When you and my sister got married, fifty-two years ago, my father hinted during the wedding dinner that Dora is, in fact, a princess from a very, very ancient family line …"

David is visiting me this morning on his own. Hector and our boys promised to come this afternoon.

I ask: "What have you been doing?"

"Rode a horse on your estate. Enjoyed walks and chats with your husband. Talking to your sons who are also staying over. Swapping yarns about the war. Perhaps I will hop over to Germany to visit my twin daughters in Emmerich. But – exactly how are you doing? I see you're not connected to your morphine tube anymore."

"I'm doing very well. The local medicine men and sorcerers are astounded. My pain is gone. Nobody can explain it. Perhaps I can be discharged next week."

"Perhaps I can explain it, I think."

"Yes?"

"You know that I have this remarkable constitution. I healed very easily from all sorts of injuries and ailments."

"I know."

"Together with that ability, it seems I also have the gift of healing. When I visited you on Tuesday, when you made your death-bed confession, I was holding your hand and grasping your fore-arm. I also did that on Wednesday and yesterday."

"I enjoyed the sensation. It did something to me. A funny and strange tingling sensation. I can't explain it."

"I think I can. Some sort of energy passed from me into your body and caused that terrible tumor inside you to dry up, get shriveled, and vanish. It has something to do with our Jewish ancestry."

"Well, I never!"

"And now I want to hear your whole story. How you hoodwinked your husband and all these blasted British bastards."

THE BOER WAR

My first war was the South African War of 1899–1902 during which I lived with my mother and little brother in Pretoria. My father joined the Boer commandoes to fight the British invaders of our free republic and after Pretoria was taken by the British forces, I started to play a very minor, yet exciting, role in this war.

Pretoria, Saturday, 8 January 1898

At breakfast, my father addresses me and my younger brother David in German – as he always does – and he warns us that we have to get dressed in our best Sunday clothes, as if we were going to church, although it is a Saturday.

Both of us get dressed directly after breakfast. We look smart, because these clothes were made by my parents. My father is a well-known tailor in this town and my mother helps him sometimes and she also deals with the money matters of their shop that is situated in one of the front rooms of our home.

An hour later, we walk from our home in Arcadia, Pretoria, to the town center where we approach a brand-new building in Market Street. I ask: "Are we going to the Jewish church?"

My dad: "That's right. Although it's not called a church, but a synagogue. You both know that I am actually a Jew from Germany, although I also worship in the Dutch Reformed Church on Church Square with you and your mother."

My mother, who was Veronica Visser before her marriage and who accompanies us, speaks in Afrikaans – as she always does: "Yes, your father is Jewish, but he is also a member of the church in which I grew up. There's nothing wrong by being Jewish. After all, Jesus and all his disciples were Jews. Both of you may be proud of the fact that your ancestors from your father's side took part in the events described in the Bible."

My dad: "I don't think that you two young ones will understand much of what will be going on today, because they will speak English and Yiddish, as well as some Hebrew. Perhaps you will understand some Yiddish because it contains some German words. But even if you don't understand much, please sit quietly, and behave yourselves. Today is a very important day for the Jewish community because the new synagogue is being inaugurated. There are about seven hundred Jews in this town."

When we enter the building, I and my mother ascend the stairs to the gallery, where all the women are seated. David and my dad get seats at the back of the hall. I don't understand a word of what is being said. There is chanting, singing, speeches, readings from a big scroll and loud applause from those present. I find it strange that many men wear hats. In our church, men always take off their hats when they enter the house of God.

The most important guest of honor is our state president, Oom[5] Paul Kruger. I recognize him immediately because we have often walked past his home where he sat on the veranda talking to people who sought his advice or help, while drinking coffee with him.

He cannot speak English (or Hebrew) and he delivers his

---

[5] Afrikaans-speaking people had the habit of addressing elder men as "Oom" (Uncle), although they were not related. It was a sign of respect.

speech in Afrikaans, although he tries his best to make it sound like Dutch, of which Afrikaans is a simplified variety.

The president assures the Jews that they are very welcome in the South African Republic, as Transvaal is officially known, and of which Pretoria is the capital. The Jews are, according to the Bible, the people of God and, therefore, he intends treating them with respect. Because the Jews only read the first half of the Bible, the Old Testament, it was decided that they could receive only one half of a building plot in Pretoria for their house of worship, while all Christian churches qualified for a whole plot.

Another guest of honor is the Reverend Hermanus Bosman, the Minister of the Dutch Reformed Church to which our family belongs.

While we are walking home afterwards, my father says: "I had a chat with the rabbi and told him that I will send David when he's bigger to be prepared for his bar mitzvah, although he will also become an adult member of the Durch Reformed Church when he turns sixteen. He was circumcised as a baby. But he was also baptized."

My mother: "How did the rabbi react to that?"

My father laughs: "He was puzzled. He said: 'How on earth is that possible? He can't be a Jew and a Christian at the same time!' I retorted: 'Why not? I'm both. My family have been able for a very long time to parade as Christians, but in our hearts, we stayed Jews all the time. We did this to escape persecution in Europe – especially from the infamous Inquisition. We managed to be both.'"

A little while later, my mother says: "David, tomorrow is your last free day. On Monday your school career is to start. How do you feel about that?"

"I don't know."

My dad: "And Dora, how do you feel about going to the high school part of your school? Ready for that? You are thirteen, after all."

"I'm excited. I can't wait to start with Latin and some other subjects. It's bad that they don't offer Hebrew in our school."

Pretoria, Saturday, 5 March 1898

David is brought home in a cart, driven by a soldier, a member of our Artillery Service from one of the forts guarding Pretoria. David holds his left arm with his right hand.

The soldier helps him off the cart and says to my dad: "He broke his arm. He had a nasty fall just outside that new fort on Klapperkop Hill."

My dad: "David, what the hell did you do there?"

David: "I wanted to see the place better after you have taken me there for the inauguration of the fortress, the other day. Then I fell and broke my arm."

My mom: "We must take you immediately to Doctor Barry to have that arm fixed."

The soldier addresses my father: "Sir, our captain requests that you come and see him at your earliest convenience. He wants to discuss your son's mishap with you."

Pretoria, Monday, 7 March 1898

When we arrive home from school for lunch, my mother immediately asks David: "How is that arm of yours?"

"The pain is gone. Doctor Barry must have done a good job when he worked on my arm, bandaging it like this."

My dad: "The captain at Fort Klapperkop told me this morning that I should not punish you too harshly because you already had your punishment by breaking an arm and experiencing lots of pain. He also said that he thinks you are an enterprising boy and that you are the type of recruit our artillery service needs, although you are still far too young to join. You also seem to have the knack of being a spy or a scout, sneaking into the fort like that"

During dinner my mother asks David: "What have you done to your bandages and the splint on your arm? Why did you remove them? The doctor said you must keep them on for at least a month."

"I took everything off. The bandages made me itch. And I feel all right. No more pain anywhere."

My dad: "Can you use all your fingers?"

"Yes."

He demonstrates his agility by picking up his plate with his left hand: "My arm feels as always. Nothing wrong with it."

Me: "That's a miracle – of the same sort of which we read in the Bible. Jesus had the ability to heal sick, lame, and blind people. The Reverend Bosman prayed in church yesterday for all the sick people in our congregation and that prayer must have helped my little brother."

My dad: "Yes, it's a miracle. I don't know how to explain it, but I'm not really surprised."

He doesn't explain why he says that.

Pretoria, Monday, 28 February 1899

The Reverend Hermanus Bosman visits our home today for an official pastoral visit. He is accompanied by Elder Josias Jooste. We all sit with our best clothes in the living room to listen to this man of God.

After he has read a chapter from the Bible and did a prayer, the reverend looks at my father: "Brother Davidsohn, there is a serious matter that I have to discuss with you."

My father nods, but stays silent.

"Brother, I could not help but to notice that you were present when the Jewish Synagogue was inaugurated last year. It has also come to my notice that you attend all the Jewish feast days and holy days in the Synogogue. How must I understand this? You are a member of the Dutch Reformed Church. That means that you must have left the Jewish faith. How do you explain that?"

My dad: "Why can't I be a member of your church and a member of the Jewish congregation at the same time? It is no secret that I was born from a Jewish family, but I also joined your congregation officially."

"No, it's impossible to be a Christian and a Jew at the same time. You can't be both."

"Why not?"

"They're two different religious faiths. They are not compatible. You can only be either a Christian, or a Jew, but not both."

"Tell me, dear Reverend, to which religion did Jesus belong?"

"Well, he was a Jew, of course, but he was also the founder of the Christian faith."

"Did he attend meetings in a synagogue and in the temple?"

"Yes, he did. The Gospels are clear about that."

"And when he was baptized by John the Baptist – was it a Christian baptism?"

"It was certainly a valid baptism."

"Was it a baptism in the Name of the Father and the Son and the Holy Spirit?"

"No, not exactly."

"Was it the Christian baptism that Jesus instituted later, or was it John's own baptism?"

"Well…, I must concede that Jesus' baptism was not exactly the Christian baptism. It wasn't performed in the Name of the Father, the Son, and the Holy Spirit. You must be right. It couldn't have been the Christiasn baptism."

"And was Jesus a Christian, as we understand Christianity?"

"No, not really. Christianity didn't exist while he was still alive."

"So – Jesus was not a Christian, but a Jew? He never received the Christian baptism?"

"No, you've made your point. Jesus was never a Christian. He was a Jew."

"And his apostles, Peter, John, James, and all the others – what were they? Were they Jews or were they Christians? Or both? Did they continue to worship in the temple, while they also recruited people to join the Christian faith?

"Yes, what can I say? It seems I'm stuck in a corner, a difficult corner, I must say. All right, yes, they were the first Christians, but they also continued to worship in the temple in Jerusalem.”

Do you agree that we may follow the example of the apostles? They were the first followers of Jesus, but they continued to worship in the temple in Jerusalem.”

“I suppose it’s all right to follow their example.”

“But do you agree that they were Jews, just like Jesus, but that they were also the first Christians – both at the same time?”

“That’s what I said. All right, I must admit – they were Jews and they were also followers of Jesus. They were also real Christians.”

“And these apostle – did they forbid any followers of Jesus to go to the temple or to attend meetings in a synagogue?”

“Not what I know of.”

“We read in the book of Acts that the apostle Paul was a Christian missionary. Am I right?”

“Certainly.”

“Do you agree that he worshipped in the temple when he visited Jerusalem for the last time, just before he was arrested?”

“I can’t deny that.”

“I advise you to read the Epistle of James in the New Testament, dear Reverend. It is specifically addressed to Jewish Christians. I was told that the Greek word for ‘meeting’ or ‘assenbly’ in Chapter 2, verse 2, is actually ‘synagogue’. That means that these Jewish Christians worshipped in synagogues, as I also do. So, you see, Reverend, I am a Jew. I can’t deny my ancestry. I worship the God of Abraham, Isaac, and Jacob. But I am also a fervent, enthusiastic, and true follower of Jesus of Nazareth. Is it wrong of me to follow the example of the apostles of whom we read in the book of Acts in the Bible?”

"Brother Davidsohn, I suppose I was wrong to criticize you for being a member of my congregation and the Jewish congregation simultaneously. It does seem as if that is possible. The apostle did it, after all. It must certainly be right to follow their examples."

Elder Jooste nods to demonstrate his agreement.

At supper, I tell my father: "Vati, that Reverend Bosman didn't like the way you pushed him into a corner, from which he could not escape."

My dad: "And how do you know that?"

"It was almost as if I could read his mind. The way he greeted us when he left, wasn't very friendly, either. I don't think he will easily forget you for proving him wrong."

Pretoria, Wednesday, 11 October 1899

When I return home from school for lunch, I observe a large number of "burgers"[6] assembling next to the church on Church Square. During school hours we often heard horsemen galloping through the streets and even firing some guns into the air. Our Grade 8 teacher forbade us to go out to watch the commotion and she did her best to continue with the lessons, but with limited success, because we continuously tried to see what was going on outside through the class room's windows.

When I reach home, I find my parents packing provisions into a bag. A big rifle lies on a chair.

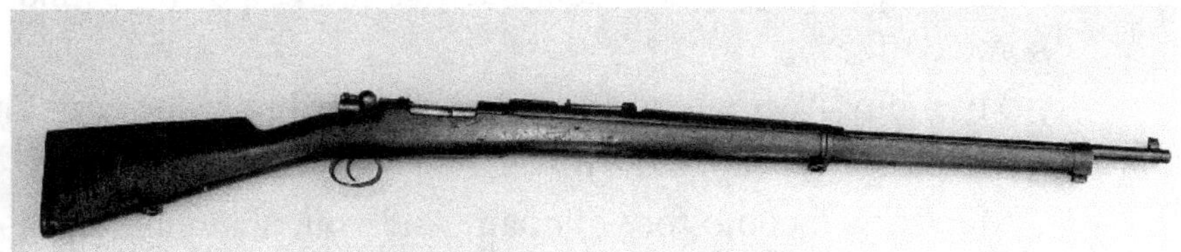

My father explains to me and my brother: "War has broken out. The blinkin' British have assembled an army on our borders and they refuse to withdraw. Oom Paul Kruger had no choice but to declare war and we have to drive them away before they attack us."

My mom adds: "Let's hope that you will be able to do that rapidly. The last war against England in 1881 took only a few weeks before the Tommys were defeated and destroyed and driven away."

David: "Will we use those big guns at the forts around Pretoria to shoot at them?"

My dad: "They have already been taken away and transported to the border with Natal. We will need them at the front."

---

[6] "Burgers": the Afrikaans word for "citizens". All males between the ages of 16 and 60 were liable to do military service in case of war.

Me: "And where did you get this gun?

"It was issued to me this morning when I reported on Church Square where all the burgers were assembling. It's a German Mauser bolt-action rifle. They also gave me a few dozen cartridges. I am part of the Pretoria Commando and our commandant is Barend de Lange. I was placed under the command of Field Cornet Carel Ferreira."

Me: "How many men are there in this commando?"

"I guess, more than a thousand. There are five field cornets and each of them has about two hundred men under him. We must provide our own horses and provisions for a few days. That's what your Mom is packing now – coffee, sugar, rusks, maize flour, dried meat, and dried fruit. Also, some nuts and apricot kernels. I'm taking a kettle and a pot to prepare food, such as maize porridge, and to brew some coffee."

My mom: "We will have to find a water bottle for you. You will also need some soap and a towel."

Me: "And a comb for your hair. And your shaving utensils."

David: "Will the Transvaal have enough men to defeat the Englishmen? My teacher told me that England is a rich country with millions of people. The queen of England rules a large part of the earth. They must have a huge army with many soldiers."

"We are, fortunately, not alone. The burgers of our sister republic, the Orange Free State, are helping us. It is the plan that we invade the Natal Colony, while they will invade the Cape Colony. We hope that many Afrikaners from Natal and the Cape Colony will join us."

David: "Will you get a uniform, just like the soldiers on Klapperkop Hill?"

"No. I'm not a professional soldier. I'm an ordinary citizen of this country who must defend our women-folk and our homes."

After my father's provisions and a roll of blankets have been packed, and he got dressed in comfortable clothes, David helps him to saddle our horse in the stable in our back yard. This horse is actually a cart horse that has to pull our two-wheeled carriage, but now he has to be used as a riding horse.

My father does a prayer while we all kneel, gives each one of us a hug and a kiss, gets onto his horse, and rides off. He turns around again and looks at my brother: "David, you are the man in the house now. Look well after your mother and your sister!"

David salutes him as he saw the artillery men do at Fort Klapperkop.

I and my brother run after him and we watch the mounted commando leaving Pretoria for the front. When we get back home, we find our mother in tears.

I put my arms around my mother's neck to console her, but I can't bring myself to tell her that I have this horrible and terrible feeling that we will lose this war.

Pretoria, Tuesday, 29 May 1900

My teacher, Miss Cora Coetzee, tells our class: "Don't go home after school. All the children of our school are to go to the residence of our president, Oom Paul Kruger. Something important is to happen there."

We are inquisitive about what is to happen at Oom Paul's house in Church Street. When we get there, a large gathering of people is already in place. The president waits on the veranda.

A boy of about sixteen years of age steps forward and shakes the hand of the president. He speaks English with a somewhat strange accent. An interpreter translates his words into Dutch with a loud voice so that all the bystanders can hear him.

The boy declares: "Mister President, I am Jimmy Smith from Philadelphia in the United States of America. Many Americans have sympathy with you in your struggle against Great Britain. We Americans can remember that our grandfathers fought against the British Army to gain our independence in 1783. You are also fighting to preserve your independence and freedom.

"We fought an invading British army during the War of 1812 and our brave men drove them away. It is our prayer that you will prevail, just as Americans have defeated British forces during two wars.

"Here I have a declaration of sympathy, support, and solidarity with your cause with the signatures of more than 29 000 American children."

With that, he hands a wooden box to the president, evidently containing the document, together with all the signatures.

The boy adds: "This box also contains some newspaper articles in which support for your cause is expressed. Our president doesn't want to upset the relationship with Great Britain and he declared that America is officially neutral in this war. That is, however, not how most Americans feel. May God bless your republic!"

Somebody in the crowd cries out: "Hurrah for America!"

Many people respond: "Hear, hear!"

Applause is given. Some of our children rush forward to shake Jimmy's hand.

Pretoria, Wednesday, 30 May 1900

It is almost winter and I don't want to leave my warm bed to get dressed in the cold. Somebody shakes my shoulder and I open my eyes. It's my father! He's home!

My first question is: "Have we won the war?"

"No, not yet. At least, we don't know yet. But get dressed and then we can talk during breakfast."

At the breakfast table, my mother is all smiles where she sits next to her husband, who is holding her hand. His face and hands are tanned because he was living in the open the last few months. He has a beard and a moustache.

My father tells us of his war experiences. He was promoted to corporal and had ten men under his command. The Boer commandoes achieved glorious victories against the khaki-clad Britishers at Colenso and other spots in Natal. Ladysmith was besieged. But then reinforcements from England turned up and the Boers had to fall back.

According to my father, the Boer forces obtained significant victories on other fronts. The most remarkable was the battle at Magersfontein, south of Kimberley, where scores of Scottish soldiers fell. Even a Scottish general did bite the dust.

Unfortunately, reinforcements, fresh from England, swarmed into the country and our men had to flee in the face of superior forces. Many burgers were captured in the process.

And now my father is back in Pretoria, together with most of his commando. It is their task to defend the town against the forces of Lord Roberts, a field marshal, which is supposed to be a super general, only two steps below the English king and four or five steps below God and his angels.

Breakfast takes longer than usual and I am late for school.

When the school breaks for lunch, I and my brother rush home to see more of our father. David hopes that he can stay for his birthday, tomorrow. We are, though, disappointed when my mother informs us that he has left again. His commando must take a stand south of Pretoria after Roberts has already taken Johannesburg to the south of Pretoria.

Pretoria, Wednesday, 21 March 1900

When I wake up, my mother and Daniel are standing next to my bed and they sing: "Happy Birthday to you, dear Dora!"

Afterwards they clap their hands while counting from one to fifteen.

David: "What do want to do on your birthday today?"

"I'm going to write a letter to our father to tell him that we miss him terribly and that we pray every day for his safety."

David: "Why don't you also pray that he will able to shoot many Englishmen very dead?"

My mother: "David, that's a nasty thing to ask from God. We must rather pray that these Englishmen come to their senses and leave us in peace. We didn't do anything to them and now they try to harm us."

David: "Our teacher read us a Psalm the other day in which King David, my hero, asked God to make his enemies become blind and lame! Why can't we ask something similar?"

Me: "And Jesus taught us to love our enemies!"

Secretly, I think that it won't really help to pray, although I can't believe that God will allow us to lose this war, because if it is a very unjust war. It is like a big boy who bullies a powerless, defenseless, and friendless little boy. But I just can't shake off this feeling that this war will end badly for us.

But, on the other hand, I was born on a very special day, autumn equinox. I also feel that I will experience exciting times and important events in future.

Pretoria, Thursday, 31 May 1900

Today is my brother's birthday and he is eight. It would have been wonderful to have my father with us, but it's not to be.

During supper, David tells us what he has done during the afternoon to celebrate his birthday: "I wandered over to the deserted Fort Klapperkop on that hill to the south of our town from where I could get a good view to the south. I immediately saw that a battle is being fought in the vicinity of Sesmylspruit (Six Mile Stream). I saw flashes and smoke from the British artillery and I could even hear the bangs of their explosions."

Me: "Were you allowed to go there at all?"

David: "Dora, you girls are all afraid of everything. Nobody stopped me there because the place is deserted. After I have watched the battle in the distance for half-an-hour, the bangs and the flashes and the smoke plumes ceased. A few minutes later, I saw a some

Boers fleeing on their horses, back to Pretoria. I decided that the English overpowered our men with their superior numbers and bigger guns."

My mother puts me to bed at eight-thirty, my usual bed-time. She gives me a few extra kisses. She blows out the candle and I lie in the dark, ready to fall asleep, although I wonder when the enemy soldiers will reach our town.

Suddenly I hear my mother exclaim: "Daniel! Thanks be to God, you're safe!"

I rush out of my bed. After my father has released my mother from his grip and he has given me a hug, he grabs David's hand: "Happy Birthday, David! I'm glad that I made it before you fell asleep."

I ask: "But, Vati, (Daddy), why are you back? Have you given up the fight?"

"No, my girl. We might have lost a minor battle today, but the fight is going on. Our generals have decided that we continue with a guerilla war in the countryside. The British forces may control our towns and villages, but they won't be able to control the countryside. We know our country and we will attack them whenever an opportunity arises. They will wish that they never invaded a peaceful country like ours."

Pretoria, Friday, 1 June 1900

Chaos and mayhem and pandemonium reign in Pretoria. People have discovered that Oom Paul Kruger and his whole government, together with all the members of the Police, have fled by train in the direction of Portuguese East Africa.

Government stores are looted and government offices are thrashed. The people are angry and anxious and afraid. There are rumors that Oom Paul absconded with all the government's gold.

Our school is closed because the teachers are too scared and terrified and petrified to show their faces outside. David goes out to join his friends to watch the turmoil. I join them.

When we get home later, my mother shouts: "You two should stay off the streets! I won't allow you to become hooligans and barbarians and thugs like that lot! People should be ashamed of themselves for behaving like that! Remember, we are honest folk, honest members of the church, honorable citizens of a free republic!"

Pretoria, Saturday, 2 June 1900

I and David sneak out of the house, shortly after daybreak. I was woken by the sounds of a multitude of horses galloping through the town. My first thought was that it must be the British soldiers entering our town, but I am wrong. It is a big Boer commando and most wield whips and sticks and clubs. That must be to get rid of the looters and anarchists and law-breakers.

It is no surprise to see my father at a distance on his horse. The commando divides into smaller groups, which start to patrol the various streets of our town.

General Louis Botha

My father sees us and comes in our direction: "David, Dora, get off the street! Oom Louis Botha has taken control and he declared martial law. People are to stay indoors until further notice."

David: "Who is this Oom Louis Botha? Never heard of him."

" Oh, he's our new commandant general after Oom Piet Joubert became sick and died some time ago. Look over there. He is sitting down to take a rest after we were busy the whole night."

My father dismounts and takes my hand to take me home, while leading his horse. He leaves us at the garden gate:

"I hope to see you all tonight. Perhaps even earlier."

My father keeps his promise and appears for supper. He looks downhearted: "I heard from our commandant that Louis Botha and the other generals think of surrendering to the Brits. They all feel that our situation is hopeless. It's only a matter of days before our capital, Pretoria, falls into the hands of our enemies. They haven't taken a final decision yet because they wanted to consult with Oom Marthinus Steyn, the president of the Orange Free State. The burgers of the Free State are, after all, our allies and we must consider their feelings."

After this long speech, we fall silent.

My mother breaks the silence after a few minutes by asking: "How do the other men in your commando – and the other commandoes – accept you, although you're not a real Boer?"

"Ha-ha. They accept me very well. They seem to like me and I'm regarded as some sort of a mascot. They call me their 'Israelite' and they hope that my presence will make the walls of Jericho come tumbling down. There are even a few men who regard me as a descendant of King David – especially because my family name is Davidsohn. The Biblical David was a great warrior and that is why they made me a corporal."

When it becomes time to go to bed, my father fetches the Bible, reads a chapter, and does a long prayer in which he asks God to give us strength, patience, faith, wisdom, and courage in this dark, dangerous, disastrous, and desperate hour.

Pretoria, Sunday, 3 June 1900

The streets and squares of Pretoria are deserted. Only a few Boer warriors are allowed to move around on horseback.

There won't be any church services today – just as the synagogue of the Hebrew congregation stayed closed yesterday. The sexton of the Dutch Reformed Church on Church Square rings the church bells three times every Sunday – at nine, at nine-thirty and just before the service starts at ten. Today, the bells are silent and we interpret that as a sign that we won't hear a sermon of the Reverend Hermanus Bosman today.

Church Square in Pretoria with the old Dutch Reformed Church and the High Court on the left

My father joins us for supper and announces: "My commandant informed us that Louis Botha and the other generals got a stinging telegram from President Steyn. He called them cowards for thinking of surrendering and he urged them to carry on with the war. The Free State commandoes won't give up the struggle against the invaders and he expects of us to do the same."

My mother: "Hurrah for good ole President Steyn! I hope these cowards in Pretoria will really feel ashamed of themselves. If

I remember correctly, you told us three days ago that it was decided to start a guerilla war – even if the soldiers of ole Queen Victoria occupy our towns."

My father: "You are truly of good Afrikaner stock. Made of the same stuff as the women who threatened to walk barefoot over the Drakensberg Mountains to get away from the hated British in Natal."

Me: "Ma, I am proud of you. And of Vati. Both of you are as brave as a lion, as strong as an ox, as wise as an owl, and as tough as a badger. That's what I also want to be."

David: "Amen, amen. Vati, what is the possibility that I may join your commando? I can ride a horse and I'm sure that I will learn how to shoot in a short time."

My Dad: "Thanks for the idea, son. But it won't work. I understand that you would like to become a warrior, but that must wait for later. Who knows – there may, perhaps, come a time when you can serve our people by becoming a soldier. But I would prefer you to become a tailor and to earn a living by providing people with clothing – just as I do. And for that, you must stay at school, even if it's war."

My mom: "Daniel Davidsohn, I suppose that you will be gone tomorrow – or the day after that. I will keep the shop open and see to it that our children go to school. You need not worry about us. You do your bit by fighting John Bull and we will do our bit by making life difficult for the poor Englishmen when they occupy this town."

My dad: "David, your dad's namesake survived a lions' den. We all will also survive this war. Please fetch the Bible for us."

Me: "Vati, if these Tommys take our town, I want to fight against them. Where can I get a rifle like yours? They will never suspect a girl like to shoot at them and helping them to lose men and horses."

My dad: "Dora, you are made of the same stuff as your Ma. But leave the real fighting to the men. Support your mother and your brother. There may be other ways of helping our war effort."

Me: "But Vati, the Boer women fought just as hard as their men during the Battle of Blood River, eighty years ago. That was when they were attacked by a Zulu army. Those women loaded the guns for the men, but a few of them also fired their guns."

My mom: "My grandmother, Anna Jacoba Scholtz, whose father was Jacob Johannes Kruger, was a crack shot a century ago. Her father was the field commandant of the Roggeveld district and he taught her how to use a gun. She won all the shooting competitions in their neighborhood. She killed the lion that attacked her husband in 1834. It's a pity that you didn't have the opportunity of getting to know her."

My dad: "That is a part of history that I am unaware of, having grown up in Germany. But unfortunately, I won't be able to find a rifle for you. There are just not enough for all the men. And, besides, ammo may be a problem, as well."

Me: "I think I know this great-grandma of mine, this Anna Jacoba Kruger. I have dreamt of her. She was a beautiful and a brave woman."

My mom: "That is certainly what my mother told me about her mother. Both were beautiful women, although I never knew my grandma very well. She died when I was only five years old. She was also a very brave woman who raised eighteen children, of which my mom was the youngest. She had two sets of twins, of which my mother was one of them."

My dad: "David, please read for us Psalm one-hundred-and-twenty-one."

Pretoria, Monday, 4 June 1900

My father joins us again for supper after spending the day with his commando

My mom: "Any news?"

My dad: "Yes. Unfortunately, not really good news. An English officer appeared in town with a white flag and a message from His Illustrious Highness, Lord Roberts, British field marshal. Roberts demanded unconditional surrender of all Boer commandoes."

My mom: "Yes?"

My dad: "Yes. Louis Botha sent this chap back with a message for Roberts – or so I've heard. Botha refused to give up, but requested that all women and children be afforded safe passage out of the town. The messenger returned an hour later. He told Botha that Roberts wouldn't allow that."

Me: "What happens now?"

My dad: "Pretoria will certainly fall into the hands of the British forces. No later than tomorrow. We have been ordered to leave the place tomorrow morning at dawn and pull back to the north."

Silence.

Me (at last): "Vati, we will miss you, of course. But we will continue to pray for you and your commando. God will certainly bless your efforts."

My dad: "David, I want you to read a passage from the Bible for us. Psalm Twenty-three."

Pretoria, Tuesday, 5 June 1900

My father left so early this morning that there wasn't any opportunity for me to say good-bye.

We were supposed to go to school today, but that was impossible. Shortly after breakfast, the British soldiers started marching into Pretoria. All inhabitants stood along Church Street to watch them proceed to the heart of the town, Church Square.

The long column was marching behind a band with drums and funny sounding wind instruments. The noise they made sounded like bleating sheep in pain and agony and despair. Somebody said that they are Scottish pipes. I cannot imagine that anybody would find that sound to be pleasant on the ear.

While watching the parade, I can suddenly understand why the British army was proceeding so slowly to reach Pretoria. Most of the men are on foot – in contrast with our commandoes that move around on horseback.

A bunch of funny-looking soldiers appear. They are all dressed in multi-colored skirts! Some of the spectators laugh at this sight. Somebody shouts at them: "Guys, do you wear knickers and bloomers under those skirts?"

When the soldiers reach Church Square, they assemble in groups and rows.

A funny flag consisting of stripes and triangles is hoisted above the Government building on Church Square. A trumpet blows and the Englishmen all lift their helmets and roar thrice: "Hurrah!" The pipe band follows with another tune and somebody mumbles: "That must be their rendering of 'God save the Queen'."

A few townspeople try to sing along, but most of the spectators stay silent. I can't help it, but I start weeping, while David holds my hand.

My mother tells us afterwards that all British prisoners-of-war were liberated by the British troops.

Pretoria, Wednesday, 6 June 1900

My mother made sure I and David attend school today.

My father, however, assured us before his departure to the north that the war certainly did not end yesterday when Pretoria was taken by the "Rooinekke".[7]

Directly after school came out and we had lunch, two of David's friends, Ben Barnard and Charles Coetzee, come and fetch him and they rush off to the Meintjeskop Hill, behind our home and north of the town. They announce that they want to see if they can observe anything of the retreating commando of which my father is a member.

Meintjeskop Hill is part of a long ridge of hills stretching for many miles, more or less in an east-west line and parallel to another ridge, the Magaliesberg Mountains, further north. These ridges are separated by a valley of a few miles' width.

During supper, David tells us what he and his friends observed: "When we reached the top of the hill, we could see over the intervening valley. It soon became clear that the Boer force has set up an ambush for the pursuing British soldiers on the Onderstepoort[8] farm where there is a narrow cleft through the Magaliesberg Range. British soldiers certainly got a beating they never expected because I saw several of them running back to Pretoria in disorder.

"We yelled at the top of our voices: 'Hurrah for the Boers!'"

---

[7] "Rooinekke" – Red Necks; the nickname given to the British "Tommys" who weren't used to the hot South African sun and whose necks became red and blistered from sun-burn.

[8] "Onderstepoort" – the Afrikaans or Dutch for "Lower Portal", a gap in the mountain range.

Pretoria, Thursday, 7 June 1900

At lunch my little brother tells us: "The three of us who got to the top of Meintjeskop Hill yesterday were treated like heroes by our class mates. Our teacher gave us an opportunity to tell the rest of the class what we saw of the Battle of Onderstepoort. Our class mates give us applause and it's clear that they like the fact that some British soldiers ran away from the battle field."

After lunch, I and my friend Lizzy Lombard, wander around to see what the "Englishmen", as these British soldiers are mostly called, are doing. We notice that they have occupied the four abandoned forts on the outskirts of the town, using the barracks to get settled in. There is also a tent village on the outskirts of the town.

It seems that most soldiers who partook in the parade two days ago, have already left again in an effort to capture or annihilate the remaining Boer commandoes.

We wander to the spot where the military horses are being kept and we see that David and his friends have made friends with a few horses. We join them. Fortunately, these animals don't know the difference between Englishmen and young Boers and they allow us to stroke them.

Pretoria, Saturday, 9 June 1900

My mother finds it impossible to keep us indoors on this Saturday. She warns us that Lord Roberts has proclaimed martial law, which means that a curfew is in place during the hours of darkness. Therefore, it won't be possible for us to wander outside after the sun has set.

My mother: "Dora, I don't think it is right for a young lady, such as you, to go for walks on the streets, even if you take a friend along. There are these English soldiers all over the place and they may molest you. After all, you look a lot older than your fifteen with that pair of round boobs of yours. Please, stay safe."

This warning doesn't apply to David and his two friends, Ben and Charles, and they saunter over to the British camp to look at their horses, their mules, their artillery pieces, their transport wagons, and their mobile kitchens.

When they return just before sunset, they tell us that they spoke to a soldier who looks after the animals.

David: "Many of those horses were stolen, the guy told us. They just took horses and mules from the farmers in the Cape Colony and Natal for use in their Army. I told him that this is theft, something forbidden in the Ten Commandments, but he only laughed. He said that Lord Roberts, the commander-in-chief, has the power to do as he wished. I regard it best not to tell this simpleton that our commandoes will give the British Army a very hard time."

Me: "That guy, this Lord Roberts, is not a commander-in-chief. He's a commander-in-thief!"

Pretoria, Monday, 11 June 1900

It was impossible to inspect the British Army's camp yesterday since it was the Lord's Day. The three of us Davidsohns attended church to listen to the Reverend Bosman. He told his congregation that we have to accept the British occupation of our town and our country because it was certainly God's will that this happened. God is, after all, in control of all affairs of mankind.

The attendance at the service was rather meagre because most men are with their commandoes. Only two octogenarian elders were sitting in the pews reserved for members of the church council.

The streets of Pretoria were more or less deserted after the service had ended. Only a few people stood around, feeling lost.

While we walked home, I proclaimed: "Mister Bosman spoke nonsense today."

My mom: "It's not proper to criticize a man of God."

Dora: "I still think he fed us with trash. I can't think that it's God's will that our country must be invaded by power-hungry and evil and horrible and greedy English-men. I don't agree – and I never will."

Today, things started moving again – but only during daylight hours. Of course, David, Ben and Charles went again to the British camp to play with the horses, while I had to sit at home, helping my mother with needlework.

At supper, David boasts about his accomplishments during the afternoon: "One of those soldiers, who looks after the horses, asked me whether he could lead me around on the back of a horse. He thought he was doing me a huge favor, because I was an ignorant and stupid little Boer boy. When I sat on the back of the horse, I galloped off, Indian style, without a saddle. When I returned the man couldn't believe his own eyes. He ran after me, shouting his head off, but I ignored him.

"Afterwards I told him: 'We Boers learn to ride when we are two months old. My father took me with him on his horse at that age.'"

Me: "That's not right that you have all the fun and games. I'm just as good as you on a horse, because Vati taught me to ride since I was very small. Ma, please keep this boy at home tomorrow. He can sew some buttons onto the shirts you are making."

David: "The three of us had some tea with this soldier, Tommy Tyndall from Yorkshire. We became friends. Perhaps I can hear some military secrets from him and his friends."

Me: "Is he perhaps a general or an important officer? Stable boys usually don't know any military secrets."

David: "He says he's a corporal, just like Vati. Actually, the artillery calls this rank a bombardier. He has five men working for him. So, he's somebody important."

Pretoria, Friday, 22 June 1900

The school holidays started today. Last year, before the war started, this winter holiday was a time for all sorts of outings – picnics at the Fountains outside the town, roaming in the hills surrounding the town, holding parties with friends, or holding sing-song evenings.

Since the war started, these activities are no longer possible. When I arrive home after school, I sink down on a kitchen chair and sigh: "Ma, what can I do during this holiday? Any ideas?"

"You are going to help me on the sewing machine and with needle and cotton string. We must make a living. Fortunately, there are people with money in this town and they need clothes. I will train you in the finer arts of needlework, which were taught to me when I studied domestic science at the teacher's college in Wellington, near Cape Town."

David gets a cheeky smile on his face: "Ma, is that the reason why Vati married you? Because you were a teacher of domestic science, who could help him with his tailor business?"

Mom: "That's right, yes. I saw an advertisement where he advertised for an assistant in his business. I applied and I got the job. And then we fell in love. And that's how I became Missus Davidsohn. My folks were not very enthusiastic about me marrying a Jew, until they got to know him better."

Me: "All right, Ma. I will help you. But I think I will also want to read some German books to improve my marks. Can you recommend any nice German books from Vati's collection?"

"Good idea. We can go and have a look."

Pretoria, Tuesday, 26 June 1900

I get a huge surprise when I enter the kitchen to get breakfast, together with David. My father is sitting next to my mother while they are holding hands and whisper in each other's ears. My father immediately puts his index finger to his lips to give us the sign to stay silent.

We both leap to him and grab him around his neck. He whispers into my left ear: "Nobody must know I'm here. It's a secret. Can you keep this secret?"

I nod my head silently up and down. David does the same.

Mom: "Your father has been ordered by Oom Barend de Lange, his commandant, to slip into Pretoria to spy on the English troops."

Dad: "And he was instructed by Oom Louis Botha to find a volunteer to do this job. I volunteered because I know Pretoria well, having lived here the past sixteen years."

After breakfast, my father orders us to go to school as we usually do. We can talk again this afternoon.

Of course, I find it impossible to pay attention in school. I struggle to control myself not to tell my friends that my father returned in secret to spy on the Rooinekke. Directly after school, I rush home. David is a few steps ahead of me.

During lunch my father tells us that there was a big battle at Donkerhoek, twenty miles east of Pretoria where Oom Louis Botha had about six thousand Boers who defended a wide front. The huge British force, containing some Australian elements, attacked on two days and suffered many losses. There were, however, too many of them and the Boers retreated without suffering significant losses.

After lunch, my father looks at my brother: "Well, David, I hear that you are fraternizing with the enemy. Tell me more."

He tells us in our usual German while whispering how it came that he, Ben, and Charles, made friends with Bombardier Tommy Tyndall. Their mutual love for horses brought them together. David and his friends visit him at least twice a week and he introduced them to the other members of his team, as well as to other soldiers. They picked up a lot of English while conversing with these guys.

My dad: "My, my, my. What a stroke of luck. You see, it's my new job to report on the comings and goings of British troops. And now you are a friend of these chaps I have to report on. I slipped through the guards on the perimeter of our town to come here. It was dark because here was no moon. I must return tomorrow night when it's new moon and I can slide through the lines. And now you, old chap, will have to become my eyes and ears within the British camp. Can you do it?"

It almost happens that he yells at full voice, but he checks himself in time: "Of course! Of course! By becoming a spy or a scout or a snoop, I will be a real Boer warrior, although I won't shoot with a gun. What do you want to know?"

"Find out which regiments are stationed here. Find out how many men there are. Find out what they think of the war. These stupid soldiers will easily talk in front of you about what's going on, without suspecting that you are reporting everything you hear. In their eyes, you and your friends are only stupid, silly, snotty small boys – harmless and innocent."

David: "May I ask Ben and Charles to help me and report to you?"

Vati: "Heavens, no! Of course not! You three may discuss between yourselves what you have observed, but they may never know that you report back to me. The less people who are in the know, the better. Agreed?"

David takes a deep breath, make his eyes wide open and declares solemnly: "You may depend upon me. Only you, Ma and Dora may know how I help the Boers. I promise to stay silent."

"Now, my boy, I leave you again tomorrow night. Go and visit your English friends tomorrow afternoon and then you come and tell me everything."

David responds: "I can already tell you that my English friends belong to the P Battery of the Third Royal Horse Artillery Regiment and that their commander is Major Williams. They don't like him because he's very strict and even cruel. They also told me that seventeen men fell during the Battle of Onderstepoort and that twenty more were wounded."

"Well, well, well. You will never know how valuable you will be for our war effort. I can only come here once a month when there is no moon. In the meantime I am now a member of the commando of Captain Naude and we hide in the 'Skurweberge', the hills to the west of Pretoria.

"We have already ambushed an English patrol and robbed them of their guns, ammunition, provisions, horses, and uniforms. We allowed them to walk back to Pretoria bare-foot and in their underclothes because we can't keep prisoners-of-war. I came here in the company of this Captain Naude, who has to get news from contacts he has in town."

My mother addresses us in her usual Afrikaans: "Please forget that you ever heard the name of this captain. Understood?"

David: "Oh, yes. Vati also never told me where his commando is hiding."

My father shakes his hand and smiles.

It is my turn to speak – in German: "Vati, what do you want me to do? Must I also make friends with some English soldiers and wriggle their secrets out of them?"

Before my father can answer, my mother quips in – in Afrikaans: "I forbid you. An innocent girl like you should never lower yourself to such a disgraceful level by mingling with these uncouth, rude, and barbaric soldiers. Behave yourself like a lady."

Me: "Then what can I do to help? I also want to be a spy, a snoop, a scout, a secret agent."

My father: "I'm afraid your mother is right. I can't allow you to get yourself into danger or into a spot where your honor is in jeopardy. These rough, rude, and rowdy Tommy's are certainly not fit company for a decent girl, like you. But you may keep your eyes and ears open. It is possible that you may pick up some gossip from your friends and their families. That will help. It will certainly help."

After a while, my mother whispers: "Daniel, can you give Dora a nice book in German to read? She wants to improve her German during the school holidays."

"I think I have the right book for her. It is a popular history of the Germanic tribes. 'Geschichte der Germanischen Stämme'.[9] It is meant for young people. I read it when I was her age. Although I am not a real German because my forebears were Israelites, I also regard myself as a German because I grew up in Germany and German is my home language. But you have real Germanic blood in your veins. From your mother's side."

My mom: "Yes, my maiden name is Visser, which is Dutch, as you know. But my mother's maiden name was Scholtz and her mother's name was Anna Jacoba Kruger. They were all from German stock."

I remember that Anna Jacoba Kruger visited me in a dream. I remember her clearly as a brave and beautiful woman who told me: "Don't despair. Things will turn out better than you ever imagined." I can't think what she meant by those words.

---

[9] "History of the Germanic Tribes".

Pretoria, Wednesday, 27 June 1900

It is shortly before sunset that David arrives home. He immediately goes to our parents' bedroom where my father is hiding during daytime.

He blurts out: "This battery has eight big guns."

My dad: "Keep your voice down. We never know who may people may overhear us."

"All right. Sorry. Anyway, this battery has sixty mules to pull these guns and ammunition carts. Six to a gun and four to a cart. There are one-hundred-and-twenty officers and men and most of them travel on horseback."

My dad: "Marvelous! Good work!"

"There are also two regiments of foot soldiers. Both have about four hundred men. There's the first battalion of the Shropshire Regiment and the third battalion of the Staffordshire Rifles."

"Marvelous! Well done!"

"My friends suspect that Lord Roberts will declare total victory very soon and return home. He will probably leave Lord Kitchener in command."

"Fantastic! You are just… fantastic!"

"There are plans to teach the foot soldiers to ride on horseback. They cannot chase the Boer commandoes while marching on their boots. The artillery people will have to teach them. They still don't know where they will get enough horses for all these foot soldiers."

"My son, I salute you! Give me your hand. Shake it!"

"The garrison commander is Colonel Watson. He gets his orders directly from Lord Roberts, although Roberts is still chasing the Boers somewhere else."

"That's something I already know. Anyway, fine work!"

After dark, a strange man appears at our back door. My father introduces him to us: "This is Captain Naudé, the man who commands our commando outside Pretoria. We are leaving this town together tonight."

David shakes the man's hand: "Captain, nice to meet you. I've already promised my father that I will immediately forget your name. Of course, I won't tell anybody that a stranger visited our home after dark tonight. Actually, you don't exist."

My mother: "But this non-existing man is welcome to share our supper tonight."

I add my voice: "Captain, I also salute you. I am sure that you will survive the war. Don't ask me how I know it. I just know it."

The captain and my parents smile at me. I can see they think that I say this just to make the captain feel good.

Pretoria, Wednesday, 25 July 1900

We expected my father already last night because it was three days before new moon with really dark winter nights. However, he arrived in the early morning hours today. Since he took one of our house keys with him, it wasn't necessary for any of us to get up and unlock the kitchen door for him.

At breakfast, David addresses his father: "You probably know that Lord Roberts is still trying to catch Oom Louis Botha and his men."

"Yes, that we do know."

"I watched how the Rooinek foot soldiers were taught to stay on horseback. It was very funny because most of them fell off after a few strides when their horses picked up speed. Some were injured rather seriously."

"So, we don't need to fight them anymore. They cause their own casualties! Ha-ha!"

"I've heard talk that the Englishmen plan to enclose Pretoria with barbed wire fences. That's to keep us inside and to keep people like you outside."

"When will they start with that?"

"As soon as stocks of barbed wire arrive by train from the Cape. Perhaps next week."

Later, my father asks me: "My lovely daughter, have you read that book about the German tribes?"

"Yes, I did. Thanks."

"Any interesting bits?"

"Yes. There was this story about this lady, a prophetess. Some people even thought she was a beautiful goddess. Her name was Veleda and she belonged to the tribe of the Bucteri. She inspired her fellow-Germans to start a rebellion against the Romans who had conquered that part of Germania. That was in the time when the Roman legions were fighting the Jews in Palestine during the Jewish Wat of the sixties of the first century after Christ."

"Unfortunately, we lost that war. That was when Jerusalem was destroyed and the temple went up in smoke and sparks. That was the biggest tragedy in the history of our people."

"And while the Romans were busy with that war against the Jews, Veleda saw that as an opportunity. She advised a German leader with the Latin name of Julius Gaius Civilis to revolt. Unfortunately, the revolt was eventually crushed, but the Romans didn't dare to catch or touch Veleda where she was living in a tower, not far from Xanten, along the lower Rhine. She also hid sometimes in a cave in the Sauerland."

"Yes, Xanten was an old fortified Roman town on the banks of the Rhine, not far from the place where I grew up, Kleve. Xanten was originally called Colonia Ulpia Traiana."

"I would like to go and visit the place. I'm sure the spirit of Veleda must still be hanging around somewhere there. I am glad that I am taking Latin in school. When I know enough of this language, I am going to read what the Roman historian Livy wrote about her. Vati, you are going to order that book for me if it isn't somewhere in a library."

"Then you should also read another book, 'Veleda, ein Zauberroman',[10] written by Benedikte Naubert. I have it somewhere and I'm sure you will enjoy it. Let me go and look for it."

A few minutes later, my father hands me an old book. It was originally written in 1795, but he has a later edition of it. There is an illustration of Veleda, the prophetess.

When I go to bed, I take the book with me and I start to read with my candle still burning. I know I must get up early tomorrow

---

[10] "Velleda, a Magic Novel".

morning to go to school and that I need my sleep, but something draws me to learn more about this mysterious woman who withstood the might of the biggest empire of those times, the Roman Empire. At this moment, our people are also revolting against the British Empire that occupied our little republic and regarding our Boer commandoes as mere rebels or gangsters who must be rooted out.

I gaze at the picture of Veleda in the book. She is sitting on top of her tower and stares at the countryside along the Rhine with the sun rising in the east. A looted Roman standard lies at her feet. She looks just like my great-grandmother who visited me in a dream, although my great-grandmother didn't expose her tits as this woman did. That was perhaps how prophetesses dressed in those days.

Pretoria, Friday, 24 August 1900

David: "Vati, how did you get here? Were you able to get through all the barbed wire fences?"

"Fortunately, a generous English officer donated his field glasses to me. Not voluntarily, of course. And with those field glasses I could see from afar where these fences were already in place. There are still some gaps through which I could slip, around midnight."

"Did you see any sentries?"

"Yes. Two chaps were sleeping under a tree and I stole their boxes of cigarettes. I could have slit their throats, but that would have been cold-blooded murder."

"But you don't smoke. What will you do with those cigarettes?"

"Give them to some of my comrades who smoke."

"Perhaps you could give them to me. With those, I can more easily get the attention of these Englishmen when I offer them some smokes."

"Good idea. Very good idea. Let's do it. But anyway, do you have anything to report?"

"Nothing, unfortunately."

"Why?"

"My friend Bombardier Tyndall and his mates were transferred somewhere else – together with their whole battery. That was two days after your previous visit. When I and my two friends went to visit them as usual, we found other soldiers at that spot and they chased us away. We might, perhaps, make friends with them by offering them some cigarettes."

It is my turn to contribute to the conversation: "I know that these Brits think the war is almost over, but they are totally wrong.

It will go on for more than a year-and-a half. They won't be able to defeat the Boer commando's and they will try some other cruel tricks."

"And how does my daughter know that?"

"I heard it somewhere."

I don't disclose that a beautiful woman communicated it to me last night in a dream.

Pretoria, Monday, 3 September 1900

The head master of our school addresses all the pupils where they are assembled: "We were ordered by the military authorities to proceed to Church Square and gather in front of the Government Building. I don't know what the reason is, but I suppose we will have to comply."

We march in a long row to Church Square. Quite a few town folks are already waiting there. A detachment of foot soldiers is standing at ease, with the stocks of their rifles resting on the ground on their left-hand side.

Precisely at nine, Colonel Watson appears on the balcony of the building with a speaking trumpet. Silence descends upon the crowd.

The colonel shouts: "Ladies and gents! Please pay attention to Field Marshal Lord Frederick Roberts. He has an important announcement to make."

Roberts steps forward and takes the speaking trumpet. He declares that the war is over. Only a few bands of brigands, highway robbers, and stupid die-hards are still holding out. All their supply routes have been blocked and they have nowhere to hide. They will be hunted and treated as criminals because they are resisting the legitimate British rule. The South African Republic is officially abolished and he declares this country to be the Transvaal Colony forthwith – one of the territories under the reign of Her Majesty, Queen Victoria.

He ends his announcement by exclaiming: "Long live the Queen!"

Almost nobody gives applause, except for a few English-speaking shop-keepers.

We return to our class rooms in silence.

I cannot help but to wonder what my father will say about this state of affairs. He hasn't appeared again since new moon in August and my mother looks worried.

During lunch, I tell my mother: "Miss Vermeulen, our music teacher started giving our class some dancing lessons. She plays a waltz or a polka or a march on her piano and we have to dance on the beat of those tunes."

My mother: "Did she bother to demonstrate all the steps to you before you started dancing? "

"Certainly. I think I got the knack of it."

David: "Did you enjoy it?

"Yes and no. I like the movements on the beat of the music. But Miss Vermeulen gave each girl a boy as a dancing partner. My partner was that little Rooinek Harold Hawkins. I hate him. He was so smug about the fact that Lord Roberts declared the war to be over and the Boer forces vanquished."

Me: "Did you tell him that Mister Roberts had it all wrong?"

"Certainly. But he just laughed at me, the stupid swine."

Pretoria, Tuesday, 4 September 1900

When David reaches home during the afternoon, my mother is very worried about his swollen eye: "David! How on earth did you get that swollen eye? It looks bad. Go and lie down on your bed and I will put a slice of cucumber on that swollen spot. And then you tell me how on earth did you get into an ugly fight. That's not how you were brought up!"

David lies down on his bed with a slice of cucumber hiding the swollen eye.

My mom: "If you got into a violent fight, then I will have no choice but to sentence you to house arrest for a whole week. Who did that to you?"

"Sergeant Chalmers."

"Who is he? A British soldier? If so, I will have to ask the Reverend Bosman to complain to Colonel Watson."

"Yes, he's a British soldier. But he was severely reprimanded by the Sergeant Major. He made him apologize to me."

"But why did he hit you? What did you do to deserve that treatment?"

"He thought we were going to harm their horses. But I was only stroking the neck of one of their animals. And then I made friends with that Sergeant Major by giving him that packet of smokes that Vati gave me."

"Was he in any way grateful?"

"Yes, he was. He invited us to go and watch tomorrow afternoon how they treat the horses' hooves."

Me: "You will have a beauty of a black eye in a few days' time. You will look like a prince of the pirates or something."

Pretoria, Wednesday, 5 September 1900

When we arrive home for lunch after school, my mother looks at David in amazement: "Well, I never. That slice of cucumber must have done some wonderful work. Your eye looks normal. There's no sign that it was swollen yesterday after that bully of a sergeant slammed you with his fist."

David looks at his own face in the mirror in my mother's bedroom and agrees with my mother that his face looks normal. There is no sign of a black eye.

I exclaim: "Jeez, that's another miracle. Just as with your broken arm that got healed within a very short time. Did anybody pray for you?"

After lunch, David collects his friends and they set off to the military camp where they will look for that sergeant major.

When David returns shortly before dusk, my mother is worried: "Where did you stay so long? How about your homework for school? You can't do that at bed time."

"I know, Ma. But I and Charles and Ben had a marvelous afternoon. We made friends with Sergeant Major William Warrick. He says he's an RSM."

Me: "What's that? It sounds like some sort of caterpillar or a beetle or some insect."

"It is the abbreviation of regimental sergeant major and his real rank is warrant officer, first class. He is the RSM of the 6th Inniskilling Regiment of Dragoons – whatever that is. I and my friends had to practice that funny name over and over until we got it right."

"And what are these dragons doing here?"

"They're not dragons. They're dragoons. That's cavalry. In other words: soldiers who fight on horseback. They're her for a short period to refit before they move on, to the Eastern Transvaal."

"Were you allowed to touch the horses?"

"Corporal Johnson had to give us riding lessons, but I think I could give him a riding lesson. You should have seen me on his horse. It was wonderful."

"That's not right! You have all the fun and games, while I must stay at home and do some nasty needlework."

"Please remember that I am doing important work as a spy for the Boers. It's really hard work."

"

Pretoria, Monday, 10 September 1900

At the breakfast table David sits and cough. My mother feels his forehead: "You are feverish. You stay in bed today. Is your nose blocked and your throat swollen?"

"Yes"

"Yes what?"

"Yes, Mother."

"No. I mean: is your nose blocked and your throat swollen? Or both?"

"Yes, mother.

"Which one of them?"

"Both of them."

"Thanks for giving me a decent answer, at last. I will run off to Doctor Barry. I know he has a wonderful cough mixture. It will help you to get rid of this cold in two ticks."

Pretoria, Tuesday, 11 September 1900

When David appears dressed at breakfast, my mother declares: "That cough medicine of Doctor Barry really picked you up. How do you feel?"

"Fit and firm and ready to fight."

"Let me feel your forehead. Ah, you're ready to go to school. Thanks be to God and Doctor Barry."

During breakfast, I ask my mother: "Ma, what happened to our vinegar in the pantry? I needed a few tablespoons full of vinegar for a domestic science project, but I found only an empty jug. How did that happen? I can clearly remember that that jug was still full a week ago."

My mom: "Search me. Perhaps the jug fell over and everything got spilt."

"But then the cupboard and the floor would have been wet…"

While we are walking to school, I tell my little brother: "Did you really swallow that stuff that the doctor gave you? I don't think so."

"Of course, I did. But it tasted horrible."

I tell myself: "Something funny is going on with David. Perhaps I will find out later on."

During the afternoon, while we walk back home, I confront my little brother: "You never swallowed all of that cough mixture. I just know it. What did you do with it?"

David smiles: "You women are funny. You can just know when something is not right. How do you do it?"

"It's called intuition. Woman just have it. God gave it to us."

"All right. Let me tell you what happened. I didn't have the heart to tell Ma that I swallowed only one table spoon full of that foul, filthy. and almost fatal fluid of Doctor Barry. It tastes horrible, horrifying, and horrific. One may describe it as a brew that was concocted by the Devil himself. I, therefore, emptied the bottle's contents into another bottle and presented the empty medicine bottle to Ma to prove that I have swallowed everything. But I had other uses for that stinking and stenchy and sickening stuff."

"How did you use it?"

"Let me tell you, but you may only tell Ma and Vati about it. Promise?"

"I promise. And I always keep my promises."

"All right. Ma put me in bed at eight, as usual. After a last kiss and a hug, she blew out the candle. Half-an-hour later she and you also went to bed. That was the sign for me to creep out of bed, get dressed again with a black pullover and I disappeared through the window. In my one hand I held the bottle with Doctor Barry's stuff and in my other hand I had a jug of vinegar."

"Aaaah! So, that's what happened with our vinegar? You are a little thief, you know."

"But it was for a good goal. While I crept through the back streets, there wasn't a soul to be seen because everybody was afraid to break the curfew. I reached the military camp safely. An almost full moon was hanging over the eastern horizon and that helped me to find my way.

"It seemed as if the 6th Dragoons were all asleep. I emptied the contents of the medicine bottle and the vinegar jug into the trough from which the horses of the 6th Dragoons have to drink. I am sure that no horse in his right mind will want to drink from that trough with the result that the lot of them will stay thirsty."

"You're cruel, very cruel. One shouldn't treat the poor animals like that. They also have feelings."

"Maybe. But my idea was to become a saboteur. I wanted to do something to help the Boers. I'm sure Vati will approve."

Pretoria, Thursday, 13 September 1900

During supper, my mother asks David: "What have you and your friends been up to this afternoon? Did you visit the military camp again?"

"Yes, Ma."

I can't help it, but I blurt out: "Ma, this little scoundrel did something very cruel to the poor horses of those English soldiers. He made them drink some poisonous and polluted water to make them sick."

David: "Ma, please tell this sister of mine not to be so cheeky. She always exaggerates things. I was only sabotaging the English war effort. Let me tell you what really happened."

My mother listens with a smile on her face while David tells his story of the cough mixture and the vinegar in the horses' drinking water. She asks: "And what did you see this afternoon? How are those poor horses? Have you killed any of them?"

"That mixture of ole Doctor Barry can certainly have that effect. But, no, no horses have died. When we got to the camp, the sergeant major told us that he had no time for us because they had a crisis. All the horses were sick. They refuse to drink any water and nibble on their fodder. That fodder is always made soft by pouring some water over it because it is otherwise very dry. He said that the horses went on a hunger strike, for no good reason."

Ma: "But you know the real reason?"

"Exactly. We walked around to inspect the horses. Just then three bare-footed men in their underclothes appeared and asked the sergeant major where they could find the colonel because they found his office locked.

"The sergeant major shouted at them that it's against regulations to walk around without being properly dressed. They told him that there is a long story to tell to explain their lack of clothes. Their squadron was looking for Boer fighters in the hills when they were ambushed. Some of the men tried to gallop off, but they didn't get very far because their horses were sick and wouldn't move fast enough. Two of them were shot dead and four were wounded. And the Boers made the rest of them surrender. They took all their guns, ammo, and provisions, and made them walk back to Pretoria on their bare feet. Their boots and horses were also looted."

Me: "They must have been a sorry sight."

"Yes, they told the sergeant major that some women-folk laughed at them. Only three of them managed to reach Pretoria. The others had to stay behind because of all the blisters and blood on their feet."

My mother and my sister start laughing. It's clear they enjoyed my story, although they feel sorry for the poor thirsty and hungry horses.

Pretoria, Saturday, 15 September 1900

David is all smiles when he tells his story after having visited the camp of the Englishmen this Saturday afternoon.

"When I got to that sergeant major, he told me that there were no riding lessons for us today. That's because they have no horses left. According to him, it is a shame that a cavalry regiment doesn't have a single horse, while they are supposed to be fighting a war."

My mother: "Have all those horses died from that poisonous and polluted mixture that you poured into the water four day ago?"

"No. The English vet thought some or other ugly bug had taken hold of the horses. They had all to be shot before the bug spreads. And now that lot can't continue with the war."

Me: "When will they get other horses?"

"Heaven knows. The sergeant major thought that they would perhaps get some fillies that have to be broken in and that will take some time before they are ready again to continue with the war."

My mom: "Did he say anything about the Boer fighters?"

"Yes. He thought they were stupid, stubborn, and silly for not realizing that they can't win the war."

Me: "I think he doesn't know our people. We won't give in so easily. This war is going to drag on for quite some time. I just know it."

Pretoria, Saturday, 22 September 1900

It's almost new moon and my father appears at the breakfast table. He must have crept into Pretoria during the night.

While having our breakfast, we keep the curtains closed and talk in whispers. We don't want to give the presence of my father away.

He has a long story to tell: "It was rather difficult to get into this place because there are so many barbed wire fences all around."

David: "I heard that these Englishmen plan to hang empty tins filled with stones onto these barbed wire fences so that they can hear when anybody is cutting the wires."

"Thanks for that news. But it wasn't necessary to cut any wires. I could slide on my belly underneath these fences."

I exclaim: "But that must have ruined your clothes!"

"Certainly. Look here, I have torn my trousers in two spots when they got stuck on the barbed wires."

My mother: "Tell us about the war. What are you doing?"

"Yes, we have had a big stroke of luck a few days ago. A big bunch of Englishmen came riding in our direction, there in the Skurweberg Mountains. Their horses were evidently sick because they could only proceed at a walking pace. We prepared an ambush and caught the lot of them, minus two who tried to chase away and were shot. We also wounded a few more and killed three of their horses.

"When they came to the sound and sane and sensible conclusion that it was best to surrender, we shook them out, as usual. We took their guns, provisions, clothes. and horses. Because we have nowhere to hold prisoners-of-war, we allowed them to walk back, back to Pretoria, in their underclothes and without boots. I don't know how far they got."

David: "Only three of them made it to Pretoria and they requested that a few wagons or carts be sent out to pick up the rest of them. I saw these three guys myself."

My dad: "So, you are still our eyes and ears in that camp! Wonderful!"

"What did you do with the horses that you took from these Tommys?"

"We saw that they were very thirsty. We took them to a little brook and after they drank some water, they started grazing. They're all right now."

"You won't be able to get any more English horses from the 6th Dragoons."

"Why's that?"

"Their vet thought that the lot of them were sick and they decided to do away with the lot of them before they infected other animals."

"That means that they won't be able to take part in the war until they get new horses, if any. Do you know what made them sick?"

"Yes. A jug full of vinegar and the contents of a medicine bottle from Doctor Barry in their drinking water did the trick."

Me: "You nasty boy! Stealing our vinegar!"

My mother: "Tell my, why didn't you take all of that cough mixture?"

"I didn't really need it. I recovered completely without that stuff."

Me: "Just as you recovered from that swollen eye. You're a walking miracle."

My father: "Yes, yes, you are a miracle. You recover easily from all sorts of injuries. You must have a remarkable constitution.

And, in addition, you immobilized a whole blooming British regiment. We need more boys of your caliber! Tell us more, please?"

"All right. On Monday night, I escaped from my room through the window with this cough mixture and the jug of vinegar. Nobody saw me as I slipped through the back streets. And then I emptied that gruesome medicine and some vinegar into the drinking troughs of the horses. Two days later, me and my friends visited those Englishmen again. They were very concerned about their horses because these animals refused to drink. They also wouldn't touch their fodder. I think that's because their dry fodder is made soft with some of their drinking water and that made them avoid that horrible smell and taste.

"And this afternoon, we visited those Tommys again. All their horses are gone."

My father: "My son, you have inflicted more damage to the British in one stroke than my whole commando was able to do in many months. And, Dora, do you have anything to tell?"

"Yes Vati. But nothing as exciting as David's story."

"Yes?"

"My friend, Lizzy Lombard, has an older sister who got on friendly terms with this English soldier. He's actually a married man with a wife and kids somewhere in England. And now he has made Lizzy's sister pregnant. Her mother asked the Reverend Bosman to lodge a complaint at Colonel Watson's office. The colonel summoned this sister and this soldier both to his office. After hearing both stories, he ordered that this man forfeit his pay for the next six months to pay for the medical expenses of the child he has fathered. He was also demoted from lance corporal to an ordinary soldier and his new job was to clean the latrines in the camp."

My mother: "So, it's not only the Englishmen who have to hang their heads in shame. Some of our Boer girls also behave badly.

What a shame."

"That's not all. Lizzy's mother ordered her to lure this soldier to their home. She did so and her mother gave this man such a hiding with a leather strap that he had to be taken to hospital."

My dad: "Let's hope that teaches the lot of them to keep their paws off our girls. One more casualty cause by a Boer woman."

Me: "The trouble is that this guy's wife and kids in England will suffer for the next six months without his pay. This soldier was so ashamed by being assaulted by a Boer woman that he didn't dare to lay a charge of inflicting grievous bodily harm against her."

Pretoria, Saturday, 3 November 1900

David tells us that some new horses for the 6th Dragoons arrived yesterday afternoon by train. Most of them are fillies. Sergeant Major Warrick allowed him and his friends to stroke the necks of some of the animals.

My mother: "You told us a while ago that these Englishmen will have to break in their new fillies. Have they started?"

David: "I persuaded the sergeant major to allow me to tame a beautiful young white Arabian stallion. He came from Egypt; the sergeant major told me. I told him that it is cruel to break in the animals and that much better results can be achieved with gentleness."

Me: "And how did you treat that horse so gently?"

"It was easy. I fed him two apples and allowed him to sniff my hand and my body to get to know my smell. Then I slit a bridle with a snaffle bit over his head and into his mouth. He allowed me to do it and then I led him around with the bridle. He followed me willingly."

My mother: "And how did that sergeant major friend of yours react to that?"

"He and Sergeant Chalmers were surprised. Even stunned. They had to admit that I know something about horses. I named the horse Firefly and promised him that I will be back on Monday with more apples."

Pretoria, Sunday, 18 November 1900

My father managed to creep through all the obstacles into town and now we are having breakfast on this Sunday morning. We feel so overjoyed by seeing him alive and well that we decide that God will understand that we don't go to church today.

"Well, David, anything to report?"

"Yes, Vati. But we need to hear from you first."

My father relates that his commando had a quiet time. Since the 6th Dragoons had no horses for a long time, they couldn't continue with their efforts to hunt the Boer units. The other regiment in Pretoria, the second battalion of the North Lancashire Mounted Rifles, didn't pose much of a threat because their soldiers were not yet at home in the saddle.

And now it's David's turn: "You can almost call me a traitor, because I was actively aiding the enemy."

My dad: "That's sad. Please don't put our family's name to shame. What exactly did you do? "

"The 6th Dragoons received the most beautiful Egyptian Arabian fillies. They wanted to break in the animals. But I couldn't allow that cruelty and I taught them how to teach the animals gently and patiently and slowly to get much better results."

"And now this regiment is ready to come and hunt us, due to your help?"

"Not quite yet. But perhaps shortly before Christmas. These fillies are not yet used to war conditions. They must be taught how to behave during a gun fight, for instance."

"And then?"

"And then we wait and see. Anyway, I see that you have been able to bring your rifle along. It's not that German Mauser you used to have."

No, it's a Lee-Metford that we scored from the khaki-clad Brits. They also donated a substantial number of rounds to go with these rifles. We couldn't use our Mausers anymore because our ammo ran out. Now we continue the fight on the account of Her Majesty's Quartermaster General. We often refer to this gun as the Point Three-Oh-Three because its rounds are point 303 inches in diameter. Unfortunately, it's not as accurate as the German rifle. I always had great faith in German products."

David continues: "Lord Roberts has already left the Transvaal for Cape Town. He thinks the war can be over within a few weeks. He left everything in the hands of Lord Kitchener to wind up a few loose strings."

My dad: "He's in for a nasty shock. There's still much fight left in us. Unfortunately, many of our men surrendered or simply deserted. Some of them even joined forces with the Englishmen to fight their own countrymen."

Me: "That's scandalous!"

"It certainly is. We call them 'Joiners' and they are held in great contempt. They are officially known as 'National Scouts', but we think of the as 'national scum' and 'domesticated Khakis'. They are an ugly, dirty, and grisly blot on our national pride. Even the brother of the Free State commandant general, Oom Christiaan de Wet, Piet de Wet, became a Joiner and the English made him a Boer general, although a traitor general who has to shoot at his own people."

My mom: "How can anybody fall so low? God isn't blind."

My dad: "And neither is the Dutch Reformed Church. One of our commando members, whose brother is a minister, says that there are plans to put these Joiners and renegades under censure or even ban them from the Church totally."

Me: "Will that mean that they will be banned to the fires and flames and foul fumes of hell?"

"One may almost say so."

Me: "I also have some news on these filthy Englishmen."

"What is it?"

"Quite a number of these English soldiers receive treatment for sores on their private parts. I heard these parts got so swollen that they struggle to march. Some of them even can't fit into their trousers anymore. It's too painful to pull up and to fasten the buttons on their trousers."

My mother: "Where did you hear that disgusting news?"

"Lizzy's sister, who is still seeing the father of her unborn child, told her. She heard it from this soldier."

"And how did they contract this terrible condition?"

"The lot of these sick men visited prostitutes, black and white, who infected them with some or other ugly, uncouth, and uncivilized disease, or something."

My dad: "Ha-ha, with those painful parts they won't be able to get onto a horse. If they dare to do it, the result will boil down to castration. They deserve this punishment from God. He's not blind. He won't allow this fornication and harlotry and whoring to continue unpunished."

Me: "Vati, what is 'fornication'?"

My mom: "I will explain that you when we are on our own. Also, the other difficult words."

David: "And what is castration?"

My dad: "I will explain that to you when we are on our own, out of earshot of the women."

Me: "I don't think I can believe what Lizzy told me. It's too fantastic."

Pretoria, Saturday, 8 December 1900

I and my brother accompany our mother on this Saturday morning to do shopping, as we often do. Each of us is carrying two empty baskets to hold our purchases. Fortunately, groceries and other stocks are still available in Pretoria, despite the war. Although the town is cut off from the outside world by barbed wire fences, the railroad link is still operational.

My father told us that many commandoes derailed trans carrying troops, animals, ammunition, and provisions and then ransacked the freight cars after convincing the guards to surrender. In this manner, the government of Her Majesty, Queen Victoria, is really financing the Boer war effort. South Africa has so many wide-open spaces that it is impossible for the Tommys to protect each and every train adequately.

However, we are on our way to buy stocks of stuff that we cannot produce ourselves – maize flour, wheat flour, coffee beans, tea leaves, sugar, salt, chicken feed, meat, and so forth. We are self-sufficient regarding fruit and vegetables, which we grow on our plot in Arcadia. Our chickens provide us with eggs.

All three of us are eager tillers of the soil. We have a large tank next to our house in which we collect rain water from the gutters on the roof for use during the dry winter months.

This all means that we are really well-fed. My mother keeps the tailoring business going and she regularly imports rolls of material from abroad. I and Dora must often help to sew on buttons or do other easier tasks. She has, therefore, mostly some cash with which we can buy stocks.

The summer fruit season has started and David and his two friends ransacked the gardens of English-speaking residents of our town so that my mother can produce dried peaches, apricots, raisins, prunes, and figs for my father to take to his commando when he visits us again.

Our garden also contains a huge cactus bush on which prickly pears are growing. It's not possible to make any dried fruit from them. The cactus produces beautiful yellow flowers this time of the year and when they fall off, the fruit may be picked and eaten after the skin has been cut open.

While we are walking back home with our baskets filled with our purchases, David asks me: "Have you noticed that officer watching you while we were walking around in town?"

"No, not really. There were so many people around that I couldn't notice anybody, really."

"Well, he's following us home. Must I ambush him and break his leg or something?"

My mom: "You will only cause unnecessary trouble if you do that. Don't try anything silly."

David addresses our mother: "Ma, I think I can understand why this officer, a young lieutenant of the North Lancashire Mounted Rifles with two pips on each shoulder, is keeping Dora under surveillance. At fifteen, she already looks like an attractive grown woman. We Davidsohns are all tall people and Dora is the tallest girl in her class at school. In addition, she can boast two well-formed tits."

My Mom: "David, stop this nonsense, talking about things that must be left unsaid."

David is unperturbed: "I don't know why men are so interested in these soft protuberances in girls. I am only too glad that I am a boy and that I don't have to worry about these vulnerable additions or annexures or appendices to the human body."

Mom: "David! Really!"

Two minutes after we have dumped our baskets on the kitchen table and elsewhere, somebody knocks on the front door. Ma goes to open the door and the two of us inquisitive siblings follow her. The lieutenant is standing on the veranda while he nervously twitches his helmet in his hands. He is rather long with a slender frame. He has red hair and freckles all over his face. He does his best to look friendly with a big grin, showing his big teeth.

My mom: "Yes?"

The man: "Good morning, Ma'am. Sorry for disturbing you. May I come in for a moment?"

"Only after you promise to get back my six dining room chairs that were requisitioned three days ago. My dining room looks awkward without them and I want them back."

"Ma'am, I promise to do my utmost to help you in this regard."

"All right. Come inside."

We all sit down in the drawing room. The man, who sits on the edge of his chair, says: "Ma'am, perhaps I should introduce myself first of all. I am Lieutenant Hector de Hacqueville of the North Lancashire Regiment here in town. If I may ask, who are you?"

My mom" I'm Missus Veronica Davidson and these are my children, Dora and David. I'm a widow. What is your business? Do you want me to make you a new suit or some smart shirts?"

"No, Ma'am. Nothing of the sort. It's something quite different. It concerns your daughter."

"What has she done that you want to discuss with me?"

"Nothing really. It... It is… actually, that…. I need a dancing partner for the New Year's celebrations at our officers' club on the thirty-first of this month. All unmarried officers are allowed to be accompanied by dancing partners. Female partners. that is."

"And you think that my daughter would be a fitting dancing partner?"

"Ma'am, hmm… exactly. Yes."

"We can discuss that as soon as my six chairs are back in my house. Understood?"

"Understood, Ma'am."

"All right. Then we talk again later. Good-bye Lieutenant Hackwell."

"It's actually de Hacqueville, Ma'am. It's really a French family name. My ancestors came with William the Conqueror during the eleventh century from Normandy in France. William became king of England."

Immediately after Lieutenant de Hacqueville has left, we hold an impromptu family meeting where we are sitting in the drawing room.

I roll my eyes and my Ma twists her handkerchief through her fingers. David declares: "If that chap tries anything funny with you, Dora, I will break his leg with a big club. I think I'm more agile that him and I will get the first hit in before he suspects anything. When his leg is broken, he won't be able to catch me."

My mom: "Stop that nonsense, David. We don't want to cause any trouble. It may somehow backfire onto your father, should he ever be caught. You must have noticed that I introduced myself as Missus Davidson – a respectable English surname – instead of the

Jewish and German Davidsohn. That was to put the man more at ease in our presence. I called myself a widow on purpose to avert the attention from your father. Many of these elevated English families have deep-seated prejudices against Jews and I want to prevent any nastiness."

Mom says again after a minute of awkward silence: "Dora?"

"Ma, I think I ought to accept his invitation. He evidently thinks that I am eighteen or nineteen – and not fifteen. But you have brought me up properly and I am sure that I will behave myself appropriately in the presence of those noble, titled, and aristocratic officers. Perhaps Lord Kitchener himself will attend."

My mom: "I will only allow you to go if you are chaperoned. By David. He must see to it that you are brought home, safely, unscathed, and with your honor intact."

David: "And when these chaps drink too much champagne they will start to boast about their military exploits. I will listen carefully and report back to Vati in January."

I giggle: "That sounds exciting! Very, really, truly exciting…"

Pretoria, Monday, 10 December 1900

The last week of the school year started this morning and we all look forward to the summer vacation of five weeks that starts on Friday.

When I and David reach our home, a cart with a mule is parked in front of our house. Two private soldiers are offloading my mother's dining room chairs and they carry them into the house.

Ma is watching everything with a satisfied smile on her face. She asks the lieutenant who supervises everything: "How did you manage this?"

"Ma'am, easily, quite… easily. I just took them with the help of two of my men."

"Where were they?"

"In the office of our battalion commander, Lieutenant Colonel Sir Lionel Lecky. Although he is my superior officer, I am actually his social superior. My father is a viscount and I am due to inherit the title after his death. Our family estate is also much older and bigger than his place. He wanted to know why I was taking the chairs from his office and I merely said that our party on New Year's Eve cannot proceed without the chairs. Hy frowned, but said nothing further."

My mom: "And you didn't tell a single lie. Well, let us sit down and discuss your wish to have my only daughter as your dancing partner."

Each one of us takes a seat. This time, the man sits comfortably on his chair, leaning backwards, evidently confident that he has impressed my mother: "Ma'am, yes. Thank you for the opportunity to discuss my wish."

My Ma: "And what made you decide that my daughter would be a fitting partner for a future viscount?"

"Ma'am, I certainly cannot think so far into the future. But when I saw you and your family in town on Saturday, it struck me how gracefully she moves. She must be an excellent dancer."

"Yes, she has been taking some dancing lessons. What else?"

"Ma'am, I promise to treat her with the utmost respect and consideration. I promise solemnly to behave as a true gentleman and a knight throughout the whole night. I will see to it that not a single hair from head gets damaged."

My mom: "Dora?"

"If this lieutenant is a better dancing partner than my previous partner, then we can give it a try."

"Miss Davidson, please accept my gratitude for your graceful acceptance of my humble invitation."

My mom: "There is one very important condition. My son is to accompany both of you during the whole occasion to ensure her safe return. He is a good friend of Sergeant Major Warrick of the 6th Dragoons and he will easily get help from that quarter if something doesn't satisfy him. Agreed?"

"Agreed, Ma'am. Totally."

"And – no alcoholic beverages for my children. And you limit your own intake to two drinks. Only two. My son will keep an eye on you. He is quite capable of counting up to two. Understood?"

"Understood, Ma'am."

"As soon as you disobey these conditions, my son is to bring his sister home. Agreed?"

"Agreed, Ma'am."

Me: "It's still three weeks before the occasion. But you will certainly be able tell me at what time you will expect me to be ready."

"We must be there at seven, when it is getting dark. Unfortunately, I don't own any wheeled vehicles and we will have to walk. That means, I will wait for you on your veranda at six-thirty."

David: "What about the mule cart outside?"

Me: "David, really!"

Pretoria, Saturday, 22 December 1900

My father materialized yesterday morning at breakfast after having crawled on his belly for a considerable distance to reach us. He told us that Kitchener is a much younger man than Roberts and that everybody expects him to treat the war situation more vigorously.

This afternoon, my Ma, David, and I work in our vegetable garden. A thunderstorm is brewing and we want to sow some tomato seeds and plant some potatoes before the water from heaven came down. My father stays indoors because it's too dangerous to show his face outside during daylight hours.

Suddenly, we hear the voice of Hector de Hacqueville as he comes around the corner of the house: "Hallo! Hallo! Hallo! I knocked on the front door but nobody came to open. I heard voices coming from the back garden. How are all of you doing?"

My mother: "Lieutenant, we didn't expect any visitors today. Please excuse us for being dressed in our working garments. It's impossible to get domestic help and gardeners nowadays and we have to do all the work ourselves. Please come inside. Please go around to the front door, which I will open for you. Dora will make some tea for us in the meantime."

My mother finds my dad in the kitchen and whispers: "It's that English officer who wants to dance with Dora. I couldn't allow him to enter through the kitchen because he might've found you. See, I'm supposed to be a widow, as far as he's concerned."

While my mother opens the front door, I wash my hands. Hector de Hacqueville is led inside and David must keep him company while my mother makes herself more presentable. I can clearly hear what they are talking.

David asks him: "What made you decide to join the Army?"

"Oh, the adventure, the comradeship, the opportunity to

serve my Queen and my country. Travelling to strange places. But it is also a family tradition that all male members must do their bit in the Army. Or the Navy."

"Where were you trained to become an officer?"

"At a place called Sandhurst. That's where all future officers have to go through all the ropes. My scholarship at a grammar school made that bit easy for me."

"And when did you come to South Africa?"

"I arrived with my unit exactly a year ago. December 1899. We took part in campaigns in the Cape Colony where we helped to lift the siege of Kimberley. And now we are guarding Pretoria and environment."

"Have you had any near brushes?"

Just before he can answer, my mother and I appear with a tray with a teapot, cups, saucers, and other paraphernalia.

The lieutenant jumps up to relieve the ladies of our burdens. That seems to impress my mother.

Initially, the conversation deals with trivialities – the weather, the scarcity of products and the Christmas celebrations.

My mother: "May I call you Hector?"

"Most certainly, Ma'am. I thought it appropriate to pay you a visit today. I am playing Father Christmas and I brought you some small gifts."

"Oh, that's not necessary."

"I must repay you for behaving so decently towards me when I visited you last time. Missus Davidson, I have found this beautiful Bible, bound in leather. I hope it will bring you some joy."

"That's very kind of you. I appreciate it."

"David, I've also brought you something to read. It's a novel: Robinson Crusoe."

David gets up to receive his gift and to shake Hector's hand.

"And now for the divine Damsel Dora: a pendant on a chan. I hope you will be able to wear it on the night we are going to the celebrations at the officers' club."

When I get up to receive my gift, he requests me to turn around so that he can fasten the ornament around my neck. I roll my eyes while looking in my mother's direction. I notice that Hector's hands shake in my presence, while he fastens the clasp of the chain.

My mom: "Hector, it suddenly strikes me that you will be very lonely over Christmas, so far from your family. Christmas Day is next Tuesday. Will you join us for lunch on that day? That is, if you don't have any other commitments?"

Hector makes a clumsy bow with his long bony body: "Ma'am, it will be an extreme honor and an extreme pleasure."

Afterwards, after Hector has left, my father remarks: "I couldn't help but to hear everything where I was hiding in the bedroom. This chap is the first decent Englishman that I have encountered. The lot of them are arrogant, callous, full of themselves and filled with silly ideas about the superiority of British culture. They have nothing to compare with what we have achieved in Germany."

My mother: "He's only behaving himself decently because he fell like a ton of stones and pebbles for your attractive daughter. He's totally besotted with her. He never suspected her Jewish background with her blonde hair, blue eyes, regular features, and the figure of a goddess."

"She may pry some military secrets out of him. Or from his friends. Dora, never forget that your German Jewish father is a Boer warrior. Your mother is the descendant of a long line of pioneers who fought ferocious barbarians to develop this country."

"Vati, you need not worry about my loyalty. I will listen carefully while in that Englishman's company."

Pretoria, Wednesday, 26 December 1900

While I was sitting in church yesterday, where I was supposed to listen to the Reverend Bosman's Christmas sermon, I couldn't concentrate on this man's voice. I just drifted off into my own thoughts. I was planning how I would behave myself later during the day when Hector was due to visit us. I decided to tease him by keeping myself in the background, while Ma and David talk to him.

The family Davidsohn (minus father) had a quiet Christmas lunch yesterday. Hector turned up with some more gifts – sausages, cheese, chocolates, and glazed fruit. I kept myself most of the time out of the conversation by serving up the dishes and pottering around in the kitchen. I couldn't help but to notice that this khaki-clad aristocrat almost made a fool of himself by staring at me whenever he got the opportunity. He had a very noticeable sad and melancholic expression on his face, perhaps since I stayed out of his reach.

After lunch, my mother announced that we usually lie down for a rest on Sundays – a custom that will be repeated on this religious holiday. We also need some time to digest the sermon of the Reverend Bosman earlier this morning. That forced Hector to leave us early.

Last night, a welcome visitor entered my dreams. I don't know whether she was Veleda, the German priestess and prophetess, or my great-grandmother, Anna Jacoba Scholtz. They look so similar that it could have been anyone of them. Or even a combination of both of them.

This woman who appeared in my dream told me with a friendly smile: "You are verrry lucky. Your life will turn out to be verrry happy, but also verrry dangerous."

And now, I am lying on my bed after I have woken up. It is still early, although the summer sun is already shining. I lie on my back with a very satisfied smile on my face, while I savor the excitement of my dream.

Pretoria, Monday, 31 December 1900

While we are trotting to the officers' club, the Honorable Lieutenant Hector de Hacqueville tells us what we can expect from the occasion, which will start with a formal miliary dinner.

"I had some sort of a dilemma, which I discussed with our club president, Colonel Watson. It was a stipulation of your mother that Dora had to be chaperoned by her brother. The problem was: where do you, David, fit in? You cannot sit at one of the tables for unmarried men who are escorting ladies to the occasion. It won't do to give you a seat at a table for the more senior married officers, whose wives stayed at Home. The solution was to give you your own table, from where you can watch everything. You will consume the same fare as anybody else, but it won't be expected of you to partake in any of the toasts that will be called."

We find that acceptable.

David's various visits to the military camp made him feel at home in a military set-up and he looks forward to what the night will offer – which promises to be exciting.

Inside the club, there is polite conversation going on at all the tables. I sit next to Hector, on his left. There are five couples at our table and all of them are young lieutenants. I hope that David will keep his ears wide open for any snippet of useful information.

Lord Kitchener

Precisely at seven, Colonel Watson enters the venue and roars: "Attention! General Viscount Horatio Kitchener!"

The commander-in-chief of the British Army in South Africa enters while everybody stands. He is greeted with applause.

He is dressed in his khaki field uniform, just as all the other officers. Hector explained that they wear their so-called mess dress, which is very smart, when they are back at Home for a formal dinner. Here, in Pretoria, it's not possible, unfortunately.

We are served soup, fish, mutton, beef, vegetables, and something sweet. Colonel Watson announces that Port Wine will now be distributed. A decanter filled with a red fluid is placed at both ends of each table. The decanter is passed on to the left after each person has filled his or her glass. Then a series of toasts are being drunk: on the health of Queen Victoria, Lord Roberts, the Prime Minister of the United Kingdom, Sir Alfred Milner (the High Commissioner for the whole of South Africa) and Lord Kitchener.

The dancing starts. A band consisting of an accordion, a violin, a clarinet, and a banjo provide the music. I cannot but help to enjoy my graceful movements in the noble arms of Hector. He proves to be very agile and moves easily on the beat of the music. It is clear that he must have had some dancing lessons. My dress is certainly the most beautiful dress in this room, since it was designed and executed by my mother.

The more senior officers, without female companions, become more and more vociferous. I suppose that it's due to the copious amount of whiskey and brandy they pour down their throats.

I ask Hector: "Where on earth did those men get all that strong stuff they are drinking? It must have cost a fortune."

"They are cleaning the last few bottles we have in stock. Colonel Watson ordered a few dozen boxes of whiskey and brandy for this occasion, but the Boers derailed the train on which these boxes were transported."

"What did the Boers do with all that liquor?"

"The committed an unforgivable sin. They smashed all those bottles of Whiskey because whiskey is a product of Scotland, part of the United Kingdom. I suppose they also thought that alcohol was invented by the devil and that it was their duty to fight this devil's brew. It's very sad because our last stocks will disappear into the throats of those men over there."

The dancing stops at eleven-fifty and the dancing couples return to their seats. I notice that David has slipped out of the venue and I know that he plans some sort of mischief. However, I pretend not to notice his departure and I keep on chatting to the people at our table.

We hear the church bell's ringing to announce the hour of midnight. A new decade and a new century have arrived. The meeting inside the officers' club breaks up and everybody steps outside. Most of the men carry glasses filled with champagne to toast the New Year. A fireworks display starts. Everybody's attention is rivetted onto the Chinese rockets flying into the air, as well as the huge Chinese crackers making loud bangs.

All of a sudden, we hear something else – the hooves of stampeding horses. They somehow escaped from their enclosures and all the bangs and noises must have made them mad or frightened or nervous. I am sure that that must have been David's doing, but I don't inform Hector of my certainty.

The officers, mostly under the influence of huge volumes of alcohol, don't know what to watch – the fireworks that are still going on or the horses running away.

David joins me and Hector after a while as we watch the mayhem and chaos. I clutch my freckled knight's arm to seek his protection at this confusing hour.

Hector: "Those poor frightened animals are not yet used to loud bangs and explosions. It's no wonder they panicked and broke out. How on earth are we going to catch all of them? Anyway, Dora and David, you must be returned to your home. Let's go."

As we walk along, we find horses roaming the streets. Some of them even entered peoples' gardens and are enjoying whatever they can consume there. When we get home, we find our mother sitting on the veranda, waiting for us.

"Hector, thank you for looking after my children. The display of fireworks was marvelous and I could enjoy everything from here where I sat. But all those poor horses stampeding! Why did the organizers of the fireworks forget to think of the fright all those bangs would cause the poor animals? By the way, there is a white stallion in our back yard, eating all the apples he can reach from our two apple trees."

After Hector has left, I accompany David to the back yard.

David: "Sis, this white stallion harvesting our apple trees, is none other than Firefly! How on earth did this animal know where I live?"

The horse refuses to be chased away and after he has consumed all the ripe apples within reach, he starts grazing on our lettuces and carrots. This cannot be tolerated and I help David to chase him away with sticks. He gallops off in a westerly direction.

Pretoria, Tuesday, 1 January 1901

Because today is a public holiday, New Year's Day, I sleep late after the excitement of last night.

David disappears with his mates to the military camp. After an hour, they are back.

"Sergeant Major Warrick doesn't know what to do because all the 'hosses' – as he calls them – have disappeared from their enclosures. The Englishmen could catch some of them, but most of them jumped over the fences surrounding our town. The Boers outside will most certainly catch them."

Ben adds: "That sergeant major thinks some of those Boers will even have the cheek to write letters of thanks to Lord Kitchener for these gifts."

I look at David and our eyes meet. We both blink our eyes with smiles on our faces. We share a secret.

Pretoria, Friday, 11 January 1901

Hector knocks on our front door during the late afternoon. My mother invites him in.

Hector: "Good afternoon, Ma'am. I thought it would be an appropriate gift if I brought you this slaughtered chicken."

David is immediately ready with a question: "Where did you steal it?"

My mom: "David! Really!"

Hector: "A black man gave it to me yesterday after I helped him to get rid of one my soldiers who wanted to get fresh with his daughter. I immediately placed the man under arrest and he will be court-martialed very soon. Some time in the detention barracks is his fate."

My mom: "Hector, thank you very much. I will prepare lunch on Sunday and we invite you to come and enjoy this chicken with us. But, please, step inside. Dora will make us some tea."

While I am preparing some tea in the kitchen, my hands shake so much that I let a saucer fall. Fortunately, it doesn't break. We are also fortunate to have enough tea leaves to make a pot of strong tea. Unfortunately, there is no milk, due to the war. I put some rusks in a bowl to serve with the tea.

Pretoria, Sunday, 13 January 1901

We went to church this morning. It was a big surprise that Hector waited for us at the church's front door with the request that he may be allowed to share a pew with us.

My mother: "Hector, will you understand the Dutch we speak in church?"

"Not really, Ma'am. But I'm willing to learn."

"All right, let's go inside."

I am sure that Hector felt dismayed, disappointed, and disheartened, because my mother engineered the situation so that I sat on her right-hand side, while David and Hector sat on the other side. There were, therefore, two people between me and Hector.

During lunch, my mother asks him to tell us more about his family. He is willing to divulge something of his family history – perhaps with the intention of impressing us, and especially me.

"My ancestors came from Norway, originally. They were Viking pirates who attacked castles and monasteries along the coasts of European countries. My ancestors were called, as far as we can gather, Hagestad. They settled in Normandy, in France, where they married French women. This part of France is still today named after these Normans. Within two or three generations, their offspring became Frenchmen. Hagestad was turned into de Hacqueville.

David: "And one of your ancestors fought with William the Conqueror to capture Britain. Isn't that so?"

"Quite right. His name was Henry de Hacqueville, the same name as my father. His grandfather, after whom he was named, was Henrik Hagestad, the captain of one of the Viking ships."

My mom: "And this Henry, where did he settle in England after the conquest?"

"William gave him an estate and made him a viscount. The

estate is called Hagdale. We suppose it has something to do with the original family name of Hagestad. That must also have been the original family farm somewhere in Norway. Our estate is in Hampshire, in the south of England and not far from Southampton. Our biggest nearby city is Winchester."

At last, I venture to speak: "You say that your father is Henry. What does this Henry do?"

"He's a brigadier general in the Army. His job is with the War Office in London as a staff officer. When he retires from the Army, he will be entitled to sit in the House of Lords, but he has very little interest in politics."

Me: "And he made you join the Army?"

"It is an ancient family tradition that all male members join the armed forces. I didn't really have much of a choice in the matter. And now I am fighting a war against you people. It's sad, very sad."

I wait that Hector asks us about our family, but it doesn't happen. I leave it to my mother to broach that subject, should it be necessary.

As Hector greets us after the meal, he asks me: "Dora, will you please accompany me to my church next Sunday? The Church of England. I will come to fetch you at a quarter-past-nine."

This is so unexpected that I don't know what to reply. I look at my mother and she nods a 'yes'.

"All right, see you then."

As Hector marches away with his helmet on his head, after having giving my mother a formal salute, my heart starts beating faster. I suddenly think of Veleda who spoke to me a while ago and told me that I may expect much happiness ahead. That is, in spite of this horrible and very sad war. I just know that she will appear again tonight and I think of all the questions I want to ask her.

Pretoria, Friday, 18 January 1901

We are relieved to have my father with us again. He had a near brush on his way here, because two Tommy sentries passed within two yards from him, without noticing him where he lay under a bush.

He tells us: "Our commando had a wonderful stroke of luck just after New Year's Day. We found two dozen horses grazing somewhere. The Rooinekke must, somehow or other, have waylaid these valuable animals. My old horse is getting worn out and I asked our commandant, Captain Naude, if I may take a beautiful young horse as my fighting horse. I want to use my old horse as a packing animal when we have to travel some distance.

"David do you still visit the military camp sometimes?"

"I certainly do, Vati. And Dora also had an opportunity of visiting the lion's den. She accompanied that freckled Englishman to their formal dinner on New Year's Eve."

I start: "Yes, Vati, it was a most fruitful and enjoyable evening. I became part of the officers' gossiping. They all expect Kitchener to start a nasty campaign against civilian Boer women and children in the near future. Most burgers leave their commandoes from time to time to go and look at their families and their farms, before they rejoin their commandoes again. They usually come back with all sorts of supplies, including slaughtered sheep. Kitchener wants to stop this. The Boer women and children will have to be rounded up and placed in so-called 'refugee camps' so that they can no longer supply the commandoes with food."

My mom: "That's criminal. Abducting non-belligerents. Will our commandoes be able to prevent that from happening?"

My dad: "What else do you expect from an Englishman? I'm not sure that we will be able to stop this. Don't think so. We can't keep tabs on every British column trekking through the country."

Me: "Anyway, that English officer who took me to that dinner, has visited me on two occasions again. He wasn't able to try any monkey tricks with me because Ma was present the whole time. He tells us that both regiments in the military camp have suffered a huge blow when all their horses fled during the fireworks display when the New Year started. They managed to retrieve less than half of the horses. That means that they can't operate effectively."

"That must be some of the horses we caught in the hills."

"And do you know how that happened?"

"No, you tell me."

"This mischievous son of yours with his misleading tactics simply opened the gates of all the horse enclosures. The fireworks made them very nervous and within two ticks they bolted in all directions. So, now you know."

"I'm very grateful for this new horse of mine. We got in a skirmish with a company of Her Majesty's soldiers. One of my friends, who rode next to me, got wounded. If my horse wasn't so fast, I might also have got nicked by an enemy bullet. I'm very much in love with my horse. David, it was a wonderful stroke of luck that you could help all those horses to stampede. Thanks. This is the second time you have sabotaged the efforts of your English friends!"

My mother: "What does this new horse of yours look like?"

My father: "One of our guys who knows something about horses, explained that these new horses are all Arabian horses. They have a characteristic skull form. They are also more sturdily built than the horses we have over here. Nevertheless, my new horse is a white stallion – a very beautiful and reliable animal."

David: "Vati, that must be Firefly. I helped to train that horse after he was delivered to the 6th Dragoons a few weeks ago."

"So, that's the name you gave to this horse? All right, I will keep that name."

Pretoria, Sunday, 20 January 1901

Hector fetches me early enough that we can march leisurely to the Church of England's chapel, built of stone.

"We have a military chaplain who conducts services for our chaps when they are in base. He also does funerals. He is, though, of the Baptist version of Christianity and I don't always like his sermons. That's why I asked my commander for permission to go to my own church."

Old St Alban's Church, Pretoria

I find the rituals in the English church somewhat strange. They kneel quite a lot, something we don't do in the Dutch Reformed Church. I follow the example of the other people,

As we stroll back, Hector asks: "Tell me something about your family, please?"

"It's only me, my mother, and my little brother. That's all."

"But who was your mother before she got married?"

"Oh, she was Vernonica Visser. She was trained as a teacher. Domestic Science. She went to the college in Wellington in the Cape Colony. That's where she was taught how to do needlework and make clothes. My late father was a tailor and he needed an assistant. He appointed her and they fell in love. I'm the result."

"Where did your mother grow up?"

"In the southern Free State. Her father was Gert Visser and her mother was Engela Scholtz. Engela was the second-youngest daughter of Joachim Hermanus Scholtz. He was one of the first white men to venture into the Transvaal where he got mauled by a lion during a hunting expedition. My mother never knew him because he died when she wasn't yet born. She only knew her grandmother, Engela. He was a great warrior and a field-cornet and he also married the daughter of another warrior. Her name was Anna Jacoba Kruger and her father was the commandant of his district in the Cape Colony, more than a century ago."

"How do you know all these things?"

"My mother inherited her mother's Bible. All these names were recorded in this Bible and that's where I saw them. I may perhaps show it to you sometime."

"Your ancestry explains why you are such an exceptional woman."

I blush when I get this compliment.

"What can you tell my about your late father?"

"He's dead. I really can't tell you anything."

I blush again because I feel ashamed after telling another lie.

Pretoria, Wednesday, 23 January 1901

Hector turns up unexpectedly at our front door during the late afternoon. He wears a black ribbon around his left arm.

My mother: "Are you joining us for supper?"

"Missus Davidson, that's very kind of you to invite me. I gladly accept. But that's not the reason for my visit."

"Yes?"

"As you can see – I'm in mourning. All military personnel are supposed to have these black ribbons on their arms. We got the sad news by telegraph that our beloved Queen, Victoria, passed away yesterday at the age of eighty-one."

"I'm so sorry to hear that."

"Thanks. Colonel Watson decreed that Friday, the day after tomorrow, be declared a day of mourning. He also approached the Reverend Bosman of the Dutch Reformed Church to help our military chaplain, Father Ambrose, with a memorial service on that day. This service must be held in the Dutch Reformed Church, which is the biggest meeting hall in town. All soldiers who can be spared from war duty, will have to attend the service. We expect a large number of people from this town to turn up as well."

"We will be there. You may count on us. Was she ill? Did she have an accident? How did she die?

"Ma'am, I'm not privy to those details, unfortunately."

David: "So, that toast you drank on her health three weeks ago didn't help much."

My mother: "David!"

Later, after Hector has left, my mother explains: "We must continue to pretend that we are on the British side during this war. That's why we are going to attend that memorial service on Friday. I suppose all the school children will also be required to go."

Pretoria, Sunday, 3 March 1901

While I and David are spending this Lord's Day in a fitting manner – that is, by sitting quietly in our rooms and reading appropriate literature – my mother calls us and leads us quietly to the kitchen window. We observe two Tommys sitting on their horses and helping themselves to our prickly pears.

Mom: "We don't do anything. Those two dumb thieves will get their punishment very soon."

Me: "How? Who will punish them?"

"God will punish them for committing a crime on his holy day. Do you notice that those two idiotic guys have no bags to carry those prickly pears? They opened their jackets and dumped the prickly pears inside their clothes, next to their chests and bellies."

David: "Ha-ha-ha. I think God is already punishing them. See how they are starting to itch from all those thousands of tiny little thorns on the prickly pears. They are getting rid of their jackets!"

Me: "And now they are indecently clothed with their ugly naked bellies exposed. I am sure it will take them at least ten days to get rid of every little devilish thorn."

David: "Look, they are leaving. They have left all the prickly pears they stole just there. I will go and pick them up later. Ma, where is your fork with those long teeth with which I can pick them up?"

Pretoria, Saturday, 23 March 1901

My sixteenth birthday happened the day before yesterday. Nothing could be made of the occasion because it was an ordinary school day. However, Hector turned up at our front door during the afternoon with a chocolate cake in his hands.

We were still in our working clothes after tending our vegetable garden, picking ripe beans, peas, and grapes, and irrigating all the veggies and fruit trees with buckets of water. Hector gave us some time to wash our hands and faces and getting into decent clothes.

When we are all seated around the dining room table and waiting for the kettle to boil, Hector stands up again: "Dear Dora, I'm not good at speeches. All I want to tell you is that I want to wish you a happy birthday, although it is already two days late. I couldn't be here because my company was guarding the rail road from the south. I only got back yesterday afternoon late and then I bribed the chef in our officers' mess to bake this cake for me. He only completed it this afternoon and here it is for our afternoon tea. May I request you to get up for a moment?"

I do so, wondering why he wants this. To my surprise, he bends over and give me a smacking kiss on my cheek.

"That is something that I always wanted to do. You know, there is an old saying about a girl: 'Sweet sixteen and never been kissed.' This doesn't apply to you anymore because you have received a kiss from a man."

My mother: "I also want a kiss!"

She gets up and Hector plants a kiss on her mouth.

David starts clapping his hands, but also exclaims: "Please don't kiss me, as well. Yik! Grrr!"

Hector: "I will only shake your hand to congratulate you for having such a beautiful sister. She must be a witch or something because she caused me to do all sorts of foolish things, like kissing her and delivering a cake as her birthday present."

My brother leaves his seat and shakes Hector's hand.

I get up to pour the boiling water on the stove into a tea pot. I get a tray ready with cups, saucers, a bowl of sugar, teaspoons, forks for the cake, a knife to cut the cake, and plates for the slices of cake. When I appear in the dining room with all the necessary tools, Hector instructs me to cut a slice of cake for each of us.

The cake is being distributed and then I pour the tea. We must drink the tea without milk because milk is unobtainable. We have, though, some sugar for the tea.

Each one of us takes two teaspoons full of sugar for our tea. Suddenly the tea starts to boil and produce a froth that spills over into our saucers. Hectors spills some tea on his trousers.

David: "Hell! Dammit! What the fuck's going on?"

My mother: "David! Your language! Really!"

David: "I'm sorry, Ma. I didn't know that this would happen. It has taken me by surprise, totally by surprise."

Me: "So, *you* are responsible for this disaster!"

Hector laughs: "This is an old trick that I used to play on my mother. This must be a case of Eno's Fruit Salts that got mixed with the sugar. This stuff looks just like sugar. David, where did you get it?"

David: "My friend Ben gave me a small packet. He swiped it from his father who got it from Doctor Barry. The packet says it helps with indigestion, malaria fever, tooth ache, dizziness, and other things. It also keeps mosquitoes away. He advised me to mix it with the sugar. That's supposed to improve everybody's health. I'm sorry."

Hector: "This fruit salt is being manufactured in Newcastle-Upon-Tyne by a certain Mister Samuel Eno. It is supposed to have some health benefits, but I don't think it was meant to be taken with tea. David, you friend Ben must have played a nasty trick on you."

Me: "I will make some fresh tea and get rid of this funny sugar. David, you are lucky. If we didn't have a guest, I would have given you a few blows over your head!"

After Hector has left again just before dark, David asks me: "Did you enjoy that kiss?"

My mother: "David! Behave yourself, please!"

I blush and just walk away. I had a dream a few nights ago where my great-grandmother – or this German priestess – told me to be ready for just that.

Pretoria, Friday, 12 April 1901

A new military unit appeared this afternoon in Pretoria. They are transporting about two dozen Boer families in carts. Some more carts arrive with tents, which the soldiers erect. The site is not far from our home, just below Meintjeskop Hill. It is impossible not to notice them because they passed not far from our house through the town.

My mom: "David, you are very inquisitive. Perhaps you should walk there and see what is going on."

David returns an hour later: "These blinking, bloody, bastards of Englishmen are the worst kind of stinking and fucking insects one can imagine."

My mother: "David! You were not brought up to use such strong language! Did you pick it up from those English soldiers you often visit?"

"Ma, that's how I feel. They're lower than dung beetles or worms that crawl in the shit."

Mom: "David!"

Me: "Why do you say that?"

"They are erecting a so-called refugee camp for defenseless women and children over there. It's really a prison camp. That's where they are keeping the families of Joiners – the men who joined the Englishmen and who are helping them to hunt the Boer fighters who refuse to surrender."

Me: "Why here?"

"Those women whose husbands gave up the fight and joined the enemy refuse to be put in the same prison camps as women whose husbands are still fighting. I talked to a little boy of my age. His name is Willie van der Walt. They were given an hour to pack some clothes and other necessities such as blankets and then they were forcibly taken away from their farm. All their crops on the fields were burnt down. The same with their farm house. All their cattle and sheep and goats were shot and left rotting where they lay. The necks of their chickens were wrung, but the soldiers took those chickens for themselves."

My mother: "That's a very serious crime to wage war against defenseless and helpless women and children. God will certainly punish them. Very harshly."

Me: "Winter is approaching and they will have to sleep in those tents. They'll freeze."

"Their black laborers were also rounded up and taken to another camp, somewhere. Willie is afraid that they will have it much worse. The Englishmen took them here inside Pretoria because it is supposed to be safe here and not somewhere else."

Me: "The officers at our table on New Year's Eve expected this thing to happen. And now it happened. We will have to help these poor people if we can."

"The guards at that camp won't allow it. They chased me away, just for talking to Willie. He's the only boy in their family. His mother, grandmother and two sisters will have to live with him in the same tent."

Pretoria, Saturday, 13 April 1901

We have to work in our garden again today to ensure that we grow enough fruit and vegetables for our own use. Hector, who is off-duty, helps us. That gives him time with me.

Shortly before dusk, David set off to Meintjeskop Hill to find his new friend, Willie van der Walt. Hector returns to his barracks.

David comes back just as the last bit of the sun disappears in the west: "Those fucking foreign fighters, those stupid soldiers, threatened to shoot me!"

My mother: "David! Your language!"

Me: "What did you do to make them angry?"

"I only wanted to talk to Willie. But they're erecting a barbed wire fence around this cursed concentration camp, as Willie calls the place. I could talk to him through this fence. He complains that there is no water, no washing facilities, no latrines. The tents are full of holes and the rain water will drop on them."

Me: "I noticed that many more carts and wagons arrived during the day, delivering some more women and children."

"And Willie complains that they haven't eaten since yesterday when they left their farm. He says he hopes his dad sees his mistake to become a Joiner. He must go back to his old commando and beg for forgiveness and start fighting these shitty soldiers of ole Queen Vic."

My mother: "David! Watch your language, please! Yes, these types of camps are really nothing but concentration camps or prison camps. They want to exterminate us Boer people and replace us with immigrants from London, Leeds, and Liverpool. Our neighbor, Missus Fouche, tells me this camp at Meintjeskop Hill is supposed to be a better type of camp because it is meant for the families of Joiners. The other camps must be much worse."

Pretoria, Sunday, 14 April 1901

Hector is waiting for us at the church door. By this time, my mom has accepted his presence in our midst, although he is part of the enemy. She even allows me to sit next to him in our pew.

While we walk back home after the service, Hector says: "Ma'am, I won't be able to stay long. Perhaps only a cup of tea. We are to leave directly after lunch. Exercises. Our new horses are used to be ridden, but they must be taught how to take part in a battle."

Me: "Where will these exercises take place?"

"I was told to the west of Pretoria. Among those hills. We believe that the Boer commando that was hiding somewhere there, has left and gone somewhere else."

Me: "Does your regiment help with the burning of farms and the killing of the cattle?"

"Heavens, no! I am actually very ashamed about the behavior of those troops who have to do that. They are low-class soldiers. We, of the North Lancashire Regiment, will never help with those criminal activities. I can't think why a civilized nation, like the inhabitants of the British Isles, can execute those types of orders."

After Hector has disappeared, my mom says: "How are we going to warn your father that a swarm of soldiers on inexperienced horses will hold exercises in their area?"

Pretoria, Wednesday, 29 May 1901

It's two days before David's birthday. He says he doesn't feel like celebrating anything because his friend Willie van der Walt in the camp below Meintjeskop Hill, is starving.

I talk to David: "I want to go with you to this camp this afternoon. I have half a loaf of bread that we can hand to Willie."

We manage to call Willie to come to the fence. David gives him the bread and Willie immediately bites off a corner. It is clear that he is very hungry.

Willie: "Thanks for this fresh bread. For breakfast, we were given stale, moldy bread. Last night, our family got a single tin of bully beef. When we opened it, we found an iron nail inside. What would have happened if my little sister swallowed that nail?"

I ask: "How is it to live in a tent?"

"It is very cramped. We are five in our tent. There are other tents with up to ten people. There's no privacy. My elder sister is sick."

During dinner, David struggles with his food, although it was prepared with care by me and my mother.

He says: "It gets stuck in my throat."

My mom: "David, are you sick? Why don't you eat your food?"

"Ma, I can't. I see in my mind those hungry eyes of that Willie chap. Those so-called refugees are suffering terribly. What can we do about it? I don't think I can sleep with a full belly when those people are starving."

My mother: "I have already spoken to the Reverend Bosman. It is the duty of the church to help people in need – even if they are our enemies. And do you know what the reverend said? 'Our hands are chopped off.' He has already spoken to Colonel Watson about those poor hungry people. The British military authorities cannot allow anybody, the church included, to interfere. So, there you have it. I will help you if you want to smuggle some food to your friend. He certainly can't help that his old man became a Joiner and a traitor."

Pretoria, Friday, 31 May 1901

Our head master, Mister Kerckhoven, announced this morning that our school, the Dutch "Staats Model School"[11], was to have its last day today. When we return on Monday, we fill find it has a new name, namely "Pretoria High School" (although it includes classes from the primary phase). Sir Alfred Milner, British High Commissioner for the whole of South Africa, has decided that English is to be the sole language of instruction in all government schools from now on. We must realize, according to him, that all inhabitants of His Majesty's colonies in South Africa, including the Transvaal Colony, must adopt the English language as only medium of communication.

The "Staats Model School" in Pretoria

Today is also David's birthday and Hector visits us during the afternoon: "Dora told me that you are nine years old today. How does that feel, hey? I've brought you a gift."

---

[11] "Staats Model School" – the Dutch for State Model School.

He produces two glass bottles, filled with little glass balls.

"These are marbles. I used to play with them when I was a school kid. "

David: "How does one play with them? I haven't seen anything like this before."

"I will show you. And then you teach your friends. I am sure that this will catch on in no time. Horowitz & Sons import them from Britain."

Pretoria, Sunday, 14 June 1901

My father is very relieved that we are still safe and sound. He asks me: "Dora, what can you tell me?"

"The Honorable Hector is still courting me. He visits me once a week when he is in town with his company. He sometimes goes to our church with us and he has picked up a few Dutch and Afrikaans expressions. At other times, he takes me to his church, although there is also a military chaplain who delivers sermons and sacraments to the troops, which I don't attend. He says he's glad that it's not his job to burn down farm buildings and the crops of the Boer farmers. He also thinks it's a shame that all the stock animals of the Boers are destroyed."

"What does he say about the concentration camps?"

"He refuses to go near them. He can't tolerate to see those starving children. He thinks the guards of those camps are all bullies – maltreating helpless people like that."

My mother: "That's what I appreciate about this young Englishman – his sensitivity and care for his fellow human beings."

My dad: "This war has brought terrible suffering to many people. Kitchener and Miller are heartless, cruel, despicable tyrants. I have often wished that I could go to England and set fire to their homes. I will give anything to see how they will take that! But, in the meantime, we have to continue with the fight over here. We can't stop without losing our self-respect."

Me: "Hector tells us that people in England are getting tired of the war that doesn't seem to end and they are putting pressure on the government to end this nonsense.

"He also tells me that the Boer commando to the west of Pretoria, in those hills, is a constant threat to them. They have been led into ambushes a few times, and each time a few men did bite the dust."

"That's our commando, of course. And, David, what are you doing?"

"Sergeant Major Warrick warned us that the 6th Dragoons may be transferred to the eastern Transvaal next month."

"Who will succeed them?"

"He doesn't know. I'm also playing the English game of marbles with my friends. Sometimes I win, sometimes I lose."

Me: "Yes, you and your marbles! Vati, the other day Hector almost broke his neck when he stepped onto a few of these marbles that your son forgot on the drawing room floor. These marbles must be declared dangerous weapons."

David: "I did say I'm sorry. Didn't I?"

Pretoria, Saturday, 10 August 1901

Our friend, Willie van der Walt, sits on the other side of the barbed wire fence of their camp while I and David chat to him.

"My mom says she hates all Englishmen."

Me: "But your dad is fighting with them? He chose their side. How can she turn against your dad?"

"She still hates all Englishmen."

"Why?"

"My sister, who is thirteen years old, is expecting a baby. The soldiers raped her while they were transporting us to this place."

"Hell."

"My mom is very angry. She says our family will never recover from the shame. No church will ever baptize that baby."

Pretoria, Saturday, 16 August 1901

Me and my little brother were sitting next to the fence of the camp next to Meintjeskop Hill and we talked to our friend Willie.

I told him: "My mom said that she is willing to look after your sister who's expecting a baby. We will smuggle her out of this camp tonight if your mother is willing to let her go. Go run to your mother and ask her if she will cooperate."

Willie appeared a quarter-of-an-hour later: "My mom and my grandma think it's a very good idea. People are making remarks about my sister who is putting on weight and they want to know where she got so much food. It will be best if she can disappear."

"How does your sister feel about this?"

"She also wants to get out of this crummy concentration camp. How are you going to do it?"

David: "She must come to this exact spot at eleven tonight. Then everybody will be asleep. I will cut a hole through the barbed wires and she can crawl through."

And now I and David are waiting for this little girl who is in the family way. The church bell strikes eleven, but nothing happens. When midnight strikes, we creep home, very disappointed.

While we waited, we could often hear children cry – probably because they are hungry or sick. These sounds make me sad, but also angry at the heartless and pitiless Lord Kitchener who devised this criminal cruelty.

Pretoria, Sunday, 17 August 1901

Directly after Hector had left after lunch, my mother declared: "Even if it's the Lord's Day today, we are going to perform a charitable deed. Both of you are going to find your friend Willie and ask him why his sister didn't appear last night."

Fortunately, when we got to our meeting spot next to the fence, Willie was waiting for us: "I'm sorry, but my sister fell ill last night. That's why she couldn't come."

Me: "Please see to it that she does come at eleven sharp, sick, or not sick. We will take care of her at our home."

And now the church bell strikes eleven. It is overcast and it is very dark. No moonlight seeps through the clouds. David has already cut a hole in the fence with our father's pliers.

We hear Willie's voice: "Psst. Are you there?"

David crawls through the hole to guide the girl back to me. She is clutching a bundle of some sort, probably her clothes.

I grab her hand and we creep on all fours not to be visible against the horizon.

Suddenly an aggressive voice yells: "Who goes there? Come here, immediately, or I will shoot!"

We continue creeping until we are far enough to sit up and scan the world. David joins us and reports in a whisper: "That stupid guard heard something, but he couldn't see anything. He won't know what to shoot at. Let's go."

David takes the girl's bundle and I hold her shaking hand while we creep through the dark streets until we reach our home. We slip in through the back door.

My mother: "Ah, here you are! Welcome my girl. What is your name?"

The timid girl whispers: "Wilma."

My mom: "Any mishaps along the way?"

David: "A guard threatened to shoot us but he couldn't see us in the dark. Our only trouble is that our clothes are somewhat full of dirt because we crept on all fours."

My mom: "Right, Wilma. This is your new home, for the time being. Have you eaten tonight? I can give you some soup."

Wilma: "Please."

My mother embraces the frightened and traumatized girl and strokes her hair: "With us you will be safe. We will take care of you and that little baby you are carrying."

Me: "When do you expect the little one to come?"

Wilma: "My mother says in January."

Me: "You will sleep with me in my room. We have prepared a bed for you. Extra blankets if you are cold."

My mother: "How old are you, Wilma?"

"I turned fourteen last month."

Pretoria, Tuesday, 12 September 1901

My father appeared during the night and we all sit around the kitchen table during breakfast to hear his stories.

My mother: "This is Wilma. She's a guest in our house. Her father is a Joiner, but we rescued her from that cruel concentration camp below Meintjeskop Hill, where she and her unborn baby would certainly have perished. She got raped by the savage soldiers who burnt down their farm and abducted her with her family. David became a friend of her brother through the fence surrounding the camp and that's how we learnt of her predicament."

My dad gets up to shake the worried Wilma's hand.

He asks: "Does she go to school here?"

Mother: "No, I teach her. After all, I am a qualified teacher, although my field of expertise is actually domestic science. Dora helps me with her. She can't go to school in her condition. She expects the baby in January. We will have to make plans after that how to treat the situation."

My father: "My wonderful wife, you have my solid support. Wilma, I'm sure that you have been told that I officially don't exist. I'm certain that you won't get any opportunity of spilling the beans and betray me."

Wilma only nods.

"Anyway, this was certainly the most difficult visit to Pretoria since the town fell to the British. It took me four hours to crawl twenty yards through the barbed wire fences. And then it took me three more hours to slip past all the sentries with their dogs."

Me: "Hector told me that Colonel Watson is very concerned about the fact that the perimeter of the town can be breached so easily. They have found spots where unknown persons have crawled through the fences. That's why they got dogs for the sentries. Vati, what will happen if they catch you?"

"Shoot me as a spy or something."

My mother: "Is your commando still able to operate at all? With all this devastation of Boer farms it seems impossible to get any food."

"We do manage. On English stocks. We still derail trains with bombs going off under the locomotives, but it's becoming more and more difficult. Kitchener is erecting blockhouses all along the rail tracks. Each blockhouse contains a squad of soldiers. We have, though, been able to capture three block houses. They were clumsily designed and the soldiers inside cannot traverse their guns to a point directly next to the structure's stone walls directly below them. We have managed to creep up unseen to spots next to some blockhouses and to surprise the poor Rooinekke inside. We threatened to blow up the building with them inside, unless they surrender. The sad and scared sods came out with their hands in the air, although we didn't really have any explosives."

Me: "And then you took all their guns, ammo and food?"

"Exactly. But this past winter was extremely difficult. We constantly lost men who fell, got sick, or were captured. But our fighting spirit is still strong and John Bull will realize some time or other that he has taken a bite that he cannot chew."

David: "Vati, there is a new British unit in the place of the Sixth Dragoons. It's the third battalion of the Royal Sussex Regiment. They haven't been long in this country yet and they are unfamiliar with local circumstances."

"And how do you know this?"

"Hector introduced me to one of their officers who needed riding lessons. The poor guy was afraid of horses after he had fallen off twice and broke an arm in the process."

Me: "Hector told me that it wasn't a surprise that that officer fell off because he was given a very ferocious animal. Even David was thrown off."

"Did you get hurt?"

David: "Vati, yes. I was somewhat seriously bruised. But with my extraordinary constitution I was able to brush it off within two days. It didn't even leave a mark."

Me: "Hector thinks David must be jinxed for recovering so easily."

My dad: "Let's talk about Wilma again. I suppose you want to keep her presence here a secret?"

My mom: "That's right. Not even Dora's boyfriend knows about her. Whenever he visits Dora, we keep him in the drawing room, while Wilma stays out of sight. When the time comes, we will get Doctor Barry here to help with the delivery. That's necessary because she is still so young. But we will be able to rely on him not to betray her. I'm teaching her some needlework and knitting and she is helping me in our business to make clothes for the people of Pretoria."

Me: "She has already made two maternity dresses for herself."

My dad: "And how is she dealing with that horrible experience she had with those barbaric British soldiers?"

Me: "During her first few nights with me in my room, she had nasty nightmares. Then I took her in my bed with me. It seems as if these nightmares have vanished. What do you say, Wilma?"

Wilma opens her mouth for the first time this morning: "Dora told me that she regards me as her little sister. She makes me feel safe here. Those nightmares are gone after I had told her of what happened and she allowed me to cry. She says she has a guardian angel who looks after her and who will also look after me."

Pretoria, Saturday, 16 September 1901

David's friend Ben teaches him and Charles how to use a sling, while I watch them.

Ben: "My mom says this is a biblical weapon. The young King David used one to knock out that giant, Goliath. That was, before he became king. Afterwards, he chopped off the giant's head. David, this ought to be your type of weapon, because your dad is actually Jewish and your family name is Davidsohn. You have the same name as this king, it seems."

A sling is easy to make. It consists of a piece of leather to hold a stone and two long strings affixed to both sides of the piece of leather to swing the stone to give it momentum. One of the strings is then released and the stone flies away at great speed.

The boys make their own slings and practice the whole Saturday afternoon until they can deliver a stone accurately at a target, a wooden board. I get a few turns and after the tenth try, I manage to hit the target at thirty feet.

Pretoria, Sunday, 17 September 1901

Because it is Sunday today, David is not allowed to go anywhere. He plays with his new toy, the sling, in our garden. I and Wilma watch him through our bedroom window.

A squad of mounted soldiers rides along our road. I am sure a wicked little devil on David's shoulder told him: "Try and hit one of those horses. Those soldiers are not supposed to ride around on the Lord's Day!"

David's first try flies over the heads of the soldiers. His second try hits the hind quarters of one of the horses. He gets such a fright that he throws his rider off and bolts away.

David hides behind the hedge on our garden's border. I and Wilma hold our bellies as we laugh. The soldier who was thrown off, bellows and howls: "My wrist is broken! Catch that bloody horse that threw me! Get me to a doctor! Dammit!"

Afterwards, David tells us that this mischievous little devil whispered into his ear: "This is great sports. Do it more often!"

I feel jealous that David gets opportunities to annoy or harm the enemy, while I must behave myself as a lady.

Pretoria, Friday, 13 December 1901

Today is the last school day of the year and some important things are supposed to happen today. We gather in the school at eight-o'-clock for religious devotions and the awarding of a few prizes. It is no surprise that I get the prize for the best pupil in my class for the subjects of mathematics and Latin. I am presented with two books: A translation of Euclid's book on Geometry and a Latin Bible, the translation by Saint Jerome. I decide to take the Latin Bible with me to church every Sunday to follow the reading from the Dutch Bible and compare it with the Latin translation.

It is, though, a surprise that I am called to appear on the stage of the hall to be named the head girl of the school for next year, my last year at school.

The head master: "Theodora, you were elected by the teachers unanimously to be the new head girl. You have leadership qualities. You are a good example for all the other pupils. You are good at your subjects, as the two prizes awarded to you do testify. We are proud of you. You may address the teachers and the pupils."

I am caught off-guard. I never expected this honor and, therefore, never thought about preparing a speech.

I, nevertheless, stammer: "Thank you, Sir. I will do my best. Thank you, Sir."

During the day, we receive our reports with the results of the exams that ended last week. I am indeed proud of my marks for Mathematics and Latin. My class teacher tells me: "Both these subjects call for clear thinking. You seem to be good at both."

When I arrive home with my new books and the news, my mother sighs: "What a pity that we can't tell your father about these achievements of yours. He went back to his commando last night and we will only see him again in a month's time, if at all."

Pretoria, Sunday, 5 January 1902

It is still school holidays. There was nothing to do during the holidays, except celebrate Christmas, New Year's Eve, pottering around in the garden, and doing some needlework. Of course, we went to church every Sunday where I followed the readings from Scripture with my Latin Bible, also called the Vulgate.

There was another formal dinner on New Year's Eve in the officers' club. It was taken for granted that I attend as Hector's dancing partner. I kept my ears open for any gossip and military secrets divulged by men who drank and talked too much.

While I was getting dressed to go to church, Wilma started sobbing: "I am all wet! Something bad happened!"

I called my mother who said: "Nothing to worry about. Your water broke. That's the sign that that little rascal inside wants to get out and see the sun for himself. Dora, trot off to Doctor Barry. I have warned him last week that he must be ready to be summoned. Let's hope he's still home and not on his way to church."

Fortunately, the good doctor came immediately. An hour later, a little boy entered the world.

Doctor Barry: "And how is this little angel to be called?"

Wilma: "I hate my father. He became a wicked Joiner. I want to call him Daniel, after my honorary father, Mister Daniel Davidsohn!"

My mother: "Doc, thank you for your help. I'm a trained teacher in domestic science and I think I know something about the care and feeding of babies. I will perform the role of nurse. And now, Wilma, you will start to nurse that baby. Your first task will be to feed him."

After the doctor has left, Wilma asks: "How will I get this little one baptized? I'm not an adult member of the church who can hold the baby during the baptism and take the vow to raise him in the right way. And, besides, the church may refuse to baptize him because he was made by men who were filled with lust."

My mother: "I will hold him during his baptism as his foster-mother. Don't worry. Your job is to produce enough milk for this little Daniel, who has escape from the lion's den, over there at Meintjeskop Hill."

Me: "What will happen if Hector comes to visit and he hears a baby cry in our house?"

"The best thing will be if you take him for a walk every time he comes. That will take him away from us. I'm sure he will enjoy being alone with you, without me and David hanging around."

Pretoria, Sunday, 30 March 1902

We have just arrived home after church when Hector comes shuffling along. He usually marches with his head held high and his strides long and resolute. But today his head hangs and his left arm is held in a sling. His left hand is bandaged heavily and he carries a bag with his right hand.

My mother: "And this, Hector?"

"Ma'am, I need a nurse. Or even two. I was in a skirmish last week and got wounded. They shot the little finger of my left hand to bits and only a stump remains. My wrist was broken when another bullet smashed the bone. My left hand is, therefore, rather somewhat useless at the moment. I was in hospital for the past week and I was discharged this morning. Now I need somebody to look after me."

"All right. We will nurse you. You can sleep with David in his room. Do we have to dress your wounds every day?"

"Fortunately, no. For that, I must report back to the hospital every morning and after they have taken care of my injuries, I am free to go again."

Me: "But why don't you sleep at your old barracks as usual?"

"I've been taken off the strength of the North Lancashire Regiment. I was declared unfit for military service. As you can see, I am in civilian clothes now."

Mom: "As far as I know, wounded soldiers are repatriated back to their families in England."

"Yes, that's what usually happens. But I have requested to get permission to stay here."

"But why?"

"Ma'am, to tell you the truth, quite honestly, really straight: I don't want to be separated from this beautiful, loving, marvelous, and intelligent damsel, named Dora. Although she may perhaps not be of English noble descent, she's a true noble lady and I would like to make her part of my life."

Me: "Is that a marriage proposal? That's silly, stupid, senseless. I'm only finishing school at the end of this year."

"You are intelligent and mature enough to know where your heart lies. You turned seventeen a week ago and I lament that I couldn't take part in the celebrations because I was out in the field at that time, where I was wounded. I know how you feel, every time I look into those deep blue eyes of yours."

Hector looks at my mother: "Ma'am, you have already invited me to stay with you. That makes me almost a member of your family. Do I have your blessing if I ask you whether you will accept me as your future son-in-law? You know full well that I haven't laid a single finger on your daughter, although I have longed to hold her in my arms. Many times."

Mother: "Hector, you make it impossible for me to say no. But that also depends on how Dora feels. I find you to be a true gentleman, a man of honor, somebody on whom we can rely. I won't stop you from becoming part of our family. But that depends upon Dora, of course. Dora?"

"Yes, Ma. I must say, he's not too bad, as Englishmen go. He's serious, dependable, faithful, and honorable. I trust that he will be a good father, judging from how he deals with David."

"Is that a yes?"

"You stupid man. I must first experience how you can hug me and how one your kisses feel before I can give a final and definitive answer. But I must also warn you that you will have to get past my father."

"Your father?" Hector looks puzzled.

"Yes, my father. He is still out there somewhere, fighting Kitchener's forces. It's entirely possible that you got wounded by members of his commando. Since you have been discharged from the Army, you may know of him. He visits us frequently since Pretoria has been shut off from the outside world. He has even seen you through a window without you knowing of his presence.

"And, may I also inform you that our family name is not really Davidson, but the German Davidsohn. Our father is a Jew from Germany who threw in his lot with his adopted countrymen when the perfidious Albion invaded our free republic in its lust for gold. Do you still want me?"

Hector gets up, rushes to my chair, lifts me up and embraces me. The tears are streaming from his cheeks, while he sobs.

I stroke his red hair.

David seems to find it silly of a grown man to shed tears, to sob, and to behave so stupidly, and he gets up to leave the room. I am sure that he can't understand what I see in this freckled, red-headed, and thin Englishman.

My mother interferes with this wonderful moment: "Hector, it is my duty to inform you that our house will be rather full with you living here as well. We have a young woman lodging with us. She is looking after her baby after the father of the child abandoned her. We suspect he's now in heaven or perhaps somewhere else. We don't know. This war has caused so many casualties. Her name is Wilma and I will introduce you to her and her baby Daniel."

While Hector makes himself at home in David's room, I look for Wilma and inform her that we are getting yet another lodger: "He must be kept under the impression that you are a young widow. At fifteen, you look old enough to have been married. Just tell him that you don't know what happened to the father of your child and that you won't be surprised if he fell somewhere. We must protect your reputation."

Wilma nods her assent.

Pretoria, Saturday, 31 May 1902

My father has managed to creep into Pretoria, for the last time, because it is expected that peace is to be declared soon. An armistice was in place since a few days ago to allow the Boer generals to hold meetings. He informs us that the leaders of the two republics met at a small railroad station on the border between them, called Vereeniging.

He brought his Point Three-Oh-Three and lots of ammunition along, which he hides in our loft. He explains that it will be expected of all Boer warriors to lay down arms – and he doesn't feel like doing that. At the breakfast table, he is introduced to the former Lieutenant the Honorable Hector de Hacqueville, who lodges with us after his discharge from the Army. Hector has found employment with the town administration and he has something to do with refuse removal. For that, he is in charge of several mule carts.

During the late afternoon, Hector fetches me and David and announces: "David, I know today is your birthday. But I propose that we celebrate it tomorrow. Pretoria has come more or less to a standstill today because it is expected that a peace treaty is to be signed. Something of profound importance may happen today. Come with me into town. We may see something."

The six Boer generals who signed the peace treaty of 31 May 1902

We do see something important. Ten Boer generals, including Oom Louis Botha and Oom Christiaan de Wet, arrive by train from Vereeniging. They are taken to Melrose House, a grand residence that was being used as the headquarters of the British Army since the days of Lord Roberts.

After about half-an-hour, the Boer leaders leave again without speaking to anybody outside, except somebody who takes a photo of six of them. They seem to be in a very somber state of mind.

Hector holds my hand to console me because I feel very sad.

Pretoria, Monday, 2 June 1901

A thanksgiving service was held in the Dutch Reformed Church yesterday. Homage was paid to all those who lost their lives – either as Boer fighters or civilian inmates in concentration camps.

The Reverend Bosman also disclosed what the main points of the peace treaty was. It boiled down to the following:

> All Boer fighters had to lay down arms and surrender;
> The Transvaal Colony and the Orange River Colony had to accept British rule;
> The amount of three million pounds was to be paid by the British government to compensate for all the damage caused by British forces;
> Limited self-rule for the colonies would be allowed after a period of time;
> Non-Boer residents of the colonies would receive the vote;
> A general amnesty would be granted; and
> All citizens would be allowed to possess licensed fire-arms.

Lunch at our home was a very subdued affair. Even Hector felt sad and he declared that he really felt ashamed for having fought against the valiant Boers. He was part of an invading Army, which had no business to commit aggression towards two peaceful republics. The Boer fighters fought for their freedom and for their country. They deserved an honorable peace.

Me: "You are forgiven. You unwittingly helped our war effort more than you will ever know."

I patted his left hand, which is almost totally healed, save for the missing part of his little finger.

My father sighed in English while he addressed Hector: "We heard that three million pounds sterling is to used to compensate the people who lost everything during the war. That amount is certainly not enough and I doubt whether our Boer people will ever see something of that money. It will be used to help the Englishmen living in this country and perhaps also a few Joiners."

Hecor got a wry smile on his face and it seemed as if he agreed with my father,

Later, Hector told us: "There is to be big victory parade tomorrow through Church Street and ending on Church Square. All British units from the surrounding areas are to take part. A contingent of National Scouts on their horses will also participate."

During the late afternoon, David visited Charles and Ben. I suspect that they planned some sort of mischief or monkey tricks.

Two scarecrows walk past our house – two Boer fighters, who have been living in the hills the last two years, who were returning home. Their clothes are shoddy and their hair and beards haven't seen scissors for ages. But they smile, because they were returning home as proud "Bitter-Enders" who never gave up or surrendered or became Joiners.

During breakfast this morning, Hector informs us about the latest news given in the local newspaper, the Pretoria News.

"It appears that Sir Alfred Milner wanted very strict punitive conditions for a peace accord. It was his intention of humiliating the Boers as much as possible. Lord Kitchener, however, won the day with more friendly and lenient peace proposals. He realized that the British authorities would need the cooperation of the Boers for a lasting peace. The Boers were able to carry on fighting for many more months, but they were concerned about their starving, dying, and sick women and children who were held hostage in these cursed concentration camps."

My dad: "Kitchener also realized that Britain's reputation suffered immensely in the international world, due to its cruelty and cold-heartedness towards innocent and impotent civilians."

I watch where David and his friends choose spots along Church Street to watch the parade. They position themselves about ten yards from each other. As little boys, they manage to get right to the edge of the sidewalk, in front of the grown-ups.

It takes a considerable time for the cavalry, infantry. and artillery to pass in front of us. At last, the troop of National Scouts appears.

I hear David shout at the top of his voice: "Now!"

Each one of them produces a paper bag filled with marbles. They roll those under the hooves of the horses. The poor horses immediately start to skid, slide, and skate on the small hard glass balls. The horses cannot keep their balance and they panic and try to run away from this strange situation. This causes more pandemonium, chaos, and mayhem. Riders are thrown off. Horses fall down and scream with pain. Some of them seem to have broken a leg.

The onlookers, who are mostly Boer people, find the scene hilarious and laugh at the antics of the hated National Scouts or Joiners. Some of them manage to catch their horses again and they try to rejoin the parade, but their horses cannot escape the mysterious glass balls under their hooves. Nobody helps those who have fallen off and injured themselves.

After three minutes of absolute humiliation for these men, most of them simply take the reins of their horses and disappear. They realize that they will never be able to survive the shame. David, Ben, and Charles disappear quietly into the background, while I follow them to congratulate them on their final blow to the hated enemy.

Pretoria, Tuesday, 3 June 1902

At breakfast, Hector tells us: "My street sweepers told me yesterday afternoon that they collected hundreds of glass marbles on Church Street, while cleaning up after the parade. David, do you know anything about that?"

He cannot lie and he admits: "That was my revenge on those Joiners. They must be taught a lesson for turning traitors. Not only did their horses throw them, but they were thoroughly humiliated."

My dad: "My son, I think you did more to disrupt the British war effort than any other boy of your age."

My mom: "Or any grown-up Boer fighter on his own, for that matter. I'm proud of you."

Hector can't help it and he gets up to shake David's hand.
It strikes me that we haven't told Hector really anything about the role my father played during the war and how I and David provided him with information about the British forces. It is certainly better to keep it that way. The war is, anyway, over and what difference will it make to divulge everything now?

THE GREAT WAR

During my second war, the so-called Great War, I helped the Germans in South West Africa and German East Africa against the Union Defense Force of South Africa that invaded these German colonies on behalf of Great Britain. This is how it happened:

Pretoria, Saturday, 28 November 1903

The wedding of Miss Theodora Davidsohn and the Honorable Lieutenant Hector de Hacqueville on this Saturday afternoon is a military affair. It is being held in the Dutch Reformed Church on Church Square and the Reverend Hermanus Bosman officiates.

I am a young bride, eighteen years old. To get married, I needed the written permission of my parents, which they willingly gave. I could not get married any earlier because I had to complete my school career first. My last exam was written a ten days ago and I am awaiting the results, but I am confident that I did very well. I took the following seven subjects: English, Latin, History, Biology, Geography, Mathematics, and Book-keeping or Accountancy. My strong point seems to be numbers. I would have liked to take Dutch as well, but that subject was abolished by the British authorities in an effort to stamp out the use of Dutch and Afrikaans. However, the Dutch Reformed Church established independent schools where Dutch had a place of honor, but I had to complete my school career in a government school because the free schools only started earlier this year from Grade One. My mother, though, ensured that I got enough exposure to Dutch and my father made sure that my German flourished. My relationship with Hector had the result that I acquired the accent of the upper classes in England. I, therefore, think that I am rather well educated for as girl of my age.

Hector got his commission as an officer back after having been declared fit for service by the good Doctor Barry. He could not rejoin his old outfit, the North Lancashire Mounted Rifles, because they had returned to Britain many months ago. He has joined, though, the Imperial Light Horse Regiment, a regiment of volunteers stationed in Johannesburg as a part-time officer. Six of his fellow officers formed a guard of honor at the entrance of the church and they are also his best men.

Hector's parents, Brigadier General Henry Viscount de Hacqueville and Henrietta Viscountess de Hacqueville, are among the guests. The general is, of course, in full uniform. He never participated in the Boer War and manned a desk at Whitehall. He has seen service in war situations when he was younger and he can boast several campaign medals – just as Hector does.

The Reverend Bosman holds his sermon in English because the guests from England don't understand a single word of Dutch. My father insisted that he reads the marriage formulary in Dutch, as it is printed at the back of our Dutch Bibles.

By this time, Hector has picked up a lot of Dutch and Afrikaans and he even joined the Dutch Reformed Church to please me and my parents. He is, therefore, able to follow the formulary and answer "Yes, I solemnly do so promise" at the appropriate moment.

The two fathers sign the marriage register as witnesses.

I am dressed, of course, in a most beautiful wedding gown, made by my parents. My bridesmaid, one of my old school friends, Lizzy Lombard, is also dressed appropriately.

It was, of course, not possible to accommodate the high visitors from England in our humble home. They stayed in the best hotel in town and that is also where the wedding dinner is being held tonight.

The first toast is being drunk on me, the bride who is eighteen years of age. The second toast s being drunk on the health of the bridegroom, who is twenty-three years old.

The toast on the parents of the bride is being called for by the viscount. He welcomes me, the bride, as a new member of the de Hacqueville family: "We are one of the proudest families in Britain. We can trace our ancestry back to the time of William the

Conqueror, who became king of England during the eleventh century. It is hoped that she will provide an heir for her husband, who has to succeed his father to the title and the estate in due time."

All the guests seem duly impressed by this illustrious, glorious, and conspicuous family from abroad.

It is my father's task to institute the last toast, the toast on the health of the bridegroom's parents. He welcomes Hector into the family: "Hector, your parents must be congratulated for instilling in you the excellent taste that you have shown by choosing Theodora Davidsohn as your bride. I must congratulate all of you for this.

"Hector, the two of us fought on different sides during the war that has ended last year. It's not impossible that we clashed directly on occasion. Who knows, it might even have been me who shot off that part of your little finger. But, in the meantime, Dora has managed to recreate you. You are now almost just as much a Boer as anybody else in this town. You speak our language and you joined our church.

"You must have recognized something in Theodora that attracted you to her as a potential life partner. Her name is actually a Greek name that means 'Gift from God'. That she is by all means. I am sure that she will provide a fitting heir to inherit the title sometime in the future.

"By the way, she shares the name of Theodora with the wife of the Roman Emperor Justinian of the sixth century after Christ. A picture of this beautiful empress in mosaic is to be found in an ancient church in the Italian town of Ravenna.

"Although we are not officially a titled family, I won't make a mistake by calling Dora a princess. Her mother's family, the Vissers, may be regarded as Boer aristocracy. And, as you all know, I have a Hebrew ancestry. I can trace my ancestors, every single one of them, back to biblical times. And by biblical times, I mean the

Old Testament times. We Davidsohns are descended from people who lived considerably more than two thousand years ago.

"We Jews had to fend for ourselves during the centuries. That is why we've learnt all sorts of crafts. I was taught to become a tailor by my father in Kleve on the border between Germany and Holland where I was born, and I taught this skill to my children. But we may call ourselves proud members of a very, very old and distinguished family. Hector, when the time comes, I may perhaps tell you our whole very proud family history.

"I must say that I find Dora's taste in men to be excellent. She chose her in-laws carefully and I propose that we all lift our glasses to toast their health."

The viscount and his wife give polite applause after my father's speech, but I can see that they are not used to be trumped by somebody whose ancestry and family history are at least three times as old as theirs.

Pretoria, Saturday, 19 December 1903

We reach the Pretoria's Railroad Station on this Saturday afternoon after a journey from Cape Town. This was the first time that I saw other parts of South Africa, having spent my whole life in and around Pretoria.

We spent our first wedding night in the hotel where the wedding dinner was held and the next day Hector took me on a train trip to Cape Town. We stayed in three different hotels, in Sea Point, Camp's Bay, and Muizenberg. He took me up onto Table Mountain, showed me the ancient Dutch Castle, walked with me through the oak-lined streets of Stellenbosch, the oldest town in South Africa after Cape Town, and we often bathed in the ocean.

Hector hires a horse and a cart with a driver to take us to his new farm outside Pretoria. He resigned from the Pretoria Town Council's service earlier this year, after he had bought a farm called Hartebeestspruit,[12] a few miles to the east of Pretoria. It belonged to the widow Hannah Henning, whose husband fell during the war. Since the couple had no children to look after the farm, she decided to sell it and take up residence inside Pretoria with her sister.

---

[12] The Dutch name can be translated as " Gateway of the Hartebeest" (a species of antelope for which no separate English names exists).

Of course, I have seen this farm with its primitive cottage shortly after Hector had bought it. The British forces burnt the cottage down in their campaign against the Boer women and children, but Hector was able to rebuild it. He hired two laborers to restore the thatched roof and he was able to replace the timber parts – roof rafters, ceiling beams, windows, and doors. As the only grandson of the late Colonel Horace Viscount de Hacqueville, he inherited a substantial sum of money with which he could buy the farm, restore the cottage, acquire some heads of cattle, and hire two black farm hands to help him with the cultivation of crops of maize and vegetables. He also planted some fruit trees and a vineyard.

I was given a free hand to furnish the cottage with furniture and other necessities in anticipation of our marriage. I could count on the good advice of my mother.

Because no agricultural activities took place during the latter part of the war, the place is wild and overgrown with trees and shrubs. There is enough grazing for the animals. The farm is watered by a little river, the Moreleta Brook. The cottage is situated on the slopes of a hill, called the Bronberg,[13] from where the whole farm can be overseen. The town of Pretoria is also visible in the distance.

We stop at my parents' home in Arcadia where we are greeted by my parents, David, and Wilma with Baby Daniel. After we have been served with coffee, I pack all my clothes and other personal items to take them to the farm.

Wilma has decided not to go back to her family. She has seen them after the end of the war when the inmates of the concentration camps were allowed to return home, but she received a very cool reception from her mother and grandmother, who didn't want to accept the baby born out of wedlock – although it wasn't her fault that she fell pregnant. She also couldn't forgive her father for becoming a traitor. My parents had little Daniel baptized in our church in their roles as foster-parents.

Me: "Wilma, what will become of you now?"

Wilma: "Your parents have agreed to let me stay here. As you know, I help with the tailoring business to earn a living for me and little Daniel."

I hug Wilma and declare: "I'm so glad that you have found a good home for your little one. You will always be welcome to visit us on the farm."

When we reach the cottage, Hector lifts me off the cart and carries me to the front door.

"Welcome to Faerie Glen!"

"Where and what is this Faerie Glen?"

"This is the new name for Hartebeestspruit. You are the fairy queen who will reign in this enchanted bush."

I remember that Veleda visited me last night while we slept in the train and announced – as usual, in ancient German – with a sly smile: "You will have magical times from now on."

---

[13] "Bronberg" can be translated as "Source Mountain".

Pretoria, Thursday, 1 September 1904

Little Henry de Hacqueville was born this morning, exactly nine months and three days after I became Missus Theodora de Hacqueville.

The poor Hector de Hacqueville knew enough about the theory of producing babies, having grown up on his father's estate in Hampshire where they had cattle and horses. About the finer points and the emotional side of the whole procedure, he was totally uninformed. Fortunately, my mother gave me very clear instructions about the art of making love in an elegant and satisfying way and I had to teach the ignorant Hector. Fortunately, he caught on very rapidly.

I insisted on the name of Henry for the baby, a family name, although I decided that I would speak Afrikaans to him and call him Hendrik, the Dutch variety of Henry or the Norwegian Henrik. I was sure that I was carrying a son and heir to the family title and estate in England. It must have been Veleda or my great-grandmother Anna who told me while I was sleeping. I can't remember whether the message was given in German or Afrikaans. Anyway, the result was that we never even considered the possibility of a name for a girl.

Little Henry or Hendrik is to be baptized in the Durch Reformed Church by the Reverend Hermanus Bosman. Since I am officially a Jew, I also insisted that he be circumcised as a member of the people of Israel. My father organized that ceremony on a week-old baby with his rabbi.

Faerie Glen, Monday, 10 October 1904

Hector takes the train every second week-end of every month to Johannesburg to take part in the activities of the Imperial Light Horse Regiment, of which he is the second-in-command of B Squadron. The ILHR has its headquarters at the so-called Drill Hall. He was issued with a rifle – the Point Three-Oh-Three that the British troops used during the war – and a pistol. Those were used for target shooting exercises at a shooting range at a place called Doornkop[14] outside Johannesburg.

Last night, he returned with a big box, which he unpacks only this morning. I look over his shoulder with little Henry – or Hendrik – on my hip.

I ask: "What is that thing for?"

"My lovely lass, this thing is called a heliograph. We used it quite a lot during the war. It's a signaling device with which you can send messages during daylight hours over long distances."

"To whom do you want to send messages?"

"My gorgeous girl, you are going to use it to signal to me where I am working some-where in the fields or the bush. That's whenever you want to tell me something. You are to shoot two shots with blanks from my revolver or rifle to draw my attention and then you send your message."

"Where did you get it?"

---

[14] "Doornkop" may be translated as "Thorny Hill".

"At the Drill Hall. They were selling off some surplus Army equipment left over from the war and I bought it."

"So, how does this thing work?"

"See this mirror? It's not an ordinary mirror, but it has a mottled surface. That reflects the sunlight towards a rather wide area so that the observers on more than one spot can see the flashes of sunlight. This is a shutter that is swiveled in front of the mirror to block the sunlight for a moment, and then it is removed again to cause another flash of sunlight. You try it. Do it with this with handle."

I pass little Henry to his father and I start playing with the apparatus.

Hector: "And now you aim that mirror so that the reflected sunlight is directed towards Meintjeskop Hill, just above your parents' home."

I do so and continue playing with the shutter.

"And how on earth will the people at the other end know what I want to tell them?"

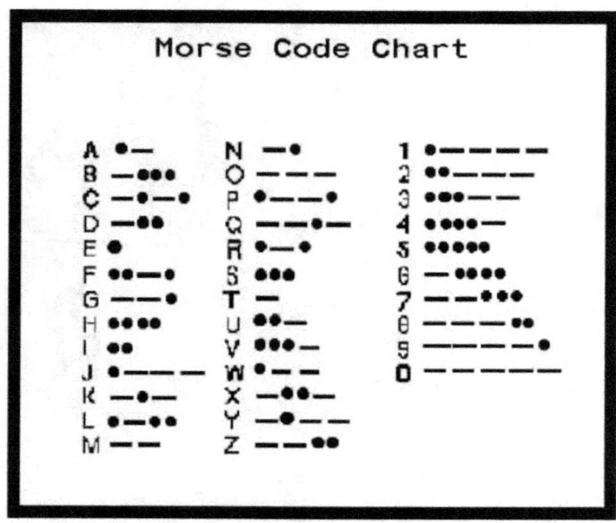

"I am going to teach you Morse Code. It consists of shorter and longer flashes to spell the different letters of the alphabet, as well as numbers. A longer pause between the flashes signals the spaces between letters. Here is a card with the Morse Code, as we used it during the war. We are going to practice it until you are used to it.""

"Are you trying to train me to become a military signaler?"

"Almost something of the sort."

Silently, I think: "This is something I could have used very well as a spy during the war. But now it's too late for that. But this does seem like a very useful thing to have."

Aloud, I say: "When do we start?"

Faerie Glen, Monday, 7 November 1904

Hector is outside, somewhere on the farm. I feel confident enough with the heliograph and the Morse Code to try it for the first time. I send the following message:

BRING ONIONS CARROTS

Hector arrives an hour later, laughing and carrying a bunch of carrots and a few onions that he has harvested from our vegetable garden: "Ah, my dear darling Dora! Congratulations! Here is a kiss, together with the vegetables you ordered."

Faerie Glen, Wednesday, 29 August 1905

Hector took off on his horse after breakfast to look at his cattle where they are grazing. I suddenly feel that I need help with the arrival of little Daniel who is due any time now.

I erect the heliograph on its tripod and aim the mirror in the general direction where Hector is supposed to be. I fire two shots in rapid succession with his revolver into the air and I start signaling:

NO 2 ALMOST HERE TAKE ME TO MA

Pretoria, Friday, 1 September 1905

Little Henry is exactly one year old today. His little brother, Daniel, arrived during the early morning hours today. I don't know how we arranged it that our second son was born exactly one year after our first son, but this is how it happened.

Hector took me to my parents' home two days ago for the delivery. I was rather long in labor. After little Daniel has arrived and I nursed him, my father explains: "Thank you for calling this little chap after me. I am sure that some or other fairy from Faerie Glen must have poured some magic stuff into the water of the Moreleta Brook to get this magical result."

Silently, I agree. That fairy's name must be Veleda, not Dora. She told me a few weeks ago one night that I am one of her descendants, on my mother's side, and that is why she is looking after me. She also informed me that I was carrying another son and that the day would come for me to visit the place where her tower stood.

Wilma also appears with her little son, who is also called Daniel, to congratulate me with my second son. She introduces me to a young man, Gideon Grobler. He is a young widower who lost his wife and little son in a concentration camp while he was fighting the British invaders of our country. His baby daughter survived due to the care given to her by other sympathetic inmates of the concentration camp.

Wilma: "Dear Gideon promised to become a father for my little Daniel, while I'm eager to take his little Geraldine as my own. We have, though, a problem. I need the written permission of my parents to get married, but my father refuses to give it to me. He says I'm a slut and he doesn't want me to be part of his family anymore."

Me: "I think he's angry that you were cared for by real Boers who can't stand Joiners like him."

Hector: "Perhaps I can do something. I will put on my Army uniform and intimidate him. Where can I find him? If he keeps on refusing permission, we may approach the court for an order. In that case, I will see to it that the Pretoria News gets the story. I don't think your old chap will like that very much. If I tell him about this alternative, he might reconsider his stubbornness and stupidity and silliness."

Gideon and Wilma both smile.

Faerie Glen, Thursday, 30 August 1906

Hector arrives home on our two-wheeled carriage, drawn by his new horse. He smiles: "We are property owners inside Pretoria since today."

"What do you mean?"

"When I visited your parents, I stumbled upon the auction of the house next to theirs. Your dad explained that Mister Jonker, his neighbor and a widower, got married for the second time and was moving to the house of his new wife. He, therefore, put his house up for auction."

"And you bought it?"

"You guessed correctly. The day after tomorrow we are going to celebrate the birthdays of Henry and Daniel at your parent's place and then you can inspect our new property."

"What are we going to do with the place? We live quite comfortably in this cottage."

"I need it as an office in town. Its cumbersome to meet business partners in a hotel lounge. It will be much better if we have a place where we are the hosts."

"And that makes us neighbors of my parents! I like that idea."

Pretoria, Saturday, 1 September 1906

We arrived early this Saturday morning at my parents' place to allow me and David to accompany my parents to the Synagogue.

My Ma baked a delicious chocolate cake after we have returned home to celebrate the second birthday of little Hendrik and the first birthday of little Daniel. Hector stayed home to look after the little ones while we were away. And now the little ones are being fed morsels of this cake, but they are far too small to understand the importance of the treat.

During the afternoon I, Hector, and Vati walk over to the house that Hector had bought.

Hector: "My dear Dora, I don't know whether you will like the furniture that came with the house. Let's have a look and if there are any items that you don't like, we discard those and get something better instead."

Some of the pieces of furniture seem decrepit and worn-out and I ask Hector whether we could replace those.

"As long as our budget can withstand your onslaughts and orders."

Hector asks my opinion about which room he should use as his office. The choice is easy: the bedroom that leads out of the drawing room. We can place a desk, chairs, and some book shelves there to convert it into a neat office. We will have to acquire some good paintings to decorate the place.

Vati: "Hector, now that you are a property owner in this town, you are eligible to stand in the coming by-election for a town councilor."

"Is there a vacancy?"

"Yes. Mister Jonker, the previous owner of this place, resigned from the Town Council after moving in with his new wife. She lives in Johannesburg and he is no longer a resident of Pretoria."

Me: "I think that the Honorable Hector de Hacqueville will be a very good town councilor. How about it?"

"I must think about it. Fortunately, I know something about the administration of this place, having been in charge of a dozen mule carts used for garbage removal."

Pretoria, Wednesday, 19 January 1906

Hector is today officially declared to be the new town councilor for the Arcadia ward. The town clerk announced that he was elected unopposed. No other candidates came forward. A notice to that effect is to be placed in the Pretoria News.

Hector: "We will have to hold an open house this Saturday. I must meet my new constituents. We will have to provide some snacks, coffee, tea, and other drinks. How are we going to manage that? I will have to place a notice to that effect in the Pretoria News."

Faerie Glen, Friday, 1 March 1907

One of Hector's farm hands reports that one of his cows struggles to deliver her new calf. Hector rushes off on horseback to attend to the cow.

Shortly afterwards, I feel that I am getting in the same position and condition as that cow because my own birth pangs are starting to cause severe cramps. I only expected little Victor a week later, but it seems as if my calculations were somewhat pessimistic.

Hector agreed with my choice of a name, namely Victor. It rhymes with Hector and it is a Latin name that fits in with the ancient Greek or Latin name of the hero Hector. But the name of Victor is also a known English name that will look good with de Hacqueville.

I drag the heliograph out and send the following signal in the direction where Hector is supposed to be, while I feel that the little one is in haste to see the world:

NO 3 COMING NEED HELP

Hector rushes back on horseback and reaches me a few minutes later. An hour later little Victor is bathed, fed, and asleep in his cot.

Me: "How is that cow doing?"

"She's just as strong and healthy as you are. She gave me a little bull calf, just as you did. Imagine, two babies on the same day!"

"Do you realize that this little boy is the result of some magic?"

"How?"

"He arrived exactly two years and six months after his eldest brother came and exactly eighteen months after his second brother. Remarkable, isn't it?"

"Yes, there must be some magic involved. That's because the fairy queen of this enchanted place is involved."

Hector gives me a hug and a kiss and declares: "Dora, congratulations with Number Three, as you called him in your signal. I'm proud of you. Also, that you are a competent signaler."

"Do you know what my wish is? I wish that none of them will ever become involved in any war. You went through the war with only a minor mishap to that little finger of yours, but it could have happened that I lost you. I don't want to lose Number One, Number Two, or Number Three."

"I don't know whether that will be in our hands."

It is as if a little voice inside my head whispers that all three my sons are doomed to pursue military careers since all their ancestors on their father's side were warriors. Some of my ancestors were also fighters.

Pretoria, Monday, 20 September 1909

Hector returns home after a meeting of the City Council: "Important and big and momentous things are going to happen to our neighborhood. The Council made some important decisions and resolutions today dealing with developments here in Arcadia."

"May I hear what happened? Or is it a secret?"

"No, certainly not."

"Why may I not hear of it?"

"No, that's not what I mean. No, it's not a secret. The Pretoria News is bound to publish the story tomorrow. Anyway, the building plans for a huge, grand, monumental, and fantastic building here on top of Meintjeskop Hill were approved. It will be the biggest building in the whole of South Africa. No doubt about it. A famous architect, a certain Sir Herbert Baker, drew up some plans for a new government building."

"Is the old Government Building on Church Square getting too small?"

"No. It's for the government of the new Union of South Africa that will come into being next year. As you well know, Cape Town will be the legislative capital of the country and Pretoria becomes the administrative capital. The new Parliament will sit in the old Parliament Building of the Cape Colony in Cape Town, but a grand new building is needed for the country's administration. It will house the office of the Prime Minister and other big shots."

"When will building work start?"

"Sometime during next year. First of all, the site must be levelled and prepared, and sand stone blocks and granite blocks must be quarried before building work can start.

Pretoria, Friday, 7 January 1910

Our household is moving to our town house today. Hector and I agreed that it would be better to raise our kids mostly in tow because Henry is due to start his school career next Tuesday. We can always move back to Faerie Glen during the school holidays. Hector will visit the farm daily or whenever needed. His duties as a town councilor calls for regular visits to his office in town.

Henry is to attend the same school as David, a school with combined English and Dutch name: the Pretoria High School for Boys – Pretoria Hogere School voor Jongens. It's called a high school, but classes start at Grade One.

The new school building was completed a year ago and was inaugurated by the Minister of Education, Oom Jannie Smuts, who was a Boer general during the war.

It was initially a unilingual English school, but Smuts managed to convert it into a dual-medium school where tuition is given in English and Dutch – an opportunity and privilege I never had.

David finished his school career last November. Hector convinced him to join his regiment, the ILHR in Johannesburg. That means that David is to receive some basic training before he can call himself a soldier – something he wanted to be since his pre-school days. Hector has been promoted to captain and he is in command of B Squadron. This is a part-time unit and part of the so-called Active Citizen Force. David will help Vati in his tailor workshop most of the time when he is not doing duty as a soldier at the Drill Hall in Johannesburg.

Pretoria, Tuesday, 29 March 1910.

The boys are glad to be back on the farm during the Easter school holidays. Henry and Daniel are already accomplished equestrians and I enjoy riding through the bush with them. I carry little Victor on my back in the same style as the black women do with their babies and toddlers. Hector is overseeing the harvest on his maize field.

When we arrive back at the cottage, we find a telegram lying on the stone pavement at the front door, secured with a stone to prevent it from flying away in the wind. Although it is addressed to Hector, I open it immediately because it may contain important news. The following words leap up into my eyes:

THE HON HECTOR DE HACQUEVILLE FAERIE GLEN
PRETORIA SOUTH AFRICA

HENRY SERIOUS HEART ATTACK PSE COME ASAP
= HENRIETTA

I immediately fetch the heliograph and send the following signal to Hector:

BAD NEWS TELEGRAM COME HOME

Cape Town, Thursday, 7 April 1910

We boarded the Dover Castle, a steamship of the Union Castle Line, this morning after having arrived by train from Pretoria. We are just in time because the ship is due to leave at four-o'-clock this afternoon for Southampton.

We were lucky to get a cabin at short notice. For that, we must thank the telegraph service in Pretoria, which enabled us to contact the shipping line's offices in Cape Town. Unfortunately, all the first-class cabins were already taken and we had to be content with second class. That's, at least, better than third class.

Hector told me when we received the telegram confirming our booking: "We are lucky, we live in the magical and magnificent and marvelous twentieth century. We are to travel on a fantastic fast steam boat that needs a mere fortnight to reach ole Blighty. In the age of sailing ships, this voyage took many months."

My parents and Wilma and her husband were more than willing to look after the boys and help Henry with his school work.

We are standing on the deck while the Dover Castle leaves Cape Town and we watch Table Mountain receding into the distance.

Hector: "Hell, here we are at last. This was a terrible week with all those arrangements. Fortunately, I got that reply from my mom three days ago to tell us that my dad is in a serious, yet stable, condition. Let's hope we find him still alive."

"My heroic husband, let's look at this as a second honeymoon. We will spend two weeks on the water, all on our own. And I am very curious to see the place where you grew up."

"Thankfully, this ship docks at Southampton. That's not too far away from our estate. We ought to reach the place before dark the same day after having arrived early enough at the docks."

"Shouldn't we go and visit your dad in hospital, first thing?"

"Perhaps, yes. Luckily, we live in the fantastic and fabulous twentieth century and we can send and receive cables from this ship and find out from my mom where my dad is."

Hagdale, Monday, 25 April 1910

After a fortnight on the water, we arrive at the de Hacqueville estate, Hagdale. Hector managed to hire a coach with two horses and a driver in Southampton to take us to his parents' home. We received a cable aboard the Dover Castle yesterday, informing us that the viscount was recuperating at home and receiving a daily visit from his doctor.

We drive through the Main Road of the village of Hursley. It is a quaint place with houses that are centuries old. Hector explains that some of them are called half-timbered houses since they have wooden skeletons or frames. There are less than a thousand inhabitants and the village consists essentially of the buildings along the Main Road and a few side streets.

He points at a very old stone structure: "I was baptized in that church. It's called the All-Saints Church. I don't know how old it is, but it dates from the Middle Ages. There is also the Old Rectory, which is just as old."

I love the place. It is situated in the middle of a wooded area or a forest with lots of trees. Spring has arrived and there are already lovely flowers blooming on the sidewalks and in the gardens.

At last, we reach Hagdale. Hector informs me: "This place was built more than a century-and-a-half ago by my great-great grandfather. He and his wife visited Italy and fell in love with a so-called little Palladian villa and they got an architect who measured the place and drew up building plans to have this place erected on their estate. The original Italian villa with the name of Villa Chiericati was built during the fifteen-hundreds, by a guy called Andrea Palladio near Vicenza. It became fashionable here in Britain to copy his designs.

I am truly delighted when we enter the grounds of Hagdale. There are many trees in the wild gardens, but also open fields where the cattle and horses roam. My eyes rest upon a beautiful building of stone. In style, it differs widely from the medieval buildings along the Main Road of Hursley because the front door is placed inside a copy of an ancient Greek or Roman temple. To my amazement, there are even statues on the roof. It looks very elegant.

Hector pays the coach man and he rings the bell at the front door. A maid with a white apron opens the door and greets us friendly: "The viscountess is in the drawing room. I will take your bags to your old room, your Honor."

My first thought is: "This place is much, much grander than our cottage on the farm and our house in Pretoria! Will I ever get used to this luxury and grandeur and elegance?"

While we enter the villa, I ask myself: "Dora, do you really belong in such a grand place? Hector is due to inherit it when his father dies, which may be very soon. Will you feel at home with all this luxury?"

As we enter the drawing room where Henrietta, Viscountess de Hacqueville, is sitting, a little voice inside me whispers (and I get the feeling that it is Veleda who speaks to me in ancient German): "Dora, you really do belong here!" I also remember that Vati said that I am supposed to be a Jewish princess. From a very, very ancient royal house.

We greet my mother-in-law who allows me to plant a peck on her cheek. Hector calls out: "Hey, Mater! Here we are, at last. How's Pater?"

"Come and greet your mother properly first. And then we can go to your dad's bedroom to see him."

Brigadier General (retired) Henry, Viscount de Hacqueville, lies in his bed, reading a newspaper. He asks gruffly: "Why did you take so long? I had this horrible heart attack already a month ago. Don't you care about me? I was on the verge of kicking the bucket with my right foot."

"Sorry, Pater. We took the very first mail ship we could get. And, as you ought to know, Pretoria and Cape Town are on the bottom parts of the earth, rather quite a few leagues from here. But, how are you doing?"

"The quacks at hospital sent me home – either to get better, or to bite the dust. Whatever. They don't seem to know which. I'm taking it easy. Doctor's orders. I'm allowed one short stroll through the garden every morning. You two are going to take me tomorrow."

I greet the Viscount with a curtsy and he grumbles: "Give me a decent kiss, girl! Thar's something the pill pushers didn't forbid me."

After chatting for a quarter-of-an-hour, my mother-in-law announces: "Dinner at seven. Formal, as usual."

While we are getting dressed in Hector's old bedroom, he takes out his Army uniform to be pressed.

"And that? We're not going to a parade, or did I miss something?"

"You can call it a blooming, blinking parade. I don't have any formal clothes, like a penguin suit. I brought this along, in case there is to be a funeral. That funeral is bound to be a military affair. He is, after all, a retired general or something."

Hagdale, Saturday, 7 May 1910

The evening newspaper is delivered to our front door. I say *"our* front door", because by now, I feel part of the set-up after staying here for the last fortnight. The maid brings the newspaper to Hector.

"Hell's bells! Mater, do you see this? King Eddie has decided to blow out his last breath last night. Heavy heart attack and bad bronchitis. I must go and tell Pater about this immediately."

We take the newspaper to the general. He scans the story on the front page briefly and barks: "Hector! You will have to represent me. There will be a royal funeral, no doubt, which will have to be attended by all the lords of the realm. Just as when ole Queen Vic died. I can't go. Too damn sick. I don't want to go the same way as His Majesty. You put on your uniform. Fortunately, you have a string of medals to decorate your chest and your belly. Go to the best tailor in Southampton to get a decent dress made for my darling daughter-in-law. Hurry up! There isn't much time!"

Hector: "All right, Pater. Tomorrow is Sunday, but I am sure that we will find a suitable tailor on Monday."

Me: "Milord, I can make my own dress. I have made all my clothes myself."

"Nonsense! You get a professional job done. Just the very best for any member of this household. I want you to look like a fairy princess."

Later, I tell Hector: "I am really going to make my own dress. We must go shopping on Monday to buy suitable material and everything else in Southampton. Or in Winchester, for that matter."

"You will also need a sewing machine. We must also buy that. We don't have something like that here."

"My father used to say: 'Fashions change, but style endures.' That is what he had in abundance – style. I hope to put that into the dress I will make. I suppose it will have to be either in black, or pure white. It must fit in with a funeral."

"Make it white. This foolish funeral is messing with our plans to go back to Pretoria. I will have to cancel our passage for next Thursday because the funeral is bound to be later than that. There must be enough time to allow all the royalty from all over Europe to get assembled and attend."

"Yes, we will have to postpone, although your dad is getting better. He doesn't seem to be lying on his death-bed anymore. We needn't stay for his funeral."

"But there is one snag."

"What?"

"I must join my regiment on the thirty-first of this month in Cape Town for that hell of a parade, I told you about. The biggest in the history of Cape Town. That is when the Union of South Africa comes into being. We will most probably have to miss it. I will have a very good excuse. Attending the funeral of the late King Edward the Seventh."

"Apart from representing your dad, you will also represent the South African Army, if something like that exists."

"Not yet. The four colonies must get united first. But the folks over here don't know it. I may easily call myself the representative of the South African Defense Force! How's that?"

"Fortunately, you are no longer a lieutenant, but a captain. That sounds better."

London, Friday, 20 May 1910

We arrived in London the day before yesterday to attend the royal funeral. The funeral directors to the Royal Household who were appointed to assist during this occasion, the family business of William Banting of St James's Street, London, contacted my father-in-law with an official invitation to the occasion. They sent a special courier with a printed invitation in golden letters.

Lord Henry informed the courier that he was extremely and exceedingly honored to be on the list of invited guests, but that he is indisposed and would, accordingly, not be in a position to accept the invitation. He, though, nominated his son and heir, the Honorable Captain Hector de Hacqueville, as his representative and replacement.

Thereafter, the courier informed Hector of our accommodation arrangements. We were to stay in a grand new hotel, built only ten years ago, called The Landmark, in Marylebone Road. On the day of the funeral, we will be transported by a coach to Buckingham Palace, from where the procession of dignitaries would proceed.

And now we are standing around in the grounds of Buckingham Palace while more and more dignitaries, notables, and celebrities arrive. There are emperors, empresses, kings, queens, crown princes, other princes, princesses, dukes, duchesses, marquesses, earls, viscounts, presidents, prime ministers, ambassadors, ministers, field marshals, admirals of the fleet, and important people without pompous titles, together with their spouses. Many of the highest noble folks are either siblings, in-laws, nephews, cousins, second cousins, or second cousins twice removed of the late king.

Hector remarks: "My wonderful wife and dearest darling, I must congratulate you with your dress. If I compare you with all these queens, princesses, duchesses, ladies, and whatever else, you deserve first prize for beauty and elegance, as well as for being the best dressed woman. I see many of those titled females with their skewed teeth and pimples on their powdered cheeks looking at you with envious eyes."

"Thanks, my honorable hubby, but I think there are a few of them who outshine me. However, I don't feel inferior to any of them."

"No, don't. Anyway, I am thirsty. Let's see if we can find something to drink inside."

We manage to slip inside the palace. We behave as if we belong there and nobody questions our presence. We wander from hall to hall, chamber to chamber.

And then we see a sight that very few people have ever seen and will ever see again: nine emperors and kings who are lined up for a group photograph. In the center we see King George V, the new king.

Directly behind him, I see the German Kaiser, Wilhelm II. I don't recognize the others, but it is certain that they must all have crowned heads. They are all heavily decorated and embellished with medals, stars, chains, ribbons, sashes, swords, and golden ropes.

We disappear before somebody chases us away.

Hector: "Somebody outside told me that Cousin Nicky, the Czar, or Emperor of Russia, couldn't come. He's a cousin of King George, just as the German Kaiser, Cousin Willy. With him present, there would have been ten crowned heads."

"How are they all cousins?"

"Oh, Wilhelm's mother was a daughter of ole Queen Victoria and a sister of our new monarch's dead father. The mother of Czar Nicholas II of all Russians was a sister of King George's mother. Both were daughters of the king of Denmark. That's how. And, in addition, Frederik VIII, the king of Denmark, is an uncle. That's also the case with King George I of the Greeks."

"Hell! It seems as if all these family members hate each other and that's why they are armed with swords. Will they fight each other during this funeral?"

"No, you silly woman. Those swords are only for show, to make them look important. They pretend to be old-time knights."

We slouch away before we are discovered and, at last, we find some bathrooms, where we can get sips of tap water.

When we join the crowd outside again, somebody with a speaking trumpet is organizing the line-up. We are placed rather towards the end, far behind the princes, dukes, and other folks with smarter titles and appellations. There must have been some or other mix-up because Hector is placed between the other viscounts, although he is only entitled to be addressed as "the Honorable". This confusion must be the result of the organizers not getting the news that old Henry cannot attend.

A carriage with the late king's coffin leads the procession. The important crowd follows. The nine emperors and kings are mounted on horses. The streets are lined with soldiers and sailors and thousands and thousands upon thousands of people watch the procession. Behind us, various bands are playing marching music – brass bands and pipe bands. As we turn a corner and I look back, I see thousands upon thousands of troops and sailors marching behind us.

Hector tells me: "I'm glad that we are young and fit. Some of these senior souls suffer, even if it is with a smile. That is the burden of being of noble descent – you may never show your displeasure or discomfort or distress or dislikes."

I agree.

The procession stops somewhere. Hector explains that we are next to the Houses of Parliament. Only the nearest family members will attend a short service in the medieval Westminster Hall, where the archbishop of Canterbury will do his bit.

Fortunately, we don't have to wait too long and we are directed to follow the carriage with the coffin again. Hector explains that we pass Hyde Park and other well-known landmarks. I would have loved to have a better look at those spots, but it is not possible to leave the procession. At last, we reach a railroad station and a sign says it is Paddington Station.

We are allotted seats in the train, according to social standing and rank. The most important souls are seated right in front, while we, the somewhat lesser nobility, must be satisfied with seats further to the rear.

To my surprise, I and Hector sit opposite a well-known figure, Field Marshal Horatio, Viscount Kitchener. Hector salutes him as a higher officer, which Kitchener reciprocates.

I can remember him from New Year's Eve, ten years ago. I whisper to Hector: "Must I kick him in the balls or on his shin?"

"Dora, if you do that ..." He stays silent, but it is clear what he means.

"All right, I won't kick him. I will only spit him in his face."

"Hell, you wild woman ..." He doesn't finish his sentence.

We sit stone-faced during the rest of the journey. I stare Kitchener down and it happens three times that I catch his eyes, but then he looks away first. That makes me feel like his superior.

I tell myself: "Although I'm supposed to be a member of the British aristocracy now, at heart I'm a Boer girl and a German woman. I'm better than this feeble and miserable field marshal."

When we disembark at Windsor where a service is to be held in the royal chapel, Kitchener is just in front of me. I take one of the long pins with which my hat is fastened onto my head. I prick him very hard on his bum and push it as deep as possible. He leaps forward because of the unexpected sting and that movement pulls the pin out and leaves it in my hand. He bumps against his wife in front of him. She almost falls. He turns around to see what happened to him.

I hiss: "You beastly, bastardly butcher! You killed thousands of innocent and defenseless Boer women and children. God will never forgive you!"

Kitchener gets red in the face, but turns around and follows his wife. There was murder in his eyes.

Hector: "My dear, damn, what have you done? Insulting a very important officer? I will have to apologize to him on your behalf."

"Too late, he has already fled. He's afraid of me. Luckily, we won't be seated next to that terrible thug in the chapel."

"Please remember that we are entering a church where a very serious and solemn service is to be held. It's called a funeral service; in case you didn't know."

"I know how to behave myself in the house of God. He will be watching me." I add in my thoughts: "With a sly and silly smile."

Inside the chapel, I sit on Hector's left side, as has to be done when a man is in uniform, so that he has his right arm free to salute, whenever necessary. I tap on his left leg with my right hand:

HUNGRY

He replies by tapping on my right thigh:

DINNER IN PALACE

Pretoria, Saturday, 26 November 1910

Hector asks me: "Are you going to wear that smart dress that you made for the royal funeral for today's event?"

"I think so. That dress fitted in nicely when we were rubbing shoulders with royalty and other important folks during May. And I am looking forward to meet good ole Queen Victoria's third son."

Although I called the dead queen "good" for Hector's sake, I think she must have been a horrible old hag. I was told that she had terrible table manners, although she was really a German princess before she became the queen of Great Britain and the empress of India.

When we returned a few months ago from Britain, we arrived in a different country than the one from which we left. By that time, the Cape Colony, the Natal Colony, the Orange River Colony, and the Transvaal Colony had united and became the Union of South Africa. The status of each of the former colonies has changed to that of provinces of the new country.

The occasion today is the laying of the corner stone of the Union Buildings, the new government building, not too far from our dwelling in town on Meintjeskop Hill. Although the spot where the corner stone is to be laid is within walking distance from our home, we take our new motor car, one of the few in Pretoria. Hector is, after all, one of the dignitaries today, being a member of the Town Council, and it wouldn't do to go on foot.

No seating is provided for the occasion and all the invited guests stand around the area where the ceremony is to take place. Exactly at twelve noon, the most distinguished guest of honor arrives: Prince Arthur, the Duke of Connaught and Strathearn.

He is welcomed by the Prime Minister of the Union of South Africa, Oom Louis Botha, the former commandant general of the

Transvaal Republic. The mayor of Pretoria also says a few friendly words.

Of course, the prince, in his uniform as a field marshal, is not able to carry the big corner stone of granite to the spot where it is to be laid. A mechanical crane does the hard work. To look important, he keeps his right hand on the stone as it is being swung into position. The crowd politely applauds his audacious and august accomplishment.

Hector whispers: "I'm sure he found this job to be easier than his previous task when he had to open the Parliament of a united South Africa in Cape Town a while ago. There he had to deliver a long speech, which we are spared today."

Me: "And now, Mister Councilor, we must move on to the town hall where lunch is to be served. Are you hungry enough?"

Johannesburg, Wednesday, 30 November 1910

We are to encounter Prince Arthur again today. Another corner stone has to be laid – this time, for a war memorial in the Saxonwold Forest, north of Johannesburg. It is to honor all troops from Johannesburg and surrounding areas who joined the British forces and lost their lives during the war.

Hector, as commander of B Squadron of his regiment, is dressed in his uniform as a captain. All his shiny medals, or "gongs" as he calls them, are hanging on their ribbons on his chest and they sound like little bells when they swing against each other as he moves.

This time, the prince delivers an oration, which he starts to read from a piece of paper, but then the wind blows it out of his hand. He, nevertheless, tries to carry on and bemoans the fact that he wasn't allowed to take part in the Boer War because he was in command of all British troops in Ireland at that time.

Lunch is being served in a big tent for all the dignitaries. The prince corners Hector and me and says: "Captain, I notice that you are wearing the com-memorative medal of the funeral of my late brother, earlier this year. How did you get there?"

Prince Arthur

"Your Royal Highness, it was really by accident. We were visiting my sick father when His Majesty passed away. I had to replace my indisposed father on the guest list."

"And who is your father, if I may ask?"

"Henry, Viscount de Hacqueville of Hagdale."

"Ah, one of the lords of the realm. It's good to meet his son and heir. And, Madam, if I may say so, but you are certainly the most beautiful rose here between all these ugly and ungainly bean stalks, strutting around in their decorated uniforms, looking like Christmas trees."

I do a curtsy: "Thank you, your Royal Highness."

"I think I have noticed you at the royal funeral."

"That is possible."

"Afterwards, Field Marshall Lord Kitchener complained to me that a South African lady pricked him with a needle or a sharp object on a tender and sensitive spot. He complained that it was rather distressing and difficult to sit down after that. Was that, perhaps, you Ma'am?"

I smile broadly: "I had to show him how I loathed him for all the terror and tears and troubles he caused on innocent civilians during the war in this country."

"Ha-ha. Good for you, my dear lady."

Although I try to behave ladylike in the presence of this British prince, I can't bring myself to think of him as an illustrious or decent person, even if he is a field marshal. I think my Hector has more integrity that the British Royals.

While we are taking the train back to Pretoria, my little brother, David, chats with us. He also attended the parade with the stone-laying today as member of the ILHR.

"We Afrikaans-speaking boys attended the occasion because we were ordered to do so. We don't like the idea of a memorial for local chaps who joined the Tommys. The fallen Boer fighters also deserve a monument. Anyway, some of the chaps in our troop call this monument the 'Khaki Monument', instead of its official name of the Rand Regiments Memorial."

Me: "They may just as well call it the Traitors' Temple or the Joiners' Joke."

Johannesburg, Wednesday 31 May 1911

Hector is wearing his uniform with decorations again today. I took the train with him to Johannesburg to the Drill Hall, the headquarters of his regiment.

Today is the first anniversary of the day when the Union of South Africa was established and it has been declared a public holiday. It is also the ninth anniversary of the end of the horrible Boer War.

The Union Defense Force, comprising all the military units of the former colonies – whether they are parts of the Permanent Force or the Active Citizen Force – is to come into being tomorrow. But tomorrow is an ordinary working day and to mark the occasion, parades are being held all over the country today.

It is to be big parade with a few thousand men taking part through the streets of Johannesburg. They came from five units: the Imperial Light Horse Regiment, the Johannesburg Mounted Riflemen, the South African Light Horse Regiment, Kitchener's Fighting Scouts, and the Transvaal Scottish Volunteers.

The newly appointed commandant general of the Active Citizen Force, Brigadier General Christiaan Beyers, a well-respected Boer general from the war, is taking the salute.

Afterwards, the members of each regiment are assembled on the Wanderer's Sports Fields, north of the railroad station, where each unit has a big tent where refreshments are being served.

General Beyers visits our tent and he is introduced to the officers. When he greets Hector, he remarks: "So, you were our unborn Defense Force's unofficial representative at the royal funeral?"

"I was forced into that role, General. I just happened to be available and go in my father's place, since his health was not quite up to it.

I am cheeky and I add: "And I had a meeting with your old enemy, Field Marshall Lord Kitchener. I gave him a piece of my mind, which he didn't like."

Hector: "I wanted to apologize to him, but there was no opportunity."

Beyers laughs: "He isn't supposed to be an enemy any-more because we made peace. But that doesn't mean that I will ever regard him as a friend. Good for you, Milady."

Brig Gen Christiaan Beyers

Afterwards, my little brother, David, who has joined the parade as a member of the ILHR, comes to us: "I want to join the Permanent Force. I was told that I may apply to be admitted to an officers' course, which will only start next year."

Hector: "Being a full-time soldier may prove to be damn dangerous. Look here at my mutilated little finger. This will prevent me from ever playing the piano or the violin."

Pretoria, Saturday, 18 November 1911

Hector warned me yesterday that he was expecting a few guests this morning. He said: "It is a business meeting and I would like you to attend. Your job will be to be my secretary and take notes of everything we discuss."

The guests arrive at ten. There are four of them – all farmers from these parts and our neighbors. Agricultural activities have recovered to a certain extent by this time after the damage done during the war and these gentlemen seem to be fairly wealthy farmers. They had the good luck of having had some money in the bank before the war with which they could start again after peace returned. Many farmers, however, lost everything during the war and they are still dirt poor and they could only survive on charity and help from farmers in the Cape Colony and Natal Colony..

Hector is the only "Rooinek" attending this meeting.

I and the boys serve coffee and rusks to put all of them in a good mood. Wilma came over to bake pancakes for the occasion.

By this time, Hector knows enough Afrikaans to conduct the meeting in this language. That creates trust between him and the other men.

Hector starts the meeting after all the coffee, rusks, and pancakes have vanished: "Men, thank you for your presence. As I told you, I have a business plan that I want to discuss with you. But I didn't tell you what my plan is. Here it is: Let us work as a team and start an export business where we sell agricultural products to markets in Europa and Britain. I propose that we export dairy products, such as butter and cheese. We can also export dried fruit. I am sure that the hides of the cattle we slaughter can be made into good leather that we can also export. How do you feel?"

A lively discussion follows and I have some difficulty to write down everything that is being said.

Hector explains that the de Hacquevilles were dairy farmers since the thirteenth century. They made butter and cheese and he was also involved with the business as a school boy. He can provide some training to the others.

I think that I can also add something to the meeting and I hold my hand up: "Gentlemen, I think that all of you see the great possibilities of this venture. The big question is: through which harbor are we going to do the exports? There are four possibilities: Cape Town, Port Elizabeth, Durban, or Lourenço Marques in Portuguese East Africa. I think Lourenço Marques is the best choice. It is the nearest harbor to Pretoria. And it is also nearer to Europe through the Suez Canal than the other harbors. We can make better profits with less expenses if we go that route."

Hector: "Hear-hear! Hurrah, my wonderful wife! You remember the geography you were taught at school. I support the idea that we go through Portuguese East Africa."

This idea finds general approval.

I have another idea: "Somebody of us ought to travel to Lourenço Marques to talk to shipping agents and consulates of European countries to hear from them exactly how we should go about it."

Ben Burger, one of the farmers: "Dora, you seem to have a few pips inside your skull, the same as Hector. I think that we ask the two of you to travel there and find out everything that has to be found out."

This idea also finds general approval, especially because it was Hector's plan in the first place to start this joint venture.

I ask for another turn to speak: "Gentlemen, friends, we should have something formal in writing. How about asking an attorney to draw up an agreement for all of us to sign. He can then register our venture as a company with the relevant authorities. He will know what to do and how to do it. I know that we Boer people are supposed to trust each other and keep our promises. But it will just be better to have something in writing to prevent any misunderstandings and make everything legal and lawful."

Hector: "My dearest darling, that's a jolly good idea. There is no doubt in my mind that you should be one of the directors of this company. What shall we call ourselves?"

Silence. Everybody starts to do some thinking. Two of the men take out their pipes to stuff some tobacco into the pipes and light the pipes.

Me: "How about 'The Farm Produce Export Company'? That describes exactly what we will be doing."

Nobody has a better name.

We all agree that each one has to acquire the necessary equipment to produce cheese, butter, dried fruit, and the tanning of leather. Some of the equipment may be acquired by the company as a whole and shared by the members.

Some more coffee is served and a jolly group of men leave our living room.

Hector grips me in a hug: "My darling Dora, what would I have done without you?"

"Thanks for the hug and the vote of confidence. But I don't think it will be the right thing for me to become a director of this company thing. If both of us sit on the board of directors the others will feel that two of us have too much voting power. Keep it at five directors – you and your four friends."

Lourenço Marques, Sunday 10 December 1911

This is the first time that we can take the boys on a vacation outside Pretoria. During the school holidays, we always retreated to the farm. But now we are watching the Indian Ocean from our hotel verandah where we enjoy breakfast. We arrived last night by train at the smart railroad station of the capital city of Portuguese East Africa, Lourenço Marques. We plan to stay till the twentieth and to return home in time for Christmas

During the day, we explore the town. We take the boys to the beach to taste the salt water of the Indian Ocean.

During our wanderings, we notice where the consulates of the following European countries are situated: Germany, Austria, Great Britain, Italy, and France. We must visit them during the following days to gather information about import permits for agricultural products into their countries via Lourenco Marques.

Lourenço Marques, Monday 11 December 1911

Our first stop was at the office of the Deutsche Ost-Afrika Linie (German East Africa Line). We have already contacted the manager of this office by telegram last week and he expected us today at nine-o'-clock.

We had no choice but to take the boys along. Thy were sternly lectured before the time to stay sitting motionlessly on the floor or the carpet and not to say a word, unless spoken to.

The manager, Herr Wolfram Wahlfahrth, was pleasantly surprised by my German, although he knows some English. Hector was even able to follow most of the German that I and our host spoke.

I explained that we need a reliable carrier for our agricultural products to various ports in Europa. I add that we will have to talk to the Union-Castle Line's office here in Lourenco Marques as well to obtain quotes. We plan to visit the offices of the Portuguese shipping line as well.

Herr Wahlfarth: "You will have to use Union-Castle to deliver your goods to Southampton or wherever in Britain. Our ships dock at Genoa in Italy, Marseilles in France, Rotterdam in Holland, and Hamburg in Germany. Our head office is in Hamburg. I can assure you that you will find us a reliable partner, should you choose to use us. We started operations more than thirty years ago and we know what we do. The aim was to link our East African Colony, Tanganyika, with the Motherland. But we also touch at Cape Town, Durban, Lourenco Marques, Dar-es-Salaam, and Alexandria before we reach Europe."

Hector: "It seems that we can talk business. Is it possible to see any of your ships, if there are any in the harbor?"

Wahlfahrth: "Oh, yes! One of our proud ships, the SS Kronprinz[15], is due to dock here this afternoon. She is a combined passenger and cargo liner. I invite you to meet me at the harbor at four so that we can have tea or coffee on the ship."

Me: "Herr Wahlfahrth, thank you for the invitation. We accept gladly."

And now we are enjoying the hospitality of the Germans. One of the stewardesses looks after the boys and she shows them all over the ship. Herr Wahlfarth introduces us to the captain and some of the officers. It is clear that these Germans want our business and, therefore, they show off their efficiency.

---

[15] The German name "Kronprinz" means "Crown Prince" in English.

Pretoria, Saturday, 23 December 1911

Our four partners visit us again and we report back about our trip to Portuguese East Africa.

Hector starts the meeting after we have had coffee, rusks, and chocolate cake: "Dear friends, we returned the day before yesterday after a very fruitful visit to Lourenco Marques. Although I went there on behalf of all of us, I won't expect you to contribute to our costs and expenses. It was simultaneously a short holiday for me and my family."

Ben Burger: "Did you achieve anything?"

Hector: "Thanks to my wonderful wife, we have provisionally contracted with various entities, provided that the directors of our as-yet unborn company agree to all the terms."

Freddy Fourie: "I am sure that we can trust your good negotiation skills and judgment. Fortunately, you also had the assistance of your clever wife. I know she was the head girl of her school and she knows how to organize and to manage things."

Hector explains that we have concluded provisional contracts with the Union-Castle Line and the German East Africa Line to transport our goods. We made contact by telegram though the good intermediate help of the consulates of Germany, Portugal, France, Austria, and Great Britain with various marketing agencies who are interested in receiving our products and distributing them throughout their countries.

It is my turn to contribute something: "Through the consulates we inquired about the prices of products like ours in Europe. If we subtract our transport costs – by train and by ship – from the money we earn, we will get a fair return on our investments and a good reward for our labors."

Ben Burger: "Three hurrahs for this wonderful woman!"

Hector: "Friends, I see a bright future for our enterprise. Thank you for your assistance. Let's hope that the world stays peaceful. If war should break out, our activities will certainly come to a stop."

Although I say nothing, some doubt is creeping into my mind about the future.

Pretoria, Monday, 6 January 1913

My father-in-law, Henry, Viscount de Hacqueville, has his birthday today. He is exactly seventy years old. I and Hector visit the telegraph office at the post office on Church Square in Pretoria to send him a telegram with our congratulations.

Because my handwriting is better than that of Hector, I complete the blank telegram form:

BRIG GEN HENRY VISCOUNT DE HACQUEVILLE
HAGDALE HURSLEY HAMPSHIRE UK

CONGRATUALTIONS WITH WONDERFUL
ACHIEVEMENT GODS BLESSINGS LOVE
= HECTOR DORA HENRY DANIEL VICTOR

The clerk behind the counter counts the number of words and calculates the cost.

I ask Hector: "Please, ask the man if we can see how they send this message? I am curious."

Hector approaches the clerk while he pays: "May we perhaps watch while this telegram is being transmitted? My wife knows the Morse Code."

The clerk: "And who are you, sir?"

"Oh, I'm Mister Hector de Hacqueville. I'm a member of the Town Council."

"Wait a minute. I will ask my manager."

He returns a minute later: "Please come this way, Sir and Madam."

He opens a door next to the counter and he takes us to a room at the back side of the building.

Me: "And who is going to transmit our message?"

A girl waves our telegram form: "Here, Madam. I will do it."

The manager waits with us for the message to be transmitted by means of a switch that is pressed down to make electrical connections according to the Morse Code.

Me: "No, you spelt 'LOVE' and 'DORA' wrong."

The manager: "Madam, how did you pick that up? I also noticed it."

The girl: "I'm sorry Ma'am. I'm not used to people peeking over my shoulder while I'm busy. That made me nervous."

The manager: "Madam, where did you pick up Morse Code?"

"My husband taught me. He was an Army officer during the war. We often communicate with a heliograph on our farm and otherwise by tapping messages to each other when we don't want other people to overhear us."

"You are a heaven-sent. I need people to man the new telegraph office in the Union Buildings that is due to be ready next month. Are you, perhaps, interested? We won't have to train you too much because you seem to be fluent in Morse."

"Perhaps. That is, if my husband is satisfied. I will be free during the day from next week when our youngest son starts school. Hector, how about it? I think I will like to have a proper job, besides being a housewife."

Hector scratches his head: "My dear, thank you for taking me into consideration. But, as I know you, you will just force me to agree with whatever, even if I don't like the idea. So, make it a 'yes'."

Pretoria, Tuesday, 14 January 1913

The manager of the telegraph office, Mister Lancelot Loxton, meets us at the almost-finished Union Buildings. He leads us to the basement in the western wing.

"This is where the telegraph office is to be situated. You will receive and send telegrams to and from the Prime Minister's office, as well as all the other offices in this building. Of course, you won't be the only person working here. We will have to recruit some more men and girls. After we have trained you, you can train the new people."

Hector: "Does that mean that my wife will become the manager of this telegraph office?"

"Exactly, Sir. I have contacted the postmaster general and he is glad that I've found a competent person for this position. She will be manager of this office, which will be a sub-office of the facility in town. She will report to me."

Hector: "She is excellent with managing people. She manages me and my farm. She was the head-girl at school."

After we have said good-bye to Mister Loxton, Hector explains the architecture of the building to me: "These two towers symbolize the two components of our society – the English-speakers and the Afrikaans-speakers. They will be united by an amphitheater and a colonnade in the middle. Next to these towers there are two wings with offices for all the civil servants. The only government department that won't work from here is the Department of Defense. They work from the Army base at Robert's Heights."

I think silently: "Will it ever be possible to get the Afrikaans-speaking part of our society to make real peace with the English-speaking part? That will only be possible if these Brits apologize for their calamitous crimes against defenseless Boer women and children in their contemptible concentration camps – as Hector has done."

Aloud, I ask: "Why are there so many of these Greek columns?"

"The architect, Sir Herbert Baker, loves the antique classical style. He visited Italy to look at the old Roman buildings. He wants this building to be a symbol of our links to the ancient Greek and Roman civilizations. That's what he told the Town Council when he explained his plans to us before we approved those plans."

Pretoria, Friday 21 March 1913

When I reach our home after my work at the post office, where I am trained to become the manager of the telegraph office in the almost-finished Union Buildings, my loving husband greets me with a hug and a kiss. I greet my three sons as well.

Hector takes me to his office and shows me an object covered by a cloth.

"Now, Missus de Hacqueville, since it is today your birthday, I ordered a special gift for you. Please unveil that painting."

I take off the cloth. It appears that I have received a painting of my future workplace, the Union Buildings, as seen from our garden in Arcadia.

"My dear, you may choose where to hang it. It's entirely up to you."

"Thanks, my magnificent and magnanimous man. I really do appreciate this loving gesture. Let's hang it in the living room where we can see it every day."

"I am very proud of you. One of these days you will be the manager of a verrrry, verrry important office, the telegraph office in the central Government Temple. You will be working right under the nose of the Prime Minister – that is, when he isn't in Cape Town during a sitting of Parliament."

Pretoria, Monday, 1 September 1913

My telegraph office in the basement of the Union Buildings is only becoming operational today. The building work on this gigantic project is not yet completed, but some government offices, including the Prime Minister's office, have already started to get established inside.

During the past five months, I was working in the central post office on Church Square. I was trained to do the job and I had to train a few girls and men on how to operate the system.

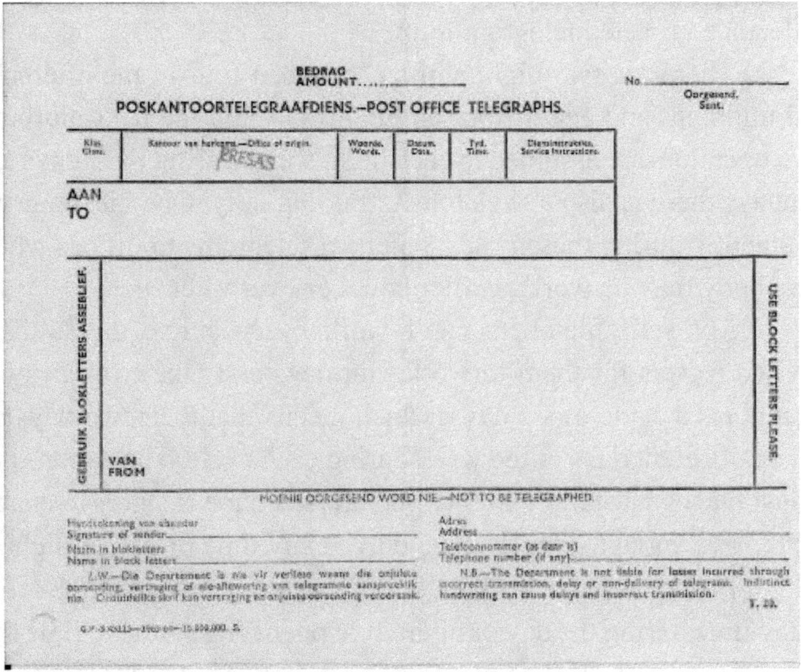

Since the beginning of August, I and Mister Loxton oversaw the installation of telegraph lines and other equipment in die basement of the building. A large stack of boxes with blank printed telegram forms was delivered last week.

And today, at last, we become operational. For me, it is a triple celebration because my two eldest sons also have their birthdays today – although we celebrated that already on Saturday, the day before yesterday.

I have four operators during daytime, between eight and four, when telegraphic traffic is at its busiest. Two must transmit messages and two must receive messages. Two messengers are at hand to deliver telegrams to the various offices in the gargantuan building. Whenever, somebody in one of the offices wants to send a telegram, somebody delivers the completed blank form to us. It may also happen that somebody may phone us and ask a messenger to collect a completed telegram form.

There are two night shifts – between four in the afternoon and midnight and again from midnight till eight the next morning. Two operators are assigned to each night shift. During Saturdays and Sundays there is also a skeleton staff doing duty. One messenger is on standby during these times to deliver telegrams to offices where somebody may be working after hours or over weekends.

My staff members can't work every single day. I have devised rosters for them to work four days and take two days off. That gives a cycle of six days, which means that their two days off fall on different days of the week during each cycle. That means that I must manage a staff of twenty operators and messengers to enable me to have enough people doing duty at any time of day or night.

I have no fixed working hours and I may appear at the office at any time during the day or night. It happens from time to time that I must relieve one of the operators to receive or send messages.

Pretoria, Monday, 8 September 1913

My duties include liaising with each government department. I have already visited each minister's office and met their private secretaries. It is necessary that we know each other to improve a smooth flow of telegrams to and from each office.

The office of the chief of British Forces in South Africa in Roberts Heights since 1905, which was taken over by the Union Defense Force in 1912.

And today, I visit the headquarters of the Defense Force at Robert's Heights, to the south east of Pretoria. This is where my little brother, David, who is a grown man now, is working. He has completed his training at the School of Infantry at Tempe, outside Bloemfontein, and he was commissioned as a second lieutenant earlier this year. With his knowledge of German, he was given the task of studying German military manuals, especially those dealing with intelligence work, and to give lectures on this topic to other members of Defense Headquarters.

David shows me around and I feel proud of my little brother who has realized his dream to become a professional soldier.

Pretoria, Friday, 7 August 1914

The local newspaper, the Pretoria News, told us three days ago that war has broken out in Europe between the United Kingdom, France, and Russia on the one hand and Germany and the Austrian Empire on the other side.

When Hector read this report, he cried out: "Crickey! This will be the end of our export business to Europe! Hell! The ship of the Deutsche Ostafrika Linie en route through the Suez Canal will be intercepted by the Royal Navy and all our cheese, butter, dried fruit, and sheets of leather will be confiscated. That is money down the damn drain. Let's hope South Africa stays out of this mess."

Me: "This war will mess with lots of other things, besides our export business. I'm sure of that."

As manager and supervisor of the telegraph office in the Union Buildings, it is my task to go through the stack of telegrams that have been received (and of which copies must be filed), as well as telegrams sent to various destinations and recipients.

And today, I get a nasty shock, although not quite unexpected. A lengthy telegram sent by the Prime Minister of the United Kingdom, H H Asquith, to Oom Louis Botha, the South African Prime Minster, comes to my attention shortly after I have arrived this morning. South Africa is requested to help the UK's war effort, especially by invading the German colonies of German South West Africa and German East Africa or Tanganyika.

This message was received a mere thirty minutes ago.

One of our messengers' steps into the telegraph office an hour later with a completed telegram form. I ask him: "Does that message come from the Prime Minister's office?"

He nods and hands me the form. Botha replies to Asquith that Britain can rely on South Africa to defend herself and to help during this conflict. All British troops still in South Africa may safely be withdrawn to Europe. I immediately request one of the operators to move away and I personally send Botha's reply off to Number 10 Downing Street in London. Afterwards, I file this message.

An hour later, I receive a phone call from Botha's office and I am requested to report to the Prime Minister immediately.

A few minutes later, I am shown into Botha's office. There are two men dressed in British military uniforms: General Louis Botha, Prime Minister, and General Jan Smuts, Minister of Defense and Botha's deputy.

The Prime Minister asks me in English, although he is Afrikaans-speaking: "Madam, are you the head of the telegraph office?"

Generals Louis Botha and Jan Smuts

I answer in my best English: "I am indeed, Sir."

"And who are you, if I may ask?"

"I'm Missus Theodora de Hacqueville. My husband is a member of the Pretoria Town Council and he is also a captain in the Imperial Light Horse Regiment in Johannesburg."

Jan Smuts: "I know of him, I think. I may have met him, as well as you, Madam."

Louis Botha: "Madam, perhaps you haven't heard the news yet. There is a great war starting in Europe and South Africa has been requested to assist."

"Mister Prime Minister, I have already read the relevant telegrams. I know."

"Good. You realize, no doubt, that secret military stuff will be passing through your hands and those of your staff members during the months to come. I expect all of you to sign the Official Secrets Act to make sure that they won't gossip about the secret telegrams they may handle. I will also require from you a list of all your staff members so that their backgrounds can be investigated. We must make sure that no security breaches take place. Every one of your staff must know that there will be serious consequences if they ever divulge military secrets to outsiders. I hope you appreciate the importance of this measure."

"Mister Prime Minister, I really and fully and completely understand your concerns. I will provide you with such a list as soon as possible. I also need twenty copies of the Official Secrets Act for my staff members to sign."

"I will instruct my private secretary to look into that."

My mind is racing while I walk through the passages and the staircase down to the basement. I tell myself: "Dora, Dora, don't act rashly. Think, think, think clearly. Use your brain cells. All of them. Go and compile that list of people in your office. And then you write down all your options, possibilities, dangers, opportunities, and anything else that comes to your mind. Don't act in haste but consider carefully that has to be done now."

I sit down with a sheet of paper. On top, I write:

LIST OF STAFF MEMBERS IN TELEGRAPH OFFICE, UNION BUILDINGS,

7 AUGUST 1914

Before I can start to write down any names, another telegram form is delivered to me. Oom Louis Botha instructs the Inspector General of the Permanent Force of the Defense Force, Brigadier General Tim Lukin, to call a meeting of all his staff officers this afternoon at Robert's Heights. He also has to assemble at least two brigades of soldiers for the invasion of South West Africa. He adds that he thinks that the relatively small number of German troops in that colony will surrender within a few weeks after the start of the operation. I send this telegram off myself and I file the telegram form.

I wonder: "How do these two gentlemen feel to fight for Great Britain after they have fought against the same Great Britain a mere twelve years ago? Have they turned themselves into something like Joiners by getting clothed like their former enemies? How many Boers will they convince to fight on the same side as the odious and despised Rooinekke?"

I suddenly remember that Louis Botha as commandant general of the Transvaal wanted to surrender to the British forces in June 1900, but relented when President Steyn of the Orange Free State called him a coward and a traitor. How much can we rely on this man? Has he turned a traitor now?"

I start writing the list of names of people working in the telegraph office. I start by providing my own details:

<u>Manager:</u>   Mrs. Theodora de Hacqueville.

D.o.b.   21 March 1885.

Married to the Hon. Capt. Hector de Hacqueville, son of Brig. Gen.

(ret.) Henry Viscount de Hacqueville of Hagdale, Hursley,

Hampshire.

Address: Faerie Glen Farm, District of Pretoria.

Of course, I don't divulge that my father was born in Germany and that we spoke German and Afrikaans in the home where I grew up.

I am confident that my marriage to an Army officer and English nobleman will convince the authorities that I am trustworthy and that my other family ties need not be investigated.

After I have completed the list and made sure that the men and girls on duty read and sign the Official Secrets Act, I start writing down my thoughts and ruminations and ideas and concerns. I use a separate page for each of the following headings:

DUTIES, OPPORTUNITIES, DANGERS, METHODS.

Before I return home at four o' clock I send off a telegram to the German consulate in Lourenco Marques, without mentioning the code of the sending office, as we usually do. I know that the consulate has its own telegraph office for diplomatic and commercial purposes. We have often used it in the past regarding our shipments of agricultural produce to Europe. The first line of my telegram, in plain German, reads:

A WIRD B USW [16]

That means that I am using a simple code in which each letter in the message is simply the previous letter in the alphabet. Thereafter, I send the rest of my message in this code, telling the Germans that future messages will be in German, English, or Latin. I tell them about all the military secrets that I have learnt today. I hope they will be able to forward my messages to Windhuk, the capital of German South West Africa and Dar-es-Salaam in German East Africa.

I am sure that the German consulate in Portuguese East Africa will not be shut down because Portugal is not taking part in the war.

---

[16] A BECOMES B ETC

I also ask the Germans to send a confirmation that they have received my telegram by sending a reply tomorrow morning exactly at eight to VELEDA at the Union Buildings, Pretoria, with a single word written in my code, namely: DANKE.[17] In code it will read: EBOLF.

The consulate is, furthermore, advised not to reply to my future messages because those replies may fall into the wrong hands and endanger my safety.

I sign the message with my code name in plain language: VELEDA. I'm sure the Germans will understand the meaning of this name – the ancient German prophetess who organized an insurrection against the cruel Roman Empire, the precursor of the British Empire

Of course, no copy of this message is filed. The telegraph offices along the way to Lourenco Marques through which my missive must pass, won't be able to decipher my message, should they ever take notice of it. I am confident that the source of my messages will stay hidden.

While I walk back home, I feel relieved and excited. My career as a spy and snoop against the bloated and bloody and bedeviled British Empire from the previous war is being resurrected and continued today. I signed the Official Secrets Act without any qualms, knowing full well that I am determined to pass on every useful secret that comes my way to the German consulate. I know that my signature will mean something very bad, like a death sentence for high treason, should I ever be caught. But I am confident that I will be careful enough to avoid something like that. I regard it as my God-given duty to fight and harm this contemptible and diabolical Empire.

---

[17] The German for THANKS.

The Honorable Hector is relieved to see me and he greets me by sweeping me off my feet and planting a warm kiss onto my mouth.

"Look at this telegram that was delivered to me this afternoon."

I read:

REPORT TO DRILL HALL SAT AT 2 PM

I ask: "What do you make of this?"

"Heaven knows. All I know is that an emergency meeting has been called. Do you perhaps know what's going on?"

"Yes, I do. But I'm not supposed to tell you. I had to sign the Official Secrets Act today and I must keep my mouth tightly and totally shut and sealed about all the messages that come to my notice. But I will, nevertheless, make an exception. War has broken out in Europe, as you know well enough, and South Africa was asked to invade German South West Africa and German East Africa. I am sure that the papers will carry the story tomorrow and then it won't be a secret anymore."

Pretoria, Saturday, 8 August 1914

The sun has just risen when my distraught mother knocks on our front door. She is in tears: "Hector, what can I do? The Police have taken my husband away!"

Hector: "Heavens! What on earth has he done?"

My mother: "Nothing. Nothing at all. The policemen said that war with Germany has broken out and all people who were born in Germany must be locked up. That is to prevent them from aiding Germany."

Me: "That's not fair. Hector, can you do anything?"

Hector: "Where are they taking him?"

My mother: "To a place in Natal called Fort Napier."

Hector: "I'm going to a meeting this afternoon. I will inquire about steps we can take. After all, my father-in-law is a law-abiding South African citizen. We must try to do something, although I'm not too optimistic."

After we have consoled my mother and she has returned home, I rush off to my telegraph office. I am just in time to put on my ear phones to receive a message from an undisclosed source, addressed to VELEDA. The message contains only one word:

EBOLF

That is a relief. The link with the consulate is established and they are grateful for that. It also means that they have grasped my code.

I make sure that the staff members who work over the weekend sign the Official Secrets Act after I have explained the need for that. I hurry back home.

A short while afterwards, David knocks on our front door: "Have you heard this atrocious news? The Police have taken Vati away, just because he was born in Germany."

Hector: "Yes, we know. I must catch the train to Johannesburg shortly for a meeting at the Drill Hall. It is, no doubt, to receive orders about the war that has broken out. I will try and find out how we can help your dad."

David: "Yes, I also know about the war and the tasks given to the Union Defense Force. We have been briefed by Jannie Smuts and Louis Botha yesterday afternoon. And Ma says that the policemen inquired about my whereabouts, but she refused to tell them anything. She says I must go into hiding or something before they lock me up."

Hector: "David, yes, I agree with Ma. They are certainly looking for you. Get out of the country. It's possible that I will have to go and fight the Germans. But, then, I'm a British subject and I cannot shirk my duty. But you're not safe around here."

David: "I'm going to join the Germans in South West. I am, after all, half-German."

Hector: "I and Dora cannot prevent you from doing that, although I don't think it will be wise. But… if you really want to join the Germans, resign your commission as an officer of the Union Defense Force first, otherwise you will be regarded as a traitor and a deserter and a renegade."

I deem it prudent not to inform David of how I feel and what I have done. The only people who may ever know that a German spy is lurking in the Union Buildings are the Germans in Lourenco Marques and Veleda who has visited me in my dreams. My husband may never suspect me of acting against the interests of Great Britain, although I may voice my concerns about the fate of my father.

Hector arrives back home after dark. Although this meeting was supposed to be confidential, he assures me that he could trust me with this information since I, anyway, see secret stuff on a daily basis and I have signed the Official Secrets Act. Hector tells me that the ILHR is to be mobilized and become part of the force that must capture German South West Africa. That means that they will start with the call-up of members and training exercises very soon.

I ask him: "When will that start? Will that mean that you will be gone from home one of these days?"

"We are to assemble at Doornkop in a fortnight's time. It will take time to send call-up papers to all the members of the regiment. It hasn't been decided yet where our training will take place. Most probably, far from here. Perhaps in a desert region, to prepare us for South West, a desert country."

"Can you refuse to go? You are, after all, not a professional soldier anymore."

"According to law, the Union Defense Force may only defend South African territory. The German colony of South West Africa is our neighbor and there are so-called 'Schutztruppe'[18], German soldiers who must protect their colony. The possibility exists that they may attack us and, therefore, we must prevent that by invading that territory first. South Africa will also send some troops to other parts, such as East Africa or Europe. Only volunteers will be used for that."

---

[18] "Schutztruppe" – the German for "Protection Troops".

Pretoria, Sunday, 9 August 1914

Last night, Veleda spoke to me: "All evil and cruel empires fall, sooner or later. They are all doomed. Be patient. Just wait."

I cannot help but to ponder her message. What she said was certainly true of the bloodthirsty Roman Empire that made life very, very difficult for my ancestors on both sides – the Jews and the Germanic tribes. But now I wonder: which empire did she mean? The British Empire or the German Reich[19]? Or both?

Directly after we have attended church this morning, I take our motor car to drive to the Union Buildings. Hector and the boys are used to my irregular working schedule and they are satisfied that I promise to be back for lunch. Hector and the boys are instructed to get everything ready for our weekly barbecue.

I run through the stack of incoming telegrams for yesterday and today. The most important items are two reports concerning German East Africa. The first report deals with an old Royal Navy battleship and two cruisers of the Cape Squadron, based at Simon's Town near Cape Town. These vessels were sent to hunt the German

---

[19] "Reich" is German for Empire.

cruiser, Königsberg, and they are presently off the coast of German East Africa, south of Dar-es-Salaam. The second report informs Louis Botha that a brigade of Indian soldiers was ordered to attack German East Africa. No date for their departure was determined yet. Botha was requested to send some South African troops to aid the Indians, when required.

Twenty minutes later, a coded message in a mixture of German and Latin is sent off to the German consulate. I use the two languages to confuse anybody who may, perhaps, intercept my message and tries to break the code. I hope the consulate has the means to warn the German ship and the German garrison in Tanganyika of these dangers.

I also inform the Germans about the meeting Hector attended yesterday. In addition, I tell them that all potential sympathizers with Germany have been rounded up and sent to a prison camp. I don't inform them that my own father is one of those who was taken and that Hector was unable to find out how we could reverse his detention. I don't want to reveal any personal details that may lead back to me, in case my messages are intercepted and decoded.

In my imagination, I can see how Veleda is smiling at me, where she is watching the Rhine and the Roman garrison in nearby Xanten.

Pretoria, Thursday, 13 August 1914

My office received a telegram form last Monday from Oom Louis Botha that had to be sent to Defense Headquarters, as well as commanding officers of all units of the Union Defense Force. They were ordered to mobilize all their troops.

There is hilarity in the telegraph office when one of the girls calls our attention to one of the replies, from a certain Colonel Coen Brits to Botha:

MOBILISATION COMPLETE. WHO MUST I FIGHT? THE GERMANS OR THE ENGLISH?

Pretoria, Friday, 14 August 1914

Botha requested Defense Headquarters three days ago to find out what the strengths of the German forces in the two German colonies are. I supposed that this information is necessary to plan the campaigns against these colonies.

And this afternoon, a detailed telegram is sent to the Prime Minister's office. The following details were received from the War Office in London:

- The commanding officer in German East Africa is Lieutenant Colonel Paul von Lettow-Vorbeck with a military garrison of 2,600 German troops and 2,472 African soldiers in fourteen Askari (black indigenous) field companies.
- The commanding officer in Windhuk, South West Africa, is Lieutenant Colonel Joachim von Heydebreck, who commands a force of almost 2 000 German Schutztruppe in twelve companies and some supporting units. There are no black troops because the indigenous people hate the Germans and they may side with a South African invading forces.

Of course, it is necessary that the Germans take note of what Britain and South Africa know about their colonial forces and I encode a message with all this information to Lourenco Marques. It is for the Germans to decide whether this intelligence is accurate.

It is impossible to forget that my little brother, David, fled South Africa to join the Germans in South West. I wonder: did he reach that territory? Were the Germans willing to recruit him? What is his function, if any? Unfortunately, we won't be able to receive any news from him while this war is raging.

Pretoria, Friday, 21 August 1914

After work, I and my family walk over to my mother's home. She has invited us to have supper with her. We find her full of smiles and she hands me the following letter in my father's handwriting:

> Fort Napier,
> Pietermaritzburg
> 16 August 1914

My darling Veronica,

Please forgive me for writing this letter in English. I have no choice in the matter. All our letters are being censored and the censors refuse to read any German letters because they may miss some hidden secret messages. The censors also don't understand Afrikaans.

Anyway, we are at last allowed to write letters and receive mail. Please write to me at the address above.

I am healthy and well. We receive enough to eat.

Fort Napier was built many years ago during the wars with the Zulus and during the Boer War it was a military base of the British forces.

We are allowed to go outside during the day, but not outside the fences around the place. That there are fences is no military secret because outsiders can see them.

It is also no military secret that we are guarded day and night. Everybody can see the guards. There is no way anybody will be able to escape.

In a certain sense, this confinement is a blessing. I have made many friends with other Germans and Austrians. These friendships may be valuable after the war. (The censors may *know this because our guards cannot prevent us from talking to each other and making friends.)*

There are some German missionaries confined with us and they provide spiritual support - something we all need.

I'm not allowed to tell you how many people are inmates in this place.
Your loving husband,
Daniel

Hector reads the letter over my shoulder: "It's clear the censors didn't like something your father has written and they blackened it out."

My mother: "At least, we know he's safe and well. Let's open a bottle of wine and drink to his health during dinner. And afterwards we may all write letters to him."

Hector: "I'm sure that incoming letters at this camp are also censored. I won't write anything about the war and my possible role in it. I will only sign it with a 'H' – which may an abbreviation of any name, like Hendrik, Harry, Hercules, or … Helmholtz."

Me: "I will sign my letter with a 'T' for Theodora, but which may mean Truida, Trudy, Thomassina, or … Tooth Fairy. The boys must sign their letters with the starting letters of their names to confuse the authorities."

Silently, I wish that I could have told my father that I am doing my little bit to aid Germany, but that will, of course, not be possible.

Pretoria, Sunday, 23 August 1914

During this Sunday afternoon, Hector is packing all his uniform pieces and other kit. He must report tomorrow morning at Doornkop, from where he and his regiment will be taken by train to Kimberley for field exercises, in anticipation of the invasion of German South West Africa.

I ask again: "Hector, do you really have to go? Why can't you just resign from your position as squadron commander and stay at home? Why must you go and shoot and kill strange people you don't know?"

I ask this because I'm concerned about my husband's safety, but also because I don't want him to shoot any Germans.

"My dear Dora, have you forgotten that our family name is de Hacqueville? All my male ancestors for the past nine centuries or more were warriors, soldiers, fighting men. Many of them were generals, such as my dad. How can I ever break this tradition and put our family name to shame by becoming a coward? I'm sure that our sons will follow in my footsteps when they are old enough."

I sob: "But you may be killed! Our seriously wounded. Those Germans will shoot back at you. I don't want to lose you …"

"That is the risk every soldier must face. Also, the soldier's wife and family, as well. And face it, I will. I must."

After supper, we all walk to my parents' home where Hector says farewell to my mother. She refused to leave her home because she must preserve the clothing business of Davidsohn (Pty) Ltd as a going concern. Fortunately, she has the help of Wilma.

Hector has already appointed Wilma's husband Gideon as the manager of his farm. Since our export business fell apart, there is less work to do. Hector has sold off some of his cattle because there is no market for all the excess milk, cream, butter, and cheese.

He also resigned as member of the Town Council because his involvement in the war will take him away from Pretoria.

My mother is more than willing to look after the three boys when I am working in the telegraph office. She loves her grandchildren and she is eager to help them with their homework, being a trained teacher. Of course, she speaks Afrikaans to them – as I also do – and they are fluent in this language. My father, who is no longer with us, taught them some German. Of course, they converse mostly in English with their father, but often also in Afrikaans – or even in German, just for the fun of it.

Pretoria, Wednesday, 2 September 1914

The Germans in Lourenco Marques get the news from me that a South African force under the command of Lieutenant Colonel Manie Maritz is on its way to the southern border of South West Africa.

Maritz made a name for himself during the Boer War as a reckless combatant and fighter who is as strong as a bull or a rhinoceros.

Pretoria, Tuesday,15 September 1914

The Pretoria News frequently carried the news that many Boers, who fought Great Britain during the previous war, are totally against South Africa's involvement in the present war. They want South Africa to stay neutral.

While I supervise the stack of incoming messages this morning, my eyes fall on a serious matter. The commandant general of the Active Citizen Force, Brigadier General Christiaan Beyers, resigns from his position and informs the Prime Minister of his decision. He refuses to take up arms against Germany and help the British Empire.

This may be welcome news for the Germans. If Beyers can persuade enough Boers in the Army to refuse to go to war, the danger for Germany's African colonies may lessen. A telegram in Latin to Lourenco Marques containing this news is sent off:

EVY CFZFST FU BM SFDVTBOU CFMMVN DPOUSB HFSMBOJBN = VELEDA

The uncoded message reads:

DUX BEYERS ET AL RECUSANT BELLUM CONTRA GERMANIAM = VELEDA[20]

I keep the message short to prevent its decoding by outsiders who may intercept it.

---

[20] GENERAL BEYERS AND OTHERS OPPOSE THE WAR AGAINST GERMANY

Pretoria, Wednesday, 23 September 1914

A flurry of telegrams were sent between Botha's office and Maritz who is encamped on the banks of the Orange River at the town of Keimoes. Botha ordered Maritz to advance in the direction of South West Africa and report how he plans to attack. Maritz refused to execute this order. Botha ordered him to return to Pretoria and hand over command to his second-in-command. Maritz refused to leave his position.

Botha then asked Maritz directly whether he had been in contact with the German authorities in Windhuk. Maritz didn't reply.

Of course, later that afternoon Lourenco Marques was notified of these developments.

Something that bothers me, is that I don't know where Hector is. I sincerely hope that he is not with Maritz, because Maritz's insolence and open rebellion will only lead to great trouble and unnecessary bloodshed. I can imagine that Botha must be very angry where he is sitting in his office. I won't be surprised if some smoke and sparks are pouring from his nose and ears.

Later, during the afternoon, a telegram arrives from the Police in the Free State town of Heilbron that General Christiaan de Wet, a Boer hero who was a constant terror and threat against the British forces during the Boer War, is assembling a commando of armed Boer rebels on horseback.

Because I am curious to see how Botha will react to this message, I decide to take it personally to his office. I refuse to hand it to his secretary and insist to give it directly to the Prime Minister, on account of its importance. Botha is the highest-ranking officer in the Union Defense Force and commander-in-chief, apart from being Prime Minister. He assumed this position after the resignation of

Beyers and he gave himself the rank of a full general, while making Jan Smuts a major general.

The secretary leads me into Botha's office where I hand him the note. He sits behind his desk in his military uniform. He immediately reads the message and becomes red in the face, slams with his fist on the desk in front of him, and yells: "Christiaan de Wet, of all people! I know he couldn't stand me. He accused me openly of being a coward. Now he has gone too far. He must be crushed, totally crushed! This can't be tolerated!

"I'm sorry, Missus de Hacqueville, for this outburst. I hope you understand that I don't like what is going on."

General Louis Botha

I reply: "General, I understand really and completely and totally how you must feel."

(Of course, I do understand his frustration and anger, which I secretly enjoy.)

Later, during the time when the day shift leaves and the evening shift takes over, another notice is transmitted to the consulate with news about Botha's state of mind and how a rebellion is brewing.

I get the feeling that de Wet's fate is sealed. Until now, he was a respected member of Parliament, but not as a member of Botha's party. Now he will become a hunted fugitive.

Pretoria, Sunday, 27 September 1914

Because I am worried about Hector's safety, but also worried about the fortunes of the Germans in South West Africa, I visit the telegraph office in the Union Buildings frequently during the weekends.

Last night, a lengthy telegram was received from General Lukin, whose brigade had landed at Port Noloth, south of the mouth of the Orange River, which forms the border between South Africa and the German colony. Lukin told Botha that a part of his force was given a hiding by the Germans at a spot called Sandfontein, in the south of the German colony, not far from the Orange River. Two squadrons of cavalry and a battery of artillery occupied Sandfontein, the only source of fresh water in the dry desert environment. The Germans surprised them, killing and wounding two dozen South Africans and killing or capturing most of their horses. The rest of the South Africans surrendered during the afternoon and were taken captive. After they were relieved of their arms, they were allowed to go because the Germans couldn't hold them.

I regard it as unnecessary to tell Lourenco Marques of this development because they must certainly have received the news from their own sources.

I feel concerned because I don't know whether Hector was part of the force that lost the Battle of Sandfontein. There is, though a possibility that he may be safe because the biggest part of Lukin's force occupied the town of Warmbad, deeper into South West Africa.

Pretoria, Saturday, 10 October 1914

Although it is a Saturday, I sit rivetted to my desk in the telegraph office. The expected rebellion against the Botha government has started and messages are pouring in and out. It is no surprise that the rebels struck today because it is the birthday of the last Transvaal president, the late Oom Paul Kruger. The following events are reported to the Prime Minister who sits in his office:

- Manie Maritz took control of the town of Keimoes on the banks of the Orange River and declared himself as head of the government of South Africa, which becomes, henceforth, totally independent from Great Britain.
- General Christiaan de Wet occupied the Free State town of Heilbron and announced that the old Republic of the Free State is resurrected.
- General Beyers threatens Pretoria with a force of 3 000 men on horseback in the hilly countryside of the Magaliesberg Range, north of Pretoria.
- Troops of the Union Defense Force are hastily sent to these points to quell the rebellion. They can move faster than the rebels because they have motorized transport – trucks and vans. The rebels only have horses and limited supplies of ammunition and food.

I took some of these messages personally to the Prime Minister's office. I wasn't allowed into his office because he was locked in a crisis meeting with Jan Smuts and other important people.

Although I am sure that newspapers world-wide will tell these stories to their readers, I send off a brief report to the Germans in Lourenco Marques. They must gather that the assault on South West Africa cannot go ahead for the time being because too many troops are necessary to fight the rebels.

Pretoria, Monday, 12 October 1914

Martial law is declared today, two days after the rebellion really started. All public gatherings, excluding religious meetings, are prohibited. Nobody may move around after sunset. Telegrams are sent to all local authorities throughout the country and to all police stations to make this step known. I and my staff work overtime and I manage to get hold of some night staff to come and help with the volume of messages.

To my regret, I inform my staff that we will have to spend the night in the Union Buildings because we won't be able to go home after dark. I send a messenger to buy some bread, butter, cheese, milk, and jam in town before it becomes dark.

When the messenger returns, he informs us that the Union Buildings are being guarded by soldiers in armored cars. I go out to watch them.

A message from Defense Headquarters to the Prime Minister estimates that there are about 12 000 rebels all over the country, but that the Union Defense Force can mobilize more than thirty thousand troops. Skirmishes and battles at various places are reported.

There is no time to transmit any news to Lourenco Marques. I believe they will receive the news through other channels anyway.

During the night, Oom Louis Botha informs Defense Headquarters that he is leaving Pretoria tomorrow morning early to take over command of the force opposing Manie Maritz along the Orange River. Jannie Smuts is left behind to manage affairs here.

Pretoria, Saturday, 24 October 1914

The rebellion by Manie Maritz seems to have failed dismally after less than a fortnight. Maritz was wounded two days ago during a battle with the Union troops under the command of Louis Botha. Botha sent a jubilant message to Jan Smuts to tell him this news.

And today I see a telegram informing Smuts that Maritz and his rebels have fled to South West Africa. He is joined by Jan Kemp, a former Boer general with a few followers. I deliver this telegram personally to Smuts who scowls when he sees the contents.

General Jan Smuts

I ask him: "Is there any response for which I must wait?"

He answers briefly: "No, nothing."

I'm not surprised that Smuts seemingly feels comfortable in his British Army uniform because he studied law at Cambridge before the Boer War and more than once expressed his admiration for the English culture. In spite of this, he served as attorney-general of the old Transvaal Republic and became a Boer general during the war. After the end of the war, his appreciation of the British Empire took over and he easily adopted the role of a British general.

Pretoria Wednesday, 28 October 1914

During lunch time, while I relieve one of the men at one of the transmitting desks, I inform the German consulate in Lourenco Marques of two brigades that sailed from Bombay in India, consisting of about 8 000 colonial troops under the command of Major General Arthur Aitken are due to land at Tanga on the German East African coast next Monday. The Indian Expeditionary Force of one brigade, consisting of 4 000 men, was to attack from British East Africa (Kenya) on the same day or the day after that.

Louis Botha, who has returned yesterday to Pretoria, got the news of these developments so that he could co-ordinate his plans with those of the War Office in London.

I also advise the Germans that Botha and Smuts plan to personally join the South African troops assembled to invade South West Africa. The rebellion seems to be largely suppressed and the war against Germany can be resumed. Botha will land at Walvis Bay and Swakopmund on the coast and Smuts will attack from the south. A brigade under Brigadier General Tim Lukin was already encamped on the Orange River, but that was something the Germans in South West Africa must already know.

Lukin has informed Defense Headquarters that his troops are in position and his message was passed on to Botha's office. He mentioned the units under his command and, to my relief, it seems that Hector with the ILHR is not part of that force. It may be that he will be part of the force that invades South West from Walvis Bay and Swakopmund, further north.

In various telegrams, Botha has expressed his concerns about the remaining rebels and how that may affect the planned incursion into South West Africa. This information is also sent to the consulate.

Pretoria Thursday, 5 November 1914

During the past few days, I kept my eyes open for any news regarding the events in German East Africa. And I get a pleasant surprise this afternoon: The British force under General Aitken was routed during a battle that went on for four days. Many British and colonial troops were killed or wounded. The Germans suffered minor casualties. Although the initial landing of troops was successful, Aitken's men met unexpected resistance from the Germans and the Askaris and they fled in disarray – especially the Indian troops who have no great love for Great Britain. Aitken was forced to order a retreat this morning, leaving behind large piles of equipment and supplies, which the Germans welcomed.

I smile while I read this filed message, which was sent for the attention of General Botha. It is, of course, unnecessary to inform Lourenco Marques of the German victory, but I, nevertheless, inform them of the British losses.

My message in code reads as follows:

UBOHB   HC   850   UPU   V   WFSXVEFU   148 WFSTDIXVOEFO = WFMFEB

In plain language, it reads:

TANGA   GB   850   TOT   U   VERWUNDET   148 VERSCHWUNDEN[21] = VELEDA

While I sign my telegram with my code name of Veleda with a smile, I can sense that this ancient prophetess also smiles. It is as if she tells me that my warning to Lourenco Marques helped von Lettow-Vorbeck to prepare an ambush for the invading British force. I am relieved that my husband and my brother were not involved.

---

[21] TANGA GB 850 DEAD AND WOUNDED 148 DISAPPEARED = VELEDA

Pretoria, Thursday, 12 November 1914

Louis Botha sends the news to Smuts in the Union Buildings that he has defeated Christiaan de Wet at a place called Mushroom Valley in the northern Free State. De Wet fled with the remnants of his force. One of those who fell during the battle was de Wet's son.

I feel sorry for this old Boer hero who was humiliated in this manner. He was commandant general of the Free State commandoes during the Boer War, while Botha was commandant general of the Transvaal units. They were supposed to be allies in those days. Now they became bitter enemies.

Pretoria, Monday, 16 November 1914

Because I don't work fixed hours as manager of the telegraph office, I decide to take this afternoon off and spend some time with my sons. I walk to my mother's home to fetch them.

Wilma opens the front door and greets me with a whisper: "Come in, quietly. Don't make a noise. We have secret visitors."

I nod quietly and follow Wilma after she has locked the front door again. I find my mother with two strange men in the dining room.

She whispers: "Dora, I want to introduce you to two of my cousins from the Free State. Daan Visser and Floors Visser."

I shake their hands in silence.

Daan whispers: "We were part of General de Wet's commando that was defeated a few days ago. We had to flee. The whole commando disintegrated. Your mother is hiding us here because the Police and the troops of the Defense Force are hunting us."

My mother: "They can't stay here indefinitely. Can you arrange for them to stay at your farm? There they will be less visible."

"Of course. Wilma, when do you expect Gideon back here?"

"Just before dusk tonight."

"When he returns to the farm tomorrow, he must take these two men with him and help them to hide in the cottage. They will have to be taken there in our motor car and their horses can follow later."

My mother serves some coffee and the two men tell us about the disaster at Mushroom Valley. I don't dare to tell them that I already got the news about this unhappy incident shortly afterwards.

Silently, I remember how I and David told our father in this same dining room about all the secrets we dug out from the British forces during the previous war. I acquired the habit during those times to be very careful about what I tell people. My career as a spy can only bear fruit if I work in total secrecy. Only the ancient Veleda in the realm of spirits knows about my identity and she sometimes guides me. The Germans in Lourenco Marques only know that an unknown person in the Union Buildings is feeding them with inside information. Perhaps, they will guess that this agent must be a woman because she uses the cover name of Veleda.

East wing of the Union Buildings in Pretoria

Pretoria, Wednesday, 2 December 1914

The Pretoria News contains the story that General Christiaan de Wet was captured yesterday near the village of Tosca while trying to escape across the border to Bechuanaland. According to the newspaper, he was caught by a unit under the command of Colonel Coen Brits. De Wet reportedly declared his gratitude that he was arrested by a Boer and not by an Englishman.

It is not necessary to let the Germans know, because they will hear of it through other channels.

I find it ironic that especially Coen Brits had to catch General de Wet. Hector told me more than once that Brits, a giant of a man who started as a field cornet during the Boer War with Botha and rose to become Botha's deputy at the end of the war, had the reputation of being a heavy drinker and a drunkard – the same as many British officers. It was this man who sent that hilarious cable to Botha when ordered to mobilize his troops at the start of the war.

Something gives me the conviction that Hector was part of the unit that caught the old Boer general.

Pretoria, Tuesday 8 December 1914

A telegram for the attention of General Botha arrived with the news that General Beyers, the former commandant general of the Active Citizen Force and one of the rebel leaders, was shot and killed at a Police road block. He and General Koos de la Rey were travelling in a motor car, ostensibly to a meeting somewhere. When they were stopped at the road block, they sped away, being rebels sought by the government. The road block was actually set up to catch some fleeing bank robbers and the Police thought that the speeding Beyers was a member of this gang and opened fire, killing him.

Botha sends a telegram to Defense Headquarters to announce that the rebellion was finally suppressed and giving the order that plans for the invasion of German South West Africa must proceed. I notify Lourenco Marques of this order.

Pretoria, Wednesday, 6 January 1915

It seems that Botha was somewhat too optimistic about the end of the rebellion because Manie Maritz and Jan Kemp managed to reach South West Africa after trekking through the Kalahari Desert.

However, this morning I see a cable from Colonel Jacob (Jaap) van Deventer, telling Louis Botha that his force of 6 000 men is waiting at Upington and Kakamas, along the Orange River, for further orders. They are poised to attack the Germans.

This news is transmitted an hour later to Lourenco Marques. I can only hope that the consulate will find a way to warn the Germans in South West Africa of this danger so that they can prepare for it.

Something tells me that Hector is not a member of Jaap van Deventer's group. He must be somewhere else as part of the group under Coen Brits. Suddenly a vision of the waves of the ocean enters my mind and vanishes after a few seconds. I ask myself: where on earth did this vision come from? Is it the Indian Ocean or the Atlantic Ocean? Something tells me it's the Atlantic Ocean.

Pretoria, Friday, 8 January 1915

A big surprise awaits me as I arrive at my mother's home after work to collect the boys. My mother smiles while she hands me an envelope: "Although your name appears on the letter, the address on the envelope is that of my house. That's why I have it. I immediately recognized Hector's handwriting but I couldn't open it because it is meant for you."

I open the envelope in two ticks. I spread the single sheet on the table so that my mother can read with me:

Cape Town

3 January 1915

My dearest delightful darling Dora!

This is the first opportunity I get of writing to you since I arrived in Cape Twon. In the past, there was no opportunity of reaching a post office to mail any letters. I hope to be able to drop this letter into a post box tonight so that it can be collected tomorrow (Monday). Fortunately, I have some postage stamps.

As you can see, I am alive and well at this moment, otherwise I would not have been able to write this.

God alone knows what will happen to me later.

We arrived here four days ago by train from Kimberley after having moved around near the border with Bechuanaland. I am not allowed to tell you what we are doing in Cape Town, but I am sure you will be able to guess.

I hope that you, the boys and my mother-in-law are well. It won't do to ask how your father is doing because you won't be able to write back to me.

I think of you every day and I pray for your safety every day. Please pray for me and my men.

Bags and bundles full of love and affection for all of you,

H de H

Of course, I know what Hector is doing in Cape Town. I saw a cable from Cape Town to the Prime Minister ten days ago with the news that the troops en route to Walvis Bay[22] arrived in Cape Town where they will be loaded onto some ships on 7 January – yesterday.

Cold shivers crawl down my spine because I already had the feeling yesterday that Hector would be at sea at that time on the Atlantic Ocean, on his way to Walvis Bay.

This means that I must contact Lourenco Marques tomorrow to warn them that a large South African force is due to arrive in Walvis Bay in a few days' time. I hope the Germans will be able to prevent the invasion without bloodshed because I can't stand the idea of Hector getting wounded. On the other hand, I don't like the idea of any Germans dying from bullet wounds, inflicted by Hector and his men.

---

[22] Walvis Bay is the only natural harbor along the coast of South West Africa (nowadays Namibia). In those days, it was a South African enclave that belonged to the Cape Province.

Hell! Why must life be so difficult? Why can't things be less complicated?

Hector mentioned my father in his letter. Fortunately, we receive a weekly letter from my father since his first letter and we are allowed to send him replies. He is healthy and strong, but extremely bored. There is very little to do at Fort Napier and, therefore, his weekly letter contains the same dreary and unexciting news every time.

Pretoria, Saturday, 20 January 1915

It is with a smile on my face that I read a report from the war in East Africa. The day before yesterday, the Germans attacked a weak force of about 300 Indian troops at the coastal town of Jassin, north of Tanga.

The commander of the Indians was killed and the rest of the troops surrendered yesterday. That enabled the Germans to capture a considerable amount of supplies, rifles, and ammunition.

It is clear to me that the German commander, Lieutenant Colonel Paul von Letow-Vorbeck, must have taken a leaf from the history books of the Boer War. The Boer commandoes managed to carry on with the war by capturing British equipment and supplies. It meant that Queen Victory actually financed the Boer war effort. Something similar was happening in East Africa. Of course, the Germans are unable to receive any supplies and reinforcements from Germany because Britannia ruled the waves and, therefore, they must capture British stocks to survive. Very clever and very nice.

Pretoria, Saturday, 5 February 1915

One of the girls who had to work today on this Saturday, fell ill and I am the only available replacement. I would rather have spent some time with my sons at the farm. I also wanted to visit the farm to hear how the two fugitive cousins of my mother are doing, but that must wait, unfortunately.

While I am waiting for incoming messages to various offices in the Union Buildings, I look at the filed telegrams that came in during the night. One of them catches my eye. It seems that a German force, led by a certain Major Hermann Ritter, executed a surprise attack on the town of Kakamas on the Orange River where a part of Jaap van Deventer's force is stationed. Their aim was to secure a crossing point on the Orange River to prevent the Union troops of attacking South West.

Unfortunately for the Germans, the attack failed. Quite a number were killed or wounded and sixteen were captured. The rest of the force, a little more than 200 men, fled back to South West.

I get the feeling that my previous warning that 6 000 troops were awaiting them, did not reach them.

There is another message that Jan Kemp has surrendered two days ago. He became sick and decided to give up the fight. He seems to be the last rebel leader who was captured.

The Pretoria News carried an article yesterday about the trials that await the rebels. They will be charged with high treason, which may lead to severe penalties and even death sentences.

I decide that it won't aid the German war effort to send them all this news. I do inform them, though, that General Louis Botha is due to leave for Swakopmund tomorrow. Most of the troops that he will command are already on their way there on transport ships. I suppose that the Germans in South West will certainly notice when the South African troops arrive.

I believe that the force of General Lukin will be called upon to advance deeper into German territory as soon as the other formations are moving as well. I somehow know that the fate of the German forces in South West is sealed because Veleda visited me again last night with a very sad expression on her face.

Pretoria, Monday, 11 July 1915

Although a large volume of messages regarding the South African campaign in South West Africa passed through my hands, there was nothing during the last five months that I could tell my German contacts that they didn't know. That meant that Veleda of the Union Buildings stayed silent during this time.

Today, the Pretoria News contains the story that the Germans have surrendered to Botha after having lost the Battle of Otavi a few days ago. Smuts and Lukin occupied the southern parts of the territory, while Botha and his force moved from Swakopmund and Walvis Bay to occupy Windhoek not long afterwards. The remnants of German Schutztruppe were pushed into the northern parts of the country, where they were overpowered.

I just know that David's efforts to aid the Germans didn't really help, but that he wasn't captured and confined to a prisoner-of-war camp, or – still worse – was charged with high treason or something horribly bad. I just know it.

Botha announced that he would return to Pretoria as soon as possible to resume his duties as head of the government.

An important telegram reaches me during the afternoon. Brigadier General Tim Lukin is appointed as the commander of the First South African Infantry Brigade, which will be formed at the town of Potchefstroom. Only volunteers will be recruited for this unit because they will have to fight in Europe against the Germans.

I decide not to send all this news to Lourenco Marques because the Germans in East Africa can't do anything with this knowledge.

Pretoria, Tuesday, 19 July 1915

Today, I feel rather downhearted. I can't pinpoint any particular reason for this feeling. I leave the telegraph office after the night shift has taken over and I shuffle homewards. Somehow or other I don't feel enthusiastic to see my mother and my sons again.

And then, suddenly, I realize why I am feeling the way I do. Hector is sitting on a wicker chair on our veranda, but his left arm is heavily bandaged. I just knew that something was wrong with him and that affected my mood already before I even saw him.

My heart suddenly misses a beat or two, but I rush towards my husband. He gets up and grabs me around the waist with his good arm. I get a good grip around his neck, while the tears suddenly start running from my eyes.

"Hey, beautiful! Why so sad? I'm not a ghost. This is really me."

"How did you get here?"

"Easily. I walked, on my two boots, from the railroad station to get here. Very simple."

"Did you arrive by train?"

"That's how people usually get to the railroad station."

"Are you finished with the war?"

"Only for the time being. As soon as this scratch on my left arm has healed, they will send me somewhere again."

I start sobbing again.

My mother and the boys join us on the verandah. My mother: "There will be a delicious dinner toning. There is a chicken pie in the oven. Dora, why are you so sad? We are all glad and happy that your husband returned home in one piece, even if he was somewhat punctured on his left arm."

Hector: "I was demobilized rather earlier than the other men from South Africa, due to my wound. I received it on the very last day of fighting. The other chaps will only return a bit later. I visited the military doctors earlier today and they replaced my bandages. I must see them in three days' time again. Perhaps the bandages can be removed totally by that time."

My mom: "What galls me, is that it was a South African bullet that pierced his arm. That's what he told us. Some or other stupid sod didn't handle his rifle correctly and nearly killed your husband."

Me: "So, the Germans didn't hurt you?"

I don't disclose the fact that I am relieved that it wasn't a German bullet that wounded my husband.

During dinner, Hector tells us about his experiences. The boys hang onto his lips and enjoy every word. He says that he never fired a shot in anger because the German Schutztruppe retreated all the time and avoided direct clashes, except where they had no other choice.

Me: "So, you didn't kill any Germans?"

"No. There was no need for that, because they always receded out of range and out of reach. The poor buggers never had a chance against us because they were outnumbered something like ten to one."

Henry asks: "Pa, what did you do when you were not chasing Germans?"

"Mostly sitting or standing around. Playing cards or other games. Some of the chaps drank a lot, but I didn't join them."

Me: "Who was your commanding officer?"

"I was part of the force under Louis Botha, but my direct commander was Colonel Coen Brits. It was rather strange to receive orders from a former Boer officer."

Of course, I know who Coen Brits is – the man who asked Botha at the outbreak of the war whom he had to attack – the Germans or die English. I also know that he has the reputation of a heavy drinker.

Hector: "Something funny happened with Brits. He likes his brandy. While we were trekking from Swakopmund to Windhoek through the desert, his supply of brandy ran out. He enquired around whether there were other men who had a supply of the stuff. It turned out that a certain corporal still had a bottle of brandy. Brits ordered him to his tent and immediately promoted this corporal to the rank of lieutenant. It is etiquette in the Army that officers may only drink with other officers – not with lower ranks. This temporary lieutenant was then invited to share his bottle of brandy with the colonel. After the contents of the bottle had disappeared, he was again demoted to corporal. Poor guy. He had the pleasure of being a lieutenant only for a couple of hours and he had to allow the colonel to empty his last bottle of brandy in exchange for that dubious honor. A poor exchange, I'd say."

After the boys have gone to bed, Hector confides in me and my mother: "I think I saw David in Walvis Bay. He has grown a beard to disguise himself."

My mom: "Did you get an opportunity to talk to him? How is he?"

"He seemed healthy enough. But I didn't want to embarrass him by approaching him. I think he was spying for the Germans. He was fraternizing with the South African troops there in Walvis Bay. I saw him once drinking one beer after the other with a South African sergeant. He was, no doubt, pumping him for information about the South African war effort."

Pretoria, Wednesday, 20 July 1915

Today is a holiday for me. Because I am the manager of the telegraph office, I don't need anybody's permission to take the day off. By this time, my staff members know their work so well that they can carry on without my supervision and help.

While the boys are in school, I, Hector, and my mother drive our motor car to the farm. We find Gideon and my mother's two cousins working hard in the vegetable garden. They are pleased to meet Hector.

I tell the two rebels: "Men, do you want to return home? I think it is now safe to do so. All the rebel leaders have been sentenced to rather light prison sentences because Louis Botha wanted to prevent them from becoming martyrs in the eyes of the Boer people. Most of the other rebels have been pardoned. So, how do you feel?"

Daan Visser: "Thank you for hiding us here. Yes, I think it is about time to go home."

As we drive back, Hector laughs: "My wonderful wife! You did something very dangerous. If these rebels were caught on our property where you hid them, you could have been accused of hiding criminals – which is also a criminal act. But I can understand your action. Those two rebels are family and you felt an obligation towards them."

"Thanks for understanding my action. But it was actually my mother's idea to hide them on the farm."

Pretoria, Tuesday, 10 August 1915

Hector is still at home. Because of his wound, he was not considered for the First South African Infantry Brigade that started to leave Potchefstroom by train yesterday. I know about these movements because Botha was kept up to date about these developments.

After supper and after the boys have gone to bed, I tell Hector (whose bandages were removed long ago): "There is a rumor that some South African troops are leaving for Europe. Do you know anything about it?"

"Yes, I do. I phoned the adjutant of the ILHR in Johannesburg this morning and he told me that the poor guys are being sent off to the trenches in Europe far too early. They haven't been trained properly yet. This brigade consists of four regiments and they barely know each other in the various regiments, which makes coordination and cooperation difficult. They will be taken by two passenger liners, starting next Monday."

"I am relieved that you're not going with them."

"My dear, don't think that I will be allowed to stay here in Pretoria very long."

Hector doesn't have to tell me why he will be leaving one of these days. Louis Botha has been requested by the War Office in London to assemble a South African force to aid the British and Belgian offensive against the Germans in East Africa. I have seen enough messages that von Letow-Vorbeck – by now a full colonel – is still playing cat and mouse with his enemies.

The request by the War Office prompted me to send a warning to Lourenco Marques that von Letow-Vorbeck may expect South Africans to attack him soon. This warning was my first message in a long time because I stayed silent during the conquest of South West Africa because the Germans must have known about everything Botha and his soldiers did.

Pretoria, Monday, 6 September 1915

My mother awaits me with the three boys on our verandah when I arrive home after another day at the telegraph office.

"Look here! A letter from David!"

I hastily grab the piece of paper and read the rather short letter without even sitting down somewhere. David tells us in Afrikaans that he is safe and in good health, although he had sustained a rather serious wound shortly before the German Schutztruppe capitulated. That wound has healed completely. He has found some work in Walvis Bay.

He also requests us not to reply to this letter because he can't give us his address. The date stamp on the envelope shows that the letter was posted in Walvis Bay but there is no return address or a name. We only know that it comes from David because we know his handwriting.

My mother: "At least, we know he's alive and well. I suppose he can't tell us anything more because he may be afraid that the Government and the Police will find him."

Me: "I think he has adopted a fictitious identity, which he can't disclose to us. It is also remarkable that he doesn't tell us anything about his role during the war. Perhaps he did things that must stay hidden."

My mother: "I'm sure you're right."

Me: "During the Boer War, he acted as a spy and a scout for the Boers and helped Vati with information about the British Army. Perhaps something like that was his job in South West."

My mother: "Who knows?"

Pretoria, Tuesday, 23 November 1915

Hector got a week's leave before returning to his new unit, the East African Expeditionary Force under the command of Jan Smuts, the Minister of Defense with the rank of major general. Hector was involved with the training of the troops for this force since September, more than two months ago.

By this time, I know it will be useless to plead with him to resign from the Army and to stay at home. It is part of his being to be a military man and it seems that our three sons can't wait to grow up and follow in the footsteps of their father.

Hector's leave is over today and this afternoon I, my mother, and the three boys take him to the newly-built Pretoria Railroad Station where he must join a contingent of this expeditionary force.

Henry asks his father while we drive the short distance to the station: "Pa, we all know you are going to East Africa to fight the Germans. How will you get there? Are you going by train all the way?"

"My boy, unfortunately, I am not allowed to tell anybody how we will go there."

Daniel: "Pa, I looked it up in that atlas we have at school. I guess that you will be taken to the harbor of Mombasa in British East Africa by boat. For that, you will have to embark in Durban. Am I correct?"

Of course, I am secretly fully aware of how Hector will reach the area of operations and Daniel is totally correct with his guess. This force is due to reach Mombasa at the end of the first week of December and I have already notified the German consulate of these plans.

Hector: "My boy, perhaps you are right. And perhaps not. I'm not allowed to tell. It's a military secret."

I also read a few days ago in an intelligence report sent to Jan Smuts that a crazy situation exists with the German Schutztruppe in East Africa. A retired German major general, a certain Kurt Wahle, was visiting his son, a farmer, in the territory last year when war broke out, which made it impossible to leave the colony. Wahle immediately offered his services to the then Lieutenant Colonel von Letow-Vorbeck, the commander. Wahle, a major general, became the second-in-command of an officer two steps lower on the military ladder.

Pretoria, Thursday, 10 February 1916

The British commander of the Second South African Infantry Division, Brigadier General Wilfrid Malleson, sent a message to General Smuts this morning, informing him that his force, consisting of Brigadier General Percival Beves' 2nd South African Infantry Brigade, an African brigade, and an Indian brigade, are poised to attack Salaita Hill just across the border from British East Africa. There is believed to be a look-out post on top of this hill with a small German detachment holding the spot and the attack is planned for early on the 12th – the day after tomorrow.

Since there is only one South African brigade in this force, it must be the brigade in which Hector is serving as a company commander.

I lose no time in informing Lourenco Marques of these plans.

Pretoria, Sunday, 13 February 1916

After I have attended church with my family this morning, I hastily visit the telegraph office and scour the filed telegrams. There is indeed a report of General Malleson to Botha and Smuts. The attack against Salaita Hill was a fiasco.

General Beves also sent a report, blaming Malleson of insufficient planning and assuming that the Germans would react in the same way as rebel forces in India, with which he was familiar. The German force on and behind Salaita Hill was much stronger than presumed and repulsed the British assault. There were 172 men lost on the British side.

Lourenco Marques receives a message from me informing the Germans of the British casualties and the fact that two British generals are at odds with each other. I believe this information will be useful.

Shortly after I have sent my message, Louis Botha appears in the telegraph office.

General Louis Botha

"Ah, Missus de Hacqueville, I am glad to find you here. My secretary doesn't work today and I had to deliver this telegram form personally. Please send it off immediately to British East Africa. It is in code and meant for the personal attention of the commander of the British forces over there."

"Mister Prime Minister, I will do so at this very moment."

It is a fairly long message and I can only guess that it contains the displeasure of Botha at the outcome of the battle of yesterday. I decide that I must get access to the codes used by the Union Defense Force. Unfortunately, Hector is too far away to help in this regard.

Pretoria, Saturday, 19 February 1016

A telegram from Smuts to Botha advises the Prime Minister that his Minister of Defense has arrived safely in British East Africa to replace Brigadier General Malleson as commander of the British forces. Smuts thanks Botha for the news that he was promoted to the rank of lieutenant general the previous day.

I waste no time in telling the Germans in Lourenco Marques of this development. I am sure that Smuts was appointed to this position on account of his experience as a Boer general during the Boer War and his experience against the Germans in South West Africa.

Pretoria, Saturday, 26 February 1016

There is no doubt in my mind that the Germans will welcome the news about the strength of the British, Indian, and South African forces in British East Africa, as supplied to Botha by Smuts. The message by Smuts was in plain text – not in code as Botha's message of a fortnight ago. That tells me that there are more or less 13 000 troops from South Africa and Rhodesia, 7 000 from India, and about the same number of African troops. In addition, there are thousands of black African carriers and porters who have to carry supplies by foot from Mombasa to the interior since there are no roads through the bush for vehicles. Smuts needs daily rations for 73 000 men.

It seems to me that this huge number of mouths to feed, as well as the equipment needed to hunt and pursue the much smaller German force, must place a huge burden on the resources of the Union Defense Force and the British war effort. If it wasn't for von Letow-Vorbeck, who was taunting and teasing the British for more than a year-and-a-half now, these resources would have been available in Europe against the Germans there.

Pretoria, Friday, 10 March 1916

A rather obscure news item in the Pretoria News of today arouses the alarm bells inside my head. The world is informed that the German Empire has declared war on Portugal yesterday because a few German ships in the harbors of Beira and Lourenco Marques were impounded and confiscated by the Portuguese authorities.

Experts declare that this development won't have any real visible consequences for the war in Europe since Portugal is very far from the front lines in France, Belgium, and Russia and Germany doesn't have the capacity to attack Portugal directly.

However, this news means that my contact with the German forces in German East Africa via the German consulate in Lourenco Marques will be severed. I compose a coded message in a mix of Latin and English to the consulate to request instructions regarding the new situation. A response in code has to be sent tomorrow morning exactly at eight to Veleda, Union Buildings, Pretoria.

I tell the young man who does duty over the week-end during the day shift that he may take the morning off because I will take his place.

Pretoria, Saturday, 11 March 1916

It so happens that Lourenco Marques contacts me exactly at eight this morning. I write down the letters as they come through my head phones to decipher the message later. After the end of the message, I reply with a brief –

PCSJGBEP = V

Decoded, this boils down to the following:

OBRIGADO = V

I can still remember this word from our visit to Lourenco Marques a few years ago. It simply means "Thank you".

I decipher the message from Lourenco Marques. It tells me that the consulate is forced to close down. The staff members have made provision for this eventuality and have obtained forged Portuguese passports with which they will be able to stay in Lourenco Marques. After living a few years in this Portuguese colony, they can speak the language well enough to disappear into the crowds. They have rented an office suite in the city under the name of Fernandez Importar e Exportar. They hope to export agricultural products to Portugal and the rest of Europe on Portuguese ships. The call sign for their new telegraph office is given.

Directly afterwards, I reply in Latin:

DPMQSFIFOEP = V

Decoded, it is as follows:

COMPREHENDO = V

This means "I understand".

Pretoria, Monday, 13 March 1916

The telephone on my desk rings and I answer immediately. It is the private secretary of the Minister of Justice who requests me to attend a meeting in the minister's office this afternoon at four. I ask: "In connection with what is this meeting?"

The voice on the other side: "Madam, frankly, I don't know."

This makes me somewhat nervous because the Minister of Justice also controls the South African Police Force.

It is fifteen minutes before the appointed time when I arrive. I have my handbag with me because I want to go home directly after the meeting. The private secretary shows me into the minister's office and I am alone. The secretary tells me that other people are also expected.

I happen to see a fairly small book of about an inch thickness on a desk with the title: "Codes and Cyphers – Defense Force of the Union of South Africa." It instantly disappears into my handbag.

Shortly afterwards, six more people are shown into the office of the Honorable Nicolaas de Wet, Minister of Justice. Mister de Wet enters after a few minutes, followed by the Minister of Posts and Telegraphs, the Honorable Thomas Watt.

Mister de Wet, a learned lawyer who studied law at Cambridge, requests all of us to sit down on the chairs provided and he welcomes us.

We all sit down.

The Hon Nicolaas Jacobus de Wet

"Dear lady and gentlemen, thank you for coming. My colleague, Mister Watts (and he points in the direction of his colleague) requested a consultation this morning with me. It concerns a serious breach of security inside our telegraph service."

Suddenly, I get a funny feeling inside my insides. I get a foul taste in my mouth. But immediately it is as if Veleda whispers to me in ancient German: "Dora, stay calm. Nothing bad will happen."

Mister de Wet continues: "I have requested the managers of the telegraph offices in Pretoria, Johannesburg, Krugersdorp, and other place nearby to attend this meeting. It has come to the notice of some officials of the Department of Posts and Telegraphs that secret messages in code are being transmitted from somewhere in the region in which you are working. It hasn't been possible to decode these messages, except for certain numbers that were sent in plain Morse Code.

"We suspect that there is a spy operating in one of the offices of which you are the managers. We need your cooperation to weed out that evil enemy agent – if it is an enemy agent who contacts unknown people somewhere. That person seems to have access to confidential information, which he or she passes on to somebody else. This must stop. The safety of our troops in Europe and East Africa may be compromised and that cannot be allowed to continue.

"Therefore, we urgently request all of you to keep your eyes and ears open for any suspicious actions by your subordinates. We know we can trust all of you because your backgrounds have been checked. Fortunately, your loyalty towards the interests of our country, and our big overseas guardian, Great Britain, cannot be questioned."

Mister Watt also speaks and impresses upon us the necessity to manage our offices according to all the rules and regulations of his department. After that, there is time for questions.

Veleda whispers into my mind: "As them how these messages were detected."

I raise my hand and I am given an opportunity to ask my question: "Mister Watt, thank you for confiding in us your concerns and worries. If I may ask: how did somebody in your department discover that possible secret messages were being sent to an unknown recipient or recipients?"

Mister Watt: "As you all know, telegrams sent to any destination very often has to pass through other stations. An observant operator in the eastern Transvaal has picked up this suspicious traffic and reported it to our department. I thought it prudent to involve the South African Police and that is why I and the Minister of Justice have convened this meeting."

Lancelot Loxton asks: "May we discuss this development with our subordinates?"

Minister de Wet: "Heavens, no! We don't want the spy or snoop or saboteur to know that he or she is being watched. Sooner or later, that person will make a mistake and then we can grab him or her. Yes, please keep your eyes and ears wide open."

After the meeting has broken up, the various managers of telegraph offices start talking to each other while walking through the corridor outside the office. Mister Loxton, the manager of the office on Church Square in town, looks at me: "Missus de Hacqueville, do you have any idea who it may be in your office? Your office in this building received many secret telegrams. What do you think?"

"The Prime Minister required of all of us at the start of the war to sign the Official Secrets Act. If it is somebody in my office, then that person may be guilty of a serious offence. Something like high treason."

"Yes, of course."

While I walk home after the meeting, I cannot help but to start trembling. This was a close call. Very close. How am I going to continue with my duty to inform the Germans of developments that concern them? How can I continue to wreak vengeance on the evil Empire of Britain for all the crimes committed during the Boer War? This very edifice in which I am working, the Union Buildings, is situated on the spot where a crushingly cruel concentration camp used to be situated. The only way will be to send messages when that suspicious operator in the eastern Transvaal is not working. And messages must be kept very brief before that operator can detect that something is being transmitted in code. Or, even better, the code has to be abandoned and messages must be sent in plain language, but in such a manner that they only make sense to the recipient in Lourenco Marques. That plain language must be in English, of course, which somebody in Lourenco Marques will be able to understand. That is the only way to avoid suspicion.

Pretoria, Tuesday, 14 March 1916

Shortly after I have entered the telegraph office this morning, the private secretary of the Minister of Justice comes to my desk.

"Missus de Hacqueville, I hope you can help me. I'm in a mess, a rather big messy mess. Actually, it's a definite disaster."

"I hope I can help. Tell me more."

"Have you perhaps noticed a code book lying on a desk in the minister's office? It was my task to tuck it away, but I forgot for a moment. I went to look for it after the meeting you attended and I suddenly couldn't find it."

"What's in that code book?"

"We became much more security conscious after some apparent leaks about military matters. It was decided that telegrams containing confidential matter should be sent in code. The code changes every day and it is rotated after the end of each month."

"I can imagine that such a valuable item has to be locked away securely."

"Exactly. My minister will give me a message to send to Defense Headquarters, or wherever, and then I must put that message in the code of the day before sending it off to your office for transmission."

"There were quite a few people at the meeting yesterday. Have you enquired with any of them?"

"Not yet. It was the easiest to start with you because you are in the same building. I will have to phone all the other people who came yesterday."

"I wish you luck with your search."

"Thanks."

After the young man has left, I feel rather relieved. It wasn't necessary to tell any lies. It also doesn't seem as if I am suspected of having taken the code book. That code book lies safely at home. I will have to hide it somewhat better, just in case our home is raided, for whatever reason. To make it inconspicuous, I will cover it with brown paper and write a misleading title on the outside and put it in a book shelf between other books.

And then, it strikes me that Hector may come home some or other time. It is absolutely necessary that he doesn't discover the secret code book in my possession.

Pretoria, Tuesday, 21 March 1916

My mother invited me this morning before I walked to work to have dinner at her home, together with the boys. It is my birthday and I am thirty-one today.

During the day, I continued to feel gloomy on account of the meeting with the Minister of Justice last week. I don't know whether that vigilant operator who reported my secret messages has kept a record of my missives. If that is the case, it may – somehow or other – lead to the decoding of the contents, although I'm not too worried about that because of the mixture of German, English, and Latin that I used.

The only clue the Police may find useful is, perhaps, my code name of Veleda. It is, however, extremely improbable that anybody in this country has ever heard of this ancient German priestess and prophetess. After all, all the Germans in this country have been rounded up and locked away at Fort Napier and they won't talk. Should anybody, somehow, find out who Veleda is or was, then it will only tell them that the German agent must perhaps be female. More than half of all the telegraph operators in the country are girls. Anyway, I recently started to sign my messages only with a "V" – not my full secret name.

As I get nearer and nearer to my mother's home, my mood improves. My mother gives me a hug when I enter her home and each one of the boys give me a kiss. Then all of them sing a song to congratulate me.

My mother: "And here is part of your birthday presents."

She hands me a letter with the address in Hector's handwriting. My heart leaps up and down within my rib cage and I immediately open the envelope.

Dar-es-Salaam

10 March 1916

My dearest delightful darling Dora!

It is my sincere wish that this letter finds you before your next birthday. It is sad that I'm unable to celebrate with you and the boys.

As you can see, I am at Dar-es-Salaam – in hospital. It's certainly no secret that we have driven the German Schutztruppe from these parts.

I am not wounded – only sick. Not malaria, although that is something some of my men are suffering from. The foul water we get to drink out there didn't accord with me and the quacks sent me to Dar-es-Salaam to get healthy again. Fortunately, the water in this hospital is potable and doesn't smell like something from a pigsty or rotten eggs.

Of course, I'm not allowed to tell you anything about the progress of the war, but I suspect that you have received enough news by other means to know what is going on.

Lots of love and kit bags full of kisses,

H de H

Hector is entirely correct. I do know what is going on. Yesterday morning I decoded a report for the attention of the Prime Minister that most units have lost a large proportion of their men due to malaria, dysentery, and other diseases, disorders, and disasters. According to the directives of the Ministers of Justice and Posts and Telegraphs, military messages are now sent in code. But I have a code book and I am able to decode the messages that I have copied at night at home.

This is useful news for the Germans and I sent the following message in plain English earlier this morning:

JANNIE AND FIVE OF HIS TEN BOYS DECLINE INVITATION TO PARTY DUE TO ILLNESS = V

My mother, who looked over my shoulder while I was reading the letter, says: "After you have read that letter to the boys, you must come and help us in the kitchen. Leg of lamb, backed potatoes, and stewed dried fruit."

Pretoria, Sunday, 16 July 1916

My emotional life is in turmoil, in trouble, in turbulence. I don't know how to define and identify all my feelings and my mood. It is difficult to describe or give a name to a mixture of sadness, worry, melancholy, anxiety, anger, love, longing, determination, and disgust.

I love my sons, my parents, and my husband.

I am angry at the hated evil Empire of Britain that stole our country and caused so much misery and mischief, even if I'm married to an English officer and nobleman.

I feel sad because I miss my husband and my lover.

I adore my father who was locked up by the Government that decided to join Great Britain in this war.

I am melancholic because the war drags on and on without any end in sight.

I am determined to help the German Empire because I can't forget my German roots.

I am worried about the welfare of my husband who is fighting the Germans.

I become anxious when I think what could happen to me and my family, should I be caught as a spy.

I decide that life is very, very arduous, baffling, confusing, difficult, and enigmatic.

And to make everything more difficult, last night Veleda visited me. She didn't say anything and only stared at me. I clearly saw her against the background of the full moon that shone its white light through my window.

The night before that, my great-grandmother Anna also visited me: "My child, I think you are doing a wonderful job. You are brave and strong. I admire you."

But I don't really feel brave and strong. It is difficult to think that I can be admired. At this moment, I am sitting with my three sons, my mother, and Wilma with her family, in our usual pew in the new Dutch Reformed Church. The old church on Church Square was broken down and this new edifice a few blocks away took its place. I contemplate my complicated life while waiting for the service to start.

The service is being led by the Reverend Herman van Broekhuizen. Our congregation has grown so much that a colleague for the Reverend Bosman had to be appointed.

The Reverend van Broekhuizen has a clear and melodious voice and he has the gift to keep the attention of his audience. He reads the story in the First Book of Samuel in the Bible of how King Saul visited a witch who had to reach the spirit of the dead prophet Samuel for him. He was deadly afraid before the start of a battle against the Philistines and he needed the guidance of Samuel's spirit.

The reverend elaborates about how wrong it is to consult the dead. Saul committed this mistake and sin, instead of relying on God and his Word. Of course, we must honor our forefathers, but God gave each one of us a good mind with which we can make careful and cautious and correct choices. It has come to his notice that there are people in this town who consult dead loved ones through the medium of so-called clairvoyants. That amounts to a grave piece of wickedness and wrongdoing.

While we walk home, I don't listen to what the others are talking. I just wish that Veleda would vanish. I don't want the same type of fate as King Saul who fell on his own sword after losing the battle. But how could I chase her away?

But, while I am battling with myself, it is as if Veleda again intrudes upon my thoughts: "Dora, Dora, you can't get rid of me. I am your destiny. The day will come that you will visit the tower in which I resided."

Suddenly, I feel sad and guilty. I have used the name of Veleda so many times in my secret messages and it means that I have almost become her reincarnation or successor and made her alive again. I suddenly wonder: did she have any sons as I do?

My emotional life is a monstruous mess. Really and truly.

When we reach home, Victor hugs me: "Ma, I love you."

I start to sob while I hold onto my youngest son.

Pretoria, Monday, 4 September 1916

Telegraph traffic between British East Africa and the Prime Minister's office doesn't contain much of interest, except for the fact that the South African troop strength is declining, due to illness – and not due to combat losses. It seems that the South Africans have captured the whole railroad line between Dar-es-Salaam and the interior, but that didn't help them to trap the German Schutztruppe.

It is rather difficult to copy incoming and outgoing telegrams between Botha and Smuts because I must do it without being observed by my staff. I have, therefore, moved my desk out of sight of the men and girls who operate the reception and dispatch of signals. I take the filed telegrams of the previous day and copy all those between Botha and Smuts in code. At night I decode those messages at home. And then I compose a message for Lourenco Marques, which I manage to send off during the next day. That has happened quite infrequently during the last few weeks and my only important message was to inform the Germans of the diminished fighting strength of the South Africans.

Today, I send the following telegram to Lourenco Marques:

BOHSJGG BVG LJTBLJ TFQ7 = V

In plain language it is as follows:

ANGRIFF AUF KISAKI SEP7 = V[23]

I am sure that von Letow-Vorbeck will immediately know how to prepare for this attack. From previous messages I know that Smuts reported that a part of the German force was stationed at Kisaki and that he wanted to eliminate the German forces bit by bit.

---

[23] German for: ATTACK ON KISAKI 7 SEP = V

Pretoria, Monday, 11 September 1916

It is with a big smile that I read a decoded message from Smuts to Botha after I have put the boys in bed.

Smuts informed Botha that the attack on Kisaki started last Thursday as planned. He sent in the Third South African Infantry Division under the command of Coen Brits (the man who loves his brandy, as Hector told me). This division was strengthened by a cavalry brigade.

It turned out that the weak German force at Kisaki was much stronger than believed. He had to call off the attack this morning after three days and sustaining heavy losses.

I don't need to inform the Germans of this event because they will certainly know everything about it. But I am sure that my warning helped them to be ready for this attack.

I just get the feeling that Hector didn't suffer any wounds or mishaps during this fight. Perhaps it was Veleda who muttered into my mind that he is safe.

Pretoria, Wednesday, 20 September 1916

Today is a sad day for me. General Botha was informed that a Belgian brigade from the Belgian Congo managed to drive a German unit under the command of Major General Kurt Wahle to the south. That happened at the Battle of Tabora, which lasted a whole week.

Wahle was outnumbered 2:1 and he had to fall back yesterday against the Belgian attack. However, the Belgians suffered something like 1 300 casualties, while Wahle only lost about 170 men. The Belgians, though, captured more than 230 of Wahle's men. It was an expensive victory for the Belgians.

Although the Germans lost the battle, they managed to extricate themselves and are ready to fight another day.

Pretoria, Monday, 8 January 1917

A very important telegram in plain language for General Botha arrived this morning. David Lloyd George, the British Prime Minister, invited Louis Botha to join his Imperial War Cabinet in London as the representative of the Union of South Africa. Since it is such an important message, I deliver it personally to Botha's office.

He reads the message with attention while I wait for a possible reaction.

"Thank you, Missus de Hacqueville. I will phone you later this afternoon when I am ready to send a reply to London."

Shortly after lunch, I get a phone call from the Prime Minister's private secretary, requesting me to report back to his office. I collect a telegram form in which Botha asks Jan Smuts, who is fighting von Letow-Vorbeck in East Africa, whether he is willing to join Lloyd George's War Cabinet in London.

I see to it that this message, also in plain language, is sent off immediately. A quarter of an hour later, Smuts replies that it would be an honor to accept the invitation. He is willing to take the first available ship from Dar-es-Salaam to Durban to report to Botha in Pretoria and then depart for London.

Another telegram form Botha tells Lloyd George that he is extremely honored by this request, but that it is not possible for him to accept the invitation. He mentions that it would be better if he sends General Jan Smuts, his deputy, and the Minister of Defense, in his place. Smuts is at this moment in charge of operations in East Africa, but he will leave as soon as possible. Smuts is a much better choice since he had studied law at Cambridge before the Boer War and was admitted as a barrister at the Middle Temple in 1894.

Pretoria, Sunday, 14 January 1917

While we are walking back home after church, Henry suddenly yells: "There's Pa!" He starts running and his two brothers follow him.

And, indeed, Hector is waiting for us on the verandah of our house: "I hoped to get a warm welcome here, but the door was locked. That forced me to sit outside and wait for you. I hoped for a better and warmer welcome…"

I don't even answer him and grab him around his neck: "I'm so glad to see you. Come inside."

The boys throw their arms around their father's body and he can't move to enter the house. I unlock the front door.

Me: "What are you doing here? Have our troops captured German East Africa?" (Of course, I know that there is still lots of fighting to be done over there.)

"No, the fighting is still going on – mostly with indigenous troops from Rhodesia, Uganda, and Kenya. Too many white troops got sick and had to be hospitalized, or even sent home. One of our regiments has less that ten percent of its strength left. Malaria, sleeping sickness, dysentery, food poisoning, you name it."

"And what is happening to you now?"

"I've been given a few days home leave and I have to join our boys on their way to Europe."

Henry shrieks: "Pa, I see you're not a captain anymore. You're a major with those little crowns on your shoulders."

"Yes, I've been promoted, Son. That's very observant of you."

My mother, who followed us when she also saw Hector on our verandah: "This calls for a celebration. Congratulations."

"While we are having lunch, I tell Hector: "I happen to know that your commander, Clever Jannie Smuts, is on his way to London to join the Imperial War Cabinet."

"And how does my dear wife know all this secret stuff?"

"It's not really a secret. In case you have forgotten, may I remind you that I am the chief telegraphist at the Union Buildings and that I handled all the telegrams between David Lloyd George, Louis Botha, and Jannia Smuts personally. I suspect that the newspapers will carry the story very soon."

"I won't be surprised if I get orders to accompany Smuts and some other men to England, from where I may be transferred to the Continent where the fighting is going on. Do you perhaps know who will succeed Smuts in East Africa?"

"Yes, I happen to know. It will be Jaap van Deventer, who also took part in the conquest of South West Africa."

"South West Africa was really a piece of cake in comparison with German East Africa. The Germans in South West didn't have the support of the natives. In East Africa it's different. Colonel von Letow-Vorbeck has recruited thousands of local black soldiers as askari's who fight for Germany. That's why we couldn't catch him yet. The terrain is also much more difficult than in South West and that makes our movement extremely arduous – apart from all the malaria mosquitos and poisonous flies and bad water."

"So, that cunning colonel from Germany is keeping our troops and the British forces very busy?"

"Exactly, his strategy is simply to draw as many soldiers away from the battle fronts in Europe to make life easier for the Kaiser's troops. And he does succeed, that cunning and crafty colonel."

Pretoria, Monday, 15 January 1917

Because I don't work fixed hours as manager of the telegraph office, I decide to take most of today off. We drive with our motor car for a brief visit to my office, which I show to Hector, and thereafter we take off to the farm.

While we are strolling around in the hot January sun to observe everything on the farm and to see whether Gideon has done his job as farm manager satisfactorily, I find it impossible not to ask Hector about his experiences in East Africa. He seems glad to have somebody who wants to listen to his stories and he tells me more or less what I already know. Of course, I don't betray my knowledge because I want to pump him for more information, if possible.

As a temporary battalion commander with the rank of major, he often attended conferences of unit commanders. That means that he has quite a lot of inside information, which he shares with me. I pretend to be ignorant about military matters, although I am married to an officer, and he patiently explains to me what happened.

"We became rather worried at some time. The Third Infantry Division's intelligence officer told us one day that it is clear that the Germans must have received some inside information from our side."

"How on earth did they find that out?"

"We have radios and it sometimes happened that we picked up messages in code meant for von Letow-Vorbeck, who also has radio sets."

"Was it possible to decode those messages? What did they tell the Germans?"

"The trouble is that those messages were usually very brief. That made decoding and deciphering extremely difficult. In fact, impossible. All we know was that the name of the sender starts with a 'V'. That could be an abbreviation for Van der Merwe or Victoria or Valiant, or whatever, any other name starting with a 'V'. "

(Secretly, I find this bit very interesting and reassuring. It seems that Lourenco Marques has sent my messages exactly as they had received them via a radio link to von Letow-Vorbeck. Because I kept the messages short and used alternatively German, Latin, and English, there was very little chance that the Brits and South Africans would have been able read my messages and warnings. The only part that I never transmitted in code, was initially my code name of Veleda and later only a V.)

Is ask: "Was it ever possible to locate the source of these radio messages?"

"Unfortunately, no. Radio waves can come from any direction, but we suspect that they came from the south. The signals were stronger when we listened to them on the southern side of a hill. It might even have been from somewhere here in Pretoria. All we could figure out was that the call sign of the recipient was that of von Letow-Vorbeck."

"Who on earth would help the Germans? All the Germans in this country have been locked up in Fort Napier."

"We suspected it must be somebody at Defense Headquarters at Roberts Heights."

"And what do you think of Jan Smuts? You have been fighting under his leadership for more than a year. So, you must have an opinion about him by this time."

"Ah, yes, hmm, Let's put it this way. He's a brilliant politician. He's a very good lawyer. It's no wonder that Louis Botha chose him to represent South Africa at the Imperial War Cabinet. I'm sure he will be a valuable member."

"And as a soldier? A s a general?"

"Rather disastrous, I'm sorry to say. The Germans ran circles around him. Never had a good idea of how to catch von Letow-Vorbeck. Over-cautious and extremely careful. Didn't know how to use his troops to the best advantage and the result was mostly catastrophic. He couldn't inspire his troops to do their utmost. Yes, he was a disaster."

"And how will Jaap van Deventer do in his place?"

"Very much the same. Or even worse, because the man can't speak English properly – just as most Boers. He constantly has to make use of an interpreter."

Pretoria, 21 March 1917

Although it is today my birthday, I don't feel like celebrating anything. Hector left for Britain a week ago, together with many new troops to strengthen the First South African Infantry Brigade in France. I do miss him after having got used to his presence during the past two months. The boys also miss him very much.

Hector was an acting battalion commander at Roberts Heights during this time, but he slept at home every night. His task was to help with the training of new troops who had to join the South African troops in France. I knew from reading telegrams to Louis Botha that this brigade had suffered horrific losses during several battles in the past. And now Hector was to join this brigade with a new understaffed battalion.

Yesterday, I received a short letter from him from Cape Town, written four days ago, to congratulate me with my birthday and with the news that their ship was to leave Cape Town that same night.

Pretoria, Wednesday, 10 October 1917

Very little of consequence happened in East Africa the last few months. There were occasional skirmishes, but no major offensives. However, Lieutenant General Jaap van Deventer sent a signal to Louis Botha – which I decoded last night at home – telling him that he planned to attack the force under Major General Kurt Wahle, who was at Nyangao at that stage, starting on 15 October.

This news prompted me to send the following message to my contacts in Lourenco Marques this morning:

JNQFUVN DPOUSB EVDFN XBIMF PDU15 = V

In Latin, decoded, it reads as follows:

IMPETUM CONTRA DUCEM WAHLE OCT15 = V[24]

I can only wonder what Jaap van Deventer's intelligence people will make of this message – that is, if they are able to listen to it.

When I arrive home during the late afternoon, I fetch the boys from my mother.

Victor, who is ten years old, confronts me: "Ma, what are we really? Grandma Veronica tells us that we are Boers. But where does our strange family name come from? I'm told it's French. And Pa speaks English. We have a grandfather who lives in England. Are we English, or Boers, or what? Or even Normans?"

"My son, what makes you ask these questions?"

"I've been reading a book Grandma gave me: 'Robin Hood and his Merry Men'. They were Saxons. Grandma says the Saxons were, in fact, a German tribe that settled in England. And Robin Hood fought against the Sheriff of Nottingham and the Normans.

---

[24] ATTACK AGAINST GENERAL WHALE OCT 15 = V

These Normans were in reality Frenchmen who conquered England – just like the Englishmen conquered our country before I was born. Do I descend from these nasty Normans with my funny French surname?"

"What do you want to be?"

"I'm a Boer. Although Pa is an Englishmen, he isn't a typical Englishman. He also speaks Afrikaans. And German. Why can't we get a proper family name that doesn't remind us of the horrible Normans who oppressed Robin Hood and his people?"

"I don't think it will be possible to change our family name. Your Pa will become an English lord as soon as your Grandpa in England dies. The name goes with the farm he will inherit in England. I've already told you about the Hagdale Estate that I saw a few years ago."

"Henry and Daniel agree with me that we are Boers and nothing else, even if we are stuck with a stupid and silly surname."

Henry joins the conversation: "Grandpa Daniel is a German Jew or a Jewish German. That makes you half German and half Jewish. But I don't feel like a Jew or a German."

Daniel: "We are Boers. We speak Afrikaans and we are proud of Grandpa Daniel who fought against the evil Englishmen during the Boer War."

Me: "If you want to be Boers, then I am proud of you. We Boers are proud, brave, and God-fearing people."

Pretoria, Saturday, 20 October 1917

Jaap van Deventer sent a lengthy report to Louis Botha about the fiasco against the Germans. I secretly made a copy of the signal in code and now, in the light of a candle, I decode it on our dining room table after the boys have gone to bed. We do have electricity for lighting, but I don't want to draw attention by keeping our lights burning till late at night and, therefore, I use a candle.

It appears that van Deventer attacked Wahle at Nyangao as planned. Wahle was ready for him, it seems, and repulsed the attack. However, Wahle fell back on the hills at Mahiwa, where he was joined by von Letow-Vorbeck. Van Deventer attacked with a Nigerian brigade, which suffered heavy losses – 2 700 men killed or wounded. He had no option but to call off the attack after three days.

Pretoria, Saturday 27 October 1917

Jaap van Deventer sent another signal to Louis Botha to tell him that the German High Command promoted Colonel Paul von Letow-Vorbeck to major general on account of his victory.

Van Deventer didn't explain how he had learnt of this, but I suppose his intelligence personnel picked up a radio message from Berlin to East Africa. I think it won't be inappropriate if I send off a message to congratulate him.

I decide to send the following message tomorrow after we have attended church:

DPOHSBUVMBUJPFT BE MFHBUVN QWMW = V

The uncoded Latin looks like this:

CONGRATULATIONES AD LEGATUM PVLV = V[25]

---

[25] CONGRATULATIONS TO GENERAL PVLV = V

Pretoria, Monday,29 October 1917

Just before lunch, one of the girls who sits at one of the receiving desks with headphones to capture incoming Morse Code messages, brings me a telegram form with a puzzled expression on her face.

"Dora, look here. I think this is a mistake. Somebody sent this message here and it is addressed to a certain Veleda. We don't have anybody or anything here with that name. And it is in a strange language. Looks like silly Dutch. What must I do with it?"

"Let me have a look at it."

I read the following message in plain German:

VELEDA UNION BUILDINGS PRETORIA
HERZLICHEN DANK = PVLV[26]

I shake my head in mock disbelief and I answer: "Yes, this must be a mistake. Some or other joker somewhere must have sent this to the wrong station. Throw it away. Or – tear it up. We can't do anything with it."

I decide to empty the waste paper basket later when the evening shift takes over and before I go home. No trace of this message must survive.

The newly promoted Major General Paul von Letow-Vorbeck certainly placed my life in danger by sending that message via Lourenco Marques, but it is also a consolation that he knows of me and appreciates my work.

Suddenly, the face of Hector intrudes into my mind. It looks as if he is in pain. It makes me very worried.

---

[26] VELEDA UNION BUILDINGS PRETORIA
HEARTFELT THANKS = PVLV

Pretoria, Wednesday, 31 October 1917

A secret message from Jaap van Deventer to Louis Botha, which I have decoded on our dining room table, makes me smile broadly.

Paul von Letow-Vorbeck has again outfoxed the British forces in German East Africa. When van Deventer thought he had him cornered against the southern border, the German general simply slipped across the border into Portuguese East Africa. He raided a Portuguese garrison at Ngomano and looted a huge amount of supplies, arms, and ammunition with which he can continue his fight.

Of course, nothing prevented the German from invading the Portuguese territory since Portugal is at war with Germany.

Pretoria, Monday, 10 December 1917

After an uneventful and boring day, I decide to go home somewhat early to spend some extra time with my sons, although we had a delightful week-end on the farm together. When I knock on the front door of my mother's home, it is Daniel that opens the door.

"Ma, come in, come in! There's a letter from Pa!"

"Where?"

"We have already opened it because it was addressed to the whole family de Hacqueville at this address. It contains good news and bad news."

"Yes?"

"He's alive but a casualty."

I rush inside to read the letter myself.

Hagdale

19 November 1917

My wonderful wife and my superb sons!

At last, there is an opportunity to write a letter to you all. As you can see, I am in very good hands, those of my mother, who is looking after me at Hagdale.

Let me explain: I was rather seriously injured on 29 October, three weeks ago. A very nasty and lousy bomb fired from a gun operated by a gang of Huns exploded not very far from me. It threw me up into the air. It is a law of nature that everything that goes up must come down again and that is exactly what happened with me. When I came down, both my legs and some ribs were broken, apart from some superficial cuts and bruises.

I lay there almost a full hour before a stretcher party came to my rescue. It wasn't possible to move on my own with two broken legs, of course. They lifted me very carefully and gently onto the stretcher and I was taken to a forward medical tent.

The good quack fixed my legs temporarily and ordered that I be taken to a military hospital far behind the front lines. There the pedlars and bone butchers decided that I needed home care and they sent me to a hospital in old Blighty, near Southampton after they have fixed my legs in very stiff and very strong plaster casts. They only shook their heads about my broken ribs and declared that those must heal all by themselves. They refused to place my rib cage in a plaster cast and I am relieved that they didn't do it because that could have very uncomfortable.

I was taken by ambulance to Hagdale yesterday. They wanted to place me in a convalescent home but I refused. I didn't want to be surrounded by medical wrecks as I was during the past three weeks. I think I deserved something better than that.

And now my mother is looking after me. She does so much better job that the blood suckers in the hospital.

It will certainly mean that I must heal completely before the Army can make use of me again.

The First South African Brigade, of which I was the second-in-command of a battalion, suffered horrific losses since they arrived in Europa shortly after the start of the war. I was one of the many replacements. Very few of the original members are still around. The rest are resting under the surface of Mother Earth inside wooden boxes or are hobbling around on crutches. I also use crutches, but they will be thrown away as soon as the plaster casts are taken off. That will probably happen during January. And then I may be called up again to serve somewhere.

Please write to me at Hagdale. I intend staying here for a while.

Your solid spouse and devoted dad,

H de H

This letter is no surprise to me. I just knew that Hector was suffering pain on 29 October.

Pretoria, Wednesday, 26 December 1917

Yesterday was the fourth Christmas of the war. I don't think anybody on the front lines felt like celebrating. It is mid-winter in Europe and the poor infantry in the trenches must be wet, miserable, hungry, and sick.

I can only imagine that the German troops and their African helpers somewhere in tropical Africa must be plagued by savage mosquitoes, poisonous ticks, deadly snakes, lack of supplies, and dangers around every corner. I regard it as my duty to lift their spirits somewhat and I send a message to congratulate General Kurt Wahle with his 62nd birthday today. I believe he must be one of the oldest soldier fighting in this war because generals and colonels usually retire before they reach the age of sixty.

Pretoria, Friday, 26 April 1918

A letter with important news from Hector arrived today. He wrote regularly during the past four months, while staying with his parents at Hagdale and regaining his strength and health. While he was in Hampshire, I didn't worry about his safety.

However, today's letter, which was written almost three weeks ago, made me feel anxious again. I read the letter many times:

Hagdale

7 April 1918

My adorable Dora and my three stupendous sons!

As you can see, I am still alive and well – otherwise I wouldn't have been able to write these words.

My mother's care caused miracles to happen. I can walk again within any trouble. I even went for a run through the countryside yesterday. I plan to go horse-riding this afternoon. All that is the result of home-cooking, a comfortable bed, lots of attention and regular visits to our local quack.

Our local medicine man and drug dealer, Dr Michael Mobbleton, declared me fit for further military deployment.

Last week, an old friend of my father, Major General (ret) Sir Nicholas Nosewhole (I knew him as a kid as Uncle Nicky Nose), visited us. He was delighted to hear of my remarkable recovery, as well of the fact that I started my military career as an officer during the Boer War in the North Lancashire Regiment, of which he also was a former member.

General Nosewhole promised to arranged my readmittance to this outfit. And just yesterday I received a telegram from the War Office, informing me that I am promoted to the temporary rank of lieutenant colonel (a major's pay) and in command of the sixth battalion of the Loyals, as the North Lancashire Regiment is also known. I gather from the fact that there is now a sixth battalion of this regiment, that it must be a newly-formed subunit of which I must take command. That will most probably entail the training of recruits, young boys just out of school, perhaps towards the end of June.

I will keep you informed about my movements and developments.

Please convey my love to your mother – as well as to your father, as soon as you write to him again.

Your steadfast spouse and fond father,

H de H

Pretoria, Sunday, 24 June 1918

Hector kept his promise and wrote regularly. His guess was correct. His new job is that of commanding officer of a new battalion, consisting of raw recruits who had to be trained within a period of three months, pending their deployment to France or Belgium towards the beginning of October.

During the last few months, no great engagements took place in Portuguese East Africa between the Germans and the British forces. Jaap van Deventer, who led a mixture of inexperienced black African troops, just didn't achieve anything worthwhile against von Letow-Vorbeck. The German general managed to stay out of reach while steadily moving southwards.

Because of van Deventer's signals to Louis Botha, I deemed it prudent to send the following warning to Lourenco Marques:

GPSJDIU GBMMF CFJ RVFMJNBOF = V

In plain German it looks like this:

FORSICHT FALLE BEI QUELIMANE = V[27]

Van Deventer was afraid that the Germans would capture the harbor town of Quelimane, steal some ships and escape. To prevent that, he asked the Portuguese to strengthen the garrison at this town and prepare for the German attack.

---

[27] BEWARE TRAP AT QUELIMANE = V

Pretoria, Wednesday, 4 July 1918

It was a very downhearted Jaap van Deventer who reported to Botha that his men had lost the battle on the Namacurra River that raged for three days and ended yesterday.

Instead of trying to capture Quelimane, as he had anticipated, the Germans turned into the opposite direction and attacked their pursuers to the north. Initially, only three German companies routed something like four British and Portuguese battalions. Many soldiers under his command simply fled when the Germans advanced against them and more than two hundred of them drowned in the flooded Namacurra River. Another two hundred were casualties and more than four hundred were taken prisoner.

Von Letow-Vorbeck's main force arrived two days after the fighting had started and that caused the rest of the British and Portuguese forces to retreat in haste – leaving behind huge heaps of supplies and ammunition.

I almost sent a congratulatory telegram to von Letow-Vorbeck because this was his biggest victory after almost four years of fighting, but I decided against such a rash move, just in case my message got intercepted and decoded.

Pretoria, Saturday, 31 August 1918

Since Henry and Daniel are celebrating their respective fourteenth and thirteenth birthdays tomorrow, we arrived at the farm yesterday afternoon for two festive days. I decided to take the whole week-end off, leaving the week-end staff to work on their own, receiving and sending mostly routine and boring and uninteresting stuff.

Should anything great happen during this time, I will be able to pick it up on Monday.

During breakfast this morning, Victor – who seems to be the brightest of the three – suddenly gets up from the table and returns with my old heliograph that is being stored in my bedroom in a cupboard.

Victor: "Ma, what is this funny thing? Can I play with it?"

Henry: "Yes, I have also noticed that thing. I remember that you used it to send some messages to Pa before the war and when we still lived here."

Victor: "Can you show us how it works?"

After breakfast, I take the boys outside and demonstrate how the heliograph works. The result is, inevitably, that I have to teach the boys Morse Code and they learn it diligently. They make copies of the card from which I initially mastered this code.

Victor: "Why don't we take this thing home in town? And then we can send messages to you at the Union Buildings."

Henry: "But how will Ma know when to look for a message?"

Victor: "She can go outside every afternoon at three sharp, and watch for a message from us, if any. Quite easy."

Daniel: "We can also use Morse Code to talk to each other when we don't want to be overheard by other kids. Those stupid souls at school won't know Morse Code."

The rest of the day is being spent in mastering Morse Code and playing with the heliograph. I can only ask myself: "Where will this end? Am I preparing my sons for military careers? Are they doomed to become soldiers and warriors and fighters, just like all their ancestors?"

A little voice inside my head tells me: "You can't escape fate." That must be the voice of Veleda.

Pretoria, Friday, 21 September 1918

The war in East Africa is dragging along. There are often optimistic messages from Jaap van Deventer to Louis Botha, promising him that the German force will be captured or annihilated very soon - which never seems to happen.

Von Letow-Vorbeck and his force has left Portuguese East Africa and entered the old German colony again, with the forces of van Deventer in pursuit. Van Deventer informed Botha yesterday that he is sure that he will be able to trap the Germans with an ambush in eastern Tanganyika.

Of course, this morning I'm ready to send off the following message to Lourenco Marques:

JOTJEJBF JO UFSSB PSJFOUBMJS = V

The uncoded Latin looks like this:

INSIDIAE IN TERRA ORIENTALIS = V[28]

---

[28] English: AMBUSH IN EASTERN COUNTRY = V

Pretoria, Monday, 30 September 1918

The fourth anniversary of the start of the Great War passed rather uneventfully almost two months ago and, yet, there doesn't seem to be an end to the war. Some experts quoted in the Pretoria News predict that the German and Austrian Empires are on their last legs and will collapse soon. I don't know whether those opinions rest on real evidence or are only wishful thinking.

Nevertheless, that smart, slippery, sly Paul von Letow-Vorbeck evaded the trap that awaited him – perhaps due to my warning. Instead, he invaded Northern Rhodesia[29] and raided some towns in the so-called Copper Belt. A dejected van Deventer sent a dejected message to Botha and Botha angrily demanded an explanation for this failure.

I send a message to Lourenco Marques and I believe that the German general will welcome the news:

CPUIB XVUFOE BVG KWE = V

The uncoded German message looks like this:

BOTHA WUTEND AUF JVD = V[30]

At three I step outside to check whether the boys have any messages for me with the heliograph. They indeed tell me that a letter from Hector has arrived. I reply and acknowledge receipt with a small mirror with which I reflect some sunlight in the direction of our home.

Hector's news is that his battalion is to join the war very shortly, as soon as transport for almost 400 troops can be arranged. He feels sorry for the boys of whom many won't survive the

---

[29] Nowadays the country of Zambia.
[30] BOTHA ANGRY AT JVD = V

trenches, the mud, the shelling, the machine guns of the Germans, the land mines, and other hardships and hazards. His task was to prepare these young men to endure all these dangers and even death or being maimed.

I don't like this type of news because it troubles me to read about the suffering of others, whether they are friends or foes.

Pretoria, 12 November 1918

There are festivities in Pretoria today. The deadly and destructive war in Europe has ended yesterday. The Germans and the Austrians have agreed to a ceasefire after their emperors had abdicated and fled. These countries are officially republics now, but according to all indications, chaos reigns as communists, republicans, democrats, and royalists fight each other. The Germans had no choice but to beg for an armistice because almost all the sailors of the Kaiserliche Marine, the German Navy, refused to fight any further. Their strike spread to other sectors of the armed forces.

Last night, Veleda intruded into my dreams. I can only remember the tears on her face and that gave me the message that she was feeling very, very sad. She must have wanted to prepare me for the horrible news that the British Empire prevailed, although only with the help of the United States of America and all former British colonies.

Heaven alone knows when Hector will be able to return home. It will certainly take some time. His new battalion most probably saw very little action during the last few weeks of the war and I feel confident that he is safe and in good health.

While I and the boys are visiting my mother for supper, there is a knock on the front door. Daniel rushes to see who is there and he is followed by Victor.

Victor rushes back and shouts: "It's Opa Daniel!"

He is followed by my father who has grown a long beard, but who seems to be in good health.

Pretoria, Thursday, 14 November 1918

Jaap van Deventer sent an uncoded message to General Louis Botha this afternoon that General Paul von Letow-Vorbeck and his troops agreed to an armistice only this morning – three days after the armistice in Europe. Apparently, he didn't receive the news of the armistice in Europe and somebody with a white flag was sent to him with the message. After he sought corroboration of this news on his radio, he agreed to lay down arms.

Van Deventer doesn't know what to do with the German general and Botha orders him to allow his former foe to return to Germany, if he so wishes.

I send my last coded message to Lourenco Marques:

WFMFEB USJUU JO SVIFTUBOE EBOLF

In good German, it looks like this:

VELEDA TRITT IN RUHESTAND DANKE[31]

A few minutes later, I receive the following answer:

XJS TDIMJFTTFO BVDI EBOLF UTDIVFTT

I decode it immediately, read the message, and stuff the completed message form immediately into my handbag:

WIR SCHLIESSEN AUCH DANKE TSCHUESS[32]

I suddenly feel lost. The reason for staying at this job has just disappeared. I decide to quit my position of manager of the telegraph office in the Union Buildings as soon as Hector returns home.

---

[31] VELEDA RETIRES THANKS
[32] WE ALSO CLOSE DOWN THANKS CHEERS

Pretoria, Saturday, 28 June 1919

For a change, I attended the service in the synagogue this morning with my father because I wanted to reaffirm my Hebrew roots. When I reach our house, Victor yells: "Ma, come! Pa is back!"

Hector rushes to embrace me. "Can I have some breakfast? I'm starving."

"Is that all you can think of? How are you? How did you get back? Where have you been all the time?"

"Give me some bacon and eggs with toast and coffee and then I will answer all your questions. But, before that, I want to find out whether you have remembered how to give me a decent kiss."

"In front of the boys?"

Later, after Hector felt satisfied after having enjoyed his breakfast, he tells us how he and his battalion were demobilized. It took a long time to be transport back to England. Only an armistice was declared last November, but a peace treaty was supposed to be signed today. That meant that the Allies had to keep some units in France after the armistice, just in case. After the German units had evaporated, his battalion could think about going home. Equipment had to be handed in and each soldier had to take part in a medal parade before allowed to go home and resume civilian life. He visited his parents at Hagdale to see whether they were still in good shape and to help them with some thorny issues, such as applying for payment for the horses the Army just took from them.

It took a long time for him to find a berth on a passenger liner, back to Cape Town. Most of the passenger liners that survived the onslaught of German submarines, were needed to evacuate troops from France and Belgium and take American troops back to America. But, in the end, he reached Cape Town and caught a train to Pretoria.

I ask: "And what did this war accomplish, if anything?"

Hector: "Yes, yes, that's a question I often asked myself. In total, a great deal of disorder, disarray, and discord. Great Britain didn't acquire any new territories, although France captured a slice of western Germany, the provinces of Alsace and Lorraine. Actually, these provinces were only taken back after the Germans had annexed them in 1871. Germany and Austria became republics after their emperors ran away. Germany lost her African colonies. Austria lost much more area when countries such as Hungary, Bohemia, Istria, Dalmatia, and others broke away and became independent. Italy grabbed Southern Tyrol. Russia was left in tatters after a bloody revolution during which the Czar was killed. Yes, one can ask: was anything of value achieved with this war?"

"But Hector, look at all those young men who lost their lives or were maimed. Look at all the misery and mischief caused in various parts of Europe. We were told this war was being fought to end all wars. I can't agree. The Germans and the Austrians, who lost more than the Allies, will try and take revenge."

(I remember that Veleda told me in a dream: "We Germans never give up!")

"You have a valid point. At this very moment, representatives of Germany are forced to sign a peace treaty drawn up by the victors. According to the newspapers, Germany must agree to disarm, renounce all territorial claims, pay a huge sum of money as punishment for all the damage they have caused, and to admit their guilt for starting this war. This is to take place in the palace of Versailles near Paris."

"The Germans won't take this humiliation lying down. They will do something about it. Watch out!"

THE SILENT WAR

Much happened after the end of the Great War. Hector inherited his late father's title and estate and we had to settle in England. Hector played with politics for a little while and returned to his military career, reaching important and exciting positions and posts, and experiencing important and exciting events.

Germany started to build up her military might to avenge the defeat of 1918 and Hector was tasked with watching this tendency while I was recruited to resume my old role as a German agent. This amounted to a silent war between Great Britain and Germany.

Pretoria, Monday, 15 January 1923

A very disturbing and depressing telegram was delivered to our front door this afternoon:

HECTOR VISCOUNT DE HACQUEVILLE ARCADIA
PRETORIA SOUTH AFRICA
MY UNPLEASANT DUTY TO INFORM YOU OF THE
DEATH YESTERDAY OF HENRY VISCOUNT DE
HACQUEVILLE DUE TO STROKE FUNERAL ON
WEDNESDAY HECTOR SOLE HEIR OF TITLE AND
ASSETS PLEASE RETURN ASAP TO SETTLE ESTATE
LETTER FOLLOWS
= JAMES JAMESON SOLICITOR HURSLEY

When Hector shows this to me, he remarks: "Of course, this is no surprise. After all, he was already eighty. I suppose he couldn't face life without my mother after her death last year."

Me: "He still seemed all right from his last letter we got a few days ago. But now, my dear, you inherited a title – as well as the estate. How do I address you from now on? Must I call you 'My Lord' or something like that now?"

Hector ignores my question: "I dreaded this day because it will mean that we will have to move to Hampshire to deal with everything regarding my dad's last will and to pay all the taxes and duties. I was living very happily and comfortably here in Pretoria – in town and on our farm – but now we must pull up our roots and build a new future at Hagdale."

"When are we leaving?"

"Not very soon. There are so many things to take care of. We must decide what to do with this house, with the farm, and with all our possessions. And all our business interests."

"Why can't we stay part of the year here and the other part over there?"

"That will be difficult. Even impossible. We can't shift the two younger boys every so often from one school to another. They need stability. There is a decent grammar school in Hursley that I attended and we can also send them there. And Henry can start with university or something during the second part of this year."

"Do you know this Mister James Jameson, the lawyer?"

"Never heard of him, but I suppose he was my father's attorney and the only one able to inform me of his death. Perhaps he had to organize the funeral and everything else, as stipulated in my father's will."

"Where will he be buried?"

"Most probably in the church yard in Hursley. That's where most of my ancestors are sleeping."

"I will really miss your father, just as I miss your mother. They were very kind and nice towards me when they visited us shortly before the start of the war, and again three years ago."

"I think that Pater fell in love with you when he first saw you at our wedding, twenty years ago. He went out of his way to be nice and considerate towards you. He totally approved of you. Mater also did. That's because you have breeding and it showed."

"They became very fond of the boys when they visited us."

"Pater was very flattered that we named Henry after his grandfather. Yes, I will also miss them, as you do."

Pretoria, Tuesday, 16 January 1923

At the breakfast table, Victor says: "Pa, I don't want to go and live in England. Sis, the place is filled with filthy Englishmen. I hate the lot of them."

Hector: "The Good Book says clearly we must love our enemies – not hate them."

"But they hate me. At school, they call me a dirty Dutchman. They're only jealous because they can only speak English, while I know four languages – Afrikaans or Dutch, German, English, and also some Latin."

Daniel: "I don't want to go to England. These Rooinekke in our school feel sour because the three of us were always the top pupils in our classes. I won't feel at home over there when I must look at Englishmen every day."

Henry: "And please remember that I am departing for Stellenbosch University in three weeks' time. I want to become a lawyer – an attorney or an advocate. I don't think I will be able to adapt to that foggy, rainy, muddy, murky…, and messy British climate. I need some sunshine."

I add my thoughts: "Hector, do you hear what our boys are telling us? I slept rather badly last night while thinking that we will have to leave Pretoria where I grew up and where we raised our children. I've lived at Hagdale for some time during 1910 and I don't know whether I will fit in there. I will feel uncomfortable whenever people address me as 'Milady'. I am a simple Boer girl with a peculiar mixed ancestry of which I am proud."

All eyes are fixed upon Hector at the head of the table. He holds up his hands to silence us: "I hear you clearly and loudly. I know how you feel because I regard myself by this time as an inhabitant of this town. I came her twenty-three years ago and I have lived more than half of my life in this place. I love this place just as much as you do. I must also admit that I don't always feel comfortable by being surrounded by Englishmen. They are loud, arrogant, and … arrogant. They think they own the world because they won the Boer War and the Great War. I really don't want to leave this place, but I have no choice.

"I can't help that I was born as the only son of an English nobleman. Fortunately, I went to an ordinary school in Hursley – not one of those so-called public schools that are, in fact, very, very private. I feel comfortable between ordinary folks. I got along very well with my Boer neighbors in these parts and I can even speak Afrikaans and I understand the Dutch sermons in church. Before the Great War, I entered a partnership with a few other famers and we could resurrect our business after the war. It will be very difficult to say good-bye to Pretoria and untangle ourselves from everything over here.

"But, I have no choice in the matter. My ancestors, who settled at Hagdale many centuries ago, will never forgive me if I just abandon the place. That is where I was born and raised and where I must return. Sorry, but I have no choice. You all will have to come with me. "

I interject: "Why don't you renounce your title and leave it to some or other cousin?"

"There are no such cousins. My father's only brother had only two daughters and they can't inherit a male title. Anyway, Henry, I can understand that you want to study at Stellenbosch. But when we go to England, I will make sure that you will be accepted at Oxford or Cambridge, or another English university. And, Victor and Daniel, you will also attain degrees from world-famous universities when you complete school over there."

We all fall silent. Everybody watches his or her plate in front of him or her. Henry plays with his fork and Victor fumbles with his napkin.

At last, Daniel mumbles: "Victor, get up. We will be late for school."

As the two boys leave home with their satchels, they embrace me and their father.

I remember what Veleda told me last night when I slept badly and fitfully: "We Germans never give up."

Hagdale, Thursday, 22 March 1923

The whole de Hacqueville family arrived at Hagdale a week ago. Much work awaited us.

The villa, which had stood empty for the past three months, had to be made habitable again. I could do that with the help of the two maids, Maud and Mary, who stayed on after my father-in-law's passing away. The cook in the kitchen, called Cheeky Carol, had to remain to feed all the other members of the personnel.

The gardener, Willy Williams, and his helpers, Tommy and Teddy, kept the garden in a presentable condition and looked after the twenty horses of the stud of Anglo-Arabians. Hector and I inspected the stables, grounds, vegetable gardens, and orchard, which they supervise. Hector grew up with horses and he was satisfied with the conditions of the animals.

The dairy business is being handled by Sam Summers and his two assistants, Ken and Kebble. As an experienced dairy farmer, Hector was able to see how well this part of the estate was attended to. Sam is also the handyman who looks after the repairs of the villa and the vehicles, a small truck for the transportation of milk to the railway station, the tractor, and my father-in-law's motor car.

Cheeky Carol, who is married to Sam, is also responsible for feeding the chickens with scraps from the kitchen and other bits. I found it almost a sacrilege when Hector explained to me that the chicken house used to be a serf's cottage, dating from the thirteen-hundreds.

"That ancient relic ought to be treated with more respect and restored to its original state. It is an insult to those poor serfs whose home is now being fouled with chicken shit."

The lawyer, Mister Jameson, took it upon himself to supervise all these workers from time to time and to handle all the money matters before our arrival – the income from the dairy business, bills that had to be paid, and the wages of all the workers – all nine of them.

Hector had to have almost daily meetings with Mister Jameson, who always addressed him as "My Lord". That was also how the personnel called him and Hector confided in me that he felt rather awkward and uncomfortable by being handled in that way – although he was used as an officer of being addressed as "Sir" or "Colonel".

Daniel and Victor both attend the local school in Hursley, while Henry is waiting at home to be enrolled at Cambridge during August or September. He often accompanies me when we go horse-riding on the grounds of Hagdale or through the countryside.

Last night, Hector told me: "It is time that I take my seat in the House of Lords. People will think there's something wrong with me if I don't do that."

Me: "Have you ever thought of resuming your military career?"

"The thought has occurred to me. Yes. Perhaps. But, in the meantime, we will have to start and pursue our social obligations.

We will have to entertain the important people from these parts. We can't live like hermits."

"That will cost a lot. Do we have the money?"

"According to Mister Jameson, we can live comfortably on my father's savings and investments, as long as we don't touch the capital. The estate generates enough income to pay all the staff members."

And today, a momentous event occurred. It fell, very literally, from the sky onto Hagdale. An airplane made an emergency landing on one of our fields. The pilot got our and walked towards the villa, where he encountered Sam, who took him to the front door. I was summoned by Maud, who answered the front door bell.

I found a strange man with a leather helmet and goggles standing on our porch: "Ma'am, I'm sorry to disturb you. My airplane encountered some engine trouble while up there in the air and I had to look for a place to do an emergency landing. I hope you won't regard me as an intruder or a trespasser. Do I have your permission to try and repair my machine where she is standing on your field?"

Me: "My good man, who are you?"

"Sorry, Ma'am. I'm Gerald Forsyth, at your service."

I turn to Sam: "Sam, can you perhaps lend this gentleman a hand? I'm sorry, my husband isn't at home at this moment, otherwise he would gladly have helped you."

Sam: "At your service, Milady."

As the two of them leave, I get Henry: "Put on your riding breeches. We are going to look at something that fell from the sky onto one of our meadows."

I and my son ride out where we find Sam and the pilot, busy tinkering with the engine of a strange contraption. This is the first time in my life that I see such a machine, except when one of them flew over Pretoria, high in the sky.

When it becomes dark, Sam informs me: "Milady, I will have to take this gent to Winchester tomorrow to buy some spare parts and oil. Also, a can of fuel. Is it all right if he leaves his machine here for the night?"

I turn to Gerald Forsyth: "You are welcome to leave this flying machine there for the night. And then you are to enjoy our hospitality for the night, till tomorrow."

"Ma'am, may I ask you a huge favor? May I please use your phone to inform my destination that they shouldn't be worried about me and that I hope to get there tomorrow?"

"The phone is in the hall. Come inside,"

Hagdale, Friday, 23 March 1923

The repairs to the flying machine came to an end just after lunch. I and Henry watched how Mister Forsyth started the engine and made sure that it ran smoothly.

Henry, the inquisitive young man, asked him: "What type of machine is this?"

"Oh, it's an Avro 504R Gosport Biplane. She's actually fairly new and I can't understand why she gave some engine trouble. Do you want a flip when I take her up? I must repay you folks somewhat for your help and hospitality."

Henry is immediately eager to try this new experience. He gets into the seat behind the pilot, puts on the goggles Forsyth provides, and they take off. The Gosport flies off into the air with a roar. Something inside me gets a huge thrill while looking at this engineering marvel. I find it an unfathomable mystery how such a thing could stay in the air. The Gosport makes a few turns in the sky and lands again.

Henry shouts: "Ma, this is the best experience I ever had in my life! You should try it!"

Geral Forsyth adds: "Ma'am, you're welcome. Hop in."

We get airborne again and I must agree that this is certainly the best experience I have ever had in my life of almost forty years. It is a strange sensation to look down onto our estate and see all the fields, orchards, gardens, and the surrounding areas. We land again, all too soon.

Mister Forsyth is invited to tea after he has switched off the engine again. I and Henry lead our horses, while taking Forsyth back. I find Hector back at home and I tell him that I have had the most exciting experience of my whole life.

Gerald: "Dear Sir, you should try it some or other time. Or, still better, buy yourself an airplane. You have a perfect landing strip on that field of yours. You can use it to travel all over England in no time."

Hector: "I don't think I will do that. I fought during the war and I saw too many fighter aircraft of the Germans and of our Royal Flying Corps being shot down. I don't think human beings are meant to fly like birds. God didn't give us wings."

Me: "You are likewise not meant to move around on wheels. God gave you two feet for walking. If he wanted you to travel more rapidly, he would have fitted you out with wheels, or four legs, like a horse."

Henry and Gerald laugh and Hector looks dismayed because his argument fell flat.

Hagdale, Sunday, 25 March 1923

It is still a strange sensation that I'm not supposed to prepare meals. Our cook, Cheeky Carol, more than once chased me out of the kitchen when I wanted to help. She insists that she is in command and that I must respect that. I can understand how she got her nickname. My role is restricted to discussing the menu for lunch and dinner with her.

So, we sit down for dinner tonight, all dressed up with our Sunday clothes. Dinner in this grand villa was always a formal affair and will remain so.

Henry asks his father: "Pa, how do I go about to join the Royal Air Force?"

Hector: "My son, it is a firm family tradition that you join the Army. You may do that after you have completed your law degree at Cambridge."

"The Royal Air Force developed out of the Army. During the Great War, it was known as the Royal Flying Corps. Now, it's a separate service of our armed forces. If I join the RAF, it will still be in accordance with our family tradition."

"Perhaps you'e right. I will ask around."

Hagdale, Friday, 13 April 1923

We are entertaining some guests tonight. They arrived by motor car and we must provide their chauffeurs also with meals. All-in-all, thirty-nine meals must be prepared.

Among our guests are Major General (retired) Sir Nicholas Nosewhole, an old family friend and a widower. Other guests include Lord Adam Barlow and his wife Charlotte, Colonel David Edmonds and his wife Fanny, Sir Gordon Hammond and his wife Innez, the solicitor James Jameson Esq with his wife Katherine, the honorable Louis Meadows, accompanied by his wife Nora, and Captain (RN, retired) Oscar Peebles and his wife Queenie – all of them neighbors of some sorts. We are also honored by the presence of the Reverend Father Richard Smurph, the local priest at All Saints Church in Hursley.

Daniel and Victor have been trained by the maids how they should act as stewards and serve the guests with drinks and snacks before dinner.

During the dinner, Henry is being lectured by Mister Jameson about his planned law course at Cambridge. Colonel Edmonds tells Henry how he must apply to become a member of the Royal Air Force – the successor of the Royal Flying Corps – and be trained as a pilot. He may even join a student squadron at Cambridge and do part of his training during weekends and holidays.

The colonel adds: "It may interest you that South Africa was the first country to create an Air Force, apart from its Army and Navy. General Smuts of South Africa, who was a member of the Imperial War Cabinet, convinced the government over here to follow South Africa's example and establish the Royal Air Force."

Captain Peebles instructs Daniel how he should go about to be admitted to the Royal Naval College at Greenwich after he had completed a degree at Cambridge.

Major General Nosewhole informs Hector how he may get back into the Army. He still has contacts with their old regiment, the North Lancashire Mounted Rifles, by holding the position of colonel-in-chief, an honorary position. He explains that it may be possible to become a part-time officer on half-pay in this unit.

Lord Adam Barlow, an earl, describes to Hector how and when he can take a seat in the House of Lords.

As hostess, it is my task to look after the comfort of all our guests and that means that I must move around sometimes.

When the party breaks up shortly before midnight, the inebriated gentlemen and ladies shuffle to their motor cars so that their chauffeurs can take them home. They have cleaned out our whole supply of red wine, Port wine, whiskey, and brandy. Twenty cigars went up in smoke. General Nosewhole fell asleep on a couch in the drawing room with a tumbler of brandy in his hand, which he graciously spilled onto the tiled floor. Lady Charlotte Barlow became very tipsy and started to tell dirty jokes, while giggling the whole time.

Missus Katherine Jameson started weeping and shed large tears while talking about a nephew who fell during the war. Colonel Edmonds disappeared through the front door to empty his bladder in the garden and came back with a very visible wet patch on his trousers. Captain Peebles, who boasted that he had commanded a cruiser during the Battle of Jutland in June 1916, flirted with me and I had trouble keeping out of his reach, while his overweight wife punched her elbows repeatedly onto his paunch.

Hector told me afterwards that this captain neglected to tell us that his light cruiser was sunk during that battle and that he had to be rescued by a German ship. He spent two-and-a half years in a prisoner-of-war camp and reached retirement age a few days after being repatriated after the armistice in November 1918. He, therefore, saw very little action during the war.

Father Richard, who had arrived on his bicycle, had to be put to bed in one of our guest rooms because it would have been too hazardous to allow him to ride back to the parsonage on his bicycle in his state in the dark.

After all the guests have left – apart from the priest – the maids start clearing up and cleaning up. I help, despite the protests of the two maids. I order Henry, Daniel, and Victor to give a hand and to help with the washing of all the crockery and glasses. That is how my mother brought me up.

When we get into bed much later, Hector holds me tightly: "My gorgeous girl, you were the most gracious and graceful hostess one can imagine. This party must be regarded as a superb and stupendous success. You and me were in the end the only people who weren't as drunk as lords, although I am a lord."

Me: "If you were drunk, I wouldn't have allowed you to hold me as you do and make love to me."

Secretly, I think that I have seen enough of the English aristocracy and gentry to loathe the lot of them – although I am also a member of that caste through marriage. I am sure that my Boer ancestors, who can be counted as Afrikaans aristocracy, knew how to behave themselves as good Christians. I insisted upon a Friday night for this party so that everybody can sober up during the Saturday and be ready to go to church on Sunday.

Hagdale, Monday, 30 November 1925

A family meeting is being held in the library of our villa after dinner. Hector starts the meeting with a speech:

"My fabulous family, it is indeed a pleasure to have all of you again under one roof. Henry and Daniel, both of you returned home from Cambridge yesterday morning after having written some tests and exams. I am truly proud of you and I salute you.

"Henry, congratulations with your flying license. I am sure that a great career awaits you as a future senior officer in the Royal Air Force. You have also completed two-and-a-half years of your law studies. I don't know what a lawyer with a pilot's license will do in the RAF, but that is the path you have chosen. After you have gotten your law degree, you will also receive your commission from His Majesty, King George, as an officer of the armed forces of the United Kingdom. You are my eldest son and the heir to my title, as well as the lion's share of this estate. I'm sure you will make a success of your life. Please marry a girl with the qualities of your marvelous mother. I need at least one grandson to whom my title and estate can go in due course.

"And Daniel, you completed one-an-a-half years of study at Cambridge. I'm proud of you, as well. When you get your degree in economics and geography, you will only be the second member of the family of the de Hacquevilles who graduates from a university. I am sorry that you don't contemplate a career in the Army, but in the Royal Navy. You will certainly be a good navigator with your knowledge of geography. You will also be a good manager of men and organizations with your knowledge of economics.

"And Victor, my son, your school career is almost at an end. Only six more months before you can enter the University of Cambridge. The fact that you want to study mathematics and physics will make you an excellent artillery officer. I foresee a brilliant career for you in our Army, should you decide to go that way. I also salute you.

"And, my dear family, from tomorrow there will be another change in our family's course through history. Your father is finished with politics. I've had enough of the House of Lords. I am bored with all those senile simpletons spewing stupid speeches that demonstrate their dementia and dumbheadedness. From tomorrow, I will be the commanding officer of the second battalion of my old outfit, the Loyals, the North Lancashire Regiment. I was appointed with the substantive rank of lieutenant-colonel, after I have held this rank on a temporary basis during the Great War. At that time, I was the commander of the sixth battalion, which saw very little action because that battalion was only formed shortly before the end of hostilities. My old regiment, as all units in the Army, was downsized with most of the men being demobilized. There are only two battalions left and I am fortunate to have been appointed as commander of one of them. I believe that I am young enough to be promoted to colonel, or even brigadier, before I retire. It's a pity that the rank of brigadier-general was abolished recently and that the rank above that of a colonel is only a brigadier, which is merely something like a senior or superior colonel. Perhaps I will reach that point.

"This position at the Loyals is not a full-time job and I will be at home quite often. I look forward to spend enough time with your maternal parent, the adorable Dora, the vivacious viscountess de Hacqueville, the home-maker at Hagdale.

"Thank you for your patience, while listening to me."

Henry holds up his hand: "Pa, I want to say what I want to say in Afrikaans, which is my first mother tongue. I congratulate you on your appointment. You were always a father to whom we could come with our problems and wishes. We trusted you always that you would do your best for your family, although we saw very little of you during the war. But millions of other children had to endure that. So, we weren't exceptions.

"We are proud of your war exploits and the decorations awarded to you. I am sure that you will wear your uniform with pride. I hope to become an officer in the Royal Air Force some or other time. I love flying. I want to make a career of flying. Our mother also loves flying. I know because I have smuggled her up into the air with my trainer after I have received my license and I was allowed to do solo flights.

"Pa, you must buy Ma an airplane. I think she's a natural. I even allowed her to take the controls of my trainer, although that was, strictly speaking, against all the rules and regulations and requirements. We have a natural landing strip on one of our meadows and we can store the machine in one of our barns."

Victor (also in Afrikaans): "Pa, if Ma gets an airplane, you won't need to take the slow train to go to London or Lancashire, or wherever. Ma can always fly you there."

Daniel (following his brothers in Afrikaans): "Pa, if I may say something. This mother of ours has a long line of audacious ancestors, all of them brave and battle-hardened Boers. She has the guts and the grit to achieve anything. Yes, I also think that you can buy her a flying machine."

Hector: "Dora?"

Me: "I think I will like to have my own airplane. Henry can give me flying lessons as soon as he gets qualified as an instructor."

Henry: "Pa, the right plane for Ma will be a Tiger Moth. It is being built by de Haviland. It's a two-seater with a seat for you as her passenger."

Hector: "I smell a rat, a scheme, a conspiracy, an intrigue. It seems I am outvoted, should I decide to vote 'no'. But then all of you must remember, I'm the chap who signs the cheques, who counts the pounds and the pennies, who pays the bills. Let's see what we can perhaps do. I can't promise anything. But that must wait until Henry becomes a qualified instructor."

Hamble, Sunday, 15 May 1927

It was not easy to convince Hector to take me to Hamble on this Sunday afternoon. He preferred to have a peaceful afternoon nap, but I insisted. Hamble is a town to the south-east of Southampton, on the Southampton Water, and halfway to Portsmouth on the coast. There are two airfields with various factories and workshops where aircraft are being built or repaired.

Hamble is hosting an air show today. It is called the Hampshire Air Pageant. All the British manufacturers of aircraft are exhibiting their products. We make sure that we get seats in the most expensive enclosure with the best view, which costs five shillings apiece. There are also seats costing half-a-crown and seats that can be bought for a shilling.

I point out to Hector that there are quite a few female pilots.

"Oh, you dragged me along to this place, just to convince me that women are also able to be pilots."

"Exactly. I think it will be a good thing if you could buy me my own plane."

Camberley, Friday, 29 June 1928

As the spouse of an officer, I had to attend many parades in the past. Today is again such an opportunity and I made a smart summer dress for the occasion. My old sewing machine, that I used to get dressed for the royal funeral eighteen years ago, is still available at Hagdale.

Both Major General Nosewhole and Colonel Edmonds vouched for Hector when he applied for a staff position at the War Office, involved with intelligence. He was subjected to the sitting of a selection board and was accepted for the position. That meant that was promoted to a full colonel.

It was also expected of him to attend a staff course for senior field officers at the Staff College at Camberley in Surrey. That meant that he was absent from home for the past six months, except over weekends.

Since all three our sons are at university in Cambridge, I was very alone at Hagdale. I filled some of my days by helping Sam to service our motor car, the tractor, and the milk truck. I think I became a rather competent mechanic.

And today, the passing-out parade at the Staff College is taking place. Hector looks splendid in his colonel's uniform with all his war-time medals.

Henry and Daniel have finished their year-end exams and they are waiting to be awarded their degrees. Daniel graduates at the same time as his elder brother because Henry's law degree took a year longer that Daniel's degree in geography and economics. They, as well as Victor who is still studying, also attend the parade of their father. Henry wears his RAF uniform as an officer cadet.

Another parade is scheduled for tomorrow. That is when Hector will take over the position of colonel-in-chief of the North Lancashire Regiment. This position is purely ceremonial and does not entail any operational duties. The previous incumbent of this position, Major General Sir Nicholas Nosewhole, decided that his diminishing strength and failing health necessitated his retirement from this position and he recommended Colonel Lord Hector de Hacqueville as his successor. Since Hector was already well-known, it was an easy choice to offer him this position. He will be welcomed by his regiment at tomorrow's parade.

This means that Hector will wear two different uniforms: the regular step-outs of staff officers at the War Office, and the ceremonial garb of the Loyals with red jackets and black trousers, with which he will attend parades and other official functions. Of course, I and the boys will also attend that occasion.

I could not stop Hector from applying for this staff job because he is a professional soldier at heart, although I knew that it would mean that we will have to spend most of our time in London in a rented apartment.

RAF Cranwell, Friday, 7 December 1928

The family de Hacqueville attends another parade today. Henry completed his training as an officer of the RAF at the Royal Air Force College Cranwell in Lancashire.

The course usually takes nine months, but he completed the basic part, which usually takes three months, while studying at Cambridge. The more advanced parts took six months and the passing-out parade is taking place today. Of course, the whole family de Hacqueville attend the ceremony.

Henry receives the rank of pilot officer, which is the equivalent of second lieutenant in the Army.

The Royal Air Force College at Cranwell

The parade is inspected by His Majesty, King George V, who wears the uniform of a marshal of the RAF, the equivalent of a field marshal. He declares that all those who have completed the course are to receive his commission. The commandant of the college, Air Vice Marshal Frederick Halahan, with a rank equivalent to that of major general, addresses the parade and congratulates the new officers for being the cream of the cream of the British armed forces. They went through a very demanding selection procedure and managed to conclude the course, literally, with flying colors.

Hagdale, Saturday, 15 December 1928

Henry disappeared this morning just after breakfast. He only said good-bye to me and when I asked where he was going, he only answered: "Somewhere."

Of course, Henry is free to go wherever he likes. After his graduation from the RAF College, he received leave till the day after New Year's Day and we enjoy his presence.

Just before lunch time, Sam, the chief gardener, calls me: "Milady, I think you should come and have a look. There's another flying machine on our meadow. It seems these things have the habit of visiting Hogdale."

I fetch Hector, who has the weekend off, where he is pottering around in a shed. We walk down to the meadow and: Lo! There is really an airplane!

The pilot is none other than Pilot Officer Henry de Hacqueville who jumps onto the grass. Hector gives me a kiss: "My delicious darling, this is your Christmas present. Henry had to go and fetch it."

Henry joins us: "Ma, when are you ready for your fist flying lesson? There is a fortnight left before I must join my new squadron and, in the meantime, we can start with Lesson One."

I ask: "What type of aircraft is this contraption?"

"Oh, she's a Tiger Moth. De Haviland Tiger Moth. Are you ready for your first lesson?"

Henry hands me a pair of goggles and we fly off, leaving Hector behind. After forty minutes of sheer delight, ecstasy, and pleasure, we return to our field.

Henry: "Ma, now you will have to endure some lectures and lessons from me. I brought my flying manuals along and I will explain them to you. You must know all about the theory of flying, weather-forecasting, navigation, and all the legal aspects of flying."

Me: "You must provide me with a manual on how to service her engine. I think I'm a masterful mechanic."

Henry: "That is certainly necessary. Pa will procure a complete set of tools and he will also erect a stand on which a huge drum of aircraft fuel can be stored."

Hector: "I can see on your face that you enjoyed the flight. I was preparing a shed where we can store this contraption, as you called her. We can't let her sleep here outside, in the rain and the wind. She needs protection. After all, she cost me a pretty penny."

"We can use her to take you to London after I have qualified. That will give you more time here at Hagdale during your off-weekends."

Hagdale, Monday, 17 December 1928

Henry is busy giving me a lecture in our library. He does it in English since the manual is written in English.

Suddenly he switches to Afrikaans: "Ma, you know, I sometimes feel like a traitor. I don't like that feeling."

"What do you mean?"

"I am an officer in the Royal Air Force, a part of the armed forces of the United Kingdom. I am part of the aristocracy of this Island nation and the day will come when people will address me as 'My Lord'."

"What is so terrible about that?"

"I don't feel like an Englishman. I don't like Englishmen and I've told you so in the past. I'm a Boer at heart. I grew up in Pretoria and my friends were all Afrikaans-speaking. My school mates got used to the fact that I have a funny-sounding family name, but they accepted me as one of them – even during the Great War when my English-speaking father was fighting on the British side. We only spoke Afrikaans during those times, although I could speak English better than many Englishmen, with the correct accent of the upper classes.

"Although I can trace my English ancestry back to the eleventh century, I can also be proud of my Boer ancestors, who were brave, courageous, honest, and God-fearing folks. I also have a German grandfather who was locked up in a prison camp, just because he was born in Germany.

"And now I am a British officer and my loyalty is supposed to be with King and Country. Bah! I loathe these English aristocrats. I've seen enough of them – the guests we entertained and some of my fellow cadets at the Air Force Academy. I stood on a higher social level than most of them because I will be able to call myself a viscount some or other time. That meant that these chaps had to treat me with respect. I didn't dare to expose my Boer heritage because they would have called me a 'dirty Dutchman' or something. In spite of it all, I even made good friends with a few of my fellow-cadets, decent types. But most of them make me sick.

"Ma, I feel like a traitor. I can't forget my Boer background. I can't forget what the British Army did during the Boer War, although I wasn't born yet at that time. You and grandma Veronica told us enough stories of how the hated English treated the Boer women and children and allowed them to die like flies in their concentration camps. Wilma told us about her experiences with bullying British soldiers."

Me: "And you wear a British uniform? I can understand that you feel like a traitor to our Boer people."

Henry: "I gladly joined the Royal Air Force because I love flying. I immediately knew that I wanted to fly when I was taken up into the air that first time. And now I've made a career of it. But, Ma, what must I do when war comes? I won't have a problem to fight the French or the Russians or the Arabs or the Turks. But what must I do if war breaks out between Britain and Germany? Please, you tell me!"

Me: "My dear son, Hendrik, may I tell you a big secret? It's meant only for your ears."

"I promise to keep it to myself."

"This mother of yours was a Boer spy during the Boer War, although I was in love with your father, who was a mere lieutenant in the British Army at that stage. He unwittingly gave me much valuable information, which I passed on to my father, who was a Boer scout who crept into Pretoria occasionally to find out what the enemy was doing. Your uncle David, who writes a letter every few months to my parents and who is presently an officer in the German

Army, was also a spy. He made friends with the British soldiers in Pretoria and heard many military secrets from them."

"Hell, Ma, what are you telling me? You never disclosed that to us."

"I just could not bring myself so far to tell your Pa. He always thought that I was a faithful and reliable supporter of the British Crown, although he shared my horror at the crimes and cruelties perpetrated by the British Army in South Africa."

"Ma, my legal studies included international law. That covers something about the law of war. There is no doubt in my mind that the British Army acted horribly wrong and illegally in our country. And now I am part of that same war machine! Hell!"

"Should war ever break out again with Germany, I will perhaps be able to help you to get over your frustrations."

I secretly decide that the time has not yet come to confide in my son regarding my exploits during the Great War. It also suddenly dawns upon me that the ancient Veleda hasn't visited me during my dreams for quite a long time. Perhaps she doesn't like the idea that I live in England now.

Greenwich, Friday, 8 June 1929

The de Hacqueville family members attend, yet again, a passing-out parade. This time, it is Daniel who becomes a commissioned officer with the rank of sublieutenant of the Royal Navy. Henry, the RAF officer, got special leave to be present.

The inspection of the parade and the salute is being taken by His Majesty, King George V in the uniform of an admiral of the fleet. The president of the Royal Naval College, Greenwich, Vice-Admiral John McClintock, delivers a speech, telling the audience of the distinguished history of this institution. The very grand and imposing buildings of the college are architectural gems.

Daniel attended this college for almost a whole year to qualify as an officer after he graduated a year ago at Cambridge.

The Royal Naval College, Greenwich

After the parade, while we are driving back home with Daniel who was granted some leave, Daniel tells us: "I must report for duty on the first of July at Portsmouth."

Me: "As a crew member of a ship or as a land-based member of the Navy?"

"Initially as a crew member of HMS Warspite, a grand battleship. I will help with navigation with my knowledge of geography. After six months, I will be assigned to the administration of the dockyard at Portsmouth with my knowledge of economics. But it is deemed necessary that I get a feeling of how life on board a big ship tastes before I help with the administration of the Navy. But later, I would like to return to the sea as a real mariner."

Hagdale, Friday, 15 June 1929

My training as a pilot proceeded rapidly and I qualified for a pilot's license a fortnight ago after completing the compulsory number of hours in the air. Daniel, the young naval officer on leave, wants to be taken up. He is somewhat jealous of his elder brother who has this glamorous job as a pilot, but he assured us that he wants to be part of the Navy. Since we visited Lourenco Marques before the Great War, he wanted to have a career connected to the sea.

After we have spent an hour in the air and I have taken Daniel out over the Channel east of Southampton and watched Portsmouth from the air, we touch Mother Earth again.

While we walk back home after the aircraft was stored in its shed, Daniel tells me in Afrikaans: "Ma, I feel like a traitor. Please tell me, how must I deal with this terrible condition?"

"You, a traitor? Tell me more, please."

"Yes, Ma. I'm an officer in His Majesty's Navy. I was trained at two of the most prestigious academic institutions in the world, the University of Cambridge, and the Royal Naval College. I'm the son of an English nobleman who can trace his ancestry to the eleventh century. But, at heart, I'm a Boer. I grew up in Pretoria and Afrikaans is my first language. My first loyalty lies with the Boer people. I really loathe these stiff Englishmen with their superior and haughty and arrogant attitude. They think they are God's favorite people and that all other nations are inferior – just as the ancient Romans felt towards all other nations in their time, whom they described as barbarians."

Me: "And now it is expected of you to be loyal towards King and Country?"

"Exactly. But my first loyalty lies with my Boer ancestors. These Brits committed the most horrible crimes and cruelties when they invaded our free republics three decades ago. I don't think we can ever forgive them, although Pa has admitted more than once that he feels ashamed about what the British soldiers did. And now I have joined them. I'm really a traitor, a despicable turn-coat. Just like the lousy Joiners you and Wilma told us about."

"Daniel, allow your mother to tell you a big secret. It's meant for your ears only. Promise me that you won't ever tell anybody?"

"I promise."

"All right. This mother of yours is married to an English nobleman, a lord. But I also have no time for these stuffy, snotty, stupid souls who call themselves Englishmen. Although I was in love with your father who was a British officer during the Boer War, I hoodwinked him by pretending to be a loyal subject of ole Queen Viccy. But, in reality, I was a Boer spy. Your father divulged more than one military secret to me, which I passed on to my father who was a Boer scout.

"My brother, your uncle David, from whom I sometimes get a letter which he sent to my parents and which they pass on to me, was also a spy at that time. As a little boy, he made friends with the English soldiers in Pretoria and heard quite a lot of secrets. He also did some sabotage, as young as he was. By the way, this uncle of yours is at present an officer in the German Army and married to a German woman. He has children of his own, your cousins, whom you probably won't ever meet. Your uncle seems to live under an assumed name in Germany because he is afraid that he will be caught as a traitor or a renegade after he joined the Germans during the Great War."

"Jeez, Ma! Should it ever happen that war breaks out between Britain and Germany, it may mean that I will have to fight against my German cousins! How on earth can I ever do that?"

"Let's hope and pray that such a war never breaks out again."

"And I have a father who is a colonel in the British Army! How can I ever turn against him?"

"Let's hope and pray that such a war never breaks out again."

I decide not to divulge anything about my work during the Great War. Perhaps later, when the time is ripe for that.

London, Monday, 15 September 1930

By this time, I am familiar with the streets and amenities and sights in London. It often happens that I take Hector on a Monday morning early in the Tiger Moth to London to be in time at his desk at the War Office. This morning, we landed again at Hendon airfield. I may use this RAF airfield because Hector as a colonel in the British Army, is entitled to make use of RAF facilities with prior notice. Hector immediately took a bus to the City, while I supervised the storage of the Tiger Moth in a shed and gave instructions to have her fueled and services for our return flight on Friday.

Thereafter, I took our luggage by bus to our rented apartment in the City, and started to walk the streets again. By this time, I have visited every old church, other ancient monuments, and all museums in this vast city. Today, the Library of the British Museum is my destination.

A friendly librarian helps me to fetch books about Veleda, the ancient German priestess and prophetess. I also find a translation of the fourth volume of Tacitus' Histories, in which he wrote about Veleda.

I learn that this remarkable woman was the daughter of a chieftain of the tribe of the Bucteri, who lived along the Lippe River, a branch of the Rhine, at the present German town of Lippstadt in Westphalia. This tribe was allied to the tribe of the Batavians, the ancestors of the Dutch. She was educated in Rome as a young girl where she learnt to speak Latin fluently. She became familiar with Roman military tactics and equipment.

I find that to be a parallel between the two of us, because I also speak English, the language of my enemies, as well as any Englishman. During the Boer war and the Great War, I learnt much about British military matters. I regard myself as a learned woman, although I haven't studied at any university. At Hagdale, I have devoured many books in the extensive library collected by Hector's father and grandfather. Here, in London, I have learnt much about history by visiting historical locations and museums. I even learnt something about astronomy by visiting the old observatory at Greenwich.

"The Conspiracy of the Batavians under Julius Civilis and Veleda" by Rembrandt (1661-1662)

Although Veleda was supposed to be a virgin, she had a fling with Gaius Julius Civilis, the Germanic military leader who was a Roman citizen with a Latin name. She had a daughter, whose name was not passed on to history. That is also something we share because I am married to a senior officer with an English name.

It transpires that Veleda was eventually captured by the Romans after the Batavians had destroyed a Roman legion at Xanten and the Romans retaliated. She was taken to Rome, where she was treated with great respect by Emperor Vespasian, who sought her advice on various matters because of her prophetic gifts. She died in Italy. I wonder whether I will ever get in a position to advise the British monarch or prime minister and whether I would eventually die in this foggy, wet, hostile country. In one of the books, I find an interesting illustration of Veleda standing on top of a cliff and directing the Germanic army with hand signals during a battle along the Rhine against the Roman legions. That reminds me of how I helped the German East African Army of Paul von Letow-Vorbeck with my signals.

I copy on a piece of paper the following excerpts from the English translation of the historian Tacitus' reports about this German priestess, prophetess, and folk heroine:

"Civilis, in accordance with a vow such as these barbarians frequently make, had dyed his hair red and let it grow long from the time he first took up arms against the Romans, but now that the massacre of the legions was finally accomplished, he cut it short (...). However, he did not bind himself or any Batavian by an oath of allegiance to Gaul, for he relied on the resources of the Germans, and he felt that, if it became necessary to dispute the empire with the Gauls, he would have the advantage of his reputation and his superior power. Munius Lupercus, commander of a legion, was sent, among other gifts, to Veleda. This maiden of the tribe of the Bructeri enjoyed extensive authority, according to the ancient German custom, which regards many women as endowed with prophetic powers and, as the superstition grows, attributes divinity to them. At this time Veleda's influence was at its height, since she had foretold the German success and the destruction of the legions. (...)

"The people of Cologne [decided]: 'We will have as arbiters Civilis and Veleda, before whom all our agreements shall be ratified.' With these proposals they first calmed the Tencteri and then sent a delegation to Civilis and Veleda with gifts which obtained from them everything that the people of Cologne desired; yet the embassy was not allowed to approach

Veleda herself and address her directly: they were kept from seeing her to inspire them with more respect. She herself lived in a high tower; one of her relatives, chosen for the purpose, carried to her the questions and brought back her answers, as if he were the messenger of a god."

While I walk back to our apartment to prepare supper, I get the conviction that this ancient woman would have agreed with my animosity against the beastly British Empire, the successor to the Roman Empire.

Woolwich, Friday, 12 June 1931

Victor, who is twenty-three years old, becomes an officer today and we attend the passing-out parade at the military academy at Woolwich, outside London.

While Victor was still studying physics and mathematics at Cambridge, he consulted his father about his future in the British Army. He decided against the Royal Air Force because he thought that aircraft were too vulnerable and prone to fatal accidents. He didn't like the Royal Navy because he was prone to sea-sickness. Only the Army remained.

Hector advised his youngest son to choose a career in either artillery or engineering in the Army with his scientific background: "For that, you must be admitted to the Royal Military Academy at Woolwich. That's where they train officers for the Royal Corps of Artillery and the Royal Corps of Engineers. Officers of the infantry and cavalry are trained at Sandhurst, where I got trained. I know the right people to secure you a place at Woolwich. The place has the nickname of 'The Shop' because it initially started in an old workshop where artillery pieces were manufactured."

When Victor arrived at the Academy, he decided not to specialize in artillery or engineering, but to be trained in signals, which was also a possibility. He wants to work with radios, telephones, and other signaling apparatus. I believe that was because I made him interested in Morse Code with my old heliograph at Faerie Glen.

And today, the whole family is attending the parade at Woolwich. Henry was promoted to flying officer, while Daniel is still a sublieutenant. We took our seats on the stands for the benefit of guests. I sit proudly next to a colonel, a flying officer, and a sublieutenant – very pleased to be the mother of the top student at the Military Academy who passed with honors. With his degree in mathematics, he was more than once tasked with teaching mathematics to the cadets who wanted to become artillery or engineering officers.

The Old Royal Military Academy, Woolwich

After the parade, which was inspected by His Royal Highness, the Prince of Wales, and where the governor, Major General Cyril Wagstaff, delivered a speech, Victor tells us about the Academy while we enjoy lunch at a restaurant in Woolwich.

"We are actually a famous lot. Do you know that the game of snooker was invented at this place, called The Shop?"

Henry: "We used to play that a lot at the Royal Air Force College. Never knew it came from this place."

Daniel: "I never played snooker, although many of my fellow-midshipmen loved it. They never knew that some land-lubbers invented it, otherwise they would have shunned it."

Victor: "Our radio room has the nickname of the 'Talking Shop'."

Hector: "Let's hope that you didn't talk too much nonsense there. By the way, Victor, I heard just yesterday that you have been given a position at the War Office. You will work with me in intelligence. We listen to German Reichswehr[33] radio stations. With your knowledge of German that you got from your German grandfather, you are an ideal snoop to help us."

Victor: "Thanks, Pa."

"You will have to work irregular hours, because radio traffic never stops. You must report for duty on the first of July."

---

[33] Reichswehr – the Défense Force of the German Reich or Empire at those times.

Hagdale, Monday, 21 September 1931

Victor helps me to push the Tiger Moth into her shed after we have landed. I took Hector very early this morning to London for a week's work and picked up Victor who has three days off. He will return to London on Wednesday night by train.

While we are sitting in the library and drinking tea, which was served by Mary, Victor starts talking in our usual Afrikaans with a worried expression on his face: "Ma, I'm in trouble. Big, big trouble. I hope you can help me."

"What trouble? Tell your mother everything."

"Ma, I joined the enemy, and I don't like the idea of being a traitor. But I really am a traitor. I commit treason every single day when I'm working at the War Office."

"How?"

"Ma, I'm a Boer, not an Englishman, although my Pa is an English lord. I grew up in Pretoria and that's an Afrikaans-speaking town. Most people there are Boers. While you were working at the Union Buildings before and during the Great War, I and my brothers were cared for by our Grandma Veronica. She's a proud descendent of the Boer families of Visser and Scholtz. She told us a lot about the Boer War and how our grandpa was a Boer warrior against the hated Englishmen who invaded our country to steal our gold mines.

"You and Wilma also told us about the British concentration camps where Boer women and children were maltreated and starved, without adequate medical care or other facilities. You told us how those terrible Tommys burnt down farm houses and the crops of the Boers with the goal of starving the Boer people.

"And now I am part of this blooming, bloody British battle machine and I must pry out the secrets of the German Reichswehr. I can't forget that my German Grandpa was thrown into a prison camp just because he was born in Germany. The Germans were always the friends of us Boers – and now I work for the enemy. I am betraying my own people."

"But you knew what you were doing when you joined the Army, not so?"

"Yes, I knew. But at that time, I didn't really know what my work would entail. And I wanted to please Pa. He sorely wanted to have a son who followed in his footsteps with a career in the Army. I wouldn't have minded to help our Army against the Russians, or the Chinese, or the Turks, or the Egyptians, or whatever. But I don't think I can fight the Germans. I eventually chose the Signal Corps because the signalers usually don't shoot guns and kill people. I can't see myself becoming a killer. What must I do, Ma? I feel terrible."

"Now, listen carefully to me, Victor. I'm going to tell you a big secret. Please keep it quiet. Please promise me."

"Yes, I promise."

"Well, this mother of yours was a spy during the Boer War. My mother allowed me to date your father, who was a British Army lieutenant, so that I could wriggle military secrets out of him. He never realized what I did. I passed those secrets on to my father, who was a Boer warrior and who visited us from time to time in Pretoria to watch what the British Army was doing. My younger brother, who is at present an officer in the German Reichswehr, was also a spy. He managed to make friends with some British soldiers and he picked up a lot of useful information. Your father doesn't know how I fooled him in those times, although I really fell in love with him. Funny, isn't it?"

"Ma, what are you telling me? Were you really a spy?"

"That's what I told you."

"And you tell me that your brother is a German officer?"

"That's what I told you."

"Ma, will it be wrong if I become a spy for the Germans? I work in the nerve center of the British Army and I may pick up some snippets of useful info. Will it be all right if I let the Germans know what I've found out?"

"Yes, but how are you going to pass those snippets on to the Germans, or whoever?"

"Yes, that's the big question. But I may provide the big brass at the War Office with skewed info about the Germans. Or I may just keep silent about important things I learn."

"That's up to you. I won't stop you, but I can't encourage you, either. But if you carry on in this way, you must be very, very careful. If you are caught, you may land into big trouble. Our whole family will be involved, in that case."

"Thanks, Ma. I know what I will do."

Hagdale, Wednesday, 23 September 1931

Veleda visited me again last night, after a long absence. Her message in ancient German was sweet and short – or short and sweet, if you like: "Alles geht gut."[34]

Of course, her words puzzled me after I woke up. What did she mean? Was she referring to my conversation with Victor the day before yesterday? Did she approve of my conversations with Henry or Hendrik and Daniel?

---

[34] "Everything goes well."

Hagdale, Friday, 12 September 1932

Hector arrived by train from London for the weekend. I stayed at home the past week to oversee the work done by the staff on the estate and to supervise the restoration the ancient chicken coop to its medieval glory. I also did some repairs on the Tiger Moth.

While Cheeky Carol is still preparing dinner in the kitchen, Hector takes me to our bedroom: "My glorious goddess, I've got important news, which mustn't be overheard by the staff."

I immediately retort: "Congratulations! Let me give you a kiss. You heard that you are being promoted. You're to become a brigadier one of these days."

"Hell! How do you know?"

"Sometimes, I just know things. You may perhaps call it female intuition."

"Well, you are right. I am to become a brigadier. But that's not all. They are appointing me as military attaché to The Hague, in Holland. That's because I understand and speak Dutch. We must start there on the first of November. That's in six weeks' time."

"You deserve another kiss. You deserve something like this."

"Thanks. My job will be intelligence gathering. I must keep an eye on Germany. My knowledge of German will come in handy. Of course, we also have an attaché in Berlin, as well as other agents who can gather intelligence. But I am supposed to contact Dutch sources, which may also keep tabs on the Germans. The War Office has also taken note of the fact that you can fly me around so that I don't have to make use of public transport. The result is that we can pop up at any spot without anybody knowing where we are going."

"Now, why is it so important to know what the Germans are doing?"

"Everybody expects a scoundrel with the name of Adolf

Hitler to become chancellor of Germany, some or other time. He's the leader of the National-Socialist Workers' Party of Germany or Nazi's for short. He wants to take revenge on the Allies for losing the Great War. He wants to enlarge German territory to create more living space for the Germans, at the expense of the Poles and the Russians. We must, yes *must* know what this gangster plans and schemes and executes and promises the Germans. That means that we will have to travel to Germany quite often."

"My father was born in Germany and I can speak German very well. I may act as your interpreter sometimes."

"I will have to take some advanced German lessons. And you will be my teacher."

"If you have to start your new job in November, then it will certainly be necessary to get lodgings there before the time, I believe."

"The Embassy will look after that. They will rent a furnished house. I also proposed to the War Office that we sell your Tiger Moth and buy something better. And bigger. Something that can cover the distance to The Hague easily enough."

"Then we should do that immediately. I will have to receive some conversion training on the new machine before we can use it."

"We will need it to visit London and Hagdale often enough. There won't be time to take the ferry and some trains every time to hop over. The War Office will subsidize our new plane and it will officially be on the inventory of the Royal Air Force, although you, as a civilian, will be empowered and authorized to be its pilot."

"You deserve another kiss. I hear the dining room bell. Let's go down for dinner and celebrate."

"Give me some time. I want to get into my formal mess dress. You get into something appropriate and hang some pearls and diamonds and other precious and shiny things on that beautiful body of yours. You must look divine. And afterwards I'm going to remove all your smart clothes and only leave the pearls and diamonds on your perfect physique."

"Please remember, I'm not the girl of fifteen for whom you fell during the Boer War. I have added a few years to my age."

"You're still my gorgeous goddess.

Hagdale, Friday, 17 September 1932

Hector arrives in a spectacular fashion from London this Friday afternoon. A brand-new twin-engine plane flies over our villa and lands on our meadow. I rush out to watch the spectacle. Hector and the pilot get out after the engines have been switched off.

Hector introduces me to the pilot: "My dear, this is Mister Mike May from the De Havilland Aircraft Company at Edgeware. He is to stay here a few days to help you to become familiar with this new beauty. And then he is to take our old Tiger Moth back to the person who bought her. Mike, this is my wife, Viscountess Theodora de Hacqueville."

I hold my hand and Mike kisses it in a gentlemanly fashion.

I admire the sleek lines of the beautiful biplane on our field.

"What type of machine is she?"

Hector wants to show off his knowledge: She is a de Havilland Dragon Rapide."

Mike adds: "Dragon Rapide DH89, to be more precise. This is a brand-new machine, one of the very first to be produced of this type."

"How is her performance? What can she do?"

"Top speed more than 150 miles per hour, but best cruising speed is about 130 miles per hour. Her ceiling is about 16 000 feet and she can reach more or less 550 miles without extra tanks. You can reach most places in Scotland with this range. Also, many destinations on the Continent. She can take eight passengers, apart from the pilot."

"When can I start with my conversion training?"

Hector: "My darling, that will only start tomorrow. Sorry. Mike will have to give you a lecture tonight about everything you need to know about her. He also must describe to you how the radio in the plane works. I can also help you with that."

"Mike, welcome to Hagdale. I didn't expect a guest, but it will be easy to accommodate you for a few days."

Hector: "This dainty Dragon is supposed to be part of the inventory of Number 24 Squadron at Hendon Aerodrome, north of London."

"Hector, since you arrived in this dazzling Dragon, I and Mike will have to take you back to London on Monday morning. That can be part of my conversion training. And then I can pop in at Hendon to meet the squadron commander."

Wassenaar, Monday, 31 October 1932

My Dragon Rapide glides down to a gentle landing at the Valkenburg airfield north of the Dutch village of Wassenaar, which lies just north of the Dutch capital city, Den Haag, in English known as The Hague. We are being met by an embassy official, who introduces himself as Captain Jonathan Johnson.

"Welcome to the Netherlands, Milord, and Milady. I'm your personal secretary and assistant. Please follow me to the staff car that has been put at your disposal. Let me help you with your luggage. The aerodrome staff will take care of your plane."

Me: "Sorry, but I must supervise what is happening with my plane. She's rather fragile because some parts are made of plywood."

Three helpers stroll along to take care of the Dragon Rapide. I tell them in Dutch to be careful and that I will watch them the whole time. It takes almost an hour before I am satisfied that my airplane is dealt with properly and stored in a covered shed.

The captain asks me: "Milady, and where did you learn to speak Dutch so fluently?"

"Oh, in church. I grew up in the Dutch Reformed Church."

"Oh. I still struggle with the language."

Hector: "Even I can speak Dutch. That's why I got this job."

"Oh."

Captain Johnson takes us to a hotel in Wassenaar where we must stay for the night since the rented home is only available from tomorrow, the first day of November. While we drive through the village, I decide Wassenaar must be a typical Dutch village with a huge windmill.

After we have booked into the hotel, I insist on inspecting our new home right away. The captain takes us and I find a woman who is cleaning the place very thoroughly.

She explains: "We Dutch are obsessed with cleanliness and neatness. I'm Missus Visser, Victoria Visser, the previous occupant's housekeeper. Pleased to meet you, Mevrouw[35]. I'm willing to stay on as your housekeeper, if you want me."

"Let's give it a try."

---

[35] "Mevrouw" – the English equivalent is "Missus" or "my lady".

Wassenaar, Tuesday, 1 November 1932

Hector is delivered to our home at five this afternoon. The staff car is driven by Staff Sergeant Samuel Smithers, Hector's orderly.

"And what did my marvelous matrimonial mate do today?" Hector asks.

"There was nothing for me to do here because Missus Visser takes care of everything. I went exploring and shopping because we need groceries and provisions. And how was your day?"

"Nothing special. I started off by reporting to the ambassador and then I was shown to my office. I have a staff of three. There is Captain Johnson, whom you met, as well as Staff Sergeant Smithers, who brought me home. He's supposed to be our chauffeur, but I think I prefer to drive the car myself as soon as I got used to drive on the other side of the road, as they do on the Continent. And then there is Mijnheer (Mister) Willem Woudstra, my office manager and interpreter. I don't think I will need him much."

Me: "And while you have an official staff car, I think we will also need our own automobile. How about that?"

"Let me think about it."

Wassenaar, Sunday, 7 November 1932

Hector sits next to me in the Reformed "Dorpskerk" or Village Church in Wassenaar. It is an ancient edifice, dating from the Middle Ages. It must have been a Catholic Church before the Reformation of the sixteenth century, when it became a Protestant congregation when the priest decided to cut his ties with the Romish Church and get married.

Everything is familiar to me: the readings from the Dutch Bible with which I grew up, Dutch Psalms and hymns, and a sermon in Dutch. During the last prayer, I tap in Morse Code on my husband's left leg:

I FEEL AT HOME HERE THANKS

He replies:

I ALSO LIKE IT HERE

After the service has ended, we go to the vestry to meet the minister of religion. His name is "Dominee" (Reverend) Hendrik de Haan. We inform him that we wish to join this church. He inquires about our names and address and promises to visit us during the coming week to get better acquainted. He tells us that there are two ministers of religion in this congregation and his colleague is Dominee Karel Kraan, whom he introduces to us.

As we stroll home, Hector quips: "That is a funny combination – Haan and Kraan. These names rhyme."

"You know that a 'Kraan' in Dutch is a water tap in English. In German, a water tap is called a 'Wasserhahn'. Another connection between their names."

"But 'Kraan' may also mean a 'crane' in English.

We laugh and feel carefree, glad, and happy to be able to see each other every day.

It suddenly dawns upon me that we are now living in Holland, the ancient home of the Batavians, the Germanic tribe that revolted against the Romans in the time of Veleda.

Wassenaar, Tuesday, 31 January 1933

By this time, I already almost forgot that we had visited Hagdale over Christmas. I must fly frequently to log enough hours in the air to keep my flying license and, therefore, we flew back home during the time when most staff members of the Embassy took off before Christmas. It was wonderful to have a family reunion on Old Year's Eve.

Henry appeared with a girlfriend, Sarah Staples, the daughter of Sir Sydney Staples MP. Daniel was accompanied by Roberta Rawlins, the daughter of Professor Ralph Rawlins who teaches geography at Cambridge. Victor came with Patricia Porter, the daughter of Doctor Peter Porter, a physician in London. They met these girls while studying at Cambridge and they kept on seeing them after joining the armed forces.

Hector also needed to see whether the butler or steward we appointed to manage the villa and the estate in our absence, Freddy Fortune, was coping with his duties. He is a retired Warrant Officer or Sergeant Major of the North Lancashire Regiment and somebody Hector trusts. Hector was quite satisfied with his supervision of all the activities at Hagdale.

We flew back on New Year's Day to enable Hector to resume duties on Monday, 2 January. And now, he is working at full steam again.

Hector comes home after work this Tuesday afternoon: "It happened as we feared. That guy Adolf Hitler was requested yesterday by 'Reichspräsident'[36] Paul von Hindenburg to form a new government. Germany went through unstable governments faster than some prostitutes go through clients. Hitler's party, the Nazis, didn't win an outright majority during the recent elections, but he managed to convince a like-minded party to join forces and

---

[36] President of the German Reich or Empire.

form a coalition with a majority in the 'Reichstag' or Parliament."

"How does this affect us?"

"Don't know. This Hitler guy promised heaven and earth to the Germans, including stopping the payment of reparations to Britain, Belgium, and France."

"What will you do now?"

"I already have an appointment with Colonel Stefanus Snijders of Dutch Military Intelligence. Perhaps he can tell me more about how the German Reichswehr will benefit from Hitler's rise to power."

"I'm sure, you will watch all these developments closely. Please remember, I'm half German, besides being a Boer girl. I'm interested in what is going on in Germany. Are we going to pay the country a visit, some or other time?"

"Certainly. Perhaps we may even visit your father's relatives over there."

Wassenaar, Monday, 27 February 1933

The radio news informs us of a dramatic event in Berlin. Firefighters are at this moment – nine o' clock at night – busy trying to douse the flames in the Reichstag, the German Parliament Building in Berlin.

Hector: "This is exactly four weeks after Hitler became chancellor or prime minister of Germany. Although he was elected during a democratic election, he's not particularly fond of democracy. He was thrown in prison a few years ago after staging a failed coup. He wanted to overthrow the government by force. He held his so-called victory speech in a beer hall in Munich before he was apprehended. I think he had too many beers before giving that speech."

"Will this fire mean that he will abolish the Parliament and stage another coup?"

"That's not necessary. He already holds enough power. But I think Germany is in for a rough time after this."

Wassenaar, Tuesday, 21 March 1933

We switch on our radio to hear the youngest news after having had our dinner. There is a recording of a speech by Hitler earlier the day at the opening ceremony of the new Parliament. Many Dutch people understand German and that's why Hitler's speech is repeated over the Dutch radio.

There were yet again new elections a fortnight ago on 6 March and the Nazis and their coalition partners, the DNVP, the Deutsche Nationale Volkspartei,[37] achieved a comfortable majority, although the Nazis only achieved 44% of the vote on their own.

Since the Reichstag building has burnt down, the opening ceremony was held in the Garrison Church in the town of Potsdam, west of Berlin.

During his speech, Hitler emphasized that his movement supports the military establishment of the country, together with the aristocracy, which still dominates the officers' corps of the armed forces.

Although Hitler could not prevent the communists from participating in the elections, despite having banned the party, his friend Hermann Göring, who is minister of the interior for the state of Prussia and who controls the Police in this state, ordered the arrest of all 81 Communist members of the Reichstag before the Reichstag constituted in Potsdam. These arrests were effected in accordance with the state of emergency, which was declared after the Reichstag fire. This step removed the most vociferous opposition to Hitler's party from Parliament and gave him a great majority.

Hector comments: "This move against the communists was not unexpected. Hitler voiced his animosity against supporters of

---

[37] German National Peoples' Party.

this political movement on many occasions."

Me: "I think most Germans will support that. Look at what happened in Russia after the communists have taken over the place. The people starve. People are thrown into prison merely for criticizing the government. I'm sure, most Germans don't want their country to go down the drain like that."

"Perhaps, you have a valid point, my dear. It is anyway clear that he wants to strengthen the German military establishment. We have information that some German pilots are already being trained in Russia. Russia was, after all, not part of the Versailles Treaty and, therefore, nothing prohibits the German pilots of being trained there. We expect the Reichswehr to acquire warplanes in the not-too-distant future, something forbidden by the Versailles Treaty, which Hitler wants to tear up. "

Wassenaar, Thursday, 23 March 1933

We hear over the radio tonight that Hitler has, in effect, achieved full and total power over Germany. He convinced the Reichstag that assembled in the Kroll Opera House to adopt a law, called the "Gesetz zur Behebung der Not von Volk und Reich".[38] This law gives him the power to issue decrees with the force of law, without consulting the Reichstag. The act was adopted by a vote of 441 for and 84 against.

I tell Hector: "That makes him a dictator, just as Mussolini in Italy and Stalin in Russia."

Hector: "He sees himself as a reincarnation of Charlemagne, Frederick Barbarossa, and Frederick the Great. He's an upstart. During the Great War, he only achieved the rank of lance corporal. He is a very common commoner and his father was merely a low public servant. He never had any academic training and he is a frustrated artist who couldn't sell any of his paintings."

"What I've heard of him, tells me he's a master orator. Very eloquent. He manages to tell people exactly what they want to hear and convince them that he's the answer to their prayers. A real demagogue. Perhaps, he may pull Germany out of the mud and the muck. Unfortunately, he hates the Jews and he blames them for all the ills in Germany and the rest of the world. That's something I don't like, for obvious reasons."

---

[38] Act to Remove the Distress of the People and the Reich.

Wassenaar, Wednesday, 10 May 1933

Hector tells me when he arrives home: "I must go to Paris in France the day after tomorrow. Secret stuff. Can you take me in your dazzling Dragon?"

"Certainly. I need those flying hours."

After supper, we listen to the radio news. We hear that some members of the SA, the "Sturmabteilung"[39] of the Nazi party, dressed in brown shirts with swastika arm bands, plundered the library of the Berlin University. They threw all books written by Jews onto a big bonfire and nobody had the courage to stop these hooligans.

I sigh: "When will they start burning Bibles? All the biblical books were written by Jews."

Hector: "Have they forgotten that Jesus and his disciples were all Jews?"

---

[39] Storm Division or storm troopers.

Paris, Sunday, 14 May 1933

Hector had talks with his German contacts yesterday afternoon. They had to meet somewhere outside Germany. Hector was wary to meet them in The Hague because there was the possibility that they would be watched by German agents. Paris was seen as a safe meeting spot.

Afterwards, Hector confided in me: "These German officers are very worried about events in Germany. They are glad that Hitler may expand the armed forces, but they don't like the way the SA and the Nazi party are behaving. Just in case, they were being followed, we agreed to meet again in Toulouse on Monday morning. Can you fly me there?"

"Yip. But what are we going to do till then?"

"We enjoy Paris."

And that's exactly what we are doing today. We plan to visits the Louvre, one of the most famous art museums in the world. We may visit other old palaces and churches and museums.

Hector: "Let's go for a walk through one of the most famous parks in the whole of France this morning before doing anything else – the Jardin du Luxembourg, which you can see from our hotel room's window. It's the garden in front of the Palais du Luxembourg, where the French Senate convenes. This palace was built by the widow of King Henry IV, but was taken over by the French Republic after the French Revolution. And then we can go for lunch in a French bistro somewhere."

The garden seems to be a popular open space in the city and many people enjoy the pleasant Spring weather under the trees. There are numerous statues and monuments. I want to learn something about French art and culture and I insist that we inspect each and every statue and monument.

We stop at a statue of a girl in a skimpy dress.

Hector: "This woman reminds me of you."

Me: "Impossible. I don't walk around with my bosom exposed like this girl."

"She, nevertheless, has something about her that makes me think of you. Let's see what the inscription says. Ah, it's a statue by a certain Etienne Hippolyte Maindron, done in 1844."

"What's it called? Who is this shameless woman?"

Hector bends over to see better: "Her name is…, let me see, …, it looks like … hmm, … Veleda! She was a pagan priestess or something. I suppose that's how pagan priestesses got dressed in the days before Christianity came to Europe."

Toulouse, Monday, 15 May1933

Hector continued his talks with his German contacts this morning. During lunch he tells me: "These chaps are glad that I understand some German, because their English is not what it should be. They eagerly want the British government to voice its protest about Hitler's plans to tear up the Versailles Treaty. They are afraid that he wants to restart the Great War in a few years' time."

Me: "Can the British government do anything, apart from making lots of noise?"

"No, unfortunately not. I had to disappoint these two chaps."

"I am sure that nothing is going to stop this Hitler guy. He managed to grasp full and absolute control of the country. Most Germans will initially support him wholeheartedly, but the time will come when they will want to curse him and erase his memory – just as the Romans wanted to forget that tyrant Nero."

"You seem to be a prophetess, or something, I'm sure."

"What are we doing the rest of the time here? We have our hotel room till tomorrow morning and we only fly back to Holland tomorrow. I like the fact that the British government is giving us these outings with all expenses paid because it's your job to spy on Germany. We must remember to keep the receipts of the fuel we tank before we take off again tomorrow and claim that money back."

"Let's go and look at that museum you see over there. I heard it's called the Musée des Augustins. That's because it's housed in an old convent that belonged to the Augustinian friars, but they were thrown out during the French Revolution when the official religion of France became the veneration of the Goddess of Reason."

"Let's do it."

We walk around in this impressive medieval building complex and watch all the paintings and statues by French artists from the past seven centuries.

Just before we ascend the staircase to the second floor, Hector looks at the statue of a reclining woman.

"This is the same woman we saw in Paris yesterday! Come and have a look!"

I am almost too afraid to have a good look because I don't want to have another shock as I had yesterday. Yet, this woman does look like the one we saw in Paris, although both her boobs are exposed, instead of only one of them.

Hector reads the inscription: "The sculptor was a guy with the name of Laurent Marqueste. It is his rendition of that pagan priestess or prophetess, Veleda. Funny name, that. Never heard of anybody called that in my life. Do you know anybody with the name of Veleda? Isn't it remarkable that we see two statues of this heathen beauty within two days?"

After staring at the statue a few seconds, he adds: "She sees something that other people can't see. She's in deep thought and looks into the future. She must have seen many good things, but also bad things. She looks sad while she's staring at her feet, without really seeing them."

I get the feeling that Veleda will visit me again during the night, very soon. It cannot be a coincidence that I saw her statues in France on two consecutive days.

Hagdale, Friday, 1 September 1933

It can be doubted whether any previous inhabitants of Hagdale ever celebrated eight events at the same time. We are celebrating the following joyous occasions tonight:

- Henry is celebrating his birthday and he is 29 years old.
- Daniel is celebrating his birthday and he is 28 years old.
- Henry is getting engaged to Sarah Staples.
- Daniel is getting engaged to Roberta Rawlins.
- Victor is getting engaged to Patricia Porter.
- Henry was recently promoted to the rank of flight lieutenant.
- Daniel was recently promoted to the rank of lieutenant (RN).
- Victor was recently informed that he was to be promoted to captain from the beginning of next year.

It took lots of planning and preparations to get to this point. The three boys often spent weekends at Hagdale during our absence and they agreed to coordinate their engagements with the birthdays of the eldest two. Hector instructed Freddy Fortune to get the villa ready for guests and order Cheeky Carol to prepare a dinner.

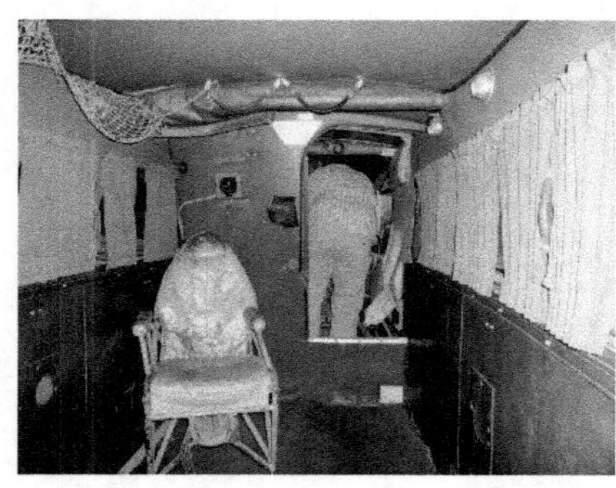

I had to receive permission from the commander of 24 Squadron, of which my Dragon Rapide is a part, to transport civilians. We took off from Valkenburg early this morning and landed at Hendon. Hector took a bus to the city to report at the War Office, while I supervised the service and cleaning of my trusted airplane.

At four the following eight passengers arrived: Brigadier Viscount Hector de Hacqueville, the Honorable Lieutenant Victor de Hacqueville (the only two military passengers), Sir Sydney Staples MP, Lady Susan Staples, Miss Sarah Staples, Doctor Peter Porter, Missus Pamela Porter, and Miss Patricia Porter. That meant the dependable Dragon was filled to capacity.

Professor Ralph Rawlins and his wife, Missus Rosalie Rawlins, together with their daughter, Miss Roberta Rawlins, arrived already yesterday by train and they were fetched from Winchester by Freddy Fortune in our motor car. Three siblings of the brides-to-be came with another train this morning and Fortune had to pick them up, as well. Daniel travelled on his own from Portsmouth and Henry flew in from his air base to our landing field on the estate in a trainer.

The dinner is, of course, a very formal affair and the four de Hacqueville males were dressed in their uniforms. Freddy Fortune was also ordered to supervise the proceedings in his old military uniform and imagine himself as still being a sergeant major.

Each of the four fathers were given an opportunity to deliver a short speech and call for toasts on each of their offspring.

We made sure that each person got only one glass of white wine and one glass of red wine. That meant that the festivities proceeded in a dignified and civilized manner.

I gathered from Hector's behavior that he approved of his prospective in-laws and I share his positive opinions of the future female additions to our family, as well as their families of origin.

While looking at all the people sitting along our long dining room table, I remember that Veleda spoke to me a few nights ago (in ancient German, of course): "There are certainly some decent Englishmen, just as there were decent Romans, while there were and are also horrible Germans."

It struck me how much she resembled her statues in France and my own face, when I look into the mirror.

Sleeping arrangements posed some minor problems. Each of the married couples were assigned to a separate bedroom, while all the young men and all the unmarried girls were bunched together in the same rooms. After all, Hagdale is not a palace, only a villa.

It is agreed that the weddings of all three couples take place in four months' time, also here at Hagdale.

Hagdale, Tuesday, 26 December 1933

A huge crowd descended upon Hagdale on Boxing Day. Fortunately, the parents of the three brides were mostly responsible for the huge amounts of food and drink that had to be consumed, the musicians, the flowers, the huge tent in which the wedding lunch was to be served, the rent of huge amounts of crockery, and the wages for a dozen waiters and waitresses to serve the guests.

Cheeky Carol was unwilling to share her kitchen with four chefs, but when I promised her a big bonus, she calmed down.

It is never easy to keep such a crowd together and satisfied. Fortunately, nobody expected us to accommodate the whole bunch of guests. We provided, though, transport in two busses to fetch the guests from and to the station in Winchester who did not come in their own automobiles. They were taken directly to the All-Saints Church in Hursley where Father Richard Smurph officiated. Thereafter, all were carried to the wedding venue in the garden of Hagdale and returned to the station in Winchester to catch the last train to London.

We provided the horses that pulled the three rented carriages in which the bridal pairs were moved from the church to Hagdale. Fortunately, there was no rain, although it was cold enough.

All five members of the de Hacqueville family arrived already last week to help with all the preparations. The wedding was, of course, a military affair with the three bridegrooms and their father in full uniform. Freddy Fortune – also in uniform – worked with a check-list to make sure that nothing was forgotten. Each bridegroom had four fellow-officers in the uniforms of the three armed services to form a guard of honor at the church and at the lunch.

Afterwards, Hector sighs: "If it wasn't for Freddy, we wouldn't have been able to handle this crowd."

Me: "I am grateful that the boys decided on a single day for their weddings. I wouldn't have been able to endure three separate weddings on different days."

"Fortunately, I have a whole week of silence and rest ahead of me before I must report back for duty at the Embassy on the second."

"I have a serious question, a rather big headache."

"Yes?"

"Did you notice that Father Richard got mixed up with the names of two of the brides? Are they really legally and legitimally married to our sons?"

"I wouldn't worry too much about that. As long as their names are entered correctly into the marriage register and all of them have received accurate marriage certificates, then things ought to work our as they should."

"It could have been a monstruous mix-up if the wrong bride was married to the wrong bridegroom."

"I think each one of them knows by this time who belongs to whom. The three bridegrooms were dressed very differently with uniforms of the RAF, Navy, and Army and nobody would confuse them – at least not the brides."

Bremen, Friday 25 May 1934

Hector announced last week: "It is necessary the I visit Bremen next week. Can you fly us there?"

"Of course. I love flying. You know that. What are you going to do there?"

"Two things. I must go and inspect the base of the Reichsmarine at Wilhelmshaven, just north of Bremen, and I want to go and meet retired General Paul von Letow-Vorbeck. I helped to fight this old guy when I served in East Africa. I would like to hear his stories, but he can also tell me a lot about Hitler's plans for the Reichswehr."

I couldn't help to smile broadly, while I remembered how I had helped this German general during the Great War with valuable information. Instead of voicing my pleasure of getting an opportunity to meet this old warrior, I rather said: "I would like to go to Germany. Then we can practice our German. Remember, German is my second home language."

"It would have been better if the British military attaché in Berlin could have done this job, but he is under constant surveillance by the German security people and he can't go anywhere without betraying his intentions. So, it will be my task to go. The German authorities don't know where that dauntless Dragon of yours will fly and they can't attach a tail to me to watch my every move."

Yesterday, we strolled around in the naval base of Wilhelmhaven. There wasn't much to see, except for a lone light cruiser and a few patrol boats. Hector managed to take some photos.

The most important part of our visit to Germany from my point of view, happens today. We ring the front door bell of the von Letow-Vorbeck home after having made this appointment already a week ago. The general opens the door and invites us to come inside.

After we have been given coffee and "Keks" or cookies by his wife, the old general says: "So, you were one of those South Africans who chased me all over East Africa!"

"I was one of those, indeed, Herr General."

"Have you ever met Jannie Smuts, who tried to catch me?"

"I have seen him a few times."

I quip in: "I used to work in the Union Buildings, where General Smuts had an office. I often talked to him when I had to deliver messages to him. That was when I was head of the telegraph office in that building."

"Ah, gnädige Frau,[40] dear Viscountess, so you bumped into him more than once. I only had the privilege of meeting him face to face eight years ago in London. We even became friends, although we were bitter enemies during the war."

After swapping yarns about the war, Hector and the general discuss the present situation in Germany. The general makes it clear that he's no supporter of Hitler, although he is a proud German patriot. He was received as a hero when he returned to Germany after the armistice in 1918 – especially because he was the only German general never to have lost a battle. He hopes that Hitler will listen to some sensible advice and forget about his hate for the Jews. His followers in the SA are mostly men without any breeding or education, low-class riff-raff.

Hector asks permission to inspect all the pictures against the walls of the living room, depicting the general's wartime exploits, and he gets up to wander around. I utilize the opportunity to put my index finger to my mouth to sign to the old general to stay silent. I hand him a little note that I have taken from my purse. It simply says: "Ich war die Veleda von 1914 bis 1918."[41]

---

[40] Esteemed Missus.
[41] "I was the Veleda of 1914 to 1918."

The general's eyes open widely and he smiles, but stays silent. It's clear, he got the message and understands that Hector is unaware of my role as Veleda.

The general asks me: "Gnädige Frau, dear Viscountess, where did you learn to speak German so well?"

"My father is a German. He was born in Kleve, on the border between Germany and Holland."

"Ah, I think I could detect the accent of those parts. It's Platt-Deutsch."[42]

When we announce that we must leave, the general accompanies us to the front door. He kisses my hand and tells Hector: "I think you have a remarkable wife. I am grateful to have made her acquaintance, as well as yours."

Hector asks the general a last favor: "May I take your photograph, please? In your uniform."

"Gerne.[43] Give me some time to get dressed in my old uniform."

He wears the *Pour le Merite* with Oak Leaves decoration awarded to him in 1917, but which he collected only after the war.

---

[42] Literally "Flat German". The German dialect that is related to Dutch and is spoken in the flat northern parts of Germany.
[43] "Gladly".

Kleve, Saturday 26 May 1934

We arrived late yesterday in the German town Kleve, where my father was born, to visit his family. We had no idea where to find them, and we found accommodation in a small hotel. This morning, we start exploring the town and a walk along the main street soon brought us to the tailor shop of Samuel and Saul Davidsohn.

The front door is locked. We ring the bell, but there is no reaction. After a few minutes, Hector exclaims: "We won't find them here. It's their Sabbath. They must be at the local synagogue."

Me: "Of course! How stupid of me. I haven't visited a synagogue in years and I almost forgot that I am a Jew – apart from being a Boer and a German."

I ask a passer-by where the local synagogue is and he directs us to the place. A notice outside says that Sabbath services start at nine. It is now a quarter-past-nine, so the service must have started only a few minutes ago.

Me: "My husband, you will only be allowed inside if you have a hat or something on your head."

"Will a handkerchief do?"

"Perhaps. Let's see."

We enter the building and find seats at the back. I look through the congregation and I notice two men with their families who could be my family. They are accompanied by their wives and five daughters between them. Of course, I can't interrupt the service and I follow the voice of the rabbi who chants Hebrew Psalms and reads from the Torah. I tap on Hectors leg:

I FEEL AT HOME HERE

Hector responds:

NICE

After almost two hours, the service ends. We exit the building and wait outside to meet my family. After a few minutes, the group of Davidsohns appear.

I can't help myself, and grab the arm of one of the men: "Excuse me, are you Samuel or Saul?"

The man looks surprised, but answers: "Samuel. And who are you, dear lady?"

I smile broadly: "Theodora Davidsohn."

"By the whiskers of all the prophets! Are you the daughter of Daniel, my brother?"

"That's me. Please meet my husband, Hector."

Samuel immediately calls his family together and tell them the good news that his niece, Theodora, has suddenly turned up. We meet Saul and the rest of the family.

Samuel: "Of course, you are coming to have lunch with us. It won't be much because we can't prepare meals on the Sabbath, but we will share everything with you."

We visit the Davidsohns the whole day. There is much news to catch up on. Both Samuel and Saul are afraid of the future because Hitler is the boss in Germany now and he hates Jews.

Saul: "We struggle to make a living. The Germans who bought our clothes in the past, are shunning us now. They seem too afraid to be associated with filthy Jews, like us."

Hector: "Have you ever thought of moving away?"

"The only place where we want to move to is Palestine. That's the country that God gave to Abraham and all his children. But our family has lived here in Kleve the last three centuries and this is where some of our ancestors are buried. We have an established business here and we can't just run away. We trust that the God of Abraham, Isaac, and Jacob will protect us."

I notice that Hector doesn't tell these Jews that he's an English titled nobleman and they spontaneously call him Hector. He explains that he is a farmer in England, but that he and his wife are visiting Europe because she wanted to trace her roots.

Hector: "Your Sabbath ends as soon as it gets dark and the stars appear. It will be all right for all of you to join us tonight for dinner at our hotel. We will warn the manager to expect nine more guests."

Kleve, Sunday 27 May 1934

Hector proposes that we go to church today. There is a Lutheran church in town and we sit in the pews when the service starts. This is the first time that I attend a German church. The hymns are unfamiliar and the liturgy is strange.

Nevertheless, I tap on Hectors left leg during the las prayer:

I FEEL AT HOME HERE

Hector responds:

NICE

The pastor announces during the service that he will be absent during the coming week, since he will be attending an extraordinary synod in Wuppertal-Barmen where the stance of Protestant Germans regarding the Nazi ideology will be discussed.

After the end of the service, we wait outside the vestry to meet the pastor, Herr Doktor Bernd Balzer. We ask him about this synod and he explains that it will not be an official synod – only a meeting of like-minded Christians who are worried about the direction the Nazi party is taking Germany.

After we have greeted the pastor, Hector proposes: "Let's go and have a look at what is happening at this synod. I suppose it will be open to the public. I will have to write a report for the War Office about the German opposition to Hitler's regime. But first of all, we must have lunch with your family this afternoon."

Xanten, Monday 28 May 1934

We get off the bus that brought us from Kleve to the old Roman town of Xanten, known to the ancient Romans as Colonia Ulpia Traiana. It was a short trip of somewhat more than thirty minutes.

When we had lunch yesterday with the Davidsohn family, I told them that my father mentioned to me that Xanten was an old Roman settlement in the vicinity of Kleve and that he hoped that I would be able to visit the site.

Saul said: "It will certainly be worthwhile to visit. There is an open-air museum where much of the ancient Roman buildings and ruins are still to be seen."

Samuel added: "You can reach it easily by bus."

And here we are. The entrance to the archaeological park is to the south-east of the partly restored wall of the ancient settlement. We buy a brochure about the history of the place at the entrance and start to wander through all the old Roman relics.

According to the guide brochure, this fortress was the home of the Eighteenth Roman Legion and the Germanic tribe of the Bucteri conquered the place in March AD 70. The Germans decimated the Roman legion. The ancient German priestess and prophetess, Veleda, made herself at home in one of the towers along the wall.

We walk around until we find Veleda's tower. It is lovingly restored and looks almost new. Without asking Hector's approval, I simply go inside and ascend the stairs. There is a window in the top story and I take in position at this window, overlooking the nearby Rhine.

I take Hector's hand and pull him nearer: "Please hold me. I want to admire the view."

Hector does as told and starts talking: "What is…?"

I gently put my index finger on his mouth and stop his words. He gets the idea that I need some silence to enjoy the moment and he holds me tightly. I place my head against his shoulder, while I continue to stare at the Rhine. I can see some boats moving up and down the river and I wonder how the Roman boats looked at the time of Veleda. I can imagine Veleda and the German general, Julius Civilis, meeting in this space.

There are buildings on the other side of the Rhine but I imagine how the scene must have looked many centuries ago when Veleda was living here. There must have been large forests over there.

After I have spent half-an-hour drinking in the atmosphere and trying to imagine how Veleda must have lived here, I loosen myself from Hector's grip and we go down the stairs.

When we are outside, Hectors starts talking again: "They say here (and he points at the brochure) that this was the tower of that ancient priestess Veleda. That's the woman whose statues we saw in France! Fancy finding her hide-out!"

I merely smile, satisfied that I have found something of the ancient Veleda. This moment is far too precious that I can spoil it by talking. Of course, I can never tell Hector that I became almost a reincarnation of this prophetess during the Great War and that she often speaks to me at night. I expect her reappearance very soon. I remember that she told me long ago that I would get the opportunity of finding her tower – and today I did exactly that.

I wonder silently how she will guide me in the time to come. Will I be able to hurt the diabolical British Empire, just as she was able to inflict some damage on the devilish Roman Empire?

Wuppertal, Friday, 31 May 1934

It was a short hop from Kleve to the industrial city of Wuppertal, east of Cologne. We arrived on Tuesday after having spent three days with my Jewish family in Kleve and visiting Xanten.

We were told by Herr Pastor Doktor Bernd Balzer that the synod was to be hosted by the Reformed congregation of Barmen-Gemarke in the northern parts of Wuppertal. The synod is scheduled to start tomorrow and end on Friday. That gives us some time to explore the city.

Hector: "I suppose they are meeting in this out-of-the-way place, and not in Berlin, to avoid the attention of the nasty Nazis. They don't want the SA hooligans to disrupt the meeting."

Me: "I must agree with you."

The "Schwebebahn" in Wuppertal

Wuppertal is famous for its suspension railroad, the "Schwebebahn", that was erected at the beginning of this century and was inaugurated by Kaiser Wilhelm II. Of course, we treated ourselves with a ride along the whole route between Oberbarmen in the north and Vohwinkel in the south, and back. The train follows mostly the Wupper, the river that gave the city its name, although it also follows some streets in the south.

The Evangelical Reformed Church
Barmen-Gemarke

I couldn't help it, and I had to boast: "You must agree that the Germans are the best engineers in the world. You won't find something like this anywhere else in the world – not in Great Britian, not in America, or anywhere else."

Hector: "That makes me afraid. If they can build something like this, they can also build better armaments – airplanes, battleships, artillery. We must be wary of their clever engineers."

We listened to the speeches at the synod since Wednesday and, today, Friday, a document is approved. It is called the Barmen Declaration and one of the authors is the famous German theologian, Professor Karl Barth.

The congregations represented at this synod call themselves

the "Bekennende Kirche".[44] The declaration makes it clear that a Christian's' first loyalty lies with Jesus Christ and not with any group or political ideology. The aim of the Nazi party to prescribe to Christians what they ought to believe is rejected.

Hector: "It is good to take note of the Christian opposition to Hitler's mad policies. Who will win the day? The Nazis or the faithful Christians? I must certainly write a report to the War Office about my impressions of this movement."

---

[44] Witnessing Church.

Wassenaar, Tuesday, 21 August 1934

Germany was brought to a standstill on the day before yesterday, a Sunday. Hitler called for a referendum after the death of Reichspräsident Paul von Hindenburg.

He wanted the approval of the German nation for assuming the combined title of "Führer und Reichskanzler"[45] since the German constitution doesn't make provision for such a state of affairs. Everybody expected an overwhelming vote of support for Hitler and last night the radio announced the result. More of less 88% of the votes went in the Führer's favor.

Hitler followed the example of Bennito Mussolini in Italy who assumed the title of "Il Duce".

Hector: "Yes, my dearest darling, you were correct. Most Germans support this tyrant because he promised them everything they wished for."

Me: "And he gave them back their human dignity and self-respect after the disastrous defeat of 1918. But the day will come when they will curse and anathemize and excommunicate and damn him and his memory."

I can say this with confidence because Veleda told me last night (in ancient German) "All dictators and despots come to an inglorious and ignominious end."

She ought to know, because she was able to charm Emperor Vespasian in Rome, but also saw how he died a stinking and sordid death due to severe diarrhea.

---

[45] Leader and Chancelor of the Reich.

Wassenaar, Friday, 30 August 1935

Hector comes home after work and asks me: "How do you feel about a walk on the beach? There are things I must discuss with you"

That is something we have often done in the past. Wassenaar is a coastal village and it boasts a beach front with some dunes covered by grass and shrubs.

The sun is still shing and we set off to the beach.

"You know that I become fifty-five in three weeks' time. That is usually the age when officers, especially senior officers, are supposed to retire. It seldom happens that they stay on any longer."

"Does that mean that we go and live at Hagdale again? May it also happen that we sometimes go back to the farm in Pretoria?"

"Perhaps. I can't say. That's what I wanted to discuss with you here in the open air. The War Office has made me an offer, which I may accept, or reject. They want me to stay on here in The Hague, even if I reach retirement age."

"But why?"

"They can't find anybody to replace me. They regard me as irreplaceable. One doesn't easily find senior British officers who can speak Dutch and German. I speak both. One doesn't easily find senior officers who have access to their own air transport. I have that. One doesn't readily find a senior officer who is a titled nobleman and who is very acceptable in diplomatic circles. I fit in with that."

"Are they satisfied with your work?"

"More than satisfied. Really delighted. How do you feel? Do you want to stay on, here in Holland, or do you want to return to Hagdale – or even to Pretoria at times."

"That's a difficult question. Really difficult. Of course, I will grab the opportunity to return to Pretoria with both hands, but I realize it won't be so easy. You have tenants who are renting the farm and it won't be so easy to throw them out. I have grown to love Hagdale. Yes, it's a difficult choice. But, how do you feel?"

"If you agree, I will like to carry on here. But only if you agree. It's an opportunity to do something worthwhile for my country. I am certainly aiding our intelligence efforts against Germany. But I don't want to keep you here against your will."

"Let's stay. If it's important for you to keep your job past retirement age, then we go for it. You are still far too young to become a pensioner. I feel up to it."

"Thanks. Then I will let the War Office know on Monday that I accept their offer to stay on here."

Kleve, Tuesday, 20 March 1936

Germans all over the country are celebrating. Hitler has removed another humiliating restriction placed on their country by the victorious Allies of the Great War by sending a few units of the Army into the Rhineland – in violation of the Versailles Treaty that ended the Great War.

The Allies had stipulated that no German soldier may tread on soil of the most western parts of the country adjoining France, Luxemburg, Belgium, and southern Holland to make the people of these countries feel more secure from possible attacks by the "Huns" or the "Boches", as the German soldiers were popularly called.

Hector got wind of this development and we flew again to Kleve in the Rhineland in time to witness this military exercise. Together with thousands of enthusiastic Germans, we stand next to the route along which the soldiers are marching, accompanied by a brass band. Our Davidsohn family members joined us.

Hector grabs my right arm to get my attention and he points to the officer at the head of a battalion: "Look, that's your brother!"

I agree with him and I start shouting: "David! David!"

Of course, it doesn't help. David keeps on marching ahead of his battalion. There is too much noise with the marching music of the brass band and the cheers of the crowd and it is impossible for him to hear my calls.

Apart from moving military units into the Rhineland, Hitler has reorganized the German armed forces. The Reichswehr was renamed the "Wehrmacht"[46] since last year and its size has increased considerably. There is a new branch of the armed forces, the "Luftwaffe" or Air Weapon. Hitler appointed his old friend, Hermann Göring, an air ace of the Great War, as chief of this service.

There was nothing the former Allies could do about these developments.

And, now, my own brother is part of this expansion of German military might. Where does it leave me? On the one hand, I don't feel comfortable with Hitler at the helm of the country. But, on the other hand, I secretly approve of the way he is running the country. He has given the Germans their self-respect back and under his guidance unemployment dropped dramatically. We see smiling faces all over Kleve as we walk around after the end of the parade. Our Jewish relatives don't smile.

---

[46] Defense Force.

Berlin, Saturday, 1 August 1936

Berlin is in a festive mood today. Today was declared a public holiday and I and Hector are sitting in the brand-new gigantic Olympic Stadium in Berlin where the Führer is to open the Summer Olympic Games. We are here to support the British and the South African teams, but also to gauge the mood of the German people.

The city of Berlin is decorated with hundreds of red swastika flags. This is an occasion where Germany can boast about her achievements for all the world to see. I secretly feel proud to be a half-German.

Hector had a meeting with his counterparts from various European countries at the British embassy yesterday. All of them travelled to Berlin to watch the Games and find out more about the Wehrmacht. Hector told me: "There is general agreement that Hitler is hell-bent on preparing for another war.

Hitler at his seat of honor at the Summer Olympics of 1936

We have a good view of the whole stadium where we sit. Suddenly, I hear Afrikaans spoken behind us. I turn around to listen better. I hear and see how two brothers, obviously twins, are discussing the program with each other. They are accompanied by two girls.

I stand up to have a better look at them and I ask: "En wat maak julle kêrels hier?"[47]

They look surprised, but they answer simultaneously: "We came to watch the Olympic Games, of course. The same as you."

"And who are you?"

They explain that they are Willie and David Scholtz who are studying in Berlin – medicine and physics. They are accompanied by their German girlfriends. They hail from the Free State and previously studied at the University of Stellenbosch. I introduce myself as a native of Pretoria, but somebody who is married to a 'Rooinek'.

Hector adds (in Afrikaans): "And I am that 'Rooinek'. Pleased to meet you guys. I caught this wonderful woman during the Boer War in Pretoria and now we live in Hampshire."

Me: "My late grandmother's maiden name was Scholtz and she also came from the Free State. Her name was Engela Visser, born Scholtz."

Willie: "Our father had an aunt with that name. That means that we may be related, somehow."

We agree to have dinner together at a restaurant in Berlin's main street, Unter den Linden.

The opening ceremony starts with a parade of all the athletes taking part. There is also a ceremony to light the Olympic Flame and speeches by the chairman of the German Olympic Committee and Hitler. The Führer's speech receives loud applause.

---

[47] "And what are you guys doing here?"

After the Olympic flame has been lighted, Hitler leaves his seat of honor and walks over to the German team on the field to wish them luck. He is photographed where he poses next to a few German girls. The crowd evidently likes this and Hitler receives some more rapturous applause.

Hector: "These Germans seem to like their dictator."

Me: "Only while there is still peace. When another war breaks out, they will despise him in the end."

"You seem to be a prophetess, just like that woman whose statue we saw in France and whose tower we visited two years ago."

All eyes are suddenly raised towards the heavens as a big flying gas bag, a Zeppelin, the Hindenburg, glides over the stadium, towing the Olympic flag, containing a picture of a huge bell with the inscription "Ich rufe die Jugend der Welt".[48] On the bell is a drawing of the German eagle on top of the five Olympic circles.

As Hitler and his entourage are leaving the stadium, a few dozen baskets containing hundreds or even thousands of pigeons are opened and the birds take to the air. To mark the official end of the opening ceremony, an artillery piece of the Army is fired. That scares the poop out the flying birds and I don't think that is something the organizers envisaged. The bird droppings rain out of the sky onto athletes and spectators alike, before the poor panicked birds disperse and disappear.

Afterwards, we locate the South African team. We enjoy seeing folks from my old country again and we wish them luck. As we say good-bye to them, the German team comes marching by. I cannot believe my own eyes because I see my brother David marching along with them. This time, he is in the garb of the German Olympic Team. I want to call him, but Hector grabs my arm and tells

---

[48] I call the youth of the world

me: "Not now. We will only cause an embarrassment if we talk to him. He will most probably ignore us, anyway."

During dinner, I and the two Scholtz boys discover that they are really my cousins, twice removed. Their father, a lawyer, is a friend of General Jan Smuts, who is presently the prime minister of South Africa, although he doesn't support all the policies of Smuts.

Willie: "Our father fought during the Boer War against the Brits and that's why we don't study in Oxford, Edinburgh, or London. We prefer Germany with our German family name."

Hector: "I was an English officer during that war, but Dora's father was a Boer warrior. I am ashamed of the atrocities perpetrated by the British Army during that war."

I ask: "Many people seem to think that Hitler is preparing for another war. What will you do when that happens? Will you choose the side of Germany or Britain?"

David: "We love our German girlfriends and we have plans to get married. We hope to go back to South Africa at the end of our studies, hopefully before any war breaks out. In that case, we won't have to choose, although our sympathy will certainly not lie on the side of Great Britain."

Hector: "And if war breaks out before your complete your studies?"

Willie: "We haven't thought so far ahead yet."

Annemarie, one of the girlfriends who seems to understand some of our Afrikaans, says in German: "We can only pray that war never breaks out. No war is ever desirable. We prefer peace."

Me: "Amen."

On my own, I wonder what will happen when war does break out again. Will I support the Germans again?

We agree to stay in touch. It's good to have family in Europe.

Berlin, Saturday, 15 August 1936

The Olympic Games ended today. We watched several athletic events, as well as the cycling races. A South African cyclist, Karl Krause, came fifth in the speed trials and the 100 kilometers race.

It is our intention of flying back to Valkenburg tomorrow because Hector must start working again on Monday. While we wait for our dinner in the dining room of our hotel, we scrutinize the evening papers. It is no surprise to see the photo of my brother David. He is called Major Thomas von Traubenstein, the trainer of two boxers who won medals.

Hector: "Now we know at last what he calls himself."

Me: "He elevated himself to the German nobility with that fancy family name. I wonder whether he uses a title such as 'Ritter', 'Freiherr', or 'Graf'."[49]

---

[49] Knight, Baron, or Count.

Wassenaar and Scheveningen, Monday, 31 August 1936

Missus Victoria Visser, our housekeeper, calls me to the telephone.

I pick up the instrument and say in Dutch: "Met burggravin Theodora de Hacqueville."[50]

A male voice on the other side says in German: "Veleda, good morning. Is it possible that we can meet somewhere this morning? How about the Kurhaus at Scheveningen at eleven?"

This is the first time that anybody addressed me in this way and a cold shudder runs down my scalp and my spine. My voice cords are suddenly paralyzed. My heart misses a few beats.

The voice continues: "It is necessary that we have a friendly chat. You need not be afraid. You are free to say no, of course, but as I know you, you won't say no. You are far too inquisitive to stay away from our meeting because you are made of the same stuff as the ancient Veleda. Will you be there?"

After about ten seconds of silence, I stammer: "All right. How will I recognize you?"

"Not necessary? I have a photo of you that was taken in Berlin a few weeks ago, while you were talking to the South African athletes. Come to the Tea Room in the Kurhaus."

Scheveningen is almost a suburb of The Hague and lies on the coast of the North Sea, west of The Hague. It is easy to reach by motor car from Wassenaar. I and Hector have enjoyed lunch more than once at the very same Kurhaus.

I reach the Kurhaus a few minutes before eleven. The Kurhaus is a giant edifice from the 1880's, with a hotel, a concert hall, a tea room, and a dining room – all overlooking the beach and the North Sea.

---

[50] You are speaking] to Viscountess Theodora de Hacqueville.

As I enter the tea room, a grey-haired gentleman gets up from a table and waves at me. He introduces himself: "Gnädige Frau, sehr geehrte Gräfin,[51] I am Wilhelm Canaris, at your service."

I extend my hand to greet him, but he kisses my hand as an old-time chevalier would do. He invites me to sit down. "Tea? Or coffee? This place has the most delicious chocolate cake. May I order something?"

"Just tea for me."

Mister Canaris waves to a waitress and places the order.

I watch him in silence and he watches me in silence. I try to stare him down as I stared Kitchener down in 1910 and he does his best to stare me down as well. Both of us sit with slight smiles on our faces.

After two or three minutes, during which no one looked away, Canaris starts talking: "Veleda, I have great regard for what

---

[51] Most esteemed Countess.

you did during the Great War. I also know of your role during the Boer War. You are just the woman we need."

"For what?"

"To tell us what is going on in Great Britain. Your husband is a brigadier who worked in the War Office and he still has the ears of the big shots there. He often confides in you. Your eldest son is an officer in the RAF. Your second son is a naval officer involved with the administration of the naval facilities at Portsmouth. Your youngest son is connected to the signals section at the War Office. We know that you and your sons are Boers at heart, although you also have German roots. You and your sons will be extremely valuable assets."

I stay silent, still staring at this man. He smiles back at me.

After a minute, he continues: "You are a woman with a strong personality. You are clever. Resourceful. Also careful. You were never caught during the Great War. You know how to cover your tracks. And, most importantly, you hate the British, although you got married into the English aristocracy. It will be almost second nature to you to aid us and recruit your sons to be your eyes and ears."

At last, I regain my voice: "Who the hell are you, Herr Canaris?"

"Yes, you have the right to know. I am Vizeadmiral[52] Wilhelm Canaris, chief of the Abwehr, the German Secret Service."

---

[52] Vice Ademiral.

"And you travelled all the way from Berlin to drink tea with me?"

"That's right. I just could not restrain myself; I had to see this remarkable woman who called herself Veleda."

"How the hell do you know that I was Veleda?"

"You admitted it to General Paul von Letow-Vorbeck. He told me much about you. He is, just as I am, a German patriot, although we both detest Adolf Hitler. I gather that you don't think much of Hitler, either."

"You are correct in that regard, Herr Vizeadmiral."

"Let me tell you something about General von Letow-Vorbeck. Last year, Hitler offered him the position of ambassador in Washington. And do you know what the old bugger's reaction was? He told Hitler straightaway: 'Go fuck yourself!' Of course, Hitler didn't like the insult, but he couldn't do anything against the old guy because he is so popular."

I can't help but to laugh. This joke makes the atmosphere less stiff.

"You deserved a medal for your work between 1914 and 1918 by helping von Letow-Vorbeck and the Schutztruppe in German South-West Africa with vital intelligence. Unfortunately, there was never an opportunity to award something like that to you. It is also better that you didn't receive any recognition for your role because that would have exposed your identity. It was very clever of you to use the cover name of that ancient German heroine, Veleda, who aided her people in their struggle against a cruel and corrupt empire. That tells me where your heart lies. How about it?"

This man caught me and made it impossible to refuse his request. Something that caught me, are his kind eyes and friendly smile. He makes the impression of an honest and solid German, the type who could have been a good friend of my father.

"All right. I will help you."

"I knew you would, Veleda. Please carry on using that name as your cover. It suits you."

I decide, I won't tell this man that the ancient Veleda often visited me in my dreams and that I almost feel like a reincarnation of this ancient German freedom fighter.

"How must I do it?"

"You have a radio in your airplane. Use the Morse Code with the same secret code you used in the past. Tap with a pen or a pencil on the microphone. An A becomes a B, a B becomes a C, and so forth. Very easy and almost impossible to break. Here is a list of the frequencies you may use. Every day of the week you use the frequency of that particular day."

"How do I know somebody will listen?"

"We understand that you will only contact us very infrequently. You won't have news on a daily basis, just as you contacted the German consulate in Lourenco Marques once every few weeks. But we will always have somebody on stand-by, listening to those frequencies. If you start transmitting and you find that somebody else is using that frequency, wait a few minutes and try again when that frequency is clear. Start with your call sign, which is a 'TH' for Theodora.

"Keep your messages brief and in different languages as you did in the past. That was clever. Use English, German, and Latin. Afrikaans or Dutch might create problems, so don't use those."

"I will memorize these frequencies because I can't afford that my husband sees something like this. Not ever."

"Nor anybody else, of course. Another cup of tea?"

"Yes please. And also a slice of that chocolate cake."

Canaris waves at a waitress and places the order.

"Veleda, I think it's important to tell you that your brother is also cooperating with us."

"David?"

"David Davidsohn. He as adopted the name of a dead boy and became Thomas Freiherr von Traubenstein."

"We wondered about his title. I saw his photo in the newspaper in Berlin. What does he do for you? He can't spy on Great Britain while commanding a German Army unit over there."

"He must tell us whether any high German officers get involved in a conspiracy to get rid of Hitler."

"Isn't it your job to protect Hitler?"

"Please, please, keep this to yourself, but I don't think you will ever get the opportunity of warning the wrong people. There are some generals and admirals who don't support Hitler. Just as the Bekennende Kirche opposes him."

"We attended the synod where the Barmen Declaration was adopted."

"I know."

"You do know a lot."

"That's my job. I also know that you had dinner with two South African students in Berlin a few weeks ago. We know that their father is a politician in South Africa, as well as a friend of General Jan Smuts, the prime minister. Are they perhaps South African and British spies, planted in Berlin?"

"No, oh no. Their father fought during the Boer War against the British and they absolutely abhor and loathe Great Britain. That's why they didn't go to Oxford or Cambridge or somewhere else in England, but to Berlin and nowhere else. They are very much pro-German. You can trust them."

"We know that your husband is supposed to watch the Wehrmacht from a distance in Holland. We can't always know where you are going and with whom he is talking because you fly him all over the place. Is it possible to let us know whenever you fly him somewhere?"

"Only if you give me a guarantee that I won't put his life in any danger. You ought to know that I happen to love that man. He's the father of my three sons."

"Nothing will happen to him. We know we will lose you if he suffers any mishaps on German soil. But this will not be the first time you pass secrets on that you have learnt from him. You did it from your first date with him."

"That is so."

It is almost as if I hear a little voice inside me: "You are doing the right thing. Well done." That must be the voice of the spirit of the real Veleda.

Nuremberg, Monday, 14 September 1936

Hector announced last week: "We must fly to Nuremberg to attend the last day of the Ninth Party Congress of the Nazi Party. I must see what type of rally the Nazi Party is able to put together. We fly on Friday. Are you ready and is that dangerous Dragon also ready?"

"You know, I'm always eager to fly. I love my Dragon, almost as much as I love you."

During the pre-flight preparations on Friday, I managed to send off the following message over the radio:

OBDI OVFSOCFSH = WFMFEB

This means:

NACH NUERNBERG = VELEDA[53]

And now we are sitting on the grandstand of the Nuremberg Rally Grounds with its monumental buildings and a gigantic parade field. We listen to one speech after the other.

The rally's theme this year is the regaining of Germany's honor after the Rhineland has been militarized successfully earlier this year.

It is clear that Hitler knows how to manipulate the crowd. After dark, there is a torch procession where much more than a hundred thousand uniformed members of the SA, SS[54], and Hitler Jugend, the Nazi Youth Movement, march past the raised platform where Hitler is taking the salute with his raised arm. Each one of them carries a torch in his right hands and a shovel over his left shoulder and they march in platoons, companies, and battalions. A brass band provides the marching music.

---

[53] TO NUREMBERG = VELEDA

[54] SS or Schulzstaffel – it means "Protection Squad", the Body Guard of Hitler.

We agree that Hitler is a master orator. He delivers a dramatic address or oration, using the gigantic public address system skillfully. He often draws loud applause from the crowd and it sounds like the sound of a huge waterfall when the people voice their approval.

Hector talks directly into my ear to be audible above the racket: "He mesmerizes these people. They seem to venerate him, almost as if he is a saint or a minor deity. The atmosphere is electric and I think we witness something great."

Me: "He inspires them with hope. People need hope when they suffer. And suffer they did the past two decades."

"He will be able to drive these people into a frenzy and they will do anything for him."

While Hitler is delivering his message, dozens of searchlights are switched on behind him. The spectacle is called the "cathedral of light".

When the rally ends, I ask myself: "Was it necessary to inform the Abwehr of our presence at this occasion? Here were so many Nazi officials, functionaries, and helpers that at least thirty pairs of eyes would have watched each and every step we take. Reports about our behavior and movements will certainly be forwarded to the Abwehr and the Secret Police, the Gestapo.[55]

---

[55] The name "Gestapo" is the abbreviation for "Geheime Staatspolizei" or Secret State Police.

Wassenaar, Thursday, I October 1936

My second opportunity to help the Abwehr comes sooner that I thought. Hector tells me this afternoon: "The War Office and the Admiralty need aerial photos of the shipbuilding works at Wilhelmshaven and Hamburg. That's where the Germans are building their submarines and battleships. Nobody is able to get near to these facilities and take pictures. The only way is to watch them from the air.

"Look at this wonderful camera I was given. I had to take a course on how to handle it. And there is a photographic laboratory at the Embassy where they can develop the negatives and get clear pictures."

Me: "If we fly over these places, what will our final destination be? The Germans will find it strange that we only fly over secret installations and then go home again."

"No, no. We spend a lazy weekend in Hamburg. We do some sight-seeing and talk with the locals. The German aeronautical authorities will only learn about our destination when we get into the air and ask for landing instructions over the radio. That won't give them enough time to put a tail on us in Hamburg."

"I will have to see whether that delightful Dragon of ours is ready. I'm taking the car to look at her in Valkenburg."

"I'm coming with you."

While Hector is inspecting the plane from the outside, I take place in the cockpit and switch on the radio. On a scrap of paper, I have the following message in English, which I transmit by tapping on the microphone, exactly at twelve minutes past six on the agreed frequency:

GMZJOH UP IBNCVSH QIPUPT PG TIJJQZBSET PO UIF
XBZ = WFMFEB

That means:

FLYING TO HAMBURG PHOTOS OF SHIPYARDS ON THE WAY = VELEDA

Wilhelmshaven and Hamburg, Friday, 2 October 1936

425

When we fly a few hundred yards to the north-east of the shipyards at Wilhelmshaven, so that Hector can get a few good shots from the side, I notice that there is much smoke over the shipyard.

Hector yells: "We will have to take more shots when we come back. These photos will be useless."

A little while later, we circle over Hamburg before landing.

Hector yells again: "Hell! There are canvas sheets all over the place. Nobody knows what is hidden under them. Perhaps even nothing."

Salzburg, Friday, 30 July 1937

A city I always wished to visit is Salzburg in Austria. A dream has come true because I and Hector are sitting in a theater in this beautiful city, situated amongst the foothills of the Alps, and we are experiencing the grand opera of Richard Wagner, Die Meistersinger von Nürnberg. Maestro Arturo Toscanini is the conductor of the orchestra.

Yesterday, we enjoyed Die Zauberflöte of Mozart and the conductor was the world-famous Bruno Walter.

Unfortunately, we will have to fly back to Wassenaar tomorrow and try and reverse our failure of a week ago. To reach Salzburg by air, we flew over Augsburg in southern Germany, where the Bayrische Flugzeugwerke[56] has its plant. We flew south of the city so that we could photograph the Lechfeld Luftwaffe Base where the aircraft of this plant are being tested. There was fog when we flew over Lechfeld and, to my relief, no photos could be taken.

We were lucky to get tickets for these musical performances of the Salzburg Festival through the good services of the British Embassy in Vienna. Of course, I notified the Abwehr of our plans in good time but it wasn't necessary for the Luftwaffe to hide their planes since the foggy weather did that for them.

---

[56] Bavarian Aircraft Works.

Augsburg, Saturday, 31 July 1937

During my pre-flight preparations at the airfield at Salzburg, I sent a message to the Abwehr exactly at twelve minutes past eight that we are due to fly again over Augsburg later today.

When we see Lechfeld to our left, Hector looks through a port hole with his camera in his hands. He exclaims: "Shit! The lousy Luftwaffe has hidden or removed all their accursed aircraft. Not a single one is visible. I can only take photographs of the runways and the sheds. Blasted!"

Of course, I sit with a smug satisfied smile on my face, which Hector can't see because I sit with my back towards him.

Berlin, Tuesday, 8 February 1938

We are sitting in the concert hall in Berlin, listening to a symphony concert by the Berliner Philharmoniker, the Berlin Philharmonic Orchestra, under the baton of the famous Wilhelm Furtwängler. I felt that an experience such as this is something that I must encounter at least once in my life.

Our tickets were organized by the British Embassy that also booked two seats next to ours for the Russian military attaché to Berlin. Hector wanted to meet him, as it were, spontaneously.

When he announced the plan to fly to Berlin, he also told me that I must plan a flight route over Münster with its huge base of the German Army. He wanted to get some photographs of this base.

I had a three-day warning before we flew off yesterday to the Tempelhof airfield in Berlin and that gave me ample time to transmit a message to the Abwehr about our plans.

When we flew over Münster, I could see the military base clearly, but all the equipment was hidden under nets and canvas sheets.

Hector shouted to be heard over the din of the aircraft engines: "Why the hell are these Germans always hiding their equipment? I don't know what they are hiding under those nets and sheets – tanks, guns, trucks, or… broomsticks?"

During the concert interval, there is time to talk to Colonel Boris Bronislav. He laughs: "That madman, Hitler, proclaimed himself chief of the Wehrmacht. Bah! He was only a Gefreiter during the Great War and he never even fired a single shot in anger. All he did was to carry messages to the front line. What does he know about military matters? I was a captain during the war and I know how much suffering a war can bring about. And now he…, he has fired a whole bunch of Generals, including the commander of the Wehrmacht, and installed himself in that position. It's clear that he is making ready for a war he can never win. He is a madman! 'Scheiße!' (shit)!'"

Hector tries to calm him down: "Herr Oberst[57], it may be dangerous to speak like that. Fortunately, we know each other well enough. But what will happen if somebody else reports you to the Gestapo?"

The colonel smirks: "They cannot fire me or shoot me. I have diplomatic immunity."

I know it will be useless to fly over Münster back to Valkenburg tomorrow because those nets and sheets will still be in place.

While we talk to the Russian colonel in the foyer, I happen to notice Vizeadmiral Wilhelm Canaris a few meters from us – too far to eavesdrop on us, but near enough to give me a sly smile while we make eye contact. That is to say "thank you" to me. It also gives me the message that he regards me as a valuable and important part of his organization and, therefore, he took the trouble of finding me here.

---

[57] An "Oberst" is a colonel in English.

Nuremberg, Monday, 12 September 1938

Hector received an order from London to attend yet another Nazi Rally at Nuremberg during September 1938. As non-party members, we weren't allowed to witness the inner party ceremonies and deliberations. We are watching, though, the closing ceremony where thousands upon thousands of SA men, SS men, and boys of the Hitler Jugend, are assembled on the huge rally grounds.

This rally is devoted to the glorification of the Third German Reich, which was recently enlarged when Austria was incorporated into Germany. A referendum held in Austria, henceforth to be called Ostmark, overwhelmingly endorsed the "Anschluss" or joining.

The parade is truly spectacular as battalion after battalion marches past Hitler where he takes the salute. These battalions are, of course, marching to the beat of the marching music provided by a massed brass band.

Apart from all the marching men, there are thousands upon thousands of spectators who applause Hitler enthusiastically and greet him with the Nazi salute.

Even Hector, the stiff English lord, gets carried away by the atmosphere and the hysteria and insanity and he also applauds Hitler's speech.

As we leave the grounds afterwards, Hector declares: "This Hitler chap certainly knows how to make the crowds eat out of his hand. He can do with them whatever he likes. That makes him so dangerous."

Me: "He is certainly a real demagogue. But not all the Germans believe all the nonsense he propagates. There are many decent people who applaud his improvement of the economy, but they don't swallow his fabrications and falsehoods and fictions about the so-called disgusting and dreadful Jews."

Hector took many photos of the event as evidence of what we saw.

RAF Upper Heyford, Thursday, 20 September 1938

Hector was summoned to the War Office in London and we landed at Hendon yesterday. He had to report about his impressions of the Nazi rally of last week, as well as other aspects of his work. We spent the night at a hotel afterwards and today we are visiting Henry at the RAF station at Upper Heyford in Oxfordshire – a short hop of about 70 miles from Hendon.

Henry is a flight lieutenant in Number 57 Squadron, RAF, and the pilot of a twin-engine light bomber, a Bristol Blenheim.

After I have set down my dashing Dragon and parked her where the voice from the control tower told me to go, Henry arrives in a truck. He takes his dad, first of all, to pay a visit to the station commander, Group Captain Bill Burrywell, to pay his respects. We enjoy lunch in the officers' mess and then Henry takes us to his plane.

"I have permission to take both of you up. Pa, you are a member of the Armed Forces and, therefore, you may fly in a military plane. Ma, although you are a civvie, you are connected to Number 24 Squadron at Hendon and, therefore, technically a member of the RAF. You are also entitled to hitch a ride in my machine."

He takes us to somewhat strange-looking aircraft with a glass-covered nose. He explains in Afrikaans: "This cockpit provides very good visibility."

We take to the air and fly northwards, away from the heavy air traffic around London. I sit in the navigator's seat and Hector has found somewhere else to sit down.

Suddenly Henry leaves his pilot's seat. "Ma, you take over. I want you to feel how she behaves."

"But I'm not licensed to fly this machine!"

"I'm a qualified instructor and I'm giving you a lesson. This is a legitimate training flight."

I take the controls. Although I only have had experience of a Tiger Moth and a Dragon Rapide, the Blenheim doesn't feel too strange. I make a few gentle turns before vacating the pilot's seat and giving Henry the opportunity to bring her down again.

After he has switched the engines off and handed the plane to the ground crew, he tells us: "Ma, you're a natural. It's a pity that the RAF doesn't use women pilots. You would have been an asset."

"There isn't a place or space for women in this part of the armed forces. I'm also too old to become a cadet. In case you have forgotten, I'm already fifty-three years old."

"Ma, you are in top form. Nothing wrong with you."

Hector: "Dora, I agree with Henry. It's a pity that you can't become a fully-qualified pilot in the RAF. They should create a hew female squadrons. And then, the Viscountess Theodora de Hacqueville can be a squadron commander."

Wassenaar, Thursday, 10 November 1938

We sit in our home for dinner and we listen to the radio news. We hear that the Führer of Germany is jubilant because he has reached an agreement with Joseph Chamberlain, Prime Minister of Great Britain, Édouard Daladier, the French Prime Minister and Benito Mussolini, the Duce of Italy, that Sudetenland, a part of Czechoslovakia, is to become part of Greater Germany. Sudetenland was part of the Austro-Hungarian Reich before the Great War and most of the inhabitants regard themselves as Germans.

We also hear that Chamberlain proclaims his satisfaction regarding the agreement that was reached after a one-day conference in Munich because the agreement will mean "peace in our time".

Hector: "Of course, Hitler threatened with a military invasion of the Sudetenland if the other powers did not agree with his demands. This agreement simply means that nobody will come to the aid of little Czechoslovakia if Hitler simply annexes the Sudeten districts and make them part of the Third German Reich – just as Germany has swallowed Austria a few months ago."

Me: "Many Germans like the strong man tactics of Hitler. They think that's the only way to deal with their enemies."

Wassenaar, Friday, 11 November 1938

We listen to the radio news while we prepare supper. It is reported that gangs of SA men attacked Jewish businesses and synagogues throughout Germany last night. They smashed windows and looted the shops. According to these SA gangs, this step is well-deserved since the Jews must be blamed for all the disasters and calamities that have befallen the German people. Now they are receiving their just reward for their crimes. Because so much broken glass lay strewn on the sidewalks, the event was dubbed the "Kristallnacht".[58]

I remark: "Those SA hoodlums and vandals don't represent ordinary, decent, civilized Germans. Was it really necessary to behave like barbarians, bastards, or bullies?"

Hector: "These gangsters tell the world that the Jews must be punished. They were the killers of Jesus!"

Me: "It was really the Romans who crucified Jesus. And not all the Jews wanted him dead. A few days before his execution, the Jews of Jerusalem welcomed him as their king because he was descended from great King David."

I feel sad about this news because I am partly from Jewish ancestry. I am also sure that these horrible hooligans don't represent the German nation, that consists mostly of decent, delightful, and God-fearing folks. It is difficult to feel loyalty towards Germany when these things happen, but then I also think about the British concentration camps and campaign of burning down all Boer farms during the Boer War. There must be more evil people in Great Britian than in Germany.

---

[58] Crystal Night.

Wassenaar, Tuesday, 15 November 1938

My husband arrives home somewhat early. He has a few passengers in his staff car and he is followed by a taxi with more passengers. I watch the strange procession from the living room window and go outside to find out what is happening.

Hector grabs my arm to pull me nearer. It suddenly dawns upon me that the people he brought home are my father's brothers, Saul and Samuel, as well as their wives and daughters.

Hector: "Please come inside, all of you. We can't congregate here on the sidewalk."

I follow all nine members of the Davidsohn family inside and Hector declares: "My superb spouse, these people have nowhere to stay for the time being. That's why I brought them here. I happened to stumble on them when they arrived at the Embassy to apply for political asylum in South Africa so that they can join your father in Pretoria."

Me: "Saul, Samuel, am I correct that you fled from Germany after the events of Crystal Night?"

Hector: "Saul, you tell the story."

Saul, who looks lost, dazed, and helpless: "We have lost everything when those Nazis looted out shop. They broke the windows, stole all our money, and smashed our sewing machines."

Samuel: "And then a miracle of biblical proportions happened. Praise be to the good God of Abraham, Isaac, and Jacob."

Saul:" Yes, it was real miracle. A German officer, who introduced himself to us as Oberstleutnant[59] von Traubenstein, helped us to draw our money from the bank and to find buyers for our property."

---

[59] Lieutenant Colonel.

Samuel: "He also convinced us to leave Germany. And this morning, he smuggled us over the border with Holland and organized transport for us to The Hague."

Saul: "And there we applied for political asylum. This German officer told us that he has Jewish family who live in Pretoria."

Me: "What did that officer call himself?"

Saul: "He said he was Oberstleutnant von Traubenstein."

Hector: "He is none other than David Davidsohn, my brother-in-law."

Samuel: "What on earth is he doing in a German Army uniform?"

Hector: "He hates Great Britain and joined the Germans during the Great War. He got married to a German woman and settled in Germany, where he continued his military career. He disappeared at the start of the Great War when he went to German South West Africa to help defend that territory against the South African forces."

Samuel: "We must see the hand of God in this. He planted our nephew in Germany to help us flee from those Nazi nuisances."

Hector turns to me: "They told me that a few more families are arriving tomorrow. They couldn't all come at the same time."

Me: "We won't be able to accommodate all those people. Hector, the Embassy will have to organize something. But my uncles, aunts, and cousins, you are welcome under our roof. The married couples can sleep in the two guest rooms and the girls can sleep in the living room. I will have to borrow some blankets and pillows from our neighbors."

Hector: "Do we have enough provisions to feed all of them?"

Me: "That's a problem that we can always overcome."

Wassenaar, Friday, 18 November 1938

My family members moved out this morning after the Embassy organized passages for all of them and their fellow-Jews who arrived a day later. They were helped to take the ferry at Hoek van Holland to Harwich in England, where the South African Embassy in London would take care of them.

Saul and Samuel insisted on paying for their passage to South Africa and they will, in due course, be taken to Southampton to board a passenger liner to Cape Town. The other Jews prefer to stay in England.

This afternoon, I escape to Valkenburg to send the following message over the radio of my dutiful Dragon:

WPO USBVCFOTUFJO IFMQFE GPSUZ KFXT UP FTDBQF = WFMFEB

In plain English, this message says:

VON TRAUBENSTEIN HELPED FORTY JEWS TO ESCAPE = VELEDA

Hagdale, Saturday, 24 December 1938

We managed to get the whole de Hacqueville family together over Christmas at Hagdale. The boys and their wives, each with a little girl and a little boy, arrived yesterday and they are due to leave again next week to spend New Year's Eve with their respective in-laws. They will also celebrate their fifth wedding anniversaries on Monday.

To my delight, I find that the little ones can speak Afrikaans with their fathers. That is what I also do. Of course, they can also speak English, the language of their mothers. This must be a somewhat unique situation: six little children who were born in England in an aristocratic family who speak Afrikaans! That tells me something about the attitudes and sentiments of their fathers.

We get the kids together around a Christmas tree and we have recruited Freddy Fortune to dress as Father Christmas. He arrives with a sack full of goodies for our grandchildren.

Freddy also delivers a crate as a present for me and Hector. Victor explains: "This is a present for our parents, from us three boys. Your old radio set is rather old and unreliable. This new set will put you in touch with the whole world. You will even be able to receive live newscasts from South Africa."

Henry: "The three of us clubbed together to provide you with this gift. Victor is the specialist in radios and we left it to him to get the right model."

Hector requests Victor to open the crate. After having had a look at the instrument, he declares: "You boys know that I operate in the world of intelligence. It is important to know what is going on in the world. We are living in dangerous times and one must know what is going on. I'm sure your mother will often use it to listen to the South African Broadcasting Corporation."

I give each of the boys a hug and I ask: "Victor, can we take this set with us to Holland? As you know, we spend very little time at Hagdale."

Victor: "Of course."

Hagdale, Tuesday, 27 December 1938

Hector is inspecting the stables for the horses and the cattle this afternoon and I use the opportunity to talk privately to the three boys in the library of the villa.

I address them in Afrikaans: "Hendrik, Daniel, Victor, this meeting never happened. No record of it will ever exist. Do I make myself clear?"

Victor: "Ma, are you going to tell us that the next war is inevitable? The three of us discussed things and we all get the impression that we are stepping nearer and nearer to the precipice. We must decide what roles we are going to play in the coming conflict. Do you want us to become German spies?"

Hendrik: "Ma, yes, the three of us have already compared notes and we agree that we don't like or love Great Britain. We are Boers, although we wear the uniforms of the enemies of our people. I only joined the RAF because I wanted to fly airplanes."

Daniel: "Yes, Ma, we have already conspired to help you to aid the Germans when war breaks out. We won't go and join the Wehrmacht. That won't ever work. But we can help you with information about British methods and movements and maneuvers. I know, for instance, about the deployment of all the warships based at Portsmouth. I am sure that you will be able to pass on all that info to the Germans, somehow or other. Our aim is to save lives – German lives, but also British lives."

I hold up my hands to silence the boys: "Boys, you astound me. I called this meeting because I wanted to recruit you as my assistants. But you have already hatched a pestilential and poisonous plot while I was working with your father in Holland and you decided that you want to thwart the British war effort. Am I right?"

Henry: "Yes, Ma, you are dead right, spot on. You told us

that you were a Boer spy during the Boer War. The three of us strongly suspect that you were also a German spy when you worked as manager at that telegraph office at the Union Buildings. You had an unparallelled opportunity of sniffing military secrets out and sending those on to the Germans in East Africa. Did we guess correctly?"

Me: "Yes, Hendrik, you're correct. I was indeed a German agent during the Great War. And I have been recruited two years ago by the German Abwehr. The chief of the Abwehr, nobody else than Vice Admiral Wilhelm Canaris, personally asked me to help him. He hoped that I could count on your assistance and cooperation. The idea was that I was to convince you to join me, but that isn't necessary anymore. You have already convinced yourselves to do so. Canaris told me as well that my brother, who is an officer in Germany, is also aiding him.

"You made it very easy for me to get involved with a highly secret intrigue with you to sabotage the war effort of these repellent Rooinekke. I want to make this clear: I love your father and I won't do anything that may put his life in danger. But it is highly unlikely that he will ever get involved with any fighting and battles. He is really past retirement age and the War Office only kept him because they can't find a replacement for him."

Henry: "Ma, fixed up. Fantastic. Then we are the Hagdale Spy Ring. We can abbreviate that to HSR. Nobody else will know what that abbreviation means. Of course, we also love our father and we will never stab him in the back. We must also be careful not to be caught because he will, inevitably, become involved as a suspected co-conspirator or accessory. Anyway, Victor will explain how you will communicate with this Canaris guy."

Victor: "Ma, yes, that new radio set that we have given you for Christmas is not only a receiver. It can also be used as a transmitter. What makes it unique is the fact that the receiver is duplicated. That means that you can listen to one frequency, while the other part is tuned to another frequency. There is a built-in microphone. With that, you can send messages in Morse Code or plain language or any other code to us or to Berlin. Hendrik and Daniel will send you messages about things in which we are involved. I will also keep my eyes and ears open where I work in the signals department of the War Office.

"I propose that you keep switched onto a certain frequency during the day and the evening on the inactive second receiver in this monster of a radio set to hear from us. We must use our call-signs, HSR2 for Hendrik, HSR3 for Daniel, and HSR4 for me, to request your attention. If you are able to respond, you reply with HSR1, your call-sign. Then we know that you are there and we can communicate by means of a code in Morse."

Henry: "Ma, can you remember how you taught us Morse Code with that old heliograph on the farm? That helped us when we did our military training and now, we can use it very nicely."

Daniel: "Ma, how did you get in touch with Berlin in the past?"

Me: "By radio, of course. The radio in my airplane. I sent short messages in Morse Code on certain frequencies, which change every day. To confuse any possible listeners, I use a secret code and use alternatively English, German, and Latin in my messages. You are to help me with information about what is going on, as Victor proposed. Your father also trusts me and he will also confide in me, without knowing that that info will reach Berlin."

Victor: "Ma, I work with signals every day. There are methods to unravel the contents of a message in code, but then those messages must be fairly lengthy and always in the same language. It's jolly clever of you to use different languages. That will, most certainly, make your coded messages unbreakable because there won't be any patterns in them that can be detected. That is to say, if anybody overhears or intercept your messages.

"I must also warn you – don't send the messages always from the same location. There are methods to pinpoint the source of a radio message. So, move around in that plane of yours if you use her transmitter. Try and send your messages when you are flying around. That will prevent any eavesdroppers from locating the source of your messages. Of course, this new radio set will, inevitably, stay in one spot. If you keep your messages brief and we use different frequences every day, there will be no time to pinpoint them on a map."

Me: "Thanks for that warning. I'll keep it in mind."

Victor: "I will draw up and schedule of frequencies for each day of the week, which we must use to communicate with each other. How does your code with Berlin work?"

Me: "It's the same code I used during the Great War. It's simple. An 'A' becomes a 'B', a 'B' becomes a 'C', and so on. That results in words that look like gibberish and nobody will guess how to decode them – especially if I use something like Latin. You also had Latin in school – so use it sometimes."

Victor: "I think we have a fool-proof system now. Does everybody understand how things will work? I will draw up a schedule of frequencies tonight."

Henry: "Grand. Thanks. We can understand why so many Boers started a rebellion in 1914. They wanted to get rid of the bloody Brits and the loathed Joiners and abhorrent traitors such as Louis Botha and Jan Smuts. They were, however, ill-prepared. We must be much more careful and stay out of trouble."

Me: "Amen, amen!"

Hagdale, Monday, 2 January 1939

Hector must report back at the Embassy tomorrow and we are preparing my dependable Dragon this morning to fly back to Valkenburg. This gives me the opportunity of sending the following message at forty-two minutes past twelve on the pre-determined frequency:

> UI IBHEBMF TQJPOFOLSFJT ITL IBU WJFS NJUHMJFEFS = WFMFEB

The message, in German, looks like this if decoded:

> TH HAGDALE SPIONENKREIS HSK HAT VIER MITGLIEDER = VELEDA[60]

I tell myself that I must keep a cool head because I will have to communicate with the boys and the Abwehr with different methods and call signs.

---

[60] TH HAGDALE SPY RING HSR FOUR MEMBERS = VELEDA

Wassenaar and Scheveningen, Monday, 14 August 1939

Veleda appeared against last night. All she said, was: "It's almost time. Be ready." She looked excited and smiled and waved at me where she was sitting on a rock with a musical instrument in her hand. Her boobs were covered decently.

Veleda (1852) by Alexandre Cabanel

This morning, a woman's voice on the telephone says in German: "Good morning, Veleda. My name is Sonja. How about a cup of tea at the Kurhaus at eleven?"

"Certainly."

This phone call was no surprise after Veleda's visit last night. I turn up in Scheveningen at the Kurhaus at eleven. An attractive woman sitting at a table in the tea room waves at me and I join her.

"My name is Sonja Schellenberg. I'm a special envoy from Vizeadmiral Canaris. He sent me with a message for you."

"Pleased to meet you.

"Tea and chocolate cake for you?"

"Please."

The order is placed.

"The Admiral has no means of reaching you as things are at present. He wants to send messages to you through radio broadcasts in Afrikaans."

"How in hell will that work?"

"Very easily. We don't need the assistance of hell. There are plans to start an Afrikaans service at Radio Zeesen, south of Berlin. We have already identified some South African students in Germany whom we can use as broadcasters."

"Are they willing to be used?"

"They don't know yet. They will only be recruited as soon as the war starts."

"War?"

"Yes. War."

"What are you telling me?"

"My admiral knows things. Hitler will attack Poland very soon, on the first day of September. Then these Afrikaans-speaking students won't be able to leave Germany because all the borders will be closed. And then we get them to work at the radio station. Their short-wave broadcasts will be directed at South Africa, but you will also be able to listen to their programs."

"And how will they send secret messages from Canaris to me? You can be sure that people from British Military Intelligence will also be listening to those broadcasts."

"They will certainly listen. But they won't understand what is being said. Your messages will be addressed to 'Our Dear Friend Theo'. Theo is, of course, the first part of your name, Theodora. But everybody who listens will think it's a man. These messages will always be directly after the nine-o'-clock news, mostly on a Sunday night, but also at other times."

"What type of messages can I expect?"

"Those will mostly be requests about plans and movements of which you may get information. It will be formulated in such a manner that you will grasp its meaning immediately, without the shitty spooks at Military Intelligence knowing what is being said. And then you respond, if you can help, by sending a message at any time, day or night. Canaris already gave you a schedule of frequencies for each day of the week. There will always be somebody who watches that frequency on that particular day. That person will also listen whether messages from other sources are coming in. So, if you hear radio traffic when you want to make contact, wait a few minutes, and try again.

"By the way, Canaris asked me to express his gratitude for the messages you have already sent. He is glad that the Hagdale Spy Ring has four members – of course, you and your three sons. Fantastic!"

"I may receive a radio message at any time from my son who works in the radio office of the War Office. If it's urgent, I will forward it immediately to you people."

"Marvelous."

"What will happen to us here in Holland when war breaks out one of these days?"

"Initially, nothing. The Wehrmacht will be busy with operations to the east."

"Hector believes that Great Britain and France will declare war against Germany if the Germans attack Poland."

"You can count on that. But they are not prepared to wage war. They will make lots of noise and send some troops to the German border, but they won't dare to attack."

"And then? That's when the Wehrmacht has finished its job in Poland?"

"Oh, then the Wehrmacht will attack the British Bulldogs and the French Frogs – just as they did during the Great War. Most of the fighting will take place on French soil."

"And we will sit safely in neutral Holland?"

"Unfortunately, no. There are plans to take Holland and Belgium together with France and Luxemburg. You must be prepared for that. See to it that your bags are packed and that you can fly away as soon as the first German troops cross the Dutch border. We don't want your husband to become a prisoner of war. His diplomatic passport won't count for anything if he is caught. He must be able to get back to London and then you can pump him for info about the British plans and actions."

"Do you have a date for this attack?"

"Sometime next year. After the winter. I understand that your plane is part of the inventory of a RAF squadron?"

"That's right. Number 24 Squadron, based at Hendon, north of London."

"Decorate your plane with the RAF roundels before you fly away. That will prevent the trigger-happy anti-aircraft gunners from blasting you to bits and pieces when you reach the British coast."

"I will anyway ask flying instructions from Hendon as soon as we are airborne to approach the coast from the right direction."

Wassenaar, Tuesday, 29 August 1939

During supper, I ask Hector: "When will the war start? Do you know?"

"What war?"

"The war that Hitler wants to unleash upon the world."

"How do you know about any wars?"

"I know things. I can just feel it. I read newspapers. I listen to our new radio. Everybody is nervous about an impending war."

Of course, I don't tell my husband about the warnings that Veleda and Sonja Schellenberg gave me.

"All right. The show is due to start this Friday. That's when the Wehrmacht will attack Poland. We know about a secret agreement the Germans have with the Russians. The Germans will attack from this side and the Russians will attack from their side. They will divide the country between themselves."

"And then?"

"Britain and France will be obliged to declare war against Germany to help Poland, as I have already told you."

"Will they also declare war against Russia?"

"That's not on the cards. There is no way we can invade Russia. They are just too far away. We don't share any borders with them. France shares a long border with Germany."

"That means, in other words, that only Germany will be punished for invading Poland, while Russia will suffer no consequences, although the Russians will be just as guilty. Is that fair?"

"That is something you will have to take up with the politicians in Westminster. I can't answer you."

THE SECOND WORLD WAR

The Second World War was very different from the Boer War and the Great War, also known as the First World War. It was the inevitable outcome of conditions that prevailed after the First World War. Airplanes played a far greater role and I was taught how to fly big bombers. Armored fighting vehicles such as tanks dominated the battle fields. I believe that I and my three sons were able to save some German and British lives.

Wassenaar, Friday, 1 September 1939

The war really started on the date that Veleda, Sonja, and Hector had predicted. I also felt it coming.

We listen to the radio news while eating our breakfast consisting of boiled eggs, bread rolls, Edam cheese, and coffee. Of course, the start of the war is great news. We are told that German troops crossed the Polish border after Polish units had opened fire on German installations.

Hector: "It's certainly a lie that those Poles opened fire first. I bet that it was German troops in Polish uniforms who did that. That gave Hitler a flimsy excuse to invade his eastern neighbors."

Me: "What will happen with us here?"

Of course, I don't disclose that Sonja has already answered that question, but I need to know what Hector knows and thinks.

"Initially, nothing. We can expect a declaration of war from Britain and France very soon. British forces will be sent to France, but they won't be enough to attack Germany directly, as they actually should do."

"What happens after the Germans – and the Russians – have occupied Poland totally and all resistance is broken? Will the Wehrmacht come this way?"

"The Dutch government has already declared their neutrality, as you have heard, just as during the Great War. We will probably be safe here. I believe Britain will also be more or less safe. That is more or less the thinking at the War Office, as far as I know. The German Navy is not strong enough to land some troops on British soil and our Royal Air Force will be able to prevent German bombing raids."

After Hector has left for work and Missus Visser has started cleaning the house, I switch on Victor's radio. I send the following message:

> UI CBUBWJB FU CSJUUBJB TF TFDVSJ TFOTVOU =
> WFMFEB

The uncoded message, in simple Latin, looks like this:

> TH BATAVIA ET BRITANIA SE SECURI SENSUNT =
> VELEDA[61]

---

[61] BATAVIA (HOLLAND) AND BRITAIN FEEL THEMSELVES SECURE = VELEDA

Wassenaar, Monday, 4 September 1939

A very smart envelope is delivered by mail to our home today. It must have taken a long time to reach us because the date stamp is a fortnight ago. Willie and David Scholtz invite us to their graduation ceremonies in Berlin during the first week of September when they will receive their doctorate is medicine and physics.

I discuss with Hector the impossible situation in which we are caught.

Hector: "I am afraid that those two cousins of yours will be caught in Germany after the start of this war and all borders are closed. We won't be allowed into Germany with our British passports, diplomatic or otherwise, if we wanted to attend those ceremonies."

"What will happen to my cousins now?"

"They will either be thrown into concentration camps, or forced to work for the German war effort. If they're prudent, they must try and get out of the country, if possible in any way. Otherwise, they may be forced to cooperate with the Nazis. I think that is what they will do since they have already declared their dislike of Great Britain."

"Hell."

Hagdale, Saturday, 30 December 1939

Hector managed to convince the Dutch "Luchtvaartminiterie"[62] to grant diplomatic immunity to my delicious Dragon, which made it possible for us to paint some RAF roundels on her sides and on top of and under her wings.

After I and Hector had performed this task, he commented: "Now the German fighters will have clear targets to shoot at. Those roundels look exactly like old-time targets used by archers who tried to hit the bull's eye in the middle.

With my plane in RAF colors, we were able to cross the North Sea and land at Hagdale without mishap. I was guided by the air controllers with whom I had radio contact throughout the flight.

None of our boys was able to spend Christmas with us because all leave was cancelled. Our daughters-in-law and their children were able to come for a few days, but they have already left.

Freddy Fortune calls me to the telephone and I announce my name. A lady's voice at the other end speaks English: "Dear Veleda,

---

[62] Air Traffic Ministry.

this is Sonja speaking. I am in Winchester now. Will it perhaps be possible to invite me to your villa? I really wish to see where you live and meet your family.”

“Only my husband is here. You are welcome to celebrate Silvester[63] with us. When can I expect you?”

Around tea-time this afternoon. And remember, when you introduce me to your charming husband, the viscount, you call me Lizzy Taylor.”

Sonja turns up on a motor cycle with a suitcase fastened on the back. I heard the motor cycle’s roar and went outside to welcome her and lead her to one of our guest rooms.

Hector enters the villa at tea-time and I introduce him to an old school friend, Elizabeth Taylor.

I explain: “We haven’t seen each other since primary school days. Her parents lived in Pretoria but they moved back to Manchester before the Boer War. And now Liz has discovered where I live and I’ve invited her to stay the night.”

Hector: “Yes, I think I can detect the accent of people from Manchester. Welcome to Hagdale.”

While dusk is settling over the countryside, I take Sonja for a walk outside. We speak alternatively German and English.

Sonja: “Thanks for making up a story about how made friends. I don’t know whether your husband swallowed that story, because I look much younger than you.”

“He believes everything I tell him. Where have you learnt to speak English with that accent?”

“Where else than in Manchester? What do you think?”

“When was that?”

“Just after school. I have an aunt who is married to an Englishman and I stayed with them for a year in Manchester.

---

[63] New Year’s Eve in German.

Thereafter, I studied English and German literature in Berlin to become a teacher. And then I joined the Abwehr with my excellent knowledge of English."

"And why are you called Elizabeth Taylor?"

"That's the name on my forged passport with which I reached England via Spain, Portugal, and Ireland."

"Just to come and have tea with me?"

"This is my second visit to England after the start of the war. My job is to find out as much as I can about coastal defenses before the German Army invades England. Actually, I must report on the feasibility of such an operation."

"Where do I fit in?"

"We hope you will be able to take photos of the Channel coast of England when you fly back to Holland."

"I don't know. It will probably not be possible while I fly the aircraft as the pilot. Hector will also notice what I am doing and that will give the game away."

"I will fix a movie camera to the undercarriage of your plane tomorrow morning. I will also fit a long strong string with which you can operate the trigger to start the camera as soon as you are over Portsmouth. It will run for about thirty minutes. And when you arrive at Valkenburg, you simply dismantle the camera without your husband noticing. I will send somebody to collect the camera with the exposed film. Just let us know exactly when you will arrive at Valkenburg."

"Won't it cause alarm if I fly over all the coastal Defenses?"

"Nobody will know that you are making a film movie. That plane of yours is painted in RAF colors, anyway. Nobody at ground level will think that you are really a spy plane. Your best route to Valkenburg is, in any case, all along the southern English coast. You must fly over Portsmouth and carry on till you reach the narrowest bit of the Channel. There you cross the Channel and you reach French territory at Calais. From there, you just carry on along the Belgian coast and the Dutch coast till you reach Valkenburg. Easily done.

"You may even explain your route to the air controllers, your husband, and anybody else as the easiest and simplest route to navigate because it is easy and simple to hug the coast of England, France, Belgium, and Holland. That will prevent you from getting lost."

Hagdale, Sunday, 31 December 1939

We take our guest to the Sunday morning service to hear father Richard Smurph in the old church in Hursley. After having had some tea afterwards, I take Sonja outside so that she can fit her movie camera with its long string to the undercarriage of my dedicated Dragon.

"You must fly at ten thousand feet and pull this string when you reach Portsmouth. That will ensure that you get pictures of all fucking coastal installations – machine gun pits, radar stations, artillery pieces, every piss pot, and so forth. This will be an extremely important job. We won't be able to do it any other way. Our Luftwaffe aircraft can sometimes sneak over the Channel, but they won't be able to see much before they are chased away or shot down."

After this job of fitting the camera was finished, I tell Sonja: "You seem to know much about aircraft."

"Yes, I think I do. My husband is a Luftwaffe bomber pilot. Incidentally, he also comes from South Africa."

"That's a surprise. How did you meet?"

"We both participated in the Olympic Games three years ago. He's really a German South African, or a South African German, if you will. He speaks Afrikaans fluently and I can understand some of it. His name is Karl Krause."

"Then I must have met him because I and Hector went to wish the South African Olympic team good luck directly after the opening ceremony."

"Oh, that was the day when all the athletes and the spectators were splattered with pigeon shit."

"I seem to remember him as a cyclist."

"That's him."

While we are taking a stroll through the estate, I ask a favor: "Will it be possible for you to find out what happened to my cousins in Germany? David and Willie Scholtz. David is a medical practitioner and Willie is a scientist."

"I'll try. If I find out, I will send a message to you via Radio Zeesen's Afrikaans Service on a Sunday night."

Sonja gives me a list: "Learn these codes by heart. Whenever you get news that an air raid by British bombers on a German city is due, you immediately let us know. Always use this list of frequencies, one for each day of the week, day, and night. Somebody will be listening at all times. Use the call sign of TH, which is the abbreviation for Theodora and sign it with V for 'Veleda'.

"All you do is to transmit your call sign, followed by the abbreviation of the German city that is to be the target that night. Just the letter designated to that city, straight, using your usual code. Your message will be so brief that it is extremely unlikely to be picked up by anybody for whom it isn't intended. For your other messages, you carry on as in the past."

I look at the list of German cities with their symbols, that I must learn by heart:

Aachen	AA
Augsburg	AU
Berlin	BE
Bremen	BR
Chemnitz	CH
Dortmund	DO
Dresden	DR
Emden	EM
Essen	ES
Frankfurt	FR

and so forth….

Wassenaar, Sunday, 14 February 1940

It became my habit of listening to the Afrikaans Service of Radio Zeesen every Sunday night. I explained to Hector that I like to hear Afrikaans radio programs.

Directly after the news at nine tonight, some personal messages are being sent. The announcer reads the following message: "Our dear friend Theo, your two cousins send their regards. David is being trained to look after wounded soldiers and Willie is doing research."

Hector seems not to have paid any attention to the message, but I grasp its meaning immediately. Both these cousins are working with the Germans. David seems to have become a military doctor and Willie is helping to develop some or other war machine. They are, at least, alive and well. They didn't succeed in leaving Germany.

Wassenaar, Thursday, 10 May 1940

Life in Holland seemingly carried on more or less as usual, even after the German Wehrmacht had attacked Denmark and Norway at the beginning of last month. Denmark capitulated within a few hours, but the Norwegians held out much longer. All our neighbors in Wassenaar seem to be nervous, expecting something bad to happen, but unable to know what to expect.

The Prime Minster spoke on radio to the country and encouraged all Dutchmen to carry on with life as usual, since Holland is to stay neutral in this war.

I remarked: "My heroic husband, do you believe that prime minister? Does he really think that the Germans won't invade Holland? Look at what happened with Denmark and Norway. It's clear, Hitler wants to conquer the whole of Europe. I'm sure, he will attack Holland, Belgium, and France very soon. What do you think?"

"My clever companion, you have it. You're dead right. That's what we at the Embassy also think."

Of course, I don't disclose what Sonja Schellenberg has told me in confidence.

Early this morning, we woke up with the roar of dozens of German bombers flying overhead. We could hear how bombs explode somewhere.

Hector: "I must rush to the Embassy to clear out all my secret documents, or incinerate them. The Germans will arrive very soon, within perhaps four days, and then we must be far away."

Me: "Please say 'thank you, Dora', because I have already started to pack our clothes and other personal items."

Missus Visser unexpectedly turned up for work this morning. I paid her off because we are leaving. She begged to come with us, but I had to disappoint her because there won't be any space in my daunting Dragon.

During the day, I drive to Valkenburg to see to the service of the airplane for the last time on Dutch soil and to load our luggage, including Victor's valuable radio. Hector arrives at three with some boxes and cases, for which I must also find space inside the cockpit.

I tell him: "Hector, Rabbi Mordechai Isaacson of the Hebrew Congregation in The Hague visited me this morning and begged me to take him, his wife, and his two sons and daughter to England. He is terrified of what would happen to them when the Germans arrive. I promised him that they can come, but only with a minimum of luggage."

"Hell, Dora, we will be overloaded. I promised my personal secretary, Captain Billy Brown, that he and his wife and their baby can come with us."

"Impossible. There are the two of us, the five Jews, and three Browns. That makes a total of ten passengers, apart from the pilot, while there is only place for eight. And then there are all our cases and boxes. I can't allow the diligent Dragon to become overloaded."

"Then who will have to stay behind?"

"Not the rabbi and his family. Billy Brown can leave with the rest of the diplomatic personnel and the British government must look after them. But we are the only help the poor rabbi will ever get. Unfortunately, his whole congregation will have to stay behind, unless they get onto boats to escape to England."

The rabbi and his family turn up at about four-o'-clock and I start to warm up the engines of the daring Dragon. Hector's staff car, our private motor vehicle, and the Rabbi's little truck are left behind. Just before I can roll out onto the runway, the runway is being blocked by a glider with the black crosses of the Luftwaffe on her body. A squad of German paratroopers rush out of the glider. I see more gliders in the air, diving down onto the Valkenburg air field.

I yell: "Hold on tight! We must get away!"

There is no possibility to use the runway and I steer the Dragon onto the grass field next to the runway. The surface is somewhat bumpy and the poor Dragon groans and moans as I push her over the rough terrain. Just before we reach the fence at the end of the air field, I forced just enough speed out of her to get airborne.

Hector bellows: "Those troops are shooting at us!"

Judah, the eldest son of the rabbi screams: "My leg!"

In my mirror, I can see how Hector grabs the first aid box to help the boy while I do my best and pray as I have never prayed before to guide the airplane over the trees and the dunes in an effort to reach the coast.

I keep on flying directly in a westerly direction, just above the waves to stay as invisible as possible.

I call Hector to come forward: "Has this dashing Dragon suffered any damage when those soldiers shot at us?"

"Only six bullet holes. Four on the fuselage and two on that boy's leg."

After more than an hour I see the English coast ahead of us. I have managed to make contact with some or other air controller and I am guided to enter British air space over Colchester. I increase height and land twenty minutes later at Hendon, the home station of my determined Dragon.

I have already asked the conning tower to send an ambulance to the spot where I stop to pick up a wounded passenger.

As I look around, I see five pale faces. The palest face is that of young Judah Isaacsohn. Despite Hector's best efforts, he has lost a lot of blood and some of that blood is spilt onto the floor of my plane.

After the wounded boy has been taken off the plane and into an ambulance, Hector takes our guests with their few pieces of luggage to the first aid station to be with Judah. I stay behind to look after my plane and to refuel.

Hector comes back after an hour: "I was able to organize temporary lodgings for these fugitives without passports. I also contacted the War Office. They told me to go home for a day or two and then report back to London."

"We can't fly now to Hagdale because I can't land on our field in the dark. It will be dark by the time we get there. Where can we sleep?"

"Perhaps at the officers' mess. Otherwise, we will have to use this dirty Dragon as a bedroom."

"She isn't so dirty anymore. I have cleaned up all Judah's blood while you were gone."

Hagdale, Saturday, 11 May 1940

It was possible to phone Freddy Fortune at Hagdale from Hendon and warn him that we will arrive home later today and that he must see to it that the villa is ready for us.

We slept very uncomfortably in the officers' mess at Hendon last night on the floor of the mess hall. There was no opportunity to talk much. Fortunately, we could use the ablution facilities and wash our faces and hands.

After a very basic breakfast, I get permission to fly off with my darling Dragon and about forty minutes later, we land on our meadow at home.

Cheeky Carol prepared a tasty lunch and while we drink some coffee in the library afterwards, Hector can start to tell me what to expect next: "The War Office gave me two days to get my life in order and then I must report back on Monday. You will have to take me back."

"Do you know what your new job will be?"

"Yes, they told me over the phone that I must report at the Directorate of Military Intelligence at the War Office. They will put me in Section 14 of British Military Intelligence, usually known as MI 14."

"What will you do there?"

"I know MI 14 as the section that deals with Germany and German-held territories. That is, I think, a logical choice for me because we have been focusing on Germany for the last eight years. I think I can tell them a lot and help them to interpret radio messages that we intercept and aerial photographs taken by the RAF of German facilities."

"You used to take some aerial photographs yourself."

"Those were amateurish. I believe they now have dedicated and specialized aircraft to do that type of job."

"Must I come and stay with you in London?"

"I don't think that will be a good thing. I haven't been told where I will stay, but it will most probably be at one of the military barracks in the city or somewhere there. Since there is a war going on, I won't have much free time to spend with you. So, fly me back on Monday morning early and return afterwards. Life will be much safer and more comfortable here. I won't be surprised of those nasty Nazis start to bomb London from the air. The Germans tried something like that during the Great War when a few Zeppilins flew over London. Now they have hundreds of bomber aircraft for that type of work."

"We also have bombers. Will we bomb Berlin?"

"Certainly. And other German cities, as well."

Hagdale, Wednesday, 15 May 1940

When we landed at Hendon on Monday, Hector immediately hitched a ride with a RAF vehicle that went to the city. I had a meeting with my squadron commander to report back from Holland and to inquire whether he had any jobs for me.

"Milady, you are a heaven-sent. I urgently need to get transport for three gentlemen to Glasgow. Can you take them?"

"Only if I will be allowed to deliver them and return home before nightfall."

The commander immediately lifted his phone and ordered his adjutant to see to it that my plane gets refueled and to locate the three gents that I must fly to Glasgow.

Less than an hour later, I was airborne with two RAF officers and a civilian. They just greeted me with a 'good morning' while they stepped into the dependable Dragon, without introducing themselves. We flew in silence. Somebody waited for them at Glasgow and I was allowed to take off again immediately after refueling.

And now I am sitting at home, not knowing what to do with myself. Suddenly the radio, which is tuned to a BBC music program, starts beeping. It's Henry's call sign. I reply with my call sign, HSR1. I grab a piece of paper to write down his message:

FTTFO WBOOBH

I immediately decode the message. It's in Afrikaans, of all languages:

ESSEN VANNAG

That means: 'Essen tonight.' I immediately hop onto the frequency Sonja gave me for today and I send off the following:

TH FT V

That means: TH ES V.

It is as if a little voice inside me – certainly that of Veleda's spirit – tells me: "Here we go!"

I hope that the Germans at Essen in the Ruhr Valley, where huge steel factories are situated, will be warned in time to get their anti-aircraft guns ready and that the Luftwaffe will be on standby to chase the RAF bombers away before they can inflict any damage.

Hagdale, Sunday, 25 August 1940

During the past three-and-a-half months, there wasn't anything that I could do to help Germany. It seemed as if the German Army and the Luftwaffe were unstoppable.

When we had to flee Holland in haste on 10 May, the Germans attacked Holland, Belgium, Luxemburg, and France at the same time. Within little more than a fortnight, the British expeditionary force, consisting of 13 divisions with almost 400 000 men, had to admit defeat and started to be evacuated from the beaches of Dunkirk in Northern France. It was a heroic effort, I must admit, and the Royal Navy, together with dozens, even hundreds of private craft, helped to take the beaten and weary British soldiers off the beaches and take them back to Britain. This operation only ended on 4 June.

Hector and Daniel, who came home for a brief two-day visit, told me that during the operation, thousands of British and French troops were either captured or became casualties. The perimeter of the Dunkirk pocket was well-defended and the Germans did not try to breach it, but the Luftwaffe did its best to bomb the poor Tommys. They sank a few destroyers of the Royal Navy and the French Navy and other craft. Tons of equipment and supplies had to be abandoned.

The French soldiers carried on as well as possible, but they surrendered on 22 June. The Germans occupied the northern part of France, while the southern half was administered from the town of Vichy by a government that had to support the German war effort.

Thereafter, the Luftwaffe started to attack Britain and concentrated on eliminating the Royal Air Force by attacking air fields and aircraft factories. According to Hector, they almost succeeded to overwhelm the Royal Air Force. He thought that these attacks were meant to soften up the British Defenses before Britain was invaded by German forces.

The first Luftwaffe attack on Southampton occurred during the afternoon of 13 August. We could hear the explosions at Hagdale, as well as see the clouds of smoke caused by the explosions and the fires that started in the dockyard area.

And today I was informed by Henry that the bombers of the Royal Air Force were ordered to hit back and start the bombing of Berlin. That prompted me to inform my contacts in Berlin to expect the bombing of Berlin for the next few days. This was only the second message I have sent since my return to Hagdale.

London, Saturday 7 September 1940

Hector phoned me yesterday with the request that I fly to London today and meet him at the War Office. He added: "It's vital. Very important. Please, do come."

Since he didn't stipulate what the reason for my visit was, I packed a bag with necessities to stay there a few days, if necessary. A cab takes me to the imposing building of the War Office at Whitehall, on Horse Guards Avenue.

At the entrance, I ask that Brigadier de Hacqueville be called and I introduce myself as his wife. I am asked to wait while Hector is summoned on a phone to come and fetch me. He is, of course, glad to see me and gives me a hug. He leads me through underground tunnels where dozens of people are working.

He warns me: "Please don't ask anybody for their names. They won't give it. People outside are not supposed to know who are the people working here. It's all confidential, secret, you see.

You and the boys are the only people who know that I work here in Section 14 of Military Intelligence.”

We reach the part of the complex occupied by Section 5.

I am introduced to a major general who invites me to sit down in his office. Hector joins me.

“Milady, thank you for coming at such short notice. Your husband vouched for you and we need your services urgently.”

I must have looked puzzled and he smiles: “You won’t do anything dangerous. What we require is simply that you keep your eyes and ears open.”

“For what?”

“We, here in Section 5, have the task of counter-espionage. We smell out enemy spies and spooks. When they are identified and caught, we can arrest them and try them and deal with them.”

I declare with a straight face: “I don’t know any enemy agents.”

“I’m sure you don’t. But you are well-placed to smoke out some of them.”

“How? I’m not a smoker.”

“Of course not. But you can help us to catch them by keeping your eyes and ears open. Your husband told me that you are fluent in German and Dutch, but that you also are of Jewish ancestry. Your father is a German Jew who lives in South Africa. You were exposed to the Jewish religion and culture by your father, although he also introduced you to some German traditions and the German language. Your husband tells me that you sometimes visit the local synagogues in Southampton and Winchester, apart from also going to a Christian church with your family – just as you frequented the Jewish synagogue in The Hague.”

“That is so. Do you suspect some jolly Jews to be nasty Nazi spies?”

"Not quite so. I am convinced that you – just as many other Germans – detest Hitler and his policies and that you wish for his downfall. Your Jewish background convinced me that you will oppose the Nazis wherever you can."

"And you expect some Jews to be secret Nazi agents?"

"Only people who masquerade as Jews. Many Jews fled from Germany and Austria after Crystal Night. Some of your relatives who managed to reach you in Holland, are examples of these fugitives. But we have the sneaking suspicion that the German Secret Service, the Abwehr, has sneaked in several agents to Britain, pretending to be Jews."

"And you expect of me to smell or smoke them out?"

"Exactly. Keep your eyes and ears open when you visit the synagogues. Also, your nose to smell them. Make the acquaintance of as many fugitives as you can. With your knowledge of German Jewish traditions, you will easily be able to identify bogus Jews. And then you let us know. Are you prepared to do your bit to defeat the forces of darkness and evil that swept over Europe?"

"Hector, what do you think? Must I take on this job?"

Hector: "I regard it as your patriotic duty as an English noblewoman. Yes. Of course, you won't be a professional agent who will be paid for your sleuthing and snooping. But then, your job will mostly be on the Jewish Sabbath when you visit the synagogues."

"All right, General, give me this job."

Secretly, I ask myself: what would Veleda have done? She would have played along and use the opportunity to warn any German agents that they may be exposed.

The general gives me a slip of paper with a telephone number on it: "Whenever you want to contact this section, phone this number, and mention your name. Somebody will contact you to hear what you can tell us. Good luck! God bless you!"

Secretly, I think: "What does God have to do with this evil English Empire? Does He also wish its destruction and demolition and disintegration?"

As we leave the general's office, Hector says: "I have booked a room for the two of us in a hotel tonight. I hoped you would approve."

"Of course."

I wander the streets of London during the rest of the day. The mood of the city seems to be gloomy, depressed, uncertain, and pessimistic. Nobody loves a war and I share their feelings.

After dinner in the hotel's dining room, we retire to our room. There is much to talk about – how we miss each other, how we miss our sons, how we miss a quiet peaceful life.

Just as we start to make love, the air raid sirens go off.

Hector groans: "Blasted! Get dressed as quickly as possible. We must get into the air raid shelter!"

While we are sitting huddled with some other hotel guests in the air raid shelter, Hector explains to me: "We have started bombing Berlin a few days ago. Now Hitler is trying to pay us back."

"Tit for tat, in other words."

We can hear how bombs are exploding and how the anti-aircraft guns bark and crack and spit flames.

One of the guests mumbles: "It sounds as if the Tilbury docks are their targets."

Hagdale, Sunday, 8 September 1940

My contacts in Berlin receive the warning that Berlin must expect another attack by the RAF tonight.

I tune my radio at nine pm to the Afrikaans program of Radio Zeesen. A man who calls himself "Neef Buurman"[64] reads the news. He mentions that an air raid is ongoing over Berlin, but that the audacious anti-aircraft gunners and the ferocious fighter pilots of the Luftwaffe are defending the city against these aggressors. Several British bombers have been shot down in flames.

I pray to the God of Abraham, Isaac, and Jacob, that Henry is not one of those casualties.

After the news, a few personal messages are being read. The announcer says: "Our dear friend Theo must take note of the fact that his uncle Wilhelm is very grateful for the letters he has received from him. It really warmed his heart."

My "Uncle Wilhelm" is, of course, Vizeadmiral Wilhelm Canaris. In other words, my messages did reach him.

After some other personal messages, a program is being aired about South African musicians who have studied in Germany.

---

[64] "Cousin Neighbour". It later transpired that he was a certain Dr Adriaan Strauss.

Hagdale, Friday, 8 November 1940

Hector asked me to fetch him and Daniel for the week-end with my dashing Dragon.

During dinner, Hector tells us that the battle against the Luftwaffe seems to have been won. When the Germans started attacking civilian targets, such as London, Coventry, and other cities, the RAF could recover from the hammer blows their air fields have been given. The Luftwaffe scaled their bombing raids considerably down, perhaps due to the many losses they had suffered.

I correct Hector's observation by telling him: "They haven't stopped their campaign against the RAF totally. Towards the end of September, there were two very heavy raids on the Spitfire factory at Hamble near Southampton. Some of the German bombers flew over us after having released their bombs and I could see them clearly in the light of the moon."

Hector reports that Henry's squadron has moved to another base at Feltwell at Norfolk, East Anglia, where they will convert to Vickers Wellington medium bombers. This news gives me the assurance that he hasn't bought it over Berlin.

Southampton, Saturday, 30 October 1940

While I sit in the Albion Place Synagogue in Southampton, I watch the congregants. Rabbi Gideon Goldstein holds a dramatic and emotional sermon about the wickedness of the ancient Philistines who worshipped false gods and suppressed the Israelites, which he compares to the Nazis who also worship false gods and oppress the descendants of Abraham, Isaac, and Jacob.

He has ample reason to be furious and emotional because the synagogue has suffered some damage during the bombing raid of two nights ago. One wall had to be propped up to prevent its collapse.

One young man listens with a smirk on his face. He looks perhaps Jewish, but it may also be that he has some southern blood from Austria. I also watch him while a Psalm is being sung.

After the service, the congregants gather in the aisles to discuss the worse bombing raid to date on Southampton. I walk over to the young man and introduce myself as Theodora Davidsohn. He mentions that his name is Sam Silbermann.

I tell him in German: "Young man, the Abwehr hasn't trained you well enough. You will certainly be caught one of these days."

The blood drains from his face and he stammers, also in German: "What do you mean?"

"Your safety is at stake, young man. You gave yourself away. You're not really a Jew. Move away from Southampton somewhere else where people will not recognize you as a Nazi spy. That is, if you value your life. Don't pretend to be a Jew, because you're not one and never will be one."

The sweat runs down his face and his eyes blink a few times, while he swallows his own saliva.

"I'm sorry for you. And, please, forget that you ever spoke to me. You could get into big, big trouble, if you don't forget this conversation and my face."

With that, I walk away, while I hope that Herr Silbermann, or whoever he is, will be more careful in the future.

I wander through the streets of Southampton, to inspect the damage done by the German bombs. I feel sorry for the people who lost their lives, their limbs, or their homes. War is always ugly when civilians get in the way. Smoke is still pouring from some ruins.

Lower High Street, Southampton after the air raids of 30 November and 1 December 1940.

Hagdale, Saturday, 4 January 1941

Christmas and New Year's Eve were horrible, solitary, cold, and uneventful, except for another Luftwaffe visit to Southampton on 5 December. To seek company, I talked to the maids, our butler, and the estate workers. I presented a Christmas lunch for all of them, which I, as the wife of the estate's lord, could not participate in.

I tinkered in the shed where my devoted Dragon stood and serviced her engines.

I feel good though, that I was able to warn the Germans a few times during the past few weeks of planned air raids by the RAF on especially Bremen and environment.

Last Sunday night, Radio Zeesen had the following message for me: "Our dear friend Theo, you are encouraged to continue with your excellent work. Many people are grateful for your efforts."

I gather that my warnings may have saved many lives.

Today, I visit the synagogue in Southampton again – just to have company. Afterwards, the rabbi invites me to visit him and his wife. They can't offer me tea because it is the Sabbath.

The rabbi tells me that he was born in England from parents who fled the Russian pogroms during the last century. He is serving this congregation for the last eighteen years and knows all the members very well.

I ask: "How many refugees from Germany have joined your congregation the last few years?"

"There are three families. They came from the German town of Kleve and they are full of praise for a German officer who smuggled them over the border with Holland. From there, they decided to settle in England. We also had a young man till a few weeks ago, but he just disappeared. Heaven knows what became of him."

I can't disclose that that German officer who smuggled the Jews over the Dutch border must have been my own brother. I also decide that these three families must be genuine fugitives and I am glad that the young man, Herr Silbermann, took my advice to heart and moved away.

Southampton, Saturday, 5 April 1941

While I listen to today's sermon of Rabbi Goldstein, I watch the members of the congregation. All of them seem shocked by the "Southampton Blitz" – the repeated bombing of the city by the Luftwaffe. I can't detect anybody who may be a secret German spy.

Afterwards, I corner the rabbi and ask him if I may again visit him and his wife at their home after the service. That helps against the loneliness.

After the conversation with the rabbi, I drive my automobile to Hamble with its aircraft factories and workshops, as well as the airfield where I and Hector watched the Air Pageant a few years ago. The place is being transformed into a fortress with anti-aircraft batteries all over the place.

This anti-aircraft emplacement on Hamble Common protected the fuel terminal and jetty.

During the past few weeks, I managed to tell Berlin to be ready for raids on Berlin, Bremen, Hamburg, and Emden. I will also inform Berlin about the defenses at Hamble.

Hamble, Monday, 22 September 1941

Sometimes, I get the feeling that the war is going along without me and I feel somewhat useless and left behind. During the Great War, I was sitting at the center point of the South African war effort. Now, I am sitting on the fringes. I was able to warn Berlin at least twice a week of planned air raids on Berlin, Bremen, Essen, Hamburg, and other targets, including French harbors being used by the German Kriegsmarine. These tasks took merely a few minutes of my time each day.

I flew towards the end of May to London to be with my husband and two of my sons. London is almost a dead city. There are few people on the streets and there are wrecked buildings in many places. Most children have been evacuated to foster-parents in the countryside. Hector told me that the worst Blitz ever occurred a few days before my visit, on 10 May. The people of London used the German expression "Blitz" (lightning) to describe the attacks by the Luftwaffe.

Since I heard very little from Daniel in Portsmouth, I flew to Portsmouth to visit him and his family. He told me that they had endure quite a few raids by the Luftwaffe, mostly on ships in the harbor, but that little damage was done. He also informed me in confidence that there wasn't much intelligence that he could pass onto me. His job in the harbor administration dealt mainly with logistics, and not with operational matters. With his background in economics, he had to manage the budget for supplies, ammunition, equipment, and fuel that had to be procured for the base and the fleet.

The Germans seemed to have become bored by watching the English coast from the French side of the Channel and they switched their attention to eastern Europa. It seems as if their plans for the invasion of Britain have been shelved. The Wehrmacht attacked

Russia on 22 June and made rapid progress. That suddenly made Russia, also called the Union of Socialist Soviet Republics, an ally of Great Britain.

Hector confided in me: "The poor Ivans were totally unprepared for this war. There are plans to supply them with some hardware to defend themselves. Otherwise, Hitler will strut around on the Red Square in Moscow, one of these days – just as he did in Paris after the fall of France."

Of course, this news was passed on to Berlin.

And today, I am taking my dignified Dragon to Hamble for repairs on one of her engines. This engine made strange noises and I wasn't able to locate their origin and, therefore, she had to be operated upon by specialists.

While waiting for the technicians to do their job, I walk around and watch how the Spitfire fighters are being assembled at the Supermarine plant. This fighter aircraft, according to Henry, was the greatest danger to German bombers entering the airspace of Britain.

I watch how a Spitfire lands on the runway outside. And then I suddenly see something that I can hardly believe: an attractive woman-pilot getting out of that Spitfire. She is evidently delivering the Spitfire for repairs, or – she took it up for a test flight and landed again.

After she has reported to wherever she had to report, I find her and we start to talk over a cup of tea in the canteen.

Me: "Since when do women fly fighter aircraft?"

"For quite some time now. Haven't you heard of the ATA yet? That's the Air Transport Auxiliary. It's a sort of a civilian appendix to the RAF. The pilots deliver aircraft to workshops for repairs and deliver new and repaired aircraft to RAF squadrons. We don't take part in battles and operations and so forth and, therefore, we weren't taught to do acrobatics or night flying. We often transport military passengers between air fields."

I ask: "How many of your pilots are women?"

"Quite a lot. We are divided into pools and we have just started Pool Number 15 here at Hamble. A pool can be compared to a regular squadron."

"How can I join?"

"Are you interested in flying? I gather so, otherwise you wouldn't have been loitering around here."

"I have my own twin-engine plane that is being repaired here and I am somehow affiliated to 24 Squadron of the RAF."

"Then you are exactly the type of woman the ATA needs. How old are you?"

"Fifty-six."

"Still young enough to join – especially if you are already an experienced pilot."

"I've been flying around the world for the past twelve odd years."

My first thought is: this type of job will help me to overcome my boredom. It will also be a perfect cover for my activities on behalf of Germany. I will certainly be flying all over the country where I can pick up bits of gossip for the benefit of Uncle Wilhelm.

My new acquaintance continues: "Our female pool has just moved into a new hangar here at Hamble. That's where we sleep between jobs."

Hagdale, Wednesday, 1 October 1941

At six-o'-clock this morning, while I am swallowing my breakfast before I return to Hamble, our phone rings. It's my happy husband, glad to catch me still at home.

"I think I have news of your brother."

"How? Did he phone you, or something?"

"No, not that. I think I've heard his voice on Radio Zeesen, last night. You know, it's part of my job to know what's going on in Berlin and what they're telling the world. There was an interview in Afrikaans with a certain Thomas. Now, we already know that your brother has adopted the name of Thomas von Traubenstein. This Thomas didn't disclose his family name, but the voice gave him away. I am fairly certain that I heard David on the radio."

"What did he say?"

"He was interviewed about his career in the German Army – his job with the German Schutztruppe in Southwest Africa and afterwards how he took part in the campaign in Norway and how he also fought against the Russians. He's a full colonel now and his last position was that of second-in-command of an infantry division."

"And what is he doing now?"

"He didn't tell. I suspect it has something to do with intelligence because that was his job when he was working at Robert's Heights before the Great War."

"If it is really him, then we know that he's alive and well enough to be interviewed in Berlin. So – he's a colonel now. That very noble name that he has chosen for himself must have helped him in his career, I'm sure."

White Waltham Airfield, Friday, 10 October 1941

This morning, I landed with my dependable Dragon Rapide at the White Waltham Airfield, in Berkshire, west of London, and now I am sitting in the office of the director of the ATA, Commodore[65] Sir Gerard d'Erlanger. He is joined by his deputy, Roy Rawlinson, and Commander Pauline Gower, the organizer of the women's section.

Hector was delighted with my decision to join the ATA and he organized my interview with Sir Gerard, who is in command of the ATA. His previous position was that of chairman of the British Overseas Airways Corporation (BOAC) and, therefore, he knows much about managing an organization involved with flying.

Sir Gerard smiles broadly after I have been invited to sit down: "Milady, thank you very much to volunteer for the ATA and become one of our so-called 'Attagirls'."

"Sir Gerard, I am thrilled and honored that you invited me to this meeting."

"I trust that you have brought your pilot's license and your flying log book along, so that we can have a look at the number of flying hours you have logged."

"Here they are (and I hold up a bag containing these documents). I have also made photographs of everything and have them validated by the local Police Chief as authentic and true copies of the originals."

"Excellent. Excellent. That means that we don't have to train you from scratch. You are familiar, as I understand it, with a twin-engine aircraft? All that remains, is to give you some conversion training on certain RAF types, such as Spitfires, Wellingtons, and so forth."

"Thank you, Sir Gerard."

---

[65] See the rank structure of the ATA in an appendix at the end of the book.

Commander Pauline Gower adds: "I propose that we now award to you the wings, the badge of competency of our organization, if Sir Gerard concurs. I have it here with me."

Sir Gerard: "I can see no reason why that shouldn't be done. She has a pilot's license, as she has just demonstrated."

Pauline asks me to stand up and receive three sets of wings, which I will have to attach to my flying overalls. 

Sir Gerard: "Milady, it is required of all new pilots to draw three sets of overalls from our stores. Also a cap or two, together with a flying helmet and flying goggles. Pauline will show you the way afterwards.

Pauline: "Milady, you will have to receive some conversion training, as Sir Gerard has indicated. It will be done at the Central Flying School at the Royal Air Force station Upavon in Wiltshire. Together with that, you will have to be instructed about all our procedures, practices, processes, and policies. You are to report there next Monday week."

"I am perfectly willing to learn everything. May I fly there with my semi-private aircraft, a Dragon Rapide?"

Sir Gerard: "Most certainly. That means that we don't have to provide the necessary transport for you. You have submitted the request to be posted to Female Pool Number 15 at Hamble, near Southampton. Since your husband's estate is in that vicinity, I think it is a fair request. You will be posted to Hamble after receiving your conversion training at Upavon and appointed in the rank of second officer. Your present rank is that of cadet. We can skip the rank of third officer in your case."

Feltwell, Sunday, 12 October 1941

My son, Henry – or Hendrik – exclaims: "Hell, Ma, when have you received those wings? I didn't know that the RAF uses women pilots. What do you fly? Spitfires? Blenheims? Wellingtons?"

"No, my dear son. This mother of yours is not a RAF pilot. Look carefully at these wings on my flying overalls. They were given to me by the Air Transport Auxiliary. I am due to receive conversion training to twin-engine flying machines from next week, and then I will be stationed at Hamble near Southampton."

"Oh, you're with the ATA? One of those Attagirls?"

"That's me."

I and Henry – by this time, promoted to squadron leader – are sitting in the officers' mess at RAF Feltwell where he is serving with No 57 Bomber Squadron. I slept in London last night after visiting Hector and Victor at the War Office to show off my new pilot's wings. Hector contacted Henry to organize permission for me to land my decorous Dragon at his base.

We are speaking Afrikaans to prevent any eavesdropping by any of his colleagues: "Hendrik, this mother of yours is as happy as a bunny in a carrot field or a horse in a cabbage bed. I'm going to fly a lot – big things. I never thought I would get into this position."

"Ma, how am I and Victor going to contact you in future with messages and warnings for Berlin? You will be flying all over the place and you will be far too busy to listen when my call sign comes through on that big radio set at home."

"That means that we will have to organize something else. I propose that we agree on a certain frequency that both of us access at exactly six-o'-clock every night to listen for a few seconds for any messages. Most of your flying and bombing raids happen later during the night. You can tune in one your plane's radio set at that time, whether you are stationary on flat Mother Earth, or already gliding through the clouds en route to some place. I will also use my radio set in whatever airplane I am sitting, either a plane that I'm ferrying, or my own dignified Dragon. How does that sound?"

"It could work. By that time, at six, we will have already been briefed about our destination for the night, but usually before we take off. Yes, let's do it that way."

"This is exactly my arrangement with Victor. By the way: How do you feel about dropping bombs on Germany?"

"I make sure that my bombs don't reach their intended targets and fall into water or onto open fields."

"But how?"

"It's simple. I'm the pilot and in command of the plane. When we approach the target, I'm supposed to slow down and allow the navigator, who is also the bomb-aimer in the nose of the Wellington, to release the bombs at the right moment. He peers at the target through a special sight. I always make it impossible for him to release his bombs at the right moment by pretending that the plane is being shaken by exploding flak or by high winds, or whatever. When the poor guy couldn't release his bombs right on time, we just jettison them somewhere else because we don't want to be burden by a heavy bomb load on our way back."

Vickers Wellington bomber

"Clever of you. And in the process, you save some lives."

"Ma, we have already inflicted real damage to some places in Germany, and I feel horrible about it. It sometimes keeps me awake when I have to sleep."

"I've seen the damage that the Southampton Blitz had caused. I can imagine that something similar must be the case over there in Germany."

Hamble, Monday, 24 November 1941

My D-class conversion training on the twin-engine bombers, the Blenheims and the Wellingtons, as well as the Douglas Dakota transport plane, proceeded smoothly. I was the only pupil or cadet during this part of the course since I joined the ATA at a time when they normally didn't take in recruits. My previous experience in the air made it necessary that I be deployed as soon as possible.

Of course, the Dakotas, Blenheims, and Wellingtons, are bigger and heavier than my dainty Dragon, but I adapted easily to their more intricate controls and instruments. I received my shoulder straps with two stripes or bars last Friday to show that I am now a second officer. Unfortunately, it wasn't possible for Hector or one of the boys to attend the occasion. The result is that the whole family de Hacqueville consists of members who have ranks – apart from titles.

And today, I am to deliver my first repaired Dakota to my old unit, No 24 Squadron at Hendon, arguably the largest squadron in the RAF with its dozens of civilian planes impressed into RAF use.

During the time of my conversion training, I was able to warn the Abwehr of a large RAF raid on Berlin on 7 November. I learned later that 20 RAF bombers were shot down and that little damage was done.

It feels like I am the Queen of the Sky, here high up in the air. I am in sole control of this marvelous machine, this technological triumph from America. Of course, I also wonder how it would feel to fly a German airplane. It won't be a surprise to me if the German machines were better.

It suddenly dawns on me, here high in the clouds, that this is a golden opportunity to do some sabotage while I am in control of an expensive war machine of the RAF. Something like this will certainly not win the war for Germany, but the nuisance value may just make life somewhat easier for the Germans.

After I have put down the aircraft at Hendon and switched off the engines, I fumble with some of the electrical wires under the instrument panel. With my nail scissors, I cut a few of them in such a manner that it won't be easily detectable. I bless Sam at Hagdale who taught me some mechanical and electrical tricks.

To see what the effect of my work is, I start the engines again. Some of the instruments on the dashboard are dead. I switch the engines off again, grab my bag, close the outside door as I get onto solid Mother Earth, and report to the conning tower that something must have gone wrong with the plane while I was flying her. Somebody must do something about it.

Thereafter, I ask the transport officer to provide a vehicle and a driver to take me to the railroad station from where I can return to my base near Southampton.

Hagdale, Sunday, 7 December 1941

Hector, Daniel, and Victor managed to get a weekend off. It is a pleasure to have my husband, as well as two of my sons and their families, with me at Hagdale. My schedule only requires of me to fetch a broken plane from somewhere near Liverpool tomorrow and deliver her to Hamble for some repairs.

While the men were busy getting dressed for dinner, I managed to contact Henry and he informed me that raids were being planned on Aachen in Germany and Brest on the French coast where some Kriegsmarine ships and submarines are based. I immediately sent a message to Berlin to warn the Germans.

After dinner, I ask the men to listen with me to Radio Zeesen. Daniel wasn't aware of this Afrikaans program, but Hector and Victor have listened to it in the past.

Hector: "Yes, it's important to know what type of lies those Nazis are telling the world."

It is pleasant to hear somebody speak Afrikaans. The news at nine contains very important items. The man reading the news and who calls himself "Neef Holm" is jubilant. Japanese planes, launched from aircraft carriers in the Pacific Ocean, attacked the American naval base at Pearl Harbor on Hawaii and sank some battleships and other craft, and damaged the harbor facilities. Unfortunately, the Russians started with a counter-attack against the Germans just outside Moscow, but the listeners are assured that the German troops are defending their positions heroically.

After the news, there are some personal messages. I listen to the following item with a straight face: "Our dear friend Theo must take note that his Uncle Wilhelm is to send him a box of 'Aachener

Lebkuchen'[66] for Christmas out of gratitude for his welcome Christmas letter with good wishes."

This tells me that Canaris is grateful for the warning regarding Aachen.

Hector coughs and growls: "Those stupid Japs have started something horrible. Mark my words, they took a bite that they won't be able to swallow. They will choke. They just brought the United States into the war. They will never have the capacity to subdue the Americans. That also means that the Americans can support us more openly and they will certainly help to supply Russia to repel the Germans from the gates of Moscow."

I and my two sons listen silently.

---

[66] "Lebkuchen" – German gingerbread.

Feltwell, Wednesday, 18 February 1942

Henry invites me to lunch in the officers' mess at RAF Feltwell where his No 57 Squadron is based. I had to deliver a repaired Wellington to this base earlier this morning.

Of course, I sabotaged the Wellington invisibly just after having landed. I brought some tools along in my overnight bag and with a hammer and chisel I punched a small hole in the hydraulic system of one of the landings wheel's. The hydraulic fluid will seep out over time and that will cause that the plane's wheel system to collapse, damaging the wing and the engine on that side.

Henry asks me in Afrikaans while we sit at a table on our own: "Ma, did you manage to warn the folks at Hamburg and Bremen that we planned to throw some bombs on them last month on more than one occasion?"

"Yes, I did."

"Good for you. Our squadron lost four Wellingtons in that raid because the German gunners must have been ready for them."

"How many bombers took part in those operations?"

"There were more than five hundred of them. Other squadrons also suffered bad losses. As far as we can gather, most of the crews were able to bail out with their parachutes. Now they are the guests of the Luftwaffe in some or other camp."

"Where does your squadron fit into the bigger picture of Bomber Command? I've heard a week ago that you have a new chief for Bomber Command."

"Yes. Our new boss is Air Marshall Arthur Harris. He was previously the commander of no 5 Group. Bomber Command comprises all the bomber squadrons and they are grouped into several groups."

"How many commands are there?"

"Quite a few. We also have Fighter Command, Training Command, Transport Command, Army Cooperation Command, Coastal Command, Maintenance Command, and so forth."

"How is this Harris chap?"

"A real butcher. A killer. Knows no mercy."

"Warfare doesn't know of any mercy, anyway. What makes him so special?"

"He issued a directive last week that we must forget about precision bombing of targets in Germany. He wants us to do what he calls 'area bombing' or 'carpet bombing'. That means that everything in the vicinity of a target must be flattened – factories, air fields, railroad stations, but also residential areas. Too bad for the poor civilians who live there. They are supposed to hide in air raid shelters when we attack. They must only see that their homes and shops are gone after the 'all clear' signal has been given."

"That's horrible."

"Indeed. He says that's wat Fat Hermann Göring's boys did during the Blitz. We are supposed to pay them back, with interest."

"And how will you deal with this directive?"

"As in the past. I will bomb open fields, lakes, the sea, or spaces that were already flattened previously. In a few cases, I have been able to remove the fuses from the bombs after they have been loaded and when I inspect the plane before take-off. That renders those bombs useless. And I will also tell you about upcoming raids."

"I've told you in the past that you have some unknown cousins in Germany. How does that make you feel when you fly over Germany?"

"Dunno. I haven't got the faintest idea where they are and whether they are part of the Wehrmacht."

"My brother, their father, is a senior Army officer. Heaven alone knows where he is serving. That is, if he's still alive."

Hagdale, Sunday, 29 March 1942

Hector managed to slip away from the War Office for a quiet weekend at home. It was possible to organize my program of flights to be with him.

Last night, we again listened to the news in Afrikaans on Radio Zeesen. Hector observed: "It's actually illegal to listen to this type of enemy propaganda. Although, with my job at the War Office, I'm authorized and even compelled to listen to all that nonsense."

The news mentioned a series of air raids by the RAF on the industrial cities of Essen and Cologne during the past fortnight. The announcer gives the assurance that little damage was done and that the Luftwaffe was able to inflict heavy losses on the enemy bombers.

I don't know how much of this news is credible, although I believe that not all of it is false propaganda because I was able to send a serious warning about the impending campaign.

After the news, I caught a message meant for me, which I heard without showing any signs: "Dear Theo, your uncle Wilhelm is inviting you to meet him at the beautiful cathedral in Cologne one of these days."

This message told me that the Cologne cathedral is unscathed and that my warning was acted upon.

During lunch on this Sunday after we have attended church in Hursley, Hector asks me: "How do you fit in with that outfit where you are working?"

"Nicely. Very nicely. I love flying. One of these days I will be sent on another conversion course, Phase E. They will teach me to fly four-engine bombers and transport planes. After that, I will be promoted to the rank of first officer – on the same level as a flight lieutenant in the RAF."

"Congratulations. I will seal that achievement with a wrestling match this afternoon on our bed after the servants have left for the day. And how do your colleagues accept you? You must be older than most of them."

"I've made quite a few friends. I don't use my noble title because that may scare them off. I'm simply Dora to most of them. And how are you doing at the War Office?"

"I'm too old to be promoted to major general or something. I'm way past retirement age and they only keep me because there's a war going on and they need all the hands they can get. But I contemplate quitting. I will become sixty-two in September and I may ask them to give me a less demanding job."

"Like what?"

"Perhaps some or other administrative job. Perhaps supervisor of a cemetery where none of the customers can talk back."

London, Friday, 28 August 1942

My first delivery of a repaired Avro Lancaster to Hendon took place this afternoon. I managed to reach Hector on the phone and we decided to spoil ourselves with a relaxing week-end in a hotel on the outskirts of London. There doesn't seem to be much danger of German air attacks nowadays and, according to Henry, the RAF and the United States' Army Air Force seem to have gained the upper hand against the Luftwaffe.

I feel proud that I was able to qualify on the heavy Lancaster and the Halifax bombers. But I certainly don't like the prospect of this particular aircraft being able to download a deadly load of exploding bombs on the homes of innocent and defenseless German civilians. I was able to sabotage this aircraft by slicing one of the fuel hoses that feeds fuel to one of the engines. As soon as the aircraft takes off again, the fuel pumps will start to push the fuel through the sliced hose and into empty spots and that will cause the aircraft to lose lots of fuel before she can reach her target. It may even happen that the flight engineer will fail to notice that the fuel tank gets empty and that it will then be too late to turn back.

During the past few weeks, I was able to send messages to Berlin regarding imminent bombing raids on Berlin, Rostock, Bremen, Hamburg, and Augsburg. Henry let me know that a plant at Augsburg was producing submarine engines.

Hector enjoys dinner with me in the hotel's dining room and we chat: "I'm getting weary of this wasteful, wrecking, worrying war. We are making some progress on certain fronts, but there are setbacks on other fronts. All the belligerents are hurting each other so much that we can all bleed to death in the end. In Africa, there's this guy called Erwin Rommel who seems to have a magic touch. His Afrikakorps is besieging the Libyan city of Tobruk where thousands of South African and British troops are surrounded and unable to get out. We foresee the fall of this city very soon."

"You told me the other day that you are going to call it a day."

"That won't be so easy. I can't just say good-bye to the lot. MI 5 called in my help the other day. They were picking up strange signals in code on certain frequencies on certain days and they suspect that it may be in German. It seems that a different frequency is being used on each day of the week. I was asked to have a look at those signals with my knowledge of German. The trouble is, they are always very brief – less that half-a-minute and it's impossible to pinpoint their source or sources. It is even possible that the source or sources are moving around to prevent being located."

"What do you think? What are those signals about?"

"The most likely explanation is that the Germans have succeeded in inserting one or more agents who are watching our Air Force and Army and Navy. There seems to be some sort of a pattern. They were always picked up shortly before a major bombing raid by the RAF on Germany. It may just be that the agent observes that several bombers are taking off somewhere and he then warns the

German air defenses to be ready. But it may also be that this agent has inside knowledge about the target of that particular night."

"Hector, you can remember that MI 5 tasked me with unmasking German spies who may have slipped into the country under the guise of Jewish refugees. I must confess, I didn't apply enough effort in this regard. I did have a look at the Hebrew Congregations in Southampton and Winchester and they seem to be all above board. There was, unfortunately, no opportunity to watch and listen and smell elsewhere. And now I am rather busy with the ATA."

"I know you would do your bit. But, in the meantime, we will continue to monitor those particular wavelengths. Perhaps we will be able to catch the sleazy scoundrel. We must. By the way, the call sign is sometimes UI. Heaven knows what that signifies."

On my own I decide that I must carry on as usual with my messages to Berlin. It will look strange if the messages suddenly stop at this junction. Perhaps I can send some spurious messages, just to confuse MI 5 – and Hector, as well.

Hamble, Sunday, 30 August 1942

While I made ready to deliver another Lancaster to no 50 Squadron at RAF Waddington in Lincolnshire, I sent the following message approximately at ten in the morning on the usual frequency to Berlin:

UI WFSVDIF KFUAU OVS NJ GVFOG AV WFSXJSSFO = V

Decoded, it looks like this:

TH VERSUCHE JETZT NUR MI FUENF ZU VERWIRREN = V [67]

 When I listen to the evening news on Radio Zeesen, the following message comes through: "Dear Theo, your Uncle Wilhelm laughed heartily at your joke. Please continue with your jokes."

This tells me that my message was understood and that Canaris wants me to carry on with such confusing messages.

---

[67] "ONLY TRYING TO CONFUSE MI FIVE NOW".

Hagdale, Sunday, 6 September 1942

Henry and his family are visiting Hagdale for a few days. He got some very welcome leave last week after having completed a tour of duty of 30 missions. He has to report back for duty tomorrow, on Monday, 7 September.

Daniel, and Victor are also at home with their families for the day. I fetched all of them with my delightful Dragon.

We are celebrating no less than twelve occasions and achievements:

- Henry's 38th birthday last Tuesday, 1 September
- Henry's promotion to the rank of wing commander, which comes into effect on Tuesday, 1 September
- Henry's appointment of commanding officer of a newly established unit, no 323 Squadron at Scampton in Lincolnshire, equipped with Lancaster Bombers, which comes into effect tomorrow, on Monday, 7 September
- The award of the Distinguished Service Order to Henry two days ago, which enables him to put the abbreviation DSO after his name
- Daniel's 37th birthday last Tuesday, 1 September
- Daniel's promotion to the rank of Commander, which comes into effect on 1 October
- Daniel's appointment of second-in-command of the logistical division at Portsmouth Naval Yard last week
- Victor's promotion to the rank of major, last month
- Victor's appointment as commanding officer of the signal's unit at the War Office, last month
- The award of the Distinguished Service Order to Victor a fortnight ago, which enables him to put the abbreviation DSO after his name

- My promotion to the rank of flight captain, which comes into effect on 1 October
- My appointment to a new, more administrative, position at No 15 Female ATA Pool at Hamble

Father Richard Smurph was invited to hold a special thanksgiving service in our drawing room this afternoon. All the employees of the estate were also expected to attend.

During dinner, which is – of course – a very formal affair in full uniform for all, me included, Hector delivers a speech of congratulations to all and he proposes toasts to each of the birthdays, the promotions, the new appointments, and the new decorations.

He continues: "My dear family, I have an important announcement to make. I reach the age of sixty-two next month. That is way past the usual retirement age for military officers. I am grateful that the Army, as well as His Majesty, King George, whose commission I hold, have been able to endure me so long.

"But the end of the road has appeared for me, in a certain sense. I will become a fully-fledged pensioner at the end of next month. I have two choices in this regard: I can retire peacefully to live the quiet and relaxed life of a gentleman here at Hagdale, or I can continue to serve King and Country in another capacity. I have chosen the latter option.

"A new job has been offered to me. Something that will not be so strenuous, arduous, and adventurous as my present job at the War Office. I will become the second-in-command of a new establishment, a special prisoner-of-war camp for German generals and admirals. We have already caught a few of them in North Africa and we expect some more of them to be caught as the war progresses. They are presently being held with other prisoners-of-war at ordinary POW camps. But we want to put them into something special. I'm not allowed to divulge any details about where this camp will be or how it will operate. But it will enable me to be at home every week-end with your maternal parent. Her new position as flight captain at the ATA Pool at Hamble boils down to some sort of an administrative job and she will be able to have most week-ends free with me."

When Hector sits down, Henry rises to his feet: "Pa, thank you for your kind words. Let me propose a toast on both our old folks, our paternal parent, and our maternal parent. They are wonderful people and I am proud to be their son. I concur with the Reverend Father Richard who prayed for a long and blessed and productive life for both of them."

Hagdale, Thursday, 1 October 1942

After Hector finally became a retired brigadier of the British Army yesterday, I fetch him this morning with my dearly-appreciated Dragon.

We enjoy lunch in the garden, under a tree that hasn't shed its autumn leaves yet.

Me: "How was your farewell to the War Office yesterday?"

"Nothing special. My boss called all in our section together during tea-time. He gave a short speech in which I was thanked and praised for the work at the intelligence sections of the War Office and as a military attaché before the war. That was all. No farewell parade or something. No medals or certificates. Everything is, after all, supposed to be hush-hush in there."

"That sounds like some sort of an anticlimax."

"Yes, but also no. In a certain sense I'm relieved to be relieved and rescued from those stuffy and overcrowded tunnels and vaults and dungeons. I'm looking forward to start something new where I will see the sun every day and where I will be able to get hold of you almost every week-end."

"Where will that be?"

"At a joint called Trent Park, just outside London. There is a big old manor house in which the German generals and admirals will be housed."

"And you will be second-in-command. Who will be your boss?"

"A retired lieutenant general with the name of John Johnstone. He's three years older than me. He will be in charge of administration, while my job will be security and intelligence gathering. The idea is to make these Germans as comfortable and relaxed as possible. A unit of the Signal Corps is busy installing microphones in every bedroom and on strategic points in the bigger spaces, such as the library and the dining hall."

"So that you can eavesdrop on the conversations of these generals? That's not very polite or gentleman-like."

"Listen, this is war. No war is ever a polite affair. People try to kill each other. We hope that they will give certain secrets away, without realizing what they are doing."

"Damn clever, I must say. Talking about secrets. What happened with those secret radio messages that you people picked up? Have they located the secret sources?"

"That's a tricky issue, if you ask me. Somebody has been able to decipher and decode most of the messages. Some are in German, while others are in English … or even in Latin, of all languages. These accursed agents used a very simple code that was, in the end, easy to break. They simply shifted each letter of the alphabet one letter further on. An "A" becomes a "B", and so on. So, we are reading their messages – which isn't very polite, either. They dealt mainly with planned air raids on certain German cities and facilities.

"But the depressing and discouraging difficulty is that it is impossible to locate the sender or senders. It is possible to locate the precise direction from which certain radio signals come from. If these signals are picked up at two different spots and these observers can draw lines on a map indicating the directions from where these signals originate, then the signals must be coming from the point where the lines intersect. But these signals tend to come from different locations, as if these agents are moving around. And then these messages are so short that there is just no time to work out on a map where they come from. Very clever of him or them. And baffling for us."

"And you can't stop those signals?"

"The gentlemen from MI 5 plan to jam those particular frequencies on the days they are supposed to be used. But that won't be a permanent solution since the agent or agents will simply switch to other frequencies. And they will continue to warn the Germans of certain air raids. But that won't be my problem anymore. I will become involved in another intelligence operation, by listening to the conversations and gossiping of these German generals who will become our pampered gullible guests at Trent Park."

I cannot help but to sit with a smile while listening to my husband. He must get the impression that I am impressed with the accomplishments of British Intelligence. But I am also glad to learn that my operation is still safe. I and my two sons must simply carry on as usual, not to make MI 5 suspicious that we know of their efforts.

Hamble, Friday, 6 November 1942

There is jubilation in the tea room or No 15 Female ATA Pool at Hamble. Some of the girls sing and others dance.

I ask by friend Betsy: "What's this all about?"

"Haven't you heard? Rommel has lost a major battle in Egypt and he is running away with all his soldiers. We heard Churchill on the radio this morning and he said that there is reason for careful optimism. This may the end of the beginning or the war and even the beginning of the end of the war."

I smile because that is expected of me. Inside, though, I don't like what I hear. The blooming British Empire has just won a big bloody battle – just as they have won in South Africa forty years ago.

But all is not lost. I promise myself to continue with my warnings to Berlin, even if MI 5 can read them. But then it strikes me that MI 5 may spoil my game by sending bogus and spurious and false messages in my name. I will have to find out whether that is the case by listening to our daily radio frequencies as often as possible.

Hagdale, Saturday, 8 October 1942

Hector is strolling around on the estate to inspect the animals and the gardens. I sit in the library next to my big radio on which I listen to BBC music. Suddenly, Daniel's call sign comes through. I report immediately back that I hear him.

He sends the following message:

BMMJFT UP JOWBEF BMHFSJB FU NOSPDDP = ITS3

I decode it immediately:

ALLIES TO INVADE ALGERIA ET MOROCCO = HSR3

This means that the German Army in North Africa, that has been driven back into Tunisia, will have to face attacks in their backs.

I immediately switch over to the frequency of the day for the benefit of Berlin. There is a funny noise to be heard, almost like a huge waterfall. That can only be MI 5 that prevents me from contacting Berlin. I don't have any alternative frequencies for today and that frustrates me extremely. This may perhaps be the most important warning that I may have sent to the Germans, but it cannot be done.

Anyway, I gather that Daniel, who works in Portsmouth, must have picked up some news of this invasion.

Hamble and North Coates, Monday, 9 November 1942

After I have flown Hector back to his work place, I land at Hamble to fly another delivery of a refurbished Bristol Beaufighter to No 143 Squadron at RAF North Coates in Lincolnshire. There is nobody else available today and I took it upon myself to fly this aircraft, something I haven't done since receiving my conversion training to four-engine planes a while ago.

The Beaufighter has a dual role: it is used by Coastal Command as a torpedo bomber and a submarine hunter, and it is used as a night fighter by Fighter Command. No 143 Squadron belongs to Coastal Command and their base is situated in northern Lincolnshire, almost on the coast and just south of the estuary of the Humber.

My orders are to fly in from the north-east, over the sea. After delivery of the aircraft, I must be taken to the nearest railroad station from where I am to catch the overnight train to London, and from there to Southampton.

As I approach the runway from the north-east, over the North Sea, I suddenly get a brainwave. This aircraft must be prevented from ever catching a German submarine or sink a German ship along the coast of Norway, Denmark, or Holland. I cut the engines and make a belly landing on the water. I hope the water is deep enough so that the wreck of this Beaufighter cannot be retrieved. I see this as a small bit of revenge for Rommel's defeat in Egypt and the jamming of my message to Berlin.

While I surf along the waves and before the plane stops and sinks, I send a message: "Mayday, Mayday!" I explain briefly that the Beaufighter suddenly just ran out of juice and that I had no choice but to ditch her.

A rescue boat finds me shortly after sunset where I float with my life jacket. The aircraft has totally disappeared under the surface. The water is cold and I feel miserable, but I also feel satisfied with myself for sabotaging the British war effort somewhat. The discomfort in the water for two hours is not too much to endure.

North Coates, Tuesday, 10 November 1942

Although it was planned that I would return to Hamble as soon as possible from North Coates, my ordeal in the water made that impossible. After being rescued, I was taken to the sick bay where a quack inspected me. I was put into a bed with a hot water bottle at my feet to revive my frozen limbs.

My flying overall was washed and dried during the night and now I am sitting in the office of Wing Commander Leslie Lockwood, the commander of No 143 Squadron. I tell my story, which is simply that the engines of the Beaufighter suddenly spluttered and then cut out. I gave the fuel gauge a glance and saw that the tanks were totally empty. I suppose that the Beaufighter wasn't given enough fuel for the long flight, or that something went haywire with the fuel system, with the result that some fuel got lost.

A stenographer took down my story and typed it afterwards. After I have read through it, I sign it simply as Flight Captain T de Hacqueville ATA.

I am given the assurance that a Board of Investigation will look into the matter, but that will only be a formality and I am given permission to return to Hamble.

There is one thing that worries me while I sit in the train to London. I couldn't retrieve my overnight bag from the sinking Beaufighter. Apart from some clotting, it contains one set of keys to my distressed Dragon. I also know that it ought to worry me that I am able to tell lies so easily, but it doesn't bother me. According to my beliefs, lying to an Englishman isn't really a sin.

While I was sleeping in the sick bay last night, Veleda appeared for the first time after a long absence. She said: "You're doing fine!"

Brimsby, Monday, 14 December 1942

Today, I am taking a brand-new Lancaster to a unit that doesn't exist as yet – No 100 Squadron of the RAF, at the airfield of RAF Grimsby, near Waltham in Lincolnshire.

I was briefed that this squadron was wiped out by the Japanese in the Far East and that it was to be resurrected tomorrow on British soil as a bomber unit under Group 1 of Bomber Command, equipped with new Lancasters.

The Lancaster normally carries a crew of seven on operational sorties. Since this is merely a ferrying exercise, I am accompanied by only one crew member, a flight engineer with the name of Emily.

Since Grimsby is situated only a few miles west of North Coates, the scene of my previous "accident", it won't work to repeat my trick of last month to write off a valuable British aircraft. I will, therefore, have to devise something different to prevent this plane from dropping bombs on German cities and killing helpless people.

While approaching the runway at Grimsby, I lower the undercarriage. The moment the wheels touch the tarmac, I pull the undercarriage up again to create the impression to any possible onlooker that the undercarriage just gave way when I touched the earth.

The Lancaster starts skidding and sliding on her belly along the runway. I and a panicked Emily flee to the rear of the aircraft to avoid the inevitable impact upon her nose. We are thrown around when the Lancaster suddenly stops. We hear a loud crash and some breaking glass. And then silence descends upon us. Emily starts shaking from shock.

We creep through the entry hatch and I see three fire engines racing towards us. Their effort is, however, unnecessary because there are no flames to be seen. I and Emily are, nevertheless, taken by one of these trucks to the sick bay. As I look back, I see that I have written off a Lancaster and two Wellingtons against which the Lancaster collided with force.

A doctor and a nurse make us strip totally to investigate whether we have sustained any structural or internal damage. We display only several bruises and minor cuts, while Emily has a swollen eye where her head bumped against something or something bumped against her head, or whatever.

I demand to be taken to the station commander. He is Group Captain Harold Helmsby and he listens attentively to my story. I explain that the undercarriage must have been defective because it just buckled, got bent, and broke under the weight of the aircraft – perhaps due to shoddy work in the factory.

It is required of me to write a report, which I sign as Flight Captain T de Hacqueville ATA.

Group Captain Helmsby assures me that a thorough inspection of the wrecked aircraft will have to be done to determine the cause of the failure. I am secretly confident that the undercarriage must be so totally deformed, demolished, and destroyed by the way we skidded and slid along the runway. All evidence of possible malfunctioning will be gone, destroyed, wiped out.

Hagdale, Sunday, 20 December 1942

Hector is enjoying the last moments of his free week-end from Trent Park with me. At nine, I tune in to Radio Zeesen. According the news in Afrikaans, a huge air raid by die RAF on Frankfurt-am-Main was a failure. Many enemy bombers were shot down and little damage was done.

Hector: "Do you believe all that propaganda?"

Me: "May I remind you that you told me a while ago that much of what Radio Zeesen says, is reliable. Of course, the Germans won't broadcast their losses and failures, but they will eagerly tell the world – and especially the Boers in South Africa – of their successes."

"Maybe, you're right."

After the news I hear a message meant for me: "Our dear friend Theo, please listen carefully. Your Uncle Wilhelm feels lonely and he seeks your company. Please reconsider your routine. If you can't reach him on a Sunday, try the routine for a Monday. He understands that some nasty people may try to interfere with your phone calls."

I pick up a magazine to turn over the pages to create the impression that I'm reading something interesting. In the meantime, I understand that Canaris wants me to change the frequencies I use for my messages and warnings. I must use the frequency scheduled for a Monday on a Sunday, and so forth. Quite simple. That's what I will do tomorrow.

Hagdale, Monday, 21 December 1942

Hector has returned to Trent Park by an early train and I am back at Hamble to pick up another Lancaster to be taken to Lincolnshire.

While I am flying over the Midlands, I send the following message on Tuesday's frequency on the Lancaster's radio, although it is Monday today:

UI IJD TVN DPNQSFIFOEP = V

This looks like this in Latin:

TH HIC SUM COMPREHENDO = V[68]

I couldn't care less if MI 5 can read my message. They are, at least, not jamming this frequency today. All that matters is that the Abwehr receives my message.

Almost directly after I have finished, something comes back – not even in code and in plain Latin:

SIC[69]

---

[68] "HERE I AM I UNDERSTAND = V"

[69] "YES".

Scampton, Friday, 5 February 1943

Today was my first experience of the so-called Wooden Wonder, the De Haviland Mosquito. There are basically three variants of this aircraft, whose fuselage and wings are made mostly of wood, namely a light bomber, a photo-reconnaissance version, and a versatile fighter.

I find it a beautiful aircraft – a true work of art. It also flies beautifully and is easy to handle. My task today is to deliver a freshly-produced photo-reconnaissance model to RAF Scampton in Lincolnshire, the base where Henry is the commander of one of the bomber squadrons.

I just cannot see myself wrecking or sabotaging this beautiful piece of machinery, although I know that it will wreak havoc against Germany.

After I have delivered the Mosquito safely to whomever has to take care of her, I seek out Henry and I find him in his office.

"Ma, it's almost lunch time. Let's go and find a few bites to bite."

When we sit at a table in the officers' mess, I address my first son in our usual Afrikaans: "Hendrik, I have some news. According to your Pa, MI 5 was able to listen to my messages to Berlin and even decode them. They can read everything that I send them."

"Ma?" His eyes grow big.

"Yes. But they can't locate me. They tried to pinpoint me on a map but that didn't work. My broadcasts are very brief and that gives them no time to set up their direction-finders. And, besides, I often send my messages when I'm flying all over the place."

"So, we're safe?"

"Mostly. They tried to jam the frequencies I used to use, but I managed to switch to other frequencies, which I will not tell you about."

"Hoe about my messages to you?"

"Those are on frequencies they haven't discovered yet. Your messages are usually less that fifteen seconds – far too short to sort out. In other words: we carry on as usual. You let me know of any air raids that are being planned and I warn the Germans so that we can save lives."

"Ma, I expect that we will be going out tonight. I don't know yet where we will be going. How do you feel? Would you like to see Germany from the air?"

"Yes, why not?"

Hagdale, Saturday, 6 February 1943

Yesterday afternoon, I phoned Hector at Hagdale and told him to expect me only today. I didn't tell him what the reason for the delay was. When I arrive home this evening, I find Hector in a foul mood.

"Woman, have you forgotten that you have a husband? Have you forgotten that you have a home?"

I give my husband a heavy hug and a killer of a kiss: "Let me tell you what this lazy lady was doing last night."

"Hanging around with strange men?"

I give him a silly sly smile: "How did you guess?"

"What were you doing with them? Tell me! Out with the truth!"

"We were looking at Germany from the air. I was with Henry and his crew in their Lancaster bomber. I was the navigator. We flew over the Ruhr Valley where most of Germany's steel factories are. It was hell. The German fighters swarmed all over us and shot down two of Henry's squadron's planes. After they have left and we got nearer to the target, the flak got hot. Another Lancaster had her wing blown off. We downloaded our bombs on what we thought were steel plants."

"Did you cause much damage?"

"We don't think so. A Mosquito photo-reconnaissance plane went back this morning and took photos. We bombed forests, open fields, and … inhabited areas. Many Germans in Essen lost their homes. I was glad that I wasn't on the receiving end."

"So, you have seen something of the war. I must confess, I haven't seen anything of this war yet. During the Great War, I took part in more than one battle. But this time, I spent my days inside an office. However, after my retirement, I am fortunate to walk around in pleasant gardens at the spot where I am working at the moment."

"At Trent Park?"

"Yes. It's really a park. Our captured German generals live in beautiful surroundings. They can feel blessed and privileged. We expect more of them to join us as time goes on."

"Then you are also blessed and privileged."

"What else did Henry tell you?"

"We spoke about the Americans. Although they entered the war more than a year ago, they only started now to do their bit in the air war against Germany. They only started to fly sorties the other day."

"What is Henry's opinion of them?"

"Not very high. They are noisy, loud, full of themselves, but they haven't achieved anything real. The RAF squadrons mostly go out during the night when the Luftwaffe fighters can't see them so well. The Americans, real cowboys, decided that they can do better and throw down their bombs while the sun is still shining. They started by attacking submarine bases, but they haven't sunk one single silly submarine yet."

"They will improve. They will learn. And, remember, America has the biggest economy in the world. They can throw dollars into the water and think nothing of it. They can keep on building airplanes, tanks, guns, and battleships till they have overpowered the Germans. Just give them some time."

I shudder.

Hamble, Tuesday, 9 February 1943

The pilots of the ATA are all seasoned travelers by train. I have travelled on most of the train routes throughout England and I have seen most railroad stations. This afternoon, I returned to Hamble after having taken another Mosquito to an air field in Wales.

I sit down in the mess to enjoy a well-earned cup of tea when the air raid siren goes off. All of us scramble to reach the air raid shelters. In am one of the last and I notice that we are being attacked by a flight of Junkers JU 88 light bombers. They throw bombs onto our buildings and parked planes, but they also shoot with their machine guns from a belly position as they sweep by.

The "all clear" signal is given after a while and we all reappear to assess the damage. Some of the girls start screaming or sobbing when the body of a male pilot, Jimmy Kirby, is found, riddled with bullets. This is the first fatality that Hamble has suffered.

Hagdale, Friday, 14 May 1943

Hector is all smiles as he arrives home after a week's work at Trent Park: "My dear, things are due to become very busy at our place."

"How?"

"Let's listen to the BBC news at seven. The whole world will be told that the glorious and glamorous German army in North Africa has capitulated. The all-powerful Afrikakorps is no more."

"How did that happen?"

"General Montgomery was able to drive the Germans bit by bit westwards, away from Egypt and through Libya. The Germans ended up in Tunisia. And then we attacked them, with the help of our Yankee friends, from the west through Morocco and Algeria. They were driven into a tight corner where they were cut off from any supplies and reinforcements. The result is that the list of our guests at Trent Park will grow substantially. There are bound to be whole bunch of German generals that we will accommodate."

I feel too afraid to listen to Radio Zeesen tonight because the defeat of the Afrikakorps will certainly be treated as a minor mishap, which it isn't.

To balance my feeling of despondency, I feel good about the fact that I was able during the past few weeks to warn Berlin on more than one occasion of heavy air raids to be expected over Essen and the Ruhr Valley. There is no way to know whether my warnings made any difference.

Hagdale, Tuesday, 8 June 1943

After a strenuous day at Hamble, I managed to fly home with my darling Dragon. I look forward to a fine supper prepared by Cheeky Carol.

The phone rings and Freddy Fortune calls me: "It's Lord Hector."

Hector: "My darling, I'm so glad to reach you. I have fantastic news!"

"Yes?"

"I've seen David this afternoon. He's one of those German generals who were caught in Tunisia."

"He's a general?"

"Yes, indeed. A major general. According to his file, he was the intelligence chief of Rommel before Rommel was called back to Germany."

"So, Rommel wasn't caught?"

"No. He apparently got ill and flew back to Berlin. A certain General Hans von Arnim took over from him. He is now our most senior guest at Trent Park."

"How is David?"

"I haven't spoken to him yet, but I saw him when the assembled group of newly arrived guests was being addressed by General Johnstone. I also spoke a few words. But he seems to be in good health."

"I'm so glad to hear that. Please send him my regards when you do get the opportunity of speaking to him."

Hagdale, Friday, 11 June 1943

After dinner, Hector and I go for a walk through the estate while the midsummer-sun is still shining. We both arrived a little earlier from our respective workplaces.

Hector: "I've had a jolly interesting chat with your brother yesterday."

"Hmm?"

"Yes. The fellow initially tried to fool me by pretending not to be able to speak English and denying that he was David Davidsohn."

"How did you unmask him?"

"That was already done on a previous occasion. He was being debriefed by a captain of the Intelligence Corpse, which happened to be one of the Jews he helped to rescue from Germany in thirty-eight. This captain easily penetrated his cover as a German nobleman by recognizing him and drawing from him the truth about his real identity."

"So, he couldn't fool you?"

"No. After I had called his bluff, we sat down somewhere and had a long chat. He adopted the identity of a dead boy in the cemetery of Swakopmund during the Great War out of fear to be caught as a traitor by the South African Army. He then married a German girl whose parents returned to Germany after the end of the war. He also went there in his capacity as a former officer of the Schutztruppe. He joined the Reichswehr and eventually rose to the rank of major general in the Wehrmacht."

"I remember seeing him as a German officer in Kleve when he and his troops marched into the town in defiance of the Versailles Treaty."

"I remember. Anyway, we agreed not to talk too much with

each other in order not to create the impression of a conspiracy between us. I promised not to disclose his real identity to his fellow German generals."

"Did he tell you anything about his family?"

"Yes. He got divorced from his wife after having caught her in bed with another man. His son is an officer in the Kriegsmarine and the captain of a torpedo boat in Holland. His twin daughters are studying medicine in Tübingen."

"So, our boys do have real cousins in Germany. Members of the German nobility. Strange, isn't it?"

Hamble, Friday, 31 December 1943

The Attagirls of 15 Female ATA Pool at Hamble are in a festive mood in our canteen. Although it is the holiday season, the war drags on and on, with no end in sight – although it looks as if the Allies are gaining the upper hand.

Apart from New Year's Eve, we are celebrating my promotion to commander, which kicks in tomorrow. We will have the week-end off, though, and that is why we are celebrating late in the afternoon after having completed a few deliveries of aircraft to various air fields.

One of the girls, Lucy, tells us: "Me 'usband, whooze a major now, waz fighting in France before Dunkirk. 'E waz a lootnant at the time. One of 'is men got wounded and 'is foot wuz shot off. He cried out: 'I've lost me foot!' His stupid sergeant who stood around, said calmly: "No, me lad, it's not lost. Look, it's lying over there!'"

Another girl, Linda, retorts: "Talking about stupidity. These Jerries across the Channel are the most stupid lot you can ever imagine. That's according to me Bill, whoze a Mosquito pilot. These Jerries were constructin' a dummy air field somewhere in 'Olland – all of it made of wood – the runways, the buildings, the planes, everything. They wanted us to waste valuable ammo and time and fuel on this place. The RAF watched them patiently and when they were finished, my Bill was sent to bomb them."

Lucy: "Did he destroy everything?"

"Nope. He just released a wooden dummy bomb onto them. 'Ere I 'ave a photo 'e took before 'e took off."

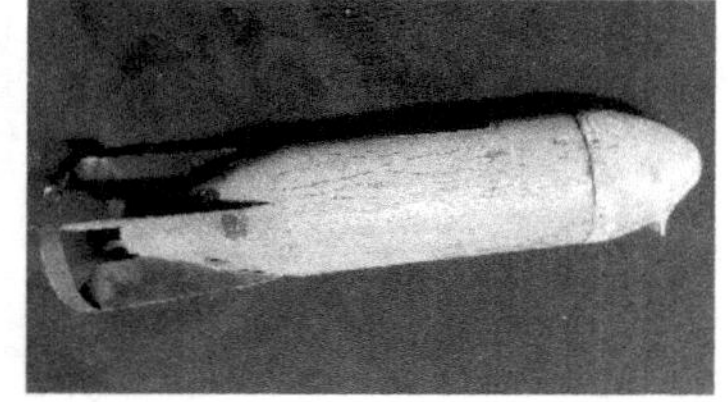

She passes the photo around.

While everybody laughs, Helen holds up her hand: "The Germans are not the only guys building dummies. We also do."

Linda: "What do you mean?"

"I flew over Dover the other day with a Dakota that I had to deliver and I saw a whole army assembled down there – tanks, trucks, tents, the tutti. Afterwards, I asked the people at the air field just beyond Dover whot was goin' on. They said: 'It's all dummies. Made of wood and rubber and canvas. To fool the Jerries. They must think we are preparin' to invade France across the narrowest bit of the Channel.'"

The thought occurs to me to go and have a look and see for myself. This is something I will have to report to Berlin, apart from all the warnings of the past few months about attacks from the air on Berlin, Essen, Hamburg, Schweinfurt, French ports, and other spots.

Hagdale, Saturday 19 February 1944

Hector has already gone to bed, while I sit in the library and listen to music from the BBC. Suddenly, a series of pips coming through grab my attention. It is a strange call sign, "SONJA".

I immediately reply with my call sign of "TH" to indicate that this Sonja has reached me.

The rest of Sonja's message follows and I write it down:

BCXFIS DMPTFE EPXO CZ IJUMFS TE PG TT UBLFT PWFS = SONJA

I hastily decode it. It is in English:

ABWEHR CLOSED DOWN BY HITLER SD OF SS TAKES OVER = SONJA

I hastily transmit back:

WHAT NEXTQ

The answer comes:

NOTHING

The name Sonja is not unfamiliar to me. She was the woman who visited me shortly before the start of the war at the Kurhaus in Scheveningen. She was Canaris' special envoy and she spoke perfect English. She also visited me at Hagdale after the start of the war.

It does seem as if Hitler has got rid of Canaris and gave his job to the SS. I can remember that Canaris told me that he didn't support Hitler and Hitler must have got wind of some or other scheme by Canaris to undermine him.

The only conclusion is that my contact with Berlin is something of the past. It won't help to try to reestablish contact. I still wanted to see for myself how the make-believe army at Dover looked like and warn the Germans not to be fooled by it, but now there is no chance to do this anymore.

I must make a point of listening to Radio Zeesen tomorrow night.

Hagdale, Sunday 20 February 1944

Hector is easily persuaded to listen to the Afrikaans newscast on Radio Zeesen tonight. He is, after all, still involved with the Intelligence Services.

The main item of the news is indeed that the Führer, Adolf Hitler, has decided to shut down the Abwehr and to transfer all its operations to the SD, the Sicherheitsdienst[70] of the SS, with Brigadeführer (Major General) Walther Schellenberg as its chief. Vizeadmiral Wilhelm Canaris has been arrested on suspicion of high treason.

Hector: "I'm not surprised. Hitler is as mad as a colony of clowns. He has lost contact with reality. He must have found out that Canaris was plotting behind his back to get rid of him, and now he is getting rid of Canaris."

I nod my head to show that I agree with him.

I sit with a magazine while the personal messages are being read to create the impression that I'm not particularly interested. There is, though, a message for me:

"Our dear friend, Theo, your uncle Wilhelm has decided to go into retirement. His niece, Sonja, will try her best to keep contact with you."

That means that I will have to wait for Sonja to do something. In the meantime, I can't do anything to warn the Germans about the RAF.

---

[70] Security Service.

Hagdale, Sunday, 27 February 1944

Henry and his family, as well as Victor and his family, are spending the week-end with us. Henry has just completed a second tour of duty and has earned a well-deserved rest period. Victor has been promoted to lieutenant-colonel and placed in command of the signals unit of VIII Corps, commanded by Lieutenant-General Sir Richard O'Connor.

During lunch, Victor tells us: "I don't have the faintest idea what this VIII Corps is. All I know, is that a corps comprises a few divisions and other units. I must report for duty the day after tomorrow at the headquarters in Somerset."

Hector: "Does that mean that you will be part of the force that invades France to drive the Nazis away?"

Victor: "I'm not privy to that type of information."

Me: "Ah, come on. Use your brain cells. You have enough of them. We know that Somerset is to the east of us, not too far from the south coast of England. There is the big harbor city of Plymouth and the naval base of Devonport nearby. Perfect embarking points for an invasion force. Of course, you will be taking part in some real warfare when France is invaded during this coming summer."

Hector: "Victor, it seems your Ma is a better strategist than your Pa. She has figured out what your role will be. I suppose you will be part of some exercises to get ready for this offensive."

Victor: "That makes sense, I believe."

Me: "And I think that you will be invading France in Normandy, the region from which the first Henry de Hacqueville came from. That is the most logical point to attack the Germans who expect you to land somewhere opposite Dover."

Hector: "That makes sense, Dora. You're clever."

Me: "I only use my brain cells. And I think I have a good

idea of the geography of England because I have been flying all over the place. I've seen Devonport and Plymouth from the air."

Victor: "Ma, I believe you're right. It does make sense."

Hector: "But will the Germans also figure that out?"

I stay silent about my knowledge of the fake wooden and rubber army near Dover.

I take Henry for a walk through the garden during the afternoon, ostensibly to show him something in my devoted Dragon. I start: "Hendrik, you must stop reporting to me about imminent air raids on German cities. My contact in Berlin has stopped operating. Hitler seems to have suspected her boss of stabbing him in the back and had him arrested. I can't reach her anymore because that whole department has been closed down."

"Sorry, Ma. Perhaps, it's better that way. I was always in a damn dilemma. I wanted to preserve the lives of innocent German civilians by warning them to be ready for our raids. But, on the other hand, I endangered the lives of my air crews who could encounter stiffer resistance and defensive measures on account of our warnings."

"May I tell you a secret? I have wrecked a few planes of the RAF. Written them off. I dumping one in the sea, sabotaged the fuel system of another one, and I did a belly landing with a Lancaster and crashed into some parked aircraft."

"Hell, Ma! What are you telling me?"

"Yes. Perhaps that is something you can also do. Every Lancaster of Halifax or Liberator written off will be one Lancaster or Halifax or Liberator less to drop bombs on German homes."

"Ma, you seem to be a better qualified pilot than I am. You have flown almost all the aircraft in the RAF's inventory. I only have experience of my initial trainer, a Blenheim, a Wellington, and a Lancaster."

During dinner, Hector tells Henry and Victor: "I don't know whether your Ma has already told you that you have three cousins in Germany."

Victor: "This is the first I hear of them."

"Your mother's brother, who is a German general, is being held as a prisoner-of-war here in England. I have spoken more than once to him. He has assumed the name of a dead boy to conceal his real identity. He calls himself the Baron Thomas von Traubenstein. His son, Sepp, is captain of a torpedo boat on the Dutch coast. His twin daughters, Gudrun and Gertrud, are studying medicine somewhere in Germany."

Henry: "When will we ever get the chance to meet them? Certainly not while this war is still going on."

Victor: "Can they speak English? We can speak a little German."

Hagdale, Friday, 21 April 1944

The first thing Hector tells me when he arrives home for the weekend: "We got rid of your brother, David."

"What do you mean?"

"He was extremely naughty and we chased him away. Good riddance!"

"Did you let him loose?"

"Hell, no. We transferred him to another camp where he won't be pampered anymore as at Trent Park."

"You say he was naughty."

"Yes, very naughty. Full of mischief. Almost made fools of us. We just couldn't afford to keep him any longer."

"Tell me more, please?"

"Because he is in the intelligence world, he suspected that all the conversations of these generals were being overheard by hidden microphones. He exploited that by telling his colleagues all sorts of tall stories with the goal of deceiving us. He pretended to know of all sorts of secret weapons of the Germans. Of course, we passed those snippets of info on and much time and effort were wasted to try and find the spots where these wonderful weapons were supposed to be manufactured."

"Ha-ha! So, he made you look like imbeciles?"

"Yes, he did. He even told his colleagues of a plan of the Abwehr to blow up the Houses of Congress in Washington by a gang of secret agents on Hitler's birthday. He made sure that everybody at Trent House knew of this plot, although he made his colleagues all swear that they wouldn't ever talk about this evil plot. Of course, they did talk and we also learnt of it. When Hitler's birthday came and went, nothing happened, naturally. We could see that all his colleagues were furious for being deceived. We were also deceived because a big manhunt was conducted in Washington to locate these fictitious agents and saboteurs."

"Ha-ha. So, he really fooled you! That's my little brother!"

"He also did some sabotage at Trent Park. He stole the boot laces of one of the other generals and constructed a sling. He shot stones at the windows of the manor house, including the office of General Johnstone. He also hurt a few military policemen who were guarding the fence from inside guard towers."

"My little brother used a sling during the Boer War to harass some British soldiers. He said that a sling is a biblical weapon. The boy David used it to knock the giant Goliath out before he sliced his head off."

"Oh, is that where he learnt that trick? Anyway, he was promptly transferred to a camp in Wales where discipline is much stricter. That was directly after we found out that the story about the bombing of the Houses of Congress was only a horrible hoax."

"It sounds as if my little brother knows how to look after himself. Watch out – he will escape from that camp in Wales. I'm certain of that. I just know it."

New Romney, Tuesday, 2 May 1944

RAF New Romney is a base on the south coast of England. There are three squadrons and other supporting units. The squadrons all fly the Hawker Typhoon, a fighter-bomber. She can engage enemy fighters and bombers, but also attack targets on the surface. For that purpose, she can be fitted with cannons or rockets.

Although I am qualified to fly four-engine aircraft, I like flying single-engine fighters. They are faster and much more maneuverable. This morning, I took one of these fighter-bombers to New Romney and I flew all along the southern coastline of England. I could clearly see the bogus army from the air, although it looked real enough.

And now I am sitting in the train on my way to London and from there to Southampton. I digest what I have seen and what I have deducted from our family conversation more than a week ago. It is clear that the War Office wants to create the impression that am invading force was aimed at Calais on the French coast, but that the invasion will take place further south.

How on earth will I be able to send this info to Berlin?

Hagdale, Sunday, 7 May 1944

We enjoy lunch with Daniel and his family who came from Portsmouth for the day. It is a celebratory lunch. Daniel was promoted a week ago to the rank of captain and he was appointed in the position of King's harbour master: Portsmouth.

Daniel explains: "Of course, I'm not in command of the whole naval base. My job is only the administration and management of the port facilities, as well as security matters. We are extremely busy now and it was tricky to take the day off. I don't think it will be possible to take another day off for the foreseeable future."

Hector: "What keeps you so busy?"

"Pa, you know I'm not allowed to divulge any secret stuff."

"So, great secret operations and activities are going on and nobody may know what's going on?"

"Pa, I may not discuss the activities and operations of the Royal Navy. Let's keep it at that."

During this conversation, I watched my son closely. It is clear that he didn't want to get into trouble, but that we wanted to give me the news that something very big was going on at Portsmouth. What else but preparations for an imminent invasion of the Continent can be the explanation for this secrecy and his lack of free time?

This knowledge fits in with my conviction that the coming invasion will take place in Normandy, not at Calais. How will I let Berlin know?

Daniel and his family say good-bye during the afternoon and leave me and Hector alone at home – apart from some staff members. After supper, we sit in the library where I listen to the BBC's music program. At nine, I switch to Radio Zeesen. After the news there is another message for me: "Dear Theo, your cousin Sonja wants to talk to you. Please contact her as in the past at the same phone number. She awaits your phone calls."

Faringdon, Monday, 8 May 1944

I find myself in a hospital bed when I open my eyes. An elderly nurse comes to look at me and I ask:

"Where am I?"

"In Faringdon, Oxfordshire, dearie. In the Cottage Hospital."

"How did I get here?"

"By ambulance. From the fire station, just around the corner from us. I don't know where you were picked up, but you were seriously injured. Ugly gash on your left leg. Our local vet patched you up because our local doctor wasn't available at the time. Our doctor and the vet often work together. And you are now connected to a blood transfusion bottle to replace all the blood you have lost."

"What time is it?"

"Six-thirty, my dear. Can I bring you some supper? We have vegetable soup and healthy brown bread with real butter."

"Yes please."

My memory slowly seeps back into my mind. I remember that while I flew back to my workplace at Hamble this morning, I thought about the message that I wanted to send to Sonja.

It was my task this morning to fly a Dakota to No 512 Squadron at RAF Broadwell in Oxfordshire. This aircraft was involved in a crash a few months ago and had to be rebuilt at Hamble.

To reach Broadwell, I had to fly almost due north for about seventy miles – not a long hop. I, therefore, hastily sent off the following message shortly after take-off on the frequency previously used on a Tuesday and I repeat it on Wednesday's frequency for good measure:

UI MBOEVHFO CFJ OPSNBOEJFO KVOJ = V

Uncoded, it read as follows:

TH LANDUNGEN BEI NORMANDIEN JUNI = V[71]

I hoped my long silence since February may have convinced MI 5 to abandon the observation of the frequencies I used to reach Berlin. It is, anyway, clear that they didn't jam these frequencies when I used them.

While I gained height, I wondered how I could sabotage this plane. She will certainly be used to drop some paratroopers in France during the coming invasion, and to transport supplies and troops to captured airfields in France.

While flying over the North Wessex downs, the port engine suddenly catches fire. That is, of course, an extremely dangerous condition because the fire can spread to the fuel tanks. My only option was to bail out after I had stopped the engine. I sent a "Mayday" message urgently to Broadwell to tell them more or less what my position was.

I steered the plane so that her nose pointed down at an open field. I rushed to the back and flew out of the door, while opening

---

[71] "HSK LANDINGS AT NORMANDY JUNE = V"

my parachute. I haven't been given much parachute training – just enough to know how to open the big mushroom above my head and how to roll over when I strike Mother Earth.

While I glided slowly down to the earth, I saw how the Dakoto exploded upon impact. That means: another airplane written off! But this time, it wasn't my doing.

I didn't know how to steer the parachute and I fell directly on top of an oak tree. The branches broke my fall, but also tore my overalls and cut my left leg. The blood started seeping out.

I must have passed out because I can't remember what happened afterwards. Somebody must have rescued me and brought me to this hospital.

After I have finished my supper, an elderly man comes to my bed: "Good evening. I'm doctor Ossie Osborne, the local medical practitioner. May I know who you are? All we know is that you were the pilot of that aircraft that crashed nearby."

"I'm Dora de Hacqueville."

"The nurse showed me your torn overalls. You seem to have had a rank or something, but you can't be from the RAF. They don't use female pilots."

"I'm a commander in the Air Transport Auxiliary. We take new and repaired aircraft back to their squadrons, and we also transport people."

"Ah, that explains it. You are very fortunate. An elderly farmer and his wife saw how you came down in your parachute onto a tree on their farm. You must have passed out due to blood loss. They called the ambulance, which brought you here. I wasn't around at the time and my friend, Casey Caswell, our local vet, was fortunately available to dress your ugly wound and put in some stitches. I came somewhat later and saw that you needed blood. That had to be brought from Oxford. And, here you are. You almost didn't make it.

"Is there anybody whom we must inform of your mishap? Are you married? A husband somewhere?"

"Yes, my husband is the retired Brigadier Hector de Hacqueville. He works as a pensioner at a POW facility. I will give you the telephone number if you want to phone him."

Faringdon, Friday, 12 May 1944

Hector is due to come and fetch me after my stay of five days at the Cottage Hospital in Faringdon, a small town in Oxfordshire.

I became a celebrity overnight and known as the lady who survived an airplane crash. The priest of the Church of England visited me on Tuesday. The old farmer and his wife who saved my life, Sam, and Sally Scofield, also visited me on Tuesday and told me how they helped me. The priest of the Catholic Church came to bless me on Wednesday. Yesterday, a deputation of the pupils of the local Grammar School brought me some flowers. This morning, two town councilors came to thank me for honoring their town with my presence.

Somehow, it got out that I was not simply Missus Dora de Hacqueville, but the Viscountess Theodora de Hacqueville. Although I insisted to be addressed simply as "Dora", the hospital staff and everybody else addressed my as "My Lady". The school kids even called me "Your Highness".

I think I will always have a soft spot for the kind people of this town. It's an irony that I, who hates the British Empire, came to love these people.

Some officials of the RAF visited me and took a statement. They promised me that a full investigation was warranted, although it would be difficult to find out what exactly went wrong with the fire in the port engine because the Dakota was totally wrecked after the impact with the earth and the ensuing explosion.

Hector arrives during the late afternoon in his automobile. I hobble out of the hospital on crutches and the staff mount a guard of honor as I leave. I receive a hug and a kiss from each one of them. Doctor Osborne gives me a certificate to state that he books me off from active duty for a whole month, due to my serious injury.

Cottage Hospital, Coxwell Road, Faringdon

I ask Hector to take me to the farm of Sam and Sally, the elderly couple who rescued me. They also bid me farewell with hugs, kisses, and tears in their eyes.

Sally says: "Dear Madam, please get better soon. You must help us to win this war! God bless you!"

I can't tell these kind people that I don't wish a victory for the British Empire.

The wreck of the Dakota hasn't been removed yet and I and Hector inspect it. Hector feels sad about the loss of this valuable piece of military hardware. I cannot show that I am relieved that this machine won't take part in this war anymore.

Hagdale, Wednesday, 7 June 1944

My wound has healed sufficiently that I can walk around without crutches. I even plan to start horse riding one of these days. I am supposed to return to my work in a few days' time.

Last night, the radio brought the news of a successful invasion of France on the beaches of Normandy – just as I have predicted. It seems as if the Germans were not prepared for this event and the initial resistance was overwhelmed relatively easily.

Freddy Fortune brings me the morning paper where I enjoy the summer weather in a wicker chair under a tree outside. The front page is filled with the story of the invasion and I eagerly read every word. It is clear that my warning of a month ago did not help. The German generals either didn't believe me, or haven't received my signal. I couldn't follow up my initial warning when I landed in hospital. That makes me wonder whether it will be worthwhile to continue with my messages.

On page 5 of the newspaper, I find the following extremely interesting item:

BRITISH BRIGADIER POSSIBLY ABDUCTED

LONDON – The War Office recruited the help of Scotland Yard in the search for the whereabouts of Brigadier Stephen Summersby (51), second-in-command of the Island Farm Prisoner-of-War camp at Bridgend in Wales.

The disappearance of the brigadier was only noted when his staff car, a station wagon, was retrieved from the harbour of Holyhead in northern Wales by harbour authorities.

Our local correspondent witnessed the retrieval of the vehicle and noted its registration number. Enquiries by our editorial staff at the War Office resulted in an official statement to the effect that Brigadier Summersby was seen leaving the camp on the evening of 31 May and that he hasn't been seen since.

One of the inmates of the camp, the German Major General Thomas von Traubenstein, disappeared at the same time. It is suspected that the prisoner forced the brigadier to smuggle him out of the camp.

It is also suspected that the German general will try to reach German-held France with his prisoner. All elements of the Royal Navy were requested to be on the look-out for suspicious-looking craft in the Channel area.

Meanwhile, our correspondent in Holyhead established that a trawler, the Jo-Anne, went missing during the night of 1 – 2 June. It is possible that the German general dumped the staff car into the harbour and stole a trawler to flee with his prisoner, either to Ireland or to France.

Enquiries at a local hotel found that a certain Brigadier Ben Burrows booked into the hotel the day before the Jo-Anne was stolen. He gave his address as Liverpool. It is assumed that this must be the missing Brigadier Summersby, or the German general, impersonating him.

According a retired expert on intelligence matters, Major General Sir Henry Harsings, the possibility exists that the brigadier was recruited by the German general to join him in a bid to reach Germany and to betray his country willingly and for personal gain.

I read this news item three times with a smile on my face. David has really escaped, just as I have promised my husband. I'm sure that he fled to neutral Ireland and not to France where the war is suddenly raging furiously. It's a mystery what happened to the British brigadier mentioned in the newspaper, but I suspect that David had escaped from him as well. I wonder what Hector's comments will be when he reads this report; certainly not very positive because David has fooled the British Army yet again.

Hagdale, Sunday, 11 June 1944

My husband must return to his workplace tomorrow early in the morning. I will take him with my determined Dragon. My leg has healed sufficiently that I can control her with ease.

We listen again to the news in Afrikaans over Radio Zeesen. The announcer quotes Field Marshall Wilhelm Keitel, the chief of the Central Command, who declared that he is full of confidence that the Allied divisions in France will be annihilated by the brave German soldiers. Afterwards the usual personal messages are read.

The following message is directed at me: "Our dearest friend Theo must listen carefully. His niece Sonja is very worried about his health and she advises him not to work so hard. She will understand if he keeps quiet for some time."

Hector suddenly sits straight: "You know, I've heard quite a few messages sent to this guy called Theo. I wonder where he lives in South Africa. He seems to have family in Germany – an uncle called Wilhelm and a niece or a cousin called Sonja. Exactly what type of job does he do for Germany while sitting in South Africa? Blowing up Police stations, railway bridges, or power stations? Or post office boxes? I'm sure the government of Jannie Smuts will find him soon enough."

Me: "I haven't paid much attention to the messages to this Theo. Yes, I also wonder who on earth he can be."

Of course, I am totally sure about the identity of this Theo, whose full name is Theodora. The latest message tells me that it won't help to send any more messages to Sonja. Nobody in Germany believes what she tells them.

Hagdale, Friday 20 July 1944

Since I started to work again about a month ago, I was kept busy with flying once or twice a week, and with administrative work. With my rank of commander of the ATA, I became second-in-command of Female Pool 15 at Hamble. I didn't perform my tasks with any degree of joy because things were going downhill for Germany, although it was clear that Great Britain also suffered much. I explained my melancholia and dejection to Hector as the result of the never-ending war with all its violence and pain and suffering and death.

Although it seemed as if the Luftwaffe has disappeared, the Germans still managed to cause explosions in places like London and Southampton. They did so by means of flying bombs – called "buzzbombs" by some people – rockets launched from France and the Low Countries in the general direction of these cities. They were not very fast and it happened that a Spitfire intercepted one of them and simply flipped it over with its wing, which caused the rocket to become confused and to drop like a solid brick without reaching its target. When they did reach British soil, they simply dropped down when their fuel ran out and they exploded with a loud bang and often caused death and destruction.

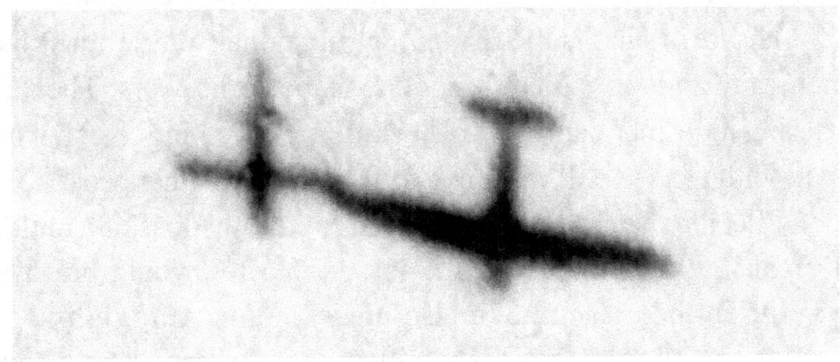

The surest sign that things were really going in a disastrous direction for Germany came to my and Hector's attention this Friday evening. According to the BBC, several generals in Germany staged a failed assassination attempt on Adolf Hitler.

We also listen to the Afrikaans news on Radio Zeesen. The announcer is almost hysterical in his condemnation of the plotters and called for their execution.

Hector smiles: "While I was still at the War Office, we often heard rumors of such a plot. We often overheard our German guests at Trent Park discussing this possibility. When they heard of this plot against Hitler this afternoon, they described it as a desperate attempt by these generals to end the war and negotiate for peace with the western Allies. I think I can agree with them. The German Army gets beaten very badly in France and it is only a matter of time before we reach the Rhine. In the meantime, the Russians are driving the Germans out of Russia with huge losses on both sides. The Russians can absorb those losses, but Germany with a much smaller population cannot afford to lose a few million men."

I have to agree with Hector diagnosis of the situation. I add: "We must be grateful that we haven't lost one of our boys yet. The war may still drag on for some time and I stay worried about the safety of Henry and Victor who are part of the shooting war. Daniel may also become a casualty if Portsmouth is attacked again."

Hector: "That is the risk any professional soldier must face. Some of my ancestors died during the Napoleonic Wars. They also fell during the American War of Liberation. Something like that may happen with us. We will just have to face it when it happens."

I decide that I won't be able just to face the loss of a child. It will break my heart – just as the loss of Hector would break my heart. And in the meantime, it also breaks my heart to think of all the suffering German civilians who lost their homes, their income, their loved ones, and their limbs. It is no wonder that I feel miserable and melancholic. I sleep badly, especially when Veleda wakes me up with her sad face.

Hector carries on: "This episode will lead to the deaths of some capable German generals. It would have been much better if they had managed to kill that damned demented dictator."

I must agree. Hitler started this war and led his people into a big mess. I remember that Veleda told me long ago that the people who supported Hitler in the beginning, will curse and condemn him in the end.

Hagdale, Monday, 25 December 1944

This is our sixth Christmas since the war started. This war is dragging on much longer than the Great War of 1914–1918. Although the Allies are clearly winning the war, the fighting is continuing.

The Germans started a surprise offensive ten days ago through the Ardennes Forest in Belgium, clearly with the object of capturing the port city of Antwerp to disrupt the arrival of supplies for British and American troops. Because of bad weather, the RAF and the USAAF couldn't take to the air and, initially, the Germans made good progress. However, their fuel supplies dried up and their armored columns got stalled and driven back, with considerable losses, which they could ill afford.

Even though Germany was on her last legs, the Britons didn't feel very well, either. Food became scarce because all young male farm workers served in the armed forces. Much agricultural land was requisitioned for the construction of airfields and army bases. Artisans and tradesmen were in short supply and there was nobody available to repair all the damage caused by German bombs. Women were increasingly being used in factories and in non-combatant roles in the armed forces. Even the eldest daughter of King George, Princess Elizabeth, became a mechanic who serviced military trucks. Ordinary products such as soap became scarce. Luxury products, such as chocolates, disappeared from shops' shelves.

Fortunately, we don't starve at Hagdale because we produce more than enough dairy products, eggs, fruit, and vegetables for our own use and to send to the markets.

Hector decided, in consultation with me, to invite all our employees to a Christmas lunch in our dining room. To be invited, everybody had to accompany us to the Christmas service in the All-Saints Church in Hursley this morning. During the lunch, we drank two toasts: on Henry whose promotion to group captain becomes effective from 2 January next year, and on me who is to be promoted to the rank of senior commander, which is the equivalent of a group captain in the RAF.

My promotion means that I will be totally in charge of Female Pool 15 of the ATA at Hamble. That will mean less flying and more administrative work. I wanted to decline this position at first, but Hector egged me on to accept it. According to him, I richly earned this honor.

After everything has been cleared up, I and Hector retire to the library where we listen to Christmas music from the BBC.

Hector: "While the ordinary people in Britain are suffering, we still pamper and spoil our captured German generals and admirals. We are becoming rather overcrowded at Trent Park because we caught quite a few of them in Italy and France. They all feel hopeless and desperate because we provide them with newspapers and they are allowed to listen to the radio. Nobody of them feels confident of a German victory anymore, although a few still cling to the hope that some miracle weapons may make some sort of a difference."

Me: "We all feel under the weather. This dark, cloudy, and wet winter weather is not conducive for high spirits. Everything looks gloomy. I can only wonder how David's family in Germany are doing."

"According to him, his daughters are studying medicine and they ought to complete their studies this coming summer. Their services will certainly be sorely needed at that time. His son is a naval officer and he didn't know whether he is still alive when we had our last conversation a few months ago."

"I don't think they are prospering at the moment. Conditions in Germany must be much worse than over here."

"Yes, quite so."

I don't tell Hector that Veleda recently gave me the insight that the present war is a repetition of the war in her time. The Germanic tribes initially wiped a Roman legion out and drove others away. But, in the end, the Roman Army prevailed and she became a prisoner of war who was abducted to Italy. She, nevertheless, had the opportunity of giving the Roman emperor a piece of her mind, directly in his face.

Hagdale, Sunday, 18 February 1945

Henry phoned me this Sunday morning early: "Ma, I've been booked off with sick leave. Can you come and fetch me and Sarah with that delicious Dragon of yours? I need a place to get some rest. Please, Ma. Can you come today?"

"Only if I will be allowed to refuel at your base for the return flight."

"No problem."

Hector flew with me to fetch our son and daughter-in-law.

When we greeted them, I asked: "Where are your kids?"

Sarah: "With my parents this week-end. They attend their public schools during the week where they stay in boarding houses."

After our guests have settled in their guest room, we sit in the library to enjoy some tea and sandwiches.

Hector: "Henry, you told your Ma over the phone that you are on sick leave. What's wrong, my boy?"

Sarah: "Pa, this husband of mine has a serious case of shell-shock, of battle weariness. He's had enough of the war. He's a crying wreck of a man at night. The nightmares make his life hell."

I and Hector both look at our son and he replies: "Ma, Pa, the shrinks think I'm not fit to fight and fly anymore. At least, not for the time being."

Me: "What led to that condition?"

"Ma, I've taken you once with my Lancaster to watch how we bombed Cologne. I endured many more such incidents over Berlin, Bremen, and other spots. As I explained to you, I usually tried to bomb a lake or an open field, and not areas where civilians live. And since Tuesday night I was the witness of the most horrible and wicked war crime of all times. It really got me. I just can't go on."

Hector: "Tell us more."

"We bombed Dresden Tuesday, Wednesday, and Thursday. I wanted to ask why we were supposed to do that while we were briefed, but I was silenced. Although I am now a group captain and in charge of a whole bomber wing, I was told by Air Chief Marshall Harris, the boss of Bomber Command, to shut up and just do what I'm told."

Me: "What type of question did you want to ask?"

"I wanted to know what type of industries we were targeting. As far as I know, Dresden has no big factories where war material was being assembled. There are also no big military installations."

Me: "And what did this Harris chap give as reason for this bombing campaign?"

"He said that the RAF and the USAAF would bomb that city, which was filled with refugees who fled from the approaching Russians, so that nothing of it would remain standing. It must convince the German High Command to sue for peace."

Hector: "Did you really smash the place?"

"I think that nothing was left intact. Our bombs caused a vicious fire storm. I believe that thousands and thousands of civilians lost their lives. I am unable to erase the sight of that fire storm from my mind. When I close my eyes, that sight intrudes upon my mind. I blame myself for being co-responsible for the deaths of an untold number of women and children. I just cannot go on."

Sarah: "I really hope that he will get some peace of mind if he stays here."

Me: "I am willing to listen to everything my son tells me. The only way to get rid of those demons and ghosts is to talk about them and get to the point where you can forgive yourself for all your crimes and sins. If we believe that God is willing to forgive us, as

He promises in the holy scriptures, then we also have the right to forgive ourselves."

Dresden after the bombing; more than 90% of the city center was destroyed

"Ma, do you think God will ever forgive me? Do you think that God will ever forgive Bomber Harris, that blood-stained butcher?"

Me: "The fact that you are feeling remorse about what you did, tells me that you are where God wants you to be. The first step to receive forgiveness is to acknowledge your guilt, to know that you have done something horrible and feel genuinely sorry about it. That is where you are now. You may then ask God to forgive you. And then you may also forgive yourself."

Sarah: "Henry calls the RAF commanders war criminals. Will God forgive them?"

Hector: "I have asked God to forgive me for the war crimes of the British Army during the Boer War. I got to the point where I could forgive myself and I am truly sorry for what we did to the Boers."

Sarah: "Henry did not only throw bombs on Dresden. Henry, tell them what you did over Holland."

"Yes. My wing flew numerous sorties to deliver food to the starving Dutch. The Wehrmacht confiscated all foodstuffs for their own starving soldiers and that left the poor Dutch with nothing to eat. We negotiated through the mediation of the Swedes and the Swiss that our bombers with supplies for the starving population would not be shot down."

Hector: "I suppose you didn't land anywhere but only dropped those supplies by parachute/"

"That's correct."

Me: "That's something you can be proud of."

We listen to the Afrikaans news on Radio Zeesen at nine. We hear that twenty-five thousand people were killed during the past few days in Dresden. The bodies were piled up in heaps to be cremated because there is no space in the cemeteries. Apart from that, there are not enough relatives to identify the dead or enough grave diggers to bury the corpses.

Henry starts sobbing when he hears this news. Sarah embraces him and I hold his hand.

Hagdale, Monday, 23 April 1945

Hector decided to quit the Army. There can be no doubt that the Allies have smashed Germany, although the Japanese still seem to hold out in the Pacific theater. I welcome his presence at home every day.

During dinner, the phone rings and Freddy Fortune calls Hector to the phone. When he returns after a few minutes, I ask him: "Who was that?"

"One of Henry's colleagues. A certain Squadron Leader Harrison."

"Why does he call on a Sunday evening?"

"Henry was flying again with his squadrons. They were on their way to bomb a submarine base in Norway, but his Lancaster developed engine trouble over the North Sea."

"Did he do a belly landing on the water?"

"Yes. Fortunately for him, a few German torpedo boats – they call these things S-Boote or Schnellboote[72] – was in the vicinity and the commander of these Germans took Harry and his crew on board. So, he's a prisoner-of-war at this moment."

"Thanks God, he survived. What will the Germans do with him?"

"Harrison thinks these German boats are based in Holland and that's where Henry and his men will be taken."

Somehow or other, I have the feeling that my son won't get to Holland and won't languish in a POW camp.

---

[72] Fast boats.

Hagdale, Wednesday, 2 May 1945

Hector is usually a calm and composed gentleman who never raises his voice. Therefore, I find it strange when he starts calling at the top of voice: "Dora! Dora! Come here! Quickly! Dora, do you hear me?"

I hear the urgency in Hector's voice and I rush to the front door where he is standing – holding onto our son, Henry.

I rush forward and also grab him around his body.

Henry: "Ho-ho. Don't squash me! You are throttling me! I'm not a ghost. I'm real! Please, let go of me!"

I see a military truck outside. That must be the vehicle with which Henry came.

We lead Henry inside and we make him sit down in the library, but he says: "I must first tell that driver that he may go back to Portsmouth."

Hector: "How the hell did you get here?"

Henry: "With that truck outside, of course. Wait, I must dismiss that driver first."

After a minute or two, Henry rejoins us: "A surprise for you two old guys, hey?"

Hector sits there with an open mouth and gapes at him. Somehow, I knew that he would come to us and I'm not surprised.

"You will never believe what I am going to tell you now. I was forced to do an emergency belly landing on the North Sea. And a German torpedo boat was friendly enough to rescue all of us. And do you know who the captain of that boat was?"

Hector: "How the hell should we know?"

"It was none other than my own cousin, Korvettenkapitän[73] Joseph von Traubenstein, The son of my uncle, David Davidsohn."

---

[73] Lieutenant Commander.

"How did you know he was your cousin?"

"I had to tell him my name and rank and service number when I was taken prisoner. And then he introduced himself. I immediately recognized that name as the family name that Uncle David had adopted during the Great War. I told this cousin what I knew about his father's real identity. Of course, we spoke in German and he was surprised that I have a German grandpa in South Africa."

Me: "Could you convince him in the end of his real identity?"

"He had no choice because I could tell him that my old man was second-in-command of the POW camp where his dad was being kept and that his real identity was unmasked."

"But how did you get back here?"

"I convinced this cousin to surrender at Portsmouth with his crew before his base in Holland was blasted to bits. He agreed that Germany was done for. It took us some time to reach Portsmouth and, on the way, we heard of the death of Hitler two days ago."

Hector: "So, you surrendered to this German skipper and then he surrendered to you? Funny, isn't it?"

Henry: "Cousin Joseph and his crew were handed over to the Naval Police at Portsmouth and I went to Daniel's office. I told him my story and he ordered the Naval Police to bring this German cousin to his office, where we had an impromptu family reunion. Afterwards, Daniel provided some transport to take me home and Cousin Joseph was locked up."

Hector: "This seems to be the end of the war for you and Cousin Joseph. Everybody expects the capitulation of Germany any day now. I can't see that you will be tasked with any other bombing raids."

Me: "How are you feeling? Still plagued by nightmares?"

"My rest period here and the motherly care I received, put me back on my feet again. But I will always remember the horror of Dresden."

Hector: "Dora, aren't we going to offer our son some tea or something?"

Hagdale, Tuesday, 8 May 1945

It is difficult to present a cheerful face at the breakfast table because Germany has suffered a crushing, humiliating, and sweeping defeat. The last bits of military resistance crumbled after Hitler had committed suicide a week ago. The top general of the Wehrmacht, Field Marshall Wilhelm Keitel, is to sign the final deed of surrender today.

I ask Hector: "Do you think the world is now in a better state than six years ago when this war started?"

"Yes, but also no. We got rid of Hitler. He started this war and we had no choice but to stop him. The world is certainly a better place without him and his Nazi gangsters and hoodlums. But, look at all the mess this war has created. Large parts of Europe have been laid waste – especially big German cities. We also suffered a lot."

"What about the Russians capturing large parts of Europe? Will they ever let go of those parts? Hitler wanted to conquer large parts of Europe and Russia to create living space for his people. Exactly the opposite has happened. Is that something positive?"

"I don't think so."

"Was it a good thing to support the Russians with huge piles of weaponry, ammunition, and other supplies? It cost us dearly to deliver all these goodies to Russia. We lost many ships with their crews and cargoes. It cost us much to donate all that war material to Stalin and his hordes."

"All those goodies were not donations. Russia must pay for all that. Let's hope they service their debt to us and America, as they have promised."

"I wonder. And they will certainly insist that they will only pay for the goodies that were delivered to them – not the stuff that ended up on the bottom of the sea. We had this conversation at the end of the previous war. We agreed that the world was in a worse shape after that war. It is again the case. Things are, in fact, far worse than in 1918."

"I agree, totally."

"When will our boys be able to go home?"

"It will take some time for them to be demobilized. Victor is part of the British Army that will have to occupy Germany. Daniel is stuck in Portsmouth harbor where ships of the Kriegsmarine will come to surrender. Henry will go back to his base and he will have to fly many sorties to Europe to deliver goods and people."

"Are we going to church on Sunday? I'm sure that there will be a thanks-giving service to celebrate peace in Europe."

"We will also have to pray for our troops and sailors and the Americans who are still fighting the Japs in the Pacific."

THE COLD WAR

569

The last war in which I became involved, albeit it very indirectly, started shortly after the end of the Second World War when the previous allies against Germany became bitter enemies. On the one side stood Great Britain, France, the United States, and other democratic countries. On the other side lurked the Soviet Union and other communist states, which were taken over from the Wehrmacht after the war, such as Poland, Hungary, Rumania, and the eastern part of Germany.

My part in this war was more or less restricted to becoming the advisor to Lord Hector de Hacqueville, who again took up politics after the war, as well as the mother of three professional warriors.

Hagdale, Saturday, 25 August 1945

Hector declares at breakfast: "I think it's time that I start doing something productive again."

"The Army won't have you. You're too old at sixty-five. What do you have in mind?"

"Yes, the Army won't have me – except in my capacity as colonel-in-chief of the North Lancashire Regiment. I will have to attend a few medal parades when the troops are being demobbed. But I'm not really old. I get bored just sitting around here and managing the estate. After Trent Park has been shut down and our guests have been removed to prisons in Germany, I became superfluous, although I've left the place somewhat earlier. I'm going back into politics."

"Do you think of renouncing your title and stand for the House of Commons?"

"Heavens, no! I can't do that. No, I will go back to the House of Lords. There are quite a few chaps there who are older than I am."

"What type of contribution will you be able to make?"

"Most of the old fools sitting there had very little exposure to the real world. My time as a battalion commander, my time in Holland, my time at the War Office, and my time at Trent Park gave me some insights and ideas and exposure. The world must hear from me. We are entering a new phase in world history after the end of the war. This morning's newspaper contains a statement by Bernard Montgomery, the guy who trounced Rommel in forty-three and who's presently the military governor of the northern parts of Germany. The occupation force, in which Victor and Henry serve, is to be renamed the Army of the Rhine. They are not there to subdue any German resistance or renewed Nazi activities, but to hold back the Red Army of the Soviet Union."

"I thought that we were demobilizing. For instance, the ATA has been disbanded and I'm officially unemployed now."

"Yes, many of our boys were demobilized and sent home. But we need to show Uncle Joe Stalin, the boss of the Russian mob, that we won't allow him to roll over the parts of Europe under our control."

"I see. So, it was a mistake not to declare war on Russia in thirty-nine? We only declared war on Germany for invading Poland, but Russia did exactly the same. And then we supported them as allies. I always thought that was absurd and stupid."

"Yes, that was a magnificent and monumental mistake. And now we are paying the price for that bloody blunder. We must keep a military force ready in Germany to stop the spread of communism. The Russians have succeeded in establishing communist governments in the countries they have liberated, or rather captured – Poland, Hungary. Romania, and others."

"And communism is an evil system?"

"In theory, it sounds good. The communists want to abolish private property. All property must be shared equally by the whole population. That sounds fantastically fair, but it isn't. It disregards human selfishness and greed that can only be held in check by a democratic system. But, in effect, communism means that the state controls everything and the state bosses live in luxury while the rest of the people live in misery. All, except for the top dogs, are equally poor and poverty-stricken and paper-thin. We can't allow that."

"So, Russia has actually created a new empire, covering eastern Europe?"

"Exactly."

"And that empire mustn't be allowed to expand?"

"Exactly."

Hagdale, Friday, 29 November 1946

An important-looking automobile stops in front of our villa and a gentleman in a smart suit gets out. I watch him through the window of the library because I heard the arrival of the strange vehicle.

Freddy Fortune answers the front door bell and leads the gentleman inside. I am called. Hector is not at home, but in London where he is attending a meeting of the House of Lords.

The gentleman bows and introduces himself as a special courier for His Majesty, King George VI. He hands me a letter in an envelope with my name and address written in golden letters.

"Milady, you are requested to consider the contents of this missive and reply in due course. His Majesty is eager to receive your reply."

I take the letter from this man, thank him and I ask Freddy to lead him out again.

This is something great, I feel it. I am no great admirer of the British Empire and its monarchy. I indeed loathe the lot of them. I put the letter down on a table, almost too afraid to touch it. And then I decide that I will only open it this evening after Hector has arrived home from his political duties in London. I will have to go and fetch him with my delightful Dragon.

I will only surprise him after dinner with this letter, which I will open in his presence, so that we can read it together.

I suddenly get a vision of Veleda who laughs at me. It is almost as if she tells me that I have been caught by the evil British Empire, but that I will get the opportunity to expose the immorality and wickedness of this empire.

Directly after dinner, for which I got dressed in the dress I made for the royal funeral of 1910, I fetch the letter and open it. Hector's eyes grow big and it's clear that this is a big surprise.

BUCKINGHAM PALACE

28th November 1946

The Honourable Viscountess Theodora de Hacqueville
Hagdale Estate
HURSLEY

INVITATION: COMMANDER OF THE BRITISH EMPIRE

It is our intention of bestowing upon you the following honour: Commander of the British Empire. Please inform us within the following ten days whether you accept this invitation so that we can announce it at the time we make our New Year's list of honours known.

You have been recommended by Sir Gerard d'Erlanger, the former director and commodore of the disbanded Air Transport Auxiliary for your exemplary devotion to duty and valuable service rendered in the interest of the British Empire during the recent war.

If you accept this invitation, the order will be bestowed upon you during the investiture at Windsor Castle on Monday, 24 March 1947, at 10 a.m. Thereafter, you will be entitled to use the abbreviation of C.B.E. after your name.

George R.I

Hector: "Well, well, well. I never! Imagine, you will meet His Majesty! He will shake your hand! You will be able to say 'hello' to him, or something. What are you going to reply? Of course, you cannot insult the King by declining this invitation!"

"Of course, I will accept. You will have to help me to write an appropriate letter of acceptance."

Although I wasn't aware of the contents of this letter before opening it, it is no real surprise to me. After all, ancient Veleda met the Roman Emperor Vespasian. If I am some sort of a reincarnation of this ancient heroine, then it is only fitting that I follow in her footsteps by meeting the British monarch. What, on earth, will I say to him, if anything?

I ask: "Exactly what does this honor entail?"

"The Order of the British Empire was created by King George V during the First World War to honor people who rendered exceptional service. There are five classes:

"The highest is the Knight Grand Cross or Dame Grand Cross of the Most Excellent Order of the British Empire. Then comes the Knight Commander or Dame Commander of the Most Excellent Order of the British Empire. Holders of these two orders may be addressed as 'Sir' or 'Dame'. These titles are not hereditary. This can't be given to you, my dear, because you are already a viscountess, which is way more important than a mere 'Dame'.

"Next is Commander of the Most Excellent Order of the British Empire, which you will receive. There are also the Officer of the Most Excellent Order of the British Empire and Member of the Most Excellent Order of the British Empire."

"Oh. Thanks."

With my knowledge of Latin, I decide that the initials R.I. after the name of George must mean "Rex" and "Imperator" – King and Emperor (of the burnt-out and broken British Empire).

Hagdale, Saturday, 22 March 1947

Hector sits with me at the breakfast table. Freddy Fortune, who is still with us, brings the newspaper to Hector.

While we are drinking our coffee, Hector hands me the paper. "Please read what you see on page two."

I open the paper on page two and I see the following report:

THE 🦁 TIMES

SATURDAY, 22 MARCH 1947

LORD HECTOR DE HACQUEVILLE CRITICAL OF WAR POLICIES

There was some angry outbursts in the otherwise calm and dignified House of Lords yesterday during a debate on foreign policy when Lord Hector de Hacqueville of Hagdale, a viscount and a retired brigadier of the British Army, lodged a fiery critique on the wartime government for making fatally wrong choices and decisions.

He declared: "We are officially in a so-called Cold War against the Soviet Union. We made the biggest mistake in our history by supporting Russia against the Germans. We must have allowed Germany and Russia to annihilate each other, but we rather helped the Russian barbarians against the civilised Germans."

He maintained that Britain must keep a large army in Germany at great cost – not to watch the impoverished and defeated Germans, but to keep dear "Uncle Joe Stalin" in check. We are even flying in supplies and food to West Berlin because the Russians have blocked all the access routes over land.

The lord added that two of his sons are involved with the Army of the Rhine as professional members of the armed forces.

"They would much rather have stayed home and be with their families than to stop Russian expansionism and imperialism."

According to him, it was extremely shortsighted not to declare war on Russia in 1939 and now we are reaping the "stinking fruits" of that omission. After all, Russai was just as guilty of aggression as Nazi Germany by invading Poland from the east during 1939.

"There were other serious miscalculations in our history. Another good example is the Boer War of 1899–1902 of which I am a veteran."

"At the moment, Nazi war criminals were being prosecuted for the atrocities they have committed. Our military and political leaders are just as guilty of war crimes," according to Lord Hector.

"The Nazis were not the inventors of concentration camps. We invented them in 1901 in South Africa and that led to the deaths of thousands of civilians. Our bombing campaign against cities such as Berlin, Cologne and especially Dresden, were barbaric and horrific. Thousands upon thousands of innocent civilians were killed or maimed for life. It's a bloody shame!"

Other members of the House of Lords called him a "Nazi-lover" for questioning Chamberlain and Churchill's decisions and calling British military leaders war criminals. Others urged him to retract his remarks.

– Our Political Correspondent

I hand the newspaper back to Hector. "Hurrah! Well done!"

Hagdale, Tuesday, 25 March 1927

Hector laughs while reading the newspaper while we wait for our breakfast to be served: "Ha-ha, my marvelous mate, my dearest darling, please read this report on page three":

THE TIMES

TUESDAY, 25 MARCH 1947

VISCOUNTESS DORA DE HACQUEVILLE CAUSES UPROAR

At a ceremony at Windsor Castle yesterday, HM King George VI bestowed honours on several individuals.

The two recipients of the Knight Grand Cross of the Most Excellent Order of the British Empire (GBE) were Lieutenant General Patrick Partridge and Sir Sydney Staples MP.

The Commander of the British Empire (CBE) was awarded to Theodora, Viscountess de Hacqueville of Hagdale, Professor Ralph Rawlins who teaches geography at Cambridge and Doctor Peter Porter, a physician in London.

Alle the recipients declared afterwards that they felt humbled and grateful for these signs of honour.

However, the Viscountess de Hacqueville added that she dedicated her order to all the Boer women and children who died during the Boer War in British concentration camps, as well as the thousands of civilians who died unnecessary when British bombs fell on cities like Dresden during the recent war.

The Times spoke to several experts on etiquette who explained that something like this is unheard of. This ceremony is certainly not the occasion to make political statements and these remarks were uncalled for.

Lord Horace Harding of Pearly Beach expressed the wish that King George would revoke the award to the viscountess due to the scandal she caused.

– *Our Correspondent*

I can only laugh with Hector. Of course, I stepped upon several sensitive and snobbish British toes with corns – just as Hector did last week. All those who complained are fully aware of the war crimes of so-called British war heroes, but it is not regarded as polite and politically correct to mention those horrors and criminal acts.

Our three sons with their families and in-laws, who were also honored, attended a feast at our country home yesterday after the ceremony to celebrate my new trinket. Henry and Victor flew over from Germany where they are stationed and Daniel came from Portsmouth where he is still working. The four people who were honored had to display their new decoration and photos were taken with all of us holding these in our hands.

Henry's daughter, little Helen, wanted to know how I experienced King George. I was honest and told my granddaughter that he was overdressed with far too many shiny things on his jacket. He reminded me of a Christmas Tree with all its golden balls and stars and ribbons.

Victor wanted to know: "Ma, are you going to use that abbreviation of CBE after your name when you sign your name?"

"Maybe. And if anybody asks me what it means I will tell him it is the abbreviation for 'Clown Bamboozling England' or even 'Chef Boiling Englishmen'."

Sir Sydney Staples, Henry's father-in-law, cornered me and said: "I overheard what you told the reporter of The Times about British war crimes. I must admit, to my shame, that you made a very valid point and that the time has come for Britain to admit to these crimes. You had great courage to expose British hypocrisy."

"That's my Boer background. We can't stand dishonesty, duplicity, and deceit."

While we went on celebrating, I wondered how on earth it could have happened that I was rewarded for service to the British Empire, while I despise this empire, aided its enemies actively, and committed sabotage to inflict some damage on this empire. I could not think of a greater irony than this. The award of this order is, anyway, a sure sign that my activities as an enemy agent stayed hidden and won't receive any recognition in the history books. I am confident that Allied investigators won't find anything about me in the Abwehr archives because my contacts with them was always face to face, or by radio with a code name, without any documentation. Nobody will find Veleda.

Although I declared to my brother-in-law that we Boers can't stand deceit and deception, I am very much guilty of that same sin by deceiving my husband and the whole country regarding who I really am. I decided that it is my fate to carry on with this farce and that I was guided by unseen forces.

London, Friday, 11 June 1948

It wasn't really a surprise when I got a phone call three days ago from the private secretary to the Prime Minister, inviting me to a meeting with the Prime Minister today at the headquarters of the Labour Party at 20 Rushworth Street, London SE1. After my meeting with the king, I had the feeling that I also needed to talk to the Prime Minister as well, just as Veleda gave advice to Emperor Vespasian in Rome.

Everybody knows that Winston Churchill isn't the Prime Minister anymore. His Conservative Party lost badly against the Labour Party during the general elections after the war in 1945 and the leader of the Labour Party, Mister Clement Attlee, moved into No 10, Downing Street, the office of the Prime Minister. However, he wanted to talk to me in his capacity as party leader and, therefore, I was invited to Rushworth Street.

My increasing age – I'm sixty-three now – as well as the shortage of aircraft fuel, necessitated the sale of my dependable Dragon a few months ago. That also meant that my pilot's license lapsed. Hector and I travelled to London by train yesterday and slept in a hotel last night.

The first thing Attlee asks after we have greeted each other, is: "Tea? Or coffee?" We both prefer coffee and after that was served, we start talking.

Attlee: "Milady, my Lord, as you know, the Labour Party represents the working class in Britain. We are busy with the nationalization of all big industries, all the mines, the Bank of

England, and the whole health system. The object is to give workers a bigger say in their workplaces and to improve the working conditions of all workers – better remuneration, better working hours, better safety standards, and so on. The British voters clearly voted for the socialism we represent and want to implement."

I nod my head to indicate that I am listening.

"We are grateful that the British public entrusted us with this important work. Britain is still in a sadly sorry state after the war. This war almost bankrupted us and, as you ought to know, everything is still in short supply. The war taught us that this country has a vast reserve of talent that wasn't utilized properly in the past. When our men were drafted into the armed forces, women had to fill their places in industry and agriculture. Women even served in the armed forces.

"For that reason, we decided to resurrect the Women's Labour League. This organization was disbanded in 1918 after women got the vote, but it becomes increasingly necessary to give women a greater voice in the Labour Movement.

"Milady, we are offering you the position of patron lady of this organization. How do you feel about it?"

"What will it entail?"

"It is purely a ceremonial function. You won't be involved with the day-to-day running of the League. You will have an advisory vote in meetings of the Central Committee, should you wish to attend those meetings. When public meetings are being held, we would like you to honour us with your presence and to deliver an address."

"Mister Prime Minister, let me make my position clear in this matter. And I'm sure that my husband will agree with me. I'm sure that you've done your homework about me and my background, otherwise you wouldn't have offered me this position. I grew up in a lower middle-class household. My father had his own tailor business and he taught me and my brother the trade. During the Great War, I was a working woman. I managed a telegraph office in Pretoria while my husband fought as an Army officer on various fronts. During the previous war, I served as a civilian pilot in the ATA and reached a responsible position. I believe that these things may have played a role in your decision to approach me."

"Milady, you are entirely correct. And your outspokenness also played a role. You are clearly on the side of those who are downtrodden and are victims of a cruel system."

"Indeed. May I add that I support certain aspects of the policies of the Labour Party. You seem to work towards the dismantling the British Empire. After the war, which made us almost bankrupt – as you've pointed out – we don't have the resources to administer a range of colonies anymore. These colonies are becoming more and more independent. It started when the Americans won their war of independence during the late eighteenth century. India gained her independence last year. Countries such as Canada, Australia, and South Africa are, for all purposes, totally independent, although the British Crown is still regarded as the binding factor.

"Last year, the Royal Family visited South Africa to strengthen the ties between Britain and South Africa. It didn't help. The National Party won the general elections a few days ago and they are determined to convert South Africa into a free republic in which the Boers form the government. With that, the inglorious victory of the British Empire over the free Boer republics will be reversed. As a Boer, I applaud this development. In case you don't know, my father fought against the blood-thirsty British Army during the Boer War.

"But I cannot support your policies of nationalization. That's exactly what communism is about. I find it ironic that the Labour Government wants to strengthen our Defenses against the Soviet Union, while emulating the failed policies of the same Soviet Union. For this reason, I decline your offer of patronage of the Women's League.

"And, besides, I and my husband have decided to spend part of the year on our farm in South Africa. When we left South Africa more than twenty years ago, my husband asked my father in Pretoria to look after the property and find tenants. Now, we intend living there a part of the year. That will prevent me from playing any part in the Labour Party."

Afterwards, while we are travelling back in the train, Hector finds time to talk to me: "Hell, Dora! You will make a wonderful politician. It's a shame that you don't have any aspirations in that regard."

"But certainly not as a member of the lame Labour Party. I can't support their silly socialism. The time will come that they will have to abandon those poisonous policies, just as they are abandoning the whole almost-extinct Empire."

Pretoria, Saturday, 18 September 1948

We arrived in Pretoria a month ago – almost at the same time as my brother David with his new wife, Harriet, a woman he had met in Ireland

After a visit to the synagogue on this Sabath, my father invites me to a meeting with his two brothers in the workshop of their thriving clothing business.

My father (in German, as usual): "Dora, now that you're back, it's high time that we tell you more about our secret family history. When you were a young woman, I hinted more than once that we have a very long family history, dating back to biblical times."

Saul: "That applies, of course, to all Jews. We can all trace our ancestry back to the time of Father Abraham who lived several millennia ago in the country of Sumer, in the ancient city of Ur, although not all Jews are able to name every and each ancestor they ever had."

Me: "Thank you for reminding me that I'm a Jew."

Samuel: "We are glad to have this opportunity of informing you where you really came from. This information must be passed on to your sons and your grandchildren, but it must only stay within our family. What we are about to tell you, is not meant for general consumption. In fact, it may be dangerous to disclose all these facts to outsiders. "

My father: "Quite so. Ecclesiastical authorities through the ages wanted to suppress this history and they even resorted to persecution, torture, and warfare to eradicate, rub out, and extinguish our family history and our legacy."

Samuel: "We are very grateful for this opportunity where all three of us can have this conversation with you. I and Saul brought the necessary family documents, including our genealogy, along from Kleve. That would have been lost, if it wasn't for your brother who rescued us from the grip of the Nazi killing machine."

My father: "The Nazis were simply continuing with the antisemitism of the Roman Catholic Church. Please remember that Hitler was actually a Catholic from Austria!"

Me: "I and Hector simply had to act when that horrible Crystal Night occurred. We had to give you shelter in our home in Wassenaar after David had rescued you and smuggled you over the border – without you really knowing who he was."

My father: "We must see the hand of Providence in all this. David was meant to become a German officer, stationed in Emmerich of all places, who could save several Jews from the gas chambers – including his own uncles and their families."

Saul: "There was, of course, no earlier opportunity of informing you of our secret family history. You only returned to Pretoria recently. You and your family had to endure the horrible Second World War in England, out of reach for us."

My father: "Indeed. You and your husband were the instruments in the hand of Gd who made it possible that our family tradition can continue. I left Germany as a young man in the previous century because there was no place for me in the family business and I had to make a new start in South Africa, where I met your mother. We could never foresee that I would be the only brother who had a son. My two brothers had only daughters and they could not continue and preserve the family name. We often corresponded and the need to pass the documents on to me was discussed, but when David disappeared in 1914 that seemed senseless."

Samuel: "But here you are also. We told David a fortnight ago what we want to tell you now."

My father: "And you and David must see to it that the family name of Davidsohn stays alive and thriving."

Me: "You make me very curious. You mentioned our family secrets repeatedly, but I still don't have the faintest idea what they entail."

My father: "It was necessary that we prepare you properly for what is to follow. Saul, show her the box."

Saul fetches a simple chest of wood, strengthened with iron straps, and secured with a padlock. A leather strap helps to keep the lid in the closed position.

Me: "I remember this box. It was part of your luggage when you stayed with us in Wassenaar."

Saul: "Yes. This box is very old. One of our ancestors had it made when he lived in Spain during the Middle Ages. It was Isaac of Navara. He had to replace an older box that became worn out and useless."

Me: "What's in it?"

Saul: "Our family history – stretching back to the times before the destruction of Jerusalem by the Romans in AD 70. Old parchments, mostly."

Me: "May I read what they contain?"

My father: "They are written in Hebrew. We had Hebrew scholars in our family who translated all of it into German – actually a mixture of Platt-Deutsch and Dutch. It was done during the early nineteenth century. After that, our great-great-grandfather started to keep the records up-to-date in Platt-Deutsch and we carried on with that. But only in standard High German."

Me: "I will certainly be able to read those translations. But I think you want to tell me yourself what they contain."

Samuel: "That's right. Anyway, when those Nazi hooligans raided our homes on Crystal Night in 1938, we were very afraid that they would burn down our homes, with this treasure along with everything inside. We had it hidden in the loft, but fortunately, they didn't go so far as to torch the place as happened elsewhere. When David came to fetch us with his Wehrmacht truck, this box went along with us."

My father: "Let me get to the gist of our family history. It is important to know that our ancestors belonged to the sect or party of the Essenes in the time before the destruction of Jerusalem by the Romans in AD 70. The name 'Essenes' doesn't occur in the New Testament, but its synonym, 'Nazorenes', occurs a few times. It is explicitly stated in more than one place in the Gospels that Jesus the Christ, Jesus the Messiah, Jesus of Nazareth, was a member of the party of the Nazoreans. The first Jewish followers of Jesus, including his apostles, were also called Nazoreans in the book of Acts."

Samuel: "Apart from these Essenes or Nazoreans, there were other sects or parties. We read in the Gospels and Acts of Pharisees, Sadducees and Zealots. They mostly didn't like the Essenes because the Essenes thought they were not obeying the laws of Moses properly and criticized them for that."

Me: "Were these Nazoreans and the Nazarenes the same people?"

Samuel: "Not quite. These names were often confused with each other in later times, even during the thirteenth century when they were mentioned by Thomas of Aquino, one of the great theologians of the Catholic Church. He used the name 'Nazarenes', but it's clear that he meant 'Nazoreans'. A 'Nazarene' was actually an inhabitant of the village of Nazareth, while a Nazorean was somebody who devoted his life to God – like the Essenes did. Some of them were also Nazarites, like John the Baptist."

Saul: "And they were also known later as the Ebionites. These people were the followers of Jesus after his crucifixion and Jesus' brother, James, afterwards became their leader in Jerusalem. The name 'Ebionites' is derived from the Hebrew word for 'The Poor Ones.' The Essenes and the Nazoreans were well-known for their sober life styles and their opposition to the rich priests in Jerusalem during the first century AD. This box contains some of the Ebionites' books – books that are thought to have been lost, but we have copies of them. Probably the only copies. One of them contains some of the sayings and wisdom of Jesus, which was later incorporated into the Gospels."

Samuel: "And when Jerusalem was destroyed by the Romans during the Jewish War of 66 to 70 AD, these Nazoreans or Ebionites fled in various directions. Some of them moved to territories to the east of the Jordan. The prophet of the Muslims, Mohammed, got his information about Jesus mostly from these people. What we read in the Qur'an about Jesus is in a certain sense quite trustworthy. But other Ebionites went to Asia Minor and to Europe, mostly to Gaul – which is France nowadays."

Saul: "Some of the followers of Jesus the Nazorean even moved to Europe much earlier. The best known of them was the apostle Peter who became the leader of the Jewish followers of Jesus in Rome."

Me: "The Catholics regard him as the first bishop of Rome and, therefore, the first pope."

Samuel: "That's what they say. The truth is a bit different. If you read the last chapter of Paul's letter to the Romans, he mentions quite a few Jews in Rome to whom he sent greetings. Peter was the leader of these Jews – not of the disciples of Paul who were mostly gentiles."

My father: "And these Jewish followers of Jesus were hunted by the Romans, just as all the other Jews and Christians were hunted after the destruction of Jerusalem. Our ancestors in Gaul joined forces with the early Christians to form a united front against the pagan Romans."

Me: "And how did we end up in Germany?"

Saul: "Oh, that's a long story – a very long story. We will give you the main points."

Me: "My ears are wide open."

Saul: "When Christianity became the official religion of the Roman Empire under Emperor Constantine, it was the Catholic variety that won the day. There were various other Christian groups, including the Nazoreans, and they were persecuted and suppressed and vilified by the Catholics. Their books were destroyed, when they could be found. Fortunately, we have some of them in this box."

My dad: "And when the Muslims conquered large parts of Spain during the eighth century, our Nazorean or Ebionite ancestors decided to move to Spain to escape from the clutches of the Catholic Church. They generally had a peaceful existence under Muslim rule."

Samuel: "There were other groups in France with which our ancestors had good relationships, although these people believed some strange things. They are known as the Cathars and the Catholic Church killed thousands of them in order to stamp out their dangerous doctrines and ideas."

Saul: "The Muslims in Spain were much more tolerant towards the Jews in those days and that's why our ancestors moved to Spain. The family leader at that stage was Jonathan of Marseilles. He became Jonathan of Toledo."

Me: "And then the Christians managed to chase the Muslims out of Spain a few centuries later. I know that from the history that I was taught in school."

Samuel: "That's correct. And then the trouble started all over again. The Spanish Inquisition, a series of ecclesiastical courts that reported directly to the Pope, had the task of ridding Spain of all heretics, witches, and Jews. They blamed the Jews for being the killers of Jesus, although it was the Romans who crucified him."

Saul: "There was much hardship. In order to hide their Jewish background, they joined the Catholic Church on the surface, but continued to practice their brand of Judaism in secret."

Me: "And that's why you, Vati, explained to the Reverend Bosman many years ago that it was all right to attend meetings in the synagogue, as well as in the Dutch Reformed Church?"

My dad: "Exactly. I'm glad you remember that."

Samuel: "Our family leader of the time, Eliud of Seville, convinced the whole clan to move to Portugal, the neighboring country to Spain. There they lived in peace for some time, but then the Portuguese Inquisition started to make life also difficult. Their leader of the time, John of Porto, decided in 1540 that they had to move to Holland. Many other Jews did the same and most of these other Portuguese Jews ended up in Amsterdam. Most Dutchmen adopted the Protestant variety of Christianity at that time, which seemed a better bet than the Portuguese Catholics."

Me: "And then some of our ancestors decided to settle in Kleve, which was part of a Dutch duchy in those times?"

Samuel: "Yes, the Duchy of Nijmegen. Kleve became German territory only later, but the people continued with their version of German and Dutch – Platt-Deutsch, in other words. That was when our clan became known as 'Davidsohn' – the German translation of their Spanish and Portuguese name. In Dutch it was 'Davidzoon' with a 'z', which sounds exactly the same

My father: "During the Middle Ages and afterwards, the Jews were not allowed to follow professional careers, such as becoming doctors, professors, lawyers and so forth. So, we all learnt some or other craft. The lot in Kleve decided to become tailors – besides being students of the Bible."

Me: "You mentioned that Jesus was a member of the sect of the party of the Essenes or Nazoreans. Where does he fit in with our family history?"

Saul: "He was indeed a Nazorean, yes. The Gospels are quite clear about that, although most translations rendered it as 'Nazarene' – a man from Nazareth. But as we explained, the words 'Nazorean' and 'Nazarene' are two different words, although they sound similar and that's why many biblical scholars confused the two with each other."

My father: "Another well-known figure who was associated with the Essenes was John the Baptist. The Essenes lived together in most cities and towns of Palestine, but they had their headquarters in the desert, at a spot nowadays called Qumran, overlooking the Jordan Valley. John was active in those parts, as well as in Galilee."

Saul: "Their library was found in big jars in a number of caves nearby, more or less a year ago. Nobody knows yet what these books of the Essenes will reveal, but it will certainly be a rich source of information. Perhaps some are copies of the books we have kept."

Samuel: "The most important thing that you must know about Jesus, is that he was an ordinary human being – not a supernatural divine being who adopted a human body by being born from a virgin, as conventional Christians believe. The Ebionites or Nazoreans, who were the original followers of Jesus in Judea and Jerusalem and who knew hm best, were quite adamant that he was conceived and born in the normal way, that Joseph was his biological father and that he was simply a mortal human being."

Me: "How did it come that the Christians regard him as the eternal divine Son of God, the Father?"

Samuel: "The apostle Paul came to that conclusion. You must remember that Paul never knew Jesus personally. He had all sorts of visions and revelations – most probably hallucinations – in which Jesus appeared to him as a celestial being."

Saul: "He wrote extensively about his visions in the letters contained in the New Testament. Go and read them."

Me: "But we read often in the Gospels that Jesus called himself the son of God. How must I understand that?"

My father: "Yes, he often called himself the son of God and he called God his father. With that, he conveyed the message that he was destined to become the next king of Israel. He was, after all, a descendant of King David. One must remember that only the kings of Israel were called sons of God in the Hebrew Scriptures and Jesus, the orthodox Jew, used this expression in that sense."

Me: "Just as the Egyptian Pharaohs called themselves sons of Osiris, one of their gods?"

Saul: "Quite right. The Roman emperors also claimed a divine ancestry to legitimize their claim to the throne. Jesus' favorite topic was the kingdom of God in his sermons. He taught his disciples to pray to God that his kingdom would come – a kingdom with Jerusalem as its capital, as in the days of King David. This was to be an earthly kingdom in which the dynasty of David would again occupy the throne and the hated pagan Romans driven away with the aid of an army of angels from heaven. Many Jews believed Jesus and, therefore, he was hailed by the crowds as the king of Israel, the son of David, when he entered Jerusalem on the back of a donkey. That was clearly a staged and organized and choreographed event to act out the fulfillment of an Old Testament prophecy"

Me: "And that must be the reason why the Roman governor, Pontius Pilate, had a notice placed on Jesus' cross to the effect that he was condemned to death for being the king of the Jews."

Saul: "That's exactly the reason why Jesus was crucified. He was about to start a rebellion against the Romans by proclaiming himself king of Israel. The Roman governor of Judea couldn't tolerate that and he had Jesus arrested and he sentenced him to death on the cross."

The 17th-century painting *Christ Crucified* by Diego Velázquez (Museo del Prado in Madrid)

My father: "Yes, he cheated death. Any other man would have died from all those horrible wounds, but he survived with the help of his friends and the women who nursed him in his tomb after his body had been removed from the cross. He only went into a state where he was seemingly dead, due to the drugged wine or vinegar the women gave him while he was hanging on the cross. The drug was probably opium, which was in widespread use in those times.

That knocked him out and he was declared dead – although he recovered sufficiently two days later to appear to his disciples and friends."

Saul: "That's more or less what we read in the Qur'an, which seems to preserve the tradition of the Nazoreans or Ebionites."

Me: "Did he ascend into heaven?"

Saul: "Only much later when he really died of old age. He promised his followers that he would return some or other time, but that never happened. He and his family fled from Judea and they settled in Gaul where the Roman authorities would not look for him."

Me: "Jesus had a family?"

Saul: "Yes, certainly. It was expected of all learned rabbis to have a wife and a family. Our family records show that he had a wife – Mary Magdalene. They had a son called Joseph, after Jesus' father. This son became the leader of the Nazoreans in exile in Gaul. This position was always inherited by the eldest son of the eldest son."

Me: "And how exactly does Jesus fit into our family history?"

My father: "It's important that you ask that question. Our family records show that we are the descendants of Jesus the Messiah, Jesus of Nazareth, Jesus the Nazorean. You are also one of his offspring. Many of our forebears inherited from him the ability to overcome serious injuries in a short period of time."

Me: "And that must be the reason why David was able to overcome various injuries and maladies and wounds exceptionally rapidly. He must have inherited that ability from him."

Saul: "Yes, he also inherited that remarkable constitution. That is a sign that you and David are really descended from him."

My father: "And you, Dora, also inherited from him the gift of prophecy. Just as Jesus, you can see the future."

Me: "And where does the name, Davidsohn, come from?"

Saul: "Simple. We are sons of King David."

My father: "We can truly trace our ancestry without interruption back to the time of King David. Our genealogy is explained on these documents in this box and it is supplemented by genealogies contained in the Bible."

Me: "And the Bible also provides us with the genealogy of David back to Adam. The Gospels of Matthew and Luke contain two genealogies of Jesus, back to King David. They seem to contradict each other. Which one must we accept?"

Samuel: "Both. The genealogy in Matthew contains the biological father of Joseph and Jesus' real grandfather. He died young and Joseph was brought up by a step-father, the man mentioned in the Gospel of Luke. You see – there can't be the slightest doubt about your ancestry."

Veleda by Charles Landelle, 1874

It suddenly dawns upon me that I have two very remarkable ancestors, who both lived during the first century AD – Jesus of Nazareth and Veleda of Xanten, the prophetess. Both rebelled against the Roman Empire. My gift of seeing the future must come from both. Just as Veleda foresaw the dissolution of the Roman Empire in the end, I also saw the termination of the British Empire.

Rheindahlen, Wednesday, 1 September 1954

Henry and Victor booked a suite for me and Hector in the Hotel and Restaurant Haus Schüppen, outside the small village of Rickerath. This village is two miles to the west of the Rheindahlen Joint Headquarters of the British Army of the Rhine and the RAF HQ for the Federal Republic of Germany, the western parts of Germany that was occupied by Britain, America, and France at the end of the Second World War. Rheindahlen is a German town to the south-east of the military complex and not far from the Dutch border.

Henry, now an air commodore, is a senior staff officer: operations at the RAF HQ. Victor, promoted to the rank of brigadier, is a senior staff officer: signals and communications of the Army of the Rhine. We are celebrating Henry's 50th birthday today in the restaurant of this hotel, which is situated in a beautiful wooded area.

Hector proposed three months ago that we retrace our steps through continental Europe to celebrate fifty years of marriage. We started in Holland, at Wassenaar. We visited Paris in France and I made sure to revisit Veleda's statue in the Luxembourg Gardens.

From Paris, we took the fast train to Berlin, which is a divided city today. The western part belongs to the Federal Republic of Germany and some western troops are stationed there to deter the Russians from annexing this enclave. We had a look at the old Olympia Stadium where we watched the Olympic Games of 1936.

We turned around and visited Kleve, where my father grew up and we had another look at the partly restored ancient Roman fortress at Xanten, where I again spent some time in Veleda's tower. I could hear her whisper: "The British Empire is gone! Germany really won the war!"

We travelled to the Sauerland to have a look at the cave in which Veleda reportedly hid when the Romans were seeking her blood and where the ancient Germans came to pay homage to her. This famous cave is open to the public and walkways have been constructed to allow visitors to move around in comfort. I convinced Hector to visit this spot, merely because it is a famous tourist attraction, without telling him of my connection to this ancient priestess and prophetess.

We undertook another ride on Wuppertal's Schwebebahn and saw lots of ruined buildings, left-overs from the war. We plan to travel to Nuremberg later, and look at the Alpine regions after that.

But now, we are enjoying the company of our two sons in a lovely restaurant. It is a pity that Daniel cannot join us, since it is also his birthday. He works at the Admiralty in London nowadays with the rank of commodore.

Henry: "We both got these jobs because we can speak German. We often have to talk to the local authorities. There are plans for the West Germans to establish their own Defense Force one of these days and we will have to liaise with those guys as well. There are some old Wehrmacht generals and admirals who will take over these new West German armed forces."

Victor: "This Army and RAF HQ is situated as far to the west as possible, in case the Russians start to invade western Germany. The plan is to stop them long before they can reach us here. Their most likely targets with an invasion will be the north German cities where the countryside is flat – ideal for armored formations – and to reach the Dutch coast."

Henry: "It is ironic that we are now protecting Germany, the erstwhile enemy of Great Britain, against the Soviet Union, the previous ally of the UK. It is, of course, a good thing that the world got rid of Hitler and his notorious Nazi bootlickers, but we exchanged that for something far more sinister and spooky, namely the Soviet Union deep inside Europe. In other words, the whole World War was a waste of lives, time, effort, and money and we ended in a far worse situation than before the war."

Victor: "Many former German officers and soldiers told me that they would have licked the Russians if it wasn't for the help Russia received from Britain and America. Their soldiers were badly trained and their equipment was inferior. Things only turned against them when the Ivans received American and British equipment."

Hector: "Do we have enough troops to stop the Russians? I warned more than once during speeches in the House of Lords that we cannot trust these Ruskis and that it was a bloody blunder to prop them up during the last war."

Henry: "We believe we will be able to stop them and annihilate them. We have much better weaponry – jet aircraft, guns, tanks, and so forth. Our troops are of a much better quality. Better training and better motivation."

Me: "So your job is actually to prevent another war?

Victor: "That's right. And one of these days the Western Germans will also become part of our alliance. The Federal Republic, which is a little more than half of the size of the pre-war Germany, has more or less the same number of inhabitants as Great Britain. Their economy is, at present, much stronger than the economy of Great Britain. They will have the means to keep a substantial army, navy, and air force."

Me: "But why is it that the German economy is stronger than that of Britain?"

Hector: "Yes, how does that work? We devastated Germany during the war and one can still see lots of ruined buildings all over the place."

Henry: "There are various reasons for that. I have spoken to many Germans all over the place and they boast that they, in reality, won the war because Germany – or the western part, then – is in a far better shape than Britain. Both of us feel the same and we are proud of it, with our late German grandfather who taught us German."

Victor: "The main reason for the rapid recovery of Germany is the fact that they work incredibly hard – much harder than the lazy British and French workers."

Henry: "The Germans benefitted from the Marshall Plan. The United States helped to pay for the rebuilding of factories and industries. Britain and France received much more than the Germans did. Britain got more than twice the amount that was given to Germany. But the lazy British Bulldogs and the sluggish French Frogs adopted socialism and they sit and wait for the state to look after them, without doing something for themselves. The Germans chose capitalism, which meant that they had to rely on their own initiative and their own brains and their own muscles. And they made a huge success of it."

Victor: "The average German has a much higher standard of living than the average Englishman or Frenchman. They travel around in Volkswagen and Mercedes Benz and Opel automobiles. The Britons can't afford Rolls Royces and have to be satisfied with mediocre Austin and Morris cars, if they can buy them.

"A German once told me, 'The Americans and the Britons really did us a favor by smashing all our outdated industries. That gave us the chance to build the most modern and most efficient plants. We built up everything from scratch and that gave us a head-start. You poor Brits are stuck with old machines and equipment that break down all the time.'"

Me: "The Britons were used to live in luxury because they plundered their colonies in the past. That made them lazy. But these colonies are no longer colonies and the British Empire is disappearing. And the Britons haven't adapted to this new situation yet. Germany really did the world a favor by weakening Great Britain and participating indirectly in the dismantling of the British Empire."

Henry: "That makes sense. Yes. But, of course, the Germans were horrified when the crimes of the Nazis came to light after the war. They knew that the Jews and political undesirables disappeared but they were oblivious of the fates of these people. They feel aggrieved that the world regards all Germans as war criminals, although only a small minority – the members of the SS, the SA, and the Nazi Party – were guilty of these atrocities in their concentration camps and elsewhere."

Me: "And who invented concentration camps in the first place? That's where defenseless people were starved and allowed to die of epidemics? Thousands upon thousands of Boer women and children, as well as black people, perished in those British camps. Concentration camps were the brain-child of Lord Horatio

Kitchener, who was hailed as a war hero. If that isn't the utmost bit of hypocrisy, I don't know."

Hector: "I'm a veteran of that war and I'm ashamed about what the British Army did. You Boer boys must return to South Africa. The country needs people like you who are hard-working."

Henry: "That's what we would like to do when we retire, although I can't loosen myself from Hagdale after your death, just as you have to look after the place, while also living in Pretoria."

Victor: "We never forgot that we are really Boers, just as Ma."

Secretly, I wonder when the time will come that I can tell Hector about the role I played during the Boer War, the First World War, the time between the wars, and the Second World War. I feel a little bit of guilt that I deceived my husband more than five decades, the whole time since my first date with him. And in that time, he trusted me. But a little voice inside me tells me that I did the right thing to oppose this evil empire, this roguish realm – even if I am a member of the aristocracy and have been rewarded for so-called meritorious service by the moron of a monarch.

Hector was never informed about the inspiration and encouragement that I've received from that ancient prophetess and pagan priestess, Veleda. He saw her statues in Paris and Toulouse, as well as her cave in the Sauerland, but he never guessed how she accompanied me through the decades in my struggle and campaign against the unholy and ungodly and ugly United Kingdom. It must stay that way.

But I must also ask myself: did she really speak to me, or was she only a dream, a product of my imagination?

I am greatly relieved that the Germans are convinced that they have, in fact, won the Second World War while getting rid of Hitler and his no-good Neanderthal Nazi gangsters in the process.

POSTSCRIPTUM

THE ✦ TIMES

FRIDAY, 5 JUNE 1992

LETTERS TO THE EDITOR

SHAMEFUL STATUE FOR BOMBER HARRIS

Air Vice Marshall Henry, Viscount de Hacqueville, of Hagdale, Hampshire, writes:

It is with the utmost horror and shame that I write this letter of protest. It has come to my attention that HM Queen Elizabeth, the Queen Mother, unveiled a statue of Marshall of the Royal Air Force Arthur "Bomber" Harris on 31 May 1992 in London.

I served under Harris during the Second World War as a member of Bomber Command and I commanded a bomber wing at the end of the war. I took part in numerous air raids over Germany. The squadrons under my command did their bit to smash German cities and they killed thousands of innocent and helpless civilians in the process.

According to reports, the mayor of the German city of Dresden

The Statue of Arthur Harris at the RAF Church of St Clement Danes

protested the erection of this statue. There were other objections.

Harris commanded all available bombers to annihilate Dresden a few weeks before the end of the war. The city contained no military targets of importance and it was filled with refugees who fled from the Russian hordes. More or less fifty thousand people lost their lives within three days.

I witnessed how Dresden experienced hell on earth when the city centre was obliterated in a fire storm. That sight gave me a nervous breakdown and I was booked off duty. It was too much for me to bear that men under my command took part in that wholesale slaughter and killing spree.

Harris was, without the slightest doubt, a war criminal. He is just as guilty as fat Hermann Göring, the head of the German Luftwaffe, who was sentenced to death in 1946, but who managed to cheat the hangman's noose by committing suicide.

Harris is just as guilty as the SS butchers and Gestapo killers who slaughtered huge numbers of opponents of the Nazi regime and other unwanted people.

Apart from being a former pilot of the RAF, I also studied Law at Cambridge. This education instilled in me a strong urge and need to promote justice and fairness. What Bomber Harris did was, without the slightest doubt, totally wrong, unfair, bad, and unjust.

It is not without significance that this statue was unveiled on 31 May 1992, exactly ninety years after the end of the infamous Boer War of 1899–1902 in South Africa. More than fifty thousand Boer civilians and black people died of starvation and lack of medical care in British concentration camps.

Bomber Harris demonstrated the same lack of humanity as Lord Horatio Kitchener, who ordered the erection of these contemptible concentration camps and the destruction of Boer farms.

I call upon the City Council of London to remove this scandalous statue forthwith and place it somewhere else, out of sight.

My brothers, Commodore (ret) Daniel de Hacqueville and Brigadier (ret) Victor de Hacqueville, read the draft of this letter and they concur.

GLOSSARY

Some parts of this story are situated in South Africa, Holland, and Germany. Therefore, many Afrikaans, Dutch, and German words and terms are used. They are given their English equivalents the first time they occur, but for the benefit of the reader a list of such words, terms, and abbreviations that are used repeatedly is given here:

Afrikaans and Dutch Expressions

Boer	Farmer – also the name given to Afrikaans-speaking people in South Africa
Burger	Citizen
Dominee	Reverend
Dorpskerk	Village church
Luchtvaartminiterie	Air Traffic Ministry
Mevrouw	Missus
Mijnheer	Mister
Neef	Cousin
Onderstepoort	Lower portal
Oom	Uncle
Pretoria Hogere School voor Jongens	Pretoria High School for Boys
Rooinekke	Red necks (the Afrikaans nickname for Englishmen)
Sesmylspruit	Six Mile Stream
Staats Model School	State Model School

German Expressions

Alles geht gut	All goes well
Angriff	Attack

Außer Dienst	Outside Service (retired)
Bekennende Kirche	Witnessing church
Brigadeführer	Major General of the SS
Danke	Thanks
Falle	Trap
Feige	Timid or cowardly
Feldwebel	Sergeant
Forsicht	Beware
Frau	Woman of Missus
Freiherr	Baron
Führer	Leader
Generalmajor	Major general
Gerne	Gladly
Geschichte der Germanischen Stämme	History of the Germanic Tribes
Gestapo	The German Secret Police
Gnädige Frau	Merciful Madam
Gothaischer Almanac	Gotha Almanac
Gräfin	Countess
Herr	Mister
Kaiser	Emperor
Keks	Cookies
Korvettenkapitän	Lieutenant commander
Kriegsmarine	War Navy of Germany
Kristallnacht	Crystal Night
Kronprinz	Crown Prince
Luftwaffe	Air Weapon or Air Force
Marine	Navy
Oberst	Colonel
Oberstleutnant'	Lieutenant Colonel
Reich	Empire

Reichsadler — Eagle of the Reich
Reichsbahn — Railway system of the Reich
Reichspräsident — President of the Reich
Reichstag — German Parliament
Reichswehr — Defense Force of the Reich or Empire
Ritter — Knight
Ruhestand — Retirement
Schliessen — Closing
Schnellboote or S-Boote — Fast torpedo boats (known in English as E-boats)
Schutzstaffel (SS) — Protection Squadron
Schutztruppe — Protection troops
Schwebebahn — Suspension railway
Sicherheitsdienst (SD) — Security service of the SS
Sturmabteilung (SA) — Storm Detachment
Tschüs — Good-bye
Vati — Daddy
Vizeadmiral — Vice Admiral
Wasserhahn — Water tap
Wehrmacht — Defense Force
Wutend — Angry

RANK STRUCTURES OF THE BRITISH ARMED FORCES

Royal Navy

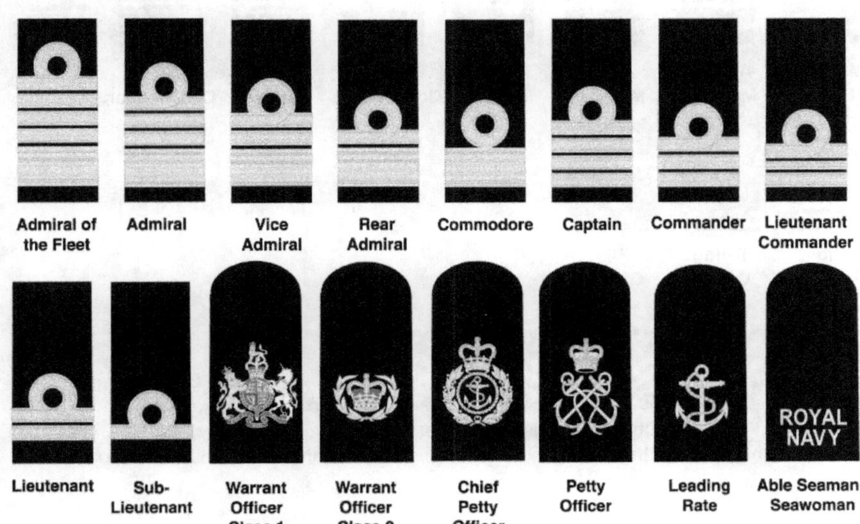

British Army

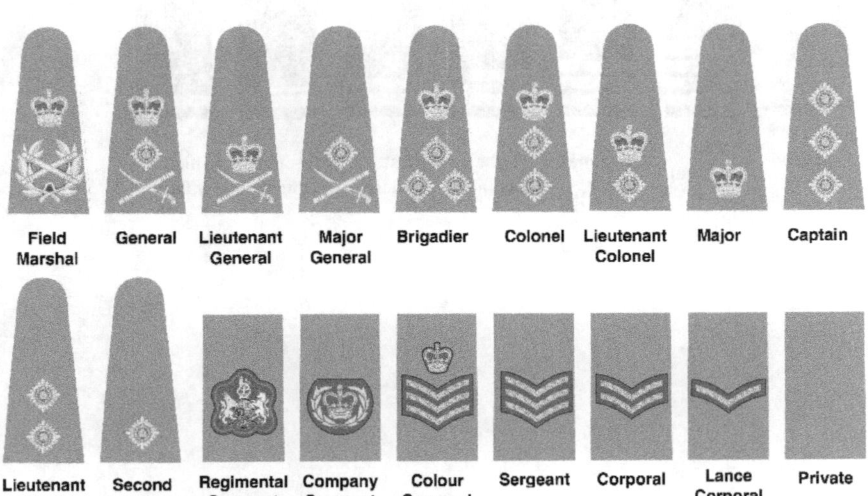

Royal Air Force

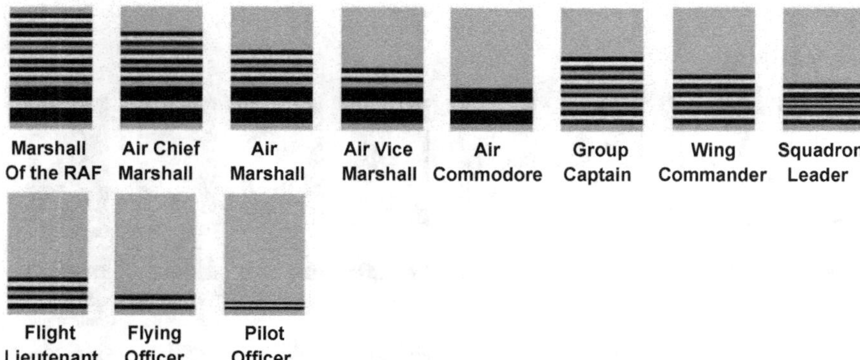

Air Transport Auxiliary

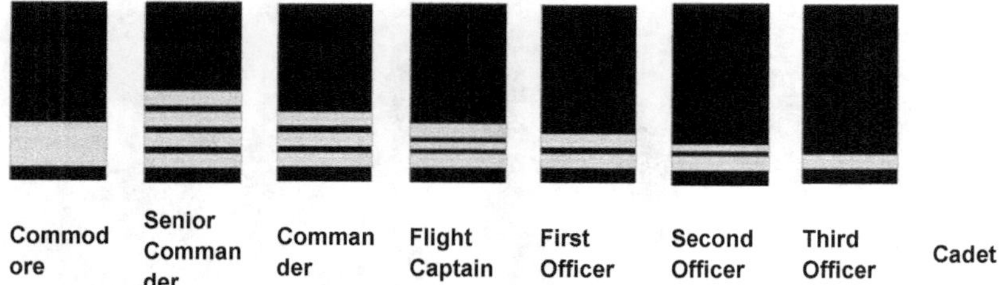

LIST OF ILLUSTRATIONS

Frontispiece
De Havilland Dragon Rapide in the colors of the RAF
https://en.wikipedia.org/wiki/De_Havilland_Dragon_Rapide

Southampton, Tuesday, 31 May 1955
Starving child in a British concentration camp.
https://allthatsinteresting.com/boer-war

Burning farm house, South African War
https://theconversation.com/concentration-camps-in-the-south-african-
war-here-are-the-real-facts-112006

Pretoria, Saturday, 8 January 1898
Old synagogue, Pretoria
http://melvinresidence.blogspot.com/2013/12/the-old-jewish-synagogue-
in-pretoria.html

State President, Paul Kruger
https://www.boerwararchive.com/commanders/joubert/

Pretoria, Monday, 28 February 1899
The Rev Hermanus Bosman
https://af.wikipedia.org/wiki/Hermanus_Bosman

Pretoria, Wednesday, 11 October 1899
Mauser rifle
https://en.wikipedia.org/wiki/Second_Boer_War

Boer commando leaving Pretoria

https://www.angloboerwar.com/unit-information/boer-units/1953-boer-forces?showall=1

Residence of Pres. Kruger
https://commons.wikimedia.org/wiki/File:5_Paul_Kruger%27s_House.jpg

Pretoria, Thursday, 31 May 1900
Fort on Klapperkop Hill
https://za.pinterest.com/pin/327355466645543614/

Pretoria, Saturday, 2 June 1900
General Louis Botha
https://commons.wikimedia.org/wiki/File:General_Louis_Botha,_1900.png

Pretoria, Sunday, 3 June 1900
Church Square, Pretoria
https://af.wikipedia.org/wiki/NG_gemeente_Pretoria

Pretoria, Tuesday, 5 June 1900
British forces entering Pretoria
https://www.wikiwand.com/en/Second_Boer_War

Victory parade, Pretoria
http://www.goldiproductions.com/angloboerwarmuseum/Boer91j_jug_pretoria.html

Pretoria, Monday, 11 June 1900
Church on Church Square, Pretoria
https://af.wikipedia.org/wiki/NG_gemeente_Pretoria

Pretoria, Tuesday, 26 June 1900
Capt. JJ Naude

G.D. Scholtz: In Dodsgevaar, die Ervarings van Kapt J J Naude. Protea Boekhuis, Pretoria, 2011: frontispiece

Pretoria, Wednesday, 5 September 1900
British soldier with a horse
http://www.rdgmuseum.org.uk/history-and-research/did-you-know/?n=horses-and-horseflesh-losses-in-the-boer-war

Pretoria, Thursday, 13 September 1900
Mounted British soldiers
https://www.battlefieldhistorytours.com.au/About_the_Boer_War.php

Pretoria, Saturday, 27 October 1900
Snaffle bit
https://www.decathlon.co.za/horse-bits/2488-39030-horse-riding-eggbutt-snaffle-bit-for-horse-and-pony-stainless-steel.html

White Arabian horse
https://pixabay.com/photos/horse-white-arabian-stallion-4575759/

Pretoria, Sunday, 18 November 1900
Lee-Metford rifle
https://en.wikipedia.org/wiki/Lee%E2%80%93Metford

Pretoria, Saturday, 8 December 1900
Prickly pear cactus
https://www.youtube.com/watch?v=hLSNfWmIntkPretoria, **Monday, 31**

December 1900
Lord Kitchener
https://en.wikipedia.org/wiki/Herbert_Kitchener,_1st_Earl_Kitchener

Pretoria, Sunday, 20 January 1901
Old St Alban's Church, Pretoria

https://www.worldanglican.com/south-africa/pretoria/the-anglican-church-of-southern-africa/christ-church-arcadia

Pretoria, Wednesday, 29 March 1901
Boer family in British concentration camp
https://theconversation.com/concentration-camps-in-the-south-african-war-here-are-the-real-facts-112006

Pretoria, Friday, 31 May 1901
Staats Model School, Pretoria
https://en.wikipedia.org/wiki/Staats_Model_School

Bottles with glass marbles
https://www.freepik.com/premium-ai-image/glass-jar-filled-with-colorful-marbles_312670131.htm

Pretoria, Saturday, 16 September 1901
Sling with stones
https://www.occpaleo.com/post/slinging-stones-slaying-giants

Pretoria, 31 May 1902
The six Boer generals who signed the peace treaty of 31 May 1902
https://www.angloboerwar.com/forum/19-ephemera/32561-postcards?start=84

Pretoria, Monday, 2 June 1902
Two Boer bitter-enders
https://earthwormexpress.com/bacon-and-the-art-of-living/the-second-anglo-boer-war/

Mounted Boer fighters
https://paraquee.com/the-boer-war-which-lasted-from-1899-to-1902-was-caused-by

Pretoria, Friday, 17 January 1910
Pretoria Boys' High School
https://en.wikipedia.org/wiki/Pretoria_Boys_High_School

Drill Hall, Johannesburg
https://www.heritageregister.org.za/node/49

Cape Town, Thursday, 7 April 1910
Dover Castle
https://en.wikipedia.org/wiki/HMHS_Dover_Castle

Hagdale, Monday, 25 April 1910
Villa Chiericati
https://en.wikipedia.org/wiki/Villa_Chiericati

London, Friday, 20 May 1910
Nine Sovereigns
https://en.wikipedia.org/wiki/Death_and_state_funeral_of_Edward_VII

Funeral train
https://www.thamesweb.co.uk/windsor/windsorhistory/royalfunerals/edwardVIIfuneral.html

Funeral Procession at Windsor
https://www.thamesweb.co.uk/windsor/windsorhistory/royalfunerals/edwardVIIfuneral.html

Pretoria, Saturday, 26 November 1910
Laying of corner stone, Union Buildings
https://www.theheritageportal.co.za/article/birth-union-buildings

Johannesburg, Wednesday, 30 November 1910
Prince Arthur

https://simple.wikipedia.org/wiki/Prince_Arthur,_Duke_of_Connaught_a
nd_Strathearn

Johannesburg, Wednesday 31 May 1911
Brig Gen C F Beyers
https://af.wikipedia.org/wiki/Christiaan_Frederik_Beyers

Lourenço Marques, Sunday 10 December 1911
Railroad station, Lourenco Marques
https://en.wikipedia.org/wiki/Maputo_Central_Railway_Station

Lourenço Marques, Monday 11 December 1911
SS Kronprinz
https://picryl.com/media/kronprinz-deutsch-ost-afrika-liniealbum-6-foto-
75-034290

Pretoria, Monday, 6 January 1913
Post Office, Pretoria
https://melvinresidence.blogspot.com/2015/02/timeline-of-pretorias-
history.html

Telegraph switch
https://www.smithsonianmag.com/arts-culture/how-the-telegraph-went-
from-semaphore-to-communication-game-changer-1403433/

Pretoria, Tuesday, 14 January 1913
Building work, Union Buildings
https://www.theheritageportal.co.za/article/birth-union-buildings

Pretoria, Friday 21 March 1913
Painting of Union Buildings
https://arra.co.za/arcadian/june_july_2021/

Pretoria, Monday, 1 September 1913
Blank telegraph form
https://www.bobshop.co.za/rep-of-south-africa-telegram-form-as-illustrated/p/251865118

Pretoria, Monday, 8 September 1913
Building in Robert's Heights, Pretoria
https://www.sahistory.org.za/place/official-residence-commander-british-forces-south-africa-roberts-heights-pretoria

Pretoria, Friday, 7 August 1914
Gen Louis Botha and Gen Jan Smuts
https://the-past.com/feature/smuts-guerrilla-politician-warlord/

Pretoria, Sunday, 9 August 1914
The prophetess Veleda
https://en.wikipedia.org/wiki/Veleda

Pretoria, Tuesday,15 September 1914
Masthead, Pretoria News
https://www.facebook.com/PretoriaNewsSA/?locale=af_ZA

Pretoria, Wednesday, 23 September 1914
Gen Louis Botha
https://ww1live.wordpress.com/tag/louis-botha/

Pretoria, Monday, 12 October 1914
Soldiers with an armored vehicle
https://www.linkedin.com/pulse/ghosts-desert-james-stejskal/

Pretoria, Saturday, 24 October 1914
General Jan Smuts
https://collection.nam.ac.uk/detail.php?acc=1981-03-28-18

Pretoria, Monday, 16 November 1914
East wing of the Union Buildings, Pretoria
https://en.wikipedia.org/wiki/Union_Buildings

Pretoria, Tuesday, 23 November 1915
Pretoria Railway Station
https://www.theheritageportal.co.za/article/pretoria-railway-station-depicted-early-picture-postcards

Pretoria, Sunday, 13 February 1916
General Louis Botha
https://fineartamerica.com/featured/louis-botha-Prime-Minister-of-the-transvaal-historic-illustrations.html

Pretoria, Monday, 13 March 1916
The Hon Nicolaas Jacobus de Wet
https://www.npg.org.uk/collections/search/portrait/mw67361/Hon-Nicolaas-Jacobus-de-Wet

Pretoria, Sunday, 16 July 1916
Veleda against the Full Moon
https://x.com/GodPlaysCards/status/1759107843968426174

Pretoria, Saturday, 31 August 1918
Heliograph
https://www.iwm.org.uk/collections/item/object/30005193

Hagdale, Thursday, 22 March 1923
Villa Chiericati
https://es.wikipedia.org/wiki/Villa_Chiericati#/media/Archivo:VillaChiericati_2007_07_18_3.jpg

Avro 504R Gosport Biplane
https://en.wikipedia.org/wiki/Avro_504

Hamble, Sunday, 15 May 1927
Woman pilot
https://www.youtube.com/watch?v=HT4ge2JbThM

Camberley, Friday, 29 June 1928
Staff College at Camberley
https://en.wikipedia.org/wiki/Staff_College,_Camberley

RAF Cranwell, Friday, 7 December 1928
Royal Air Force College Cranwell in Lancashire
https://en.wikipedia.org/wiki/RAF_Cranwell

Hagdale, Saturday, 15 December 1928
De Haviland Tiger Moth Biplane
https://en.wikipedia.org/wiki/De_Havilland_Tiger_Moth

Greenwich, Friday, 8 June 1929
Royal Naval College, Greenwich
https://en.wikipedia.org/wiki/Old_Royal_Naval_College

London, Monday, 15 September 1930
"The Conspiracy of the Batavians under Julius Civilis and Veleda" by
Rembrandt (1661-1662)
https://www.wikiart.org/en/rembrandt/batavernas-trohetsed-1662

Woolwich, Friday, 12 June 1931
The Old Royal Military Academy, Woolwich
https://en.wikipedia.org/wiki/Royal_Military_Academy,_Woolwich

Hagdale, Friday, 17 September 1932
De Havilland Dragon Rapide
https://en.wikipedia.org/wiki/De_Havilland_Dragon_Rapide

Wassenaar, Monday, 31 October 1932
Dutch windmill, Wassenaar
https://commons.wikimedia.org/wiki/File:Wassenaar_molen_Windlust.jpg

Wassenaar, Sunday, 7 November 1932
Reformed "Dorpskerk", Wassenaar
https://pkn-wassenaar.nl/events/kerkdienst-vanuit-de-dorpskerk/

Paris, Sunday, 14 May1933
Statue of Veleda
https://www.eutouring.com/images_paris_statues_389.html

Toulouse, Monday, 15 May1933
Statue of Veleda
https://www.augustins.org/fr/notice/ra-974-velleda-15da958f-10f0-4b51-a3a5-8775e7afbc6e

Hagdale, Friday, 1 September 1933
Inside of Dragon Rapide
https://en.wikipedia.org/wiki/De_Havilland_Dragon_Rapide

Bremen, Friday 25 May 1934
General Paul von Letow-Vorbeck
https://kaiserreich.fandom.com/wiki/Paul_von_Lettow-Vorbeck

Kleve, Sunday 27 May 1934
Evangelical Lutheran Church, Kleve
https://commons.wikimedia.org/wiki/Category:Kleine_Kirche_%28Kleve%29#/media/File:Kleine_Kirche_(Kleve)_(3).JPG/2

Xanten, Monday 28 May 1934
Restored Roman Tower, Xanten
https://upload.wikimedia.org/wikipedia/commons/7/79/Hafentor_APX.jpg https

Wuppertal, Friday, 31 May 1934
Schwebebahn, Wuppertal
https://hr.m.wikipedia.org/wiki/Datoteka:Wuppertal_kaiserwagen.jpg

Evangelical Reformed Church, Barmen-Gemarke
https://www.evangelisch-wuppertal.de/aktuelle-meldungen-leser-1365/Barmer_Erklarrung59.html

Wassenaar, Friday, 30 August 1935
Beach, Wassenaar
https://en.wikipedia.org/wiki/Wassenaar#/media/File:Autumn_Beach_(29881666014).jpg

Kleve, Tuesday, 20 March 1936
German soldiers crossing a bridge
https://www.nationalarchives.gov.uk/education/resources/german-occupation/

Berlin, Saturday, 1 August 1936
Hitler at the Olympic Games, 1936
https://www.nbcnews.com/news/world/nazi-built-venue-1936-berlin-olympics-host-all-jewish-games-n397036

Wassenaar and Scheveningen, Monday, 31 August 1936
Kurhaus, Scheveningen
https://it.wikipedia.org/wiki/Kurhaus_di_Scheveningen

Vice Admiral Wilhelm Canaris
https://en.wikipedia.org/wiki/Wilhelm_Canaris

Neuremberg, Monday, 14 September 1936
Nazi rally, Neuremburg, 1936
https://en.wikipedia.org/wiki/Nazi_Party_Rally_Grounds

Nuremberg, Monday, 12 September 1938
Nazi rally, Neuremberg, 1938
https://www.britannica.com/topic/Nazi-Party

RAF Upper Heyford, Thursday, 20 September 1938
Bristol Blemheim, light bomber
https://en.wikipedia.org/wiki/Bristol_Blenheim#/media/File:Bristol_blen
heim_1_ExCC.jpg

Hagdale, Saturday, 24 December 1938
Villa Chiericati
https://en.wikipedia.org/wiki/Villa_Chiericati

Wassenaar and Scheveningen, Monday, 14 August 1939
Veleda (1852) by Alexandre Cabanel
https://www.ancient-origins.net/history-famous-people/legendary-
prophetess-veleda-secret-weapon-against-romans-007624

Hagdale, Saturday, 30 December 1939
De Havilland Dragon Rapide in RAF colors
https://en.wikipedia.org/wiki/De_Havilland_Dragon_Rapide

Wassenaar, Thursday, 10 May 1940
German paratroopers attacking from a glider
Bundesarchiv - Bild 101I-569-1579-14A

London, Saturday 7 September 1940
War Office, London
https://en.wikipedia.org/wiki/War_Office

Southampton, Saturday, 30 October 1940
Synagogue, Southampton

https://www.facebook.com/story.php/?story_fbid=753193073653147&id
=100068873823936&paipv=0&eav=AfZ9FAJMdXdBU1EabEIpH0pB0
W-81x31887N-eqpZJ0shDmOxvzg706420xUwOc7fCM&_rdr

Lower High Street, Southampton after the air raids of 30 November and
1 December 1940.
https://en.wikipedia.org/wiki/Southampton_Blitz

Southampto, Saturday, 5 April 1941
Coastal gun, Hamble
https://en.wikipedia.org/wiki/Hamble-le-Rice

Hamble, Monday, 22 September 1941
Assembly of Supermarine Spitfires
http://www.hamblehistory.org.uk/community/hamble-local-history-
society-12978/hambles-airfields/

Woman pilot in Spitfire
https://www.reddit.com/r/WWIIplanes/

White Waltham Airfield, Friday, 10 October 1941
ATA pilot's wings
https://en.wikipedia.org/wiki/Air_Transport_Auxiliary

Feltwell, Sunday, 12 October 1941
Vickers Wellington bomber
https://en.wikipedia.org/wiki/Vickers_Wellington_LN514

Hamble, Monday, 24 November 1941
Douglas Dakota
https://commons.wikimedia.org/wiki/File:Dakota_of_Voice_Flight_267_
Sqn_RAF_over_Malaya.jpg

London, Friday, 29 August 1942
Avro Lancaster bomber
https://en.wikipedia.org/wiki/Avro_Lancaster

Hamble and North Coates, Monday, 9 November 1942
Bristol Beaufighter
https://en.wikipedia.org/wiki/Bristol_Beaufighter

Brimsby, Monday, 14 December 1942
Avro Lancaster bomber
https://en.wikipedia.org/wiki/Avro_Lancaster

Scampton, Friday, 5 February 1943
De Havilland Mosquito
https://en.wikipedia.org/wiki/De_Havilland_Mosquito

Hamble, Tuesday, 9 February 1943
Junkers JU 88 light bomber
https://en.wikipedia.org/wiki/Junkers_Ju_88

Hamble, Friday, 31 December 1943
Wooden bomb
https://www.reddit.com/r/interestingasfuck/comments/ol3jv3/during_ww
2_the_germans_built_fake_wooden/
elds

New Romney, Tuesday, 2 May 1944
Hawker Typhoon fighter-bomber
https://en.wikipedia.org/wiki/Hawker_Typhoon

Faringdon, Monday, 8 May 1944
Douglas Dakota
https://en.wikipedia.org/wiki/List_of_Douglas_C-47_Skytrain_operators

Faringdon, Friday, 12 May 1944
Cottage Hospital, Coxwell Road, Faringdon
https://www.faringdon.org/cottage-hospital.html

Hagdale, Friday 20 July 1944
Spitfire tumbling a German "Buzzbomb"
https://en.wikipedia.org/wiki/V-1_flying_bomb

Hagdale, Sunday, 18 February 1945
Dresden after the bombing, Feb 1945
https://en.wikipedia.org/wiki/Bombing_of_Dresden

Hagdale, Wednesday, 2 May 1945
German S-Boot
https://en.wikipedia.org/wiki/E-boat

Hagdale, Sunday, 8 April 1945
All Saints' Church, Hyrsley
https://commons.m.wikimedia.org/wiki/File:All_Saints_Church_at_Hurs
ley_-_geograph.org.uk_-_5294889.jpg

Hagdale, Friday, 29 November 1946
Letterhead of Buckingam Palace
https://www.rotary-ribi.org/clubs/page.php?PgID=310570&ClubID=835

Signature of King George VI
https://www.historyforsale.com/king-george-vi-great-britain-typed-letter-
signed-02-10-1937/dc285849

Hagdale, Tuesday, 25 March 1927
King George VI
https://www.reddit.com/r/monarchism/comments/15drwt1/hm_king_geor
ge_vi_of_the_uk_looked_better_in/

Order of Commander of the British Empire
https://en.wikipedia.org/wiki/Order_of_the_British_Empire

London, Friday, 11 June 1948
Prime Minister Clement Attlee
https://en.wikipedia.org/wiki/List_of_prime_ministers_of_the_United_K
ingdom

Pretoria, Saturday, 18 September 1948
Medieval wooden box
Photo taken by the author of a box in his wife's possession

Mosaic of Jesus Christ, Hagia Sophia, Istanbul
https://commons.wikimedia.org/wiki/File:Jesus-Christ-from-Hagia-
Sophia.jpg

The 17th-century painting *Christ Crucified* by Diego Velázquez
https://www.pxfuel.com/en/search?q=inri

Veleda by Charles Landelle, 1874
https://www.meisterdrucke.ie/fine-art-prints/Charles-
Landelle/205362/Velleda.html

Rheindahlen, Wednesday, 1 September 1954
Veleda's Cave, Sauerland
https://www.wikidata.org/wiki/Q1114393

The Times, Friday, 12 June 1992
The Statue of Arthur Harris at the RAF Church of St Clement Danes
© Christopher Hilton https://www.geograph.org.uk/photo/3333572

Rank Structures of the Royal Navy, British Army and RAF
https://uklandpower.com/2018/11/07/do-we-need-to-simplify-the-
rank-structures-of-uk-armed-forces/

Rank Structure of the Air Transport Auxiliary

https://en.wikipedia.org/wiki/Air_Transport_Auxiliary